I0633247

SPARK OF INTRIGUE

A SECONDARY WORLD FANTASY

UNEXPECTED HEROES
BOOK 4

MARTY C. LEE

Bookaholics Press

BOOKS BY MARTY C. LEE

Unexpected Heroes series

Wind of Choice

Seed of War

Wave of Dreams

Spark of Intrigue

Tales of Kaiatan

Legends of Kaiatan

Nobody's Revenge (novella 0.9)

The Cat's Fortune (a Legends novella)

Unexpected Heroes: The Complete Series

Unexpected Tales: Four Short Stories of Kaiatan

(an excerpt of Tales of Kaiatan)

Return of the Fae series

The Coming of the Fae

The Peril of the Fae

The Academy of the Fae

The War of the Fae

The King of the Fae

The Heirs of the Fae

The Escape of the Fae (novella 0.5)

Spotting the Fae (novella 0.8)

AS M. CATE LEE

Relatively Haunted series (2026)

Book design and publication by Bookaholics Press LLC, Provo Utah
Edited by Martha Rasmussen
Front cover design by Brenda Camp Walter
Back cover and chapter heading illustrations by Naomi Rasmussen
Map by Michelle Allan and Naomi Rasmussen
Author photograph by Melissa C. Baxter

ISBN 13: 978-1-950230-14-3 (epub)
978-1-950230-15-0 (mobi)
978-1-950230-16-7 (paperback)
978-1-950230-17-4 (large print)
978-1-950230-29-7 (hardback)
978-1-950230-63-1 (audiobook)

Published by Bookaholics Press LLC
Provo, Utah bookaholicspress@gmail.com

Contact the author at MCLeeBooks.com

For Chris Hadfield, who will probably never know he encouraged me to be an author,
and for my Day Group, who should already know they did, too.

CONTENTS

Map of Iskra

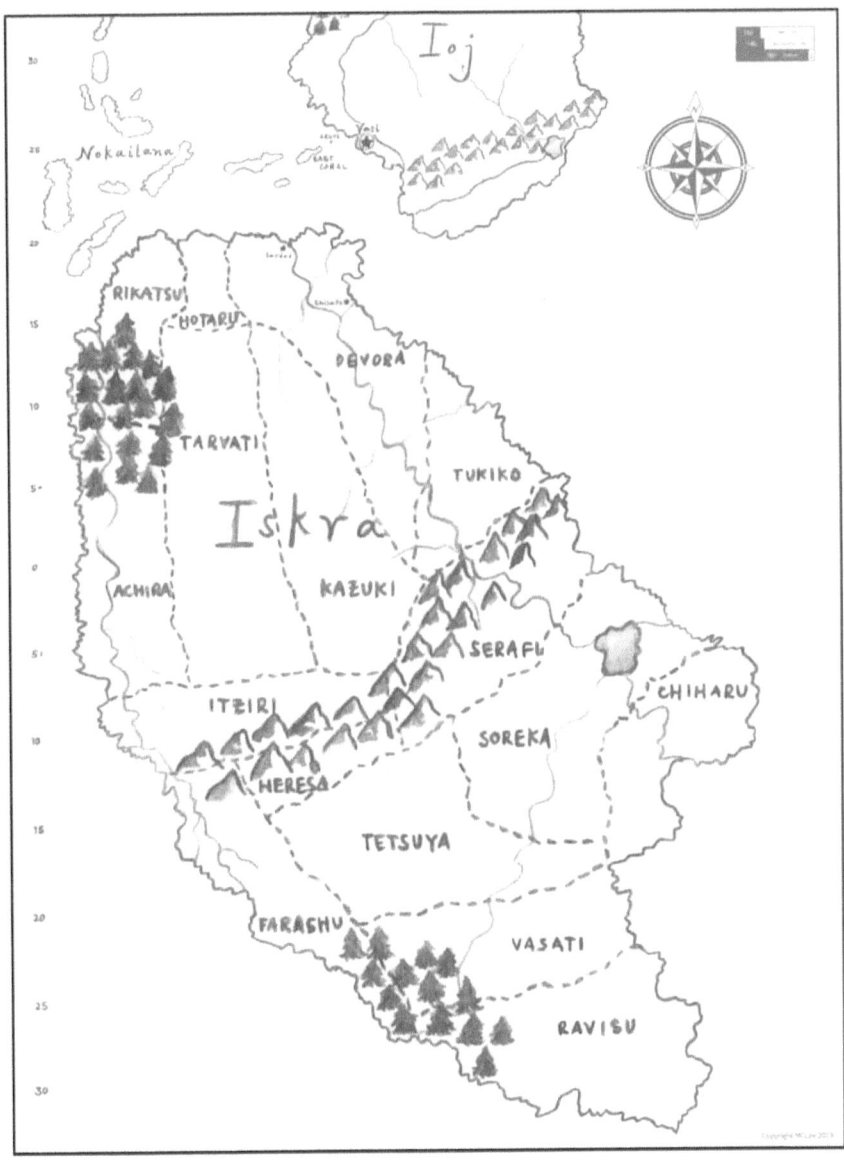

1. SEEKING

(CHISATO CITY, DEVORA DISTRICT, ISKRA)

Rarely, an infant is born with red hair, chosen of Resef and able to call fire. Distant legends tell of even fewer Iskrins becoming fire-touched as adults.

Iskrin Culture and History, vol. 3

Zefra watched the pennant with the saffron bee as if it were a mirage that would disappear if she looked away. Behind her lay the city, half stone buildings and half colorful tents, surrounded by the fertile fields next to the river. The banner flew from the last tent at the edge of the city, marking her last chance. Beyond it, the fields turned to white desert reflecting the brilliant sun as clouds raced from the apricot horizon for the afternoon rains.

After training her whole life for this task, she was ready. She had seen more of the world than caravan guides twice her age, and faced dangers from their nightmares.

If only she could convince someone else of that. Anyone else.

Zefra shook the sand off her worn robe and boots and tucked stray waves of hair under her scarf to hide its color. She straightened her sword belt to display her curved saif, a gift from her brother. Hopefully, it announced she could take care of herself.

After wiping her sweaty hands on her tan robe, she took a deep breath and ducked through the tent flap.

Two men sat cross-legged on colorful woven mats, writing on their slates, and looked up as she entered. Though both had the stark white skin and brown eyes of the Iskrin, the younger one had hair a shade more brown than the usual black. He reminded Zefra of her friend, Sayaka, who had guarded her in her first adventure. Perhaps 'twas a good omen.

Zefra bowed and sat across from them, keeping her back as straight as the staff she laid at her feet. "I seek employment as a guide. I am available immediately for any size caravan on any route."

The younger man grinned at the older one before facing her with the remnants of the smile. "I think you're in the wrong tent, youngster. This is for experienced guides. If you follow this row to the other end, there is a tent that hires the less-experienced as assistants and apprentices."

"I am experienced," Zefra protested, pressing her hands against her legs to flatten her instinctive fists. "I have already guided three expeditions and discovered a new oasis."

That was not the whole story, but close enough. When she had been strictly truthful in another hiring tent, they laughed and sent her to the tents of the storytellers to hear the "correct" tale.

The younger man raised his eyebrows. "You have, have you? How old are you?"

Zefra swallowed the insult and kept her face smooth. "I am an adult."

She had passed her survival trek, so her actual age of sixteen was irrelevant. They should ask her questions about her experience.

The older man looked her over from head to feet, and his mouth twitched. "But how long have you been an adult? We have nothing appropriate for youngsters. Come back after you get real experience."

Zefra inhaled. She had discovered an entirely new oasis while still considered a child. She helped save the world two summers ago. A few months later, she stopped war from overtaking Darrendra and brought home maps that were hundreds of years old to enrich her clan's collection. Last year, she explored the supposedly cursed Dragon Isles on behalf of the long-lost god, Kassian, and destroyed a pirate infestation. She had visited all four countries as well as the unclaimed islands. How much experience did they need to lead a simple caravan? How many of their guides had done as much by three times her age?

"I—" she began.

"Run along, girl." The younger man turned to his slate, counting on his fingers before scratching out numbers and rewriting them.

If she set him on fire, he would burn beautifully. Zefra took another deep breath. Adulthood meant one could not burn people for being rude. She could almost hear her friend, Nia, say, "Adulthood is boring." It certainly appeared useless. One obstacle after another had blocked her for over a year.

After returning from her last misadventure, she was sure her time had finally come, but reality had been disappointing. Applying for a job was as futile here as it had been in every hiring tent. Her youthful face and scrawny body made everyone ignore her practicality and capability. No one even believed her experience. And the last time she uncovered her hair to prove her identity, the men accused her of dying it for fraud. The time she proved it the other way, they doused her with water and suggested she would make a better warrior or priest. 'Twas all useless.

The older man still watched her politely, though with a faint smile.

Zefra stood and bowed to him, ignoring the younger man. "Thank you for your time."

She walked out with as much pride as despair allowed. Now where would she go?

Her home district of Hotaru was too poor to have caravan jobs for her. The Rikatsu to the west were shipbuilders and needed no land guides, though she had wasted a month asking there. She had left her parents and siblings and walked for months to reach Devora, hoping someone in the bigger, wealthier agricultural district would hire her. In each town, no matter how small, she had looked for employment, but there was none. Chisato was their biggest city and on a major trade route, and someone must need a guide.

Despite this caravan chief's assurances, the apprentice tent had not taken her, either. They had enough interest from their own district that they closed their ranks to applicants from the rest of Iskra, regardless of experience or need. If there was nothing for her here, would there be anything in any of the other cities? Must she try all sixteen districts? Iskra was large enough that it would take her years, decades perhaps, to travel to every corner.

Zefra blinked back tears. By then, at least, she would be old enough to satisfy prospective employers, though probably no larger. Body size was irrelevant for guides, and her mind was more than sufficient, if anyone would give her the chance to prove it.

As if to confirm the general opinion of her, the daily winter rains began, spitting at her from the sky. She raised her face and let the water run across her dry skin. As drops peppered her and bounced on the dusty earth, she headed for the market. By late afternoon, the dry ground would moisten. The rainy winter was good for the grain the Devora grew, though farmers still depended on irrigation for most of their water.

Her stomach growled. Her snares had been empty this morning, and there had not been enough time to hunt food *and* seek an employer before the afternoon rains. Zefra fingered the pouch hanging from her embroidered sash. Other than her slate, chalk, and a letter with a difficult question, 'twas nearly empty, without even a fire starter. The few coins she had brought were almost gone, though she had camped outside the city all week rather than rent a cot at an inn.

If she did not find a job today, she must go without dinner to save her coins for tomorrow. If she did not find a job tomorrow... No, she must find a job by tomorrow or she would eat rat and lizard as she skulked home.

Her parents would give her a job with the horses without a word of censure, or she could make maps with her grandparents. Her older brother would tease her without mercy, but even that would be better than the lecture on failure her own mind would repeat with every beat of the horses' hooves.

She needed another plan.

Zefra stood at the edge of the market square and scanned the neat rows of dull tents, tapping her slate through her pouch. Most merchants had dropped their tent flaps for an afternoon nap during the rain, but a few stalwart — or desperate — raised bright canopies to protect their goods from the moisture and called to the remaining patrons. Mingled with the local Iskrins in brown and saffron were a few wearing the colors of other clans. Even without considering clothing styles and colors, the occasional outdweller stood out with different colors of skin and hair and sometimes wings. The scents of myriad spices and roasted lamb and vegetables drifted on the breeze, and her stomach grumbled harder.

Even a day's work would give enough coin to eat and stay another day to look further. If she found a week's work, she could store enough supplies to make it to another city. There must be someone who needed a strong back and an intelligent mind, even for an afternoon.

If her experience was not enough, would asking Ahjin for a recommendation help her find permanent employment? Surely a letter from the Mouth of the Gods would be impressive. Even though he was still chasing the pirates from last year's events, he might take the time to help her.

"Zefra," someone called in an accented voice.

Zefra turned and instantly spotted a lovely Darrendrakar, taller than most Iskrins and waving one arm enthusiastically. During Nemerra's recent stay in Iskra, she had usually been too far away to visit, and Zefra had not seen her since shortly after the babies were born. She counted mentally. Far too long ago.

While she waited for her friend to wind through the thinning crowd, Zefra mentally composed a list of merchants to approach later.

As soon as Nemerra was close enough for conversation, Zefra greeted her in trade tongue. "Bright day, Nemerra. I did not realize you were in the area."

Though Nemerra had braided her russet hair in a local style, its lack of a scarf declared her an outdweller as surely as the bright colors of her hair and dress. Proper Iskrin matrons cast shocked glances at the brown skin showing below her elbows and between her knee-length hem and calf-high boots.

Nemerra nodded cheerfully to the closest shoppers and smiled at Zefra. "Good to see you. We have been traveling for Ludik's apprenticeship. This is our last stop before we go home. What are you doing here?"

Zefra shrugged with faked unconcern. "Not finding work."

"That is unfortunate," Nemerra said. "If I hear of any, I will let you know. If you aren't busy now, would you keep me company in the market?"

"You plan to continue during the rain? Perhaps it might be better to come back tomorrow. Your purchases will get wet."

Nemerra opened a palm to the sky. "This is only a gentle mist. Remember what Darrendran rain is like?"

Zefra shuddered. She liked rain, but she preferred not to drown in it. "What is on your shopping list today?"

"Supplies for our trip home, gifts for our families, and things for the babies." Nemerra shook her head. "They're growing so fast, it's nearly impossible to keep them clothed."

"Nine months is a busy time for infants," Zefra agreed. "Soon they will be walking and getting into everything."

Nemerra laughed again. "Darrendrakar babies walk sooner than that, especially in their four-legged form. They are *already* into everything, the little terrors."

Zefra could not imagine being a mother at nineteen, especially to four children, but Nemerra smiled as if she would burst from happiness. The slender young shapeshifter jumped into stories about her family's latest escapades as the two women browsed the open stalls. Nemerra piled small gifts into the basket she gave Zefra to carry, bargained to the smallest coin, then paid from a heavy purse.

"So they keep my hands full," Nemerra admitted as they moved to the next tent. "Ludik helps as much as he can, but his apprenticeship keeps him busy. Now that he's nearly finished, our mamas are eagerly awaiting the chance to spend time with the babies. I can't wait to have enough free time to return to my leather-working." She looked north, then rifled through a stack of shapeless infant robes.

"When are you leaving?" Zefra asked.

"In a day or two. Ludik has already been declared a Shri, but he has a few patients he wants to finish treating." Nemerra dropped a few robes into the basket.

Zefra's stomach growled louder than before.

Nemerra pressed her lips together. "You are welcome to stay with us until we go. We would enjoy a visit."

"I could not impose," Zefra said politely, subtly pressing her hand to her stomach to quiet it.

Apparently not subtly enough, for Nemerra's eyes flickered to her hand. "If you don't find other work, I could use help with the children until we leave. With our six ravenous appetites and Ludik's assistants and random patients, I already cook for an army."

"You could have stayed in Darrendra while he was here," Zefra said.

Nemerra rubbed one hand across the bite scar on her neck, a

souvenir from the last time she accompanied Ludik. "And be apart for nearly a year and a half? No."

The scar, or the creator of the scar, reminded Zefra of her other problem. She poked her pouch, feeling the letter inside crinkle, then finally blurted, "Lyell wants me as guardian to Tala."

"What? As a bodyguard for his daughter?" Nemerra raised her eyebrows. "Is Lyell still that distressed?"

"No, only in case something happens to him, since his wife is already dead." Zefra shifted to her other foot. "But look how busy you are with your children. If I agree to take Tala, even if only in an emergency, how would I work for a caravan? I do not have anyone to help me, and I do not wish to be responsible for a small child. I am not ready for motherhood."

Nemerra's busy hands slowed but did not stop sorting. "Don't you want to have a family?"

"Certainly." As Zefra ran her hand along the edge of the basket, her gold dowry bracelets jingled musically. She shoved them under her sleeve and clamped her other hand over her wrist. "But what is the hurry? I'm only sixteen and not ready for marriage."

Nemerra tapped Zefra's arm. "Then why advertise your availability with the bracelets?"

Zefra groaned. Even Nemerra had been in Iskra long enough to know what they meant.

"'Twas Mother's idea. I told her no, but she insisted. 'You never know, Zefra. Perhaps you will meet a wonderful man while you're gallivanting around the desert.' I do not think she understands I will be too busy as soon as I find a job. I will have time for a family in a few years, when I'm older and more experienced and can pick better jobs instead of taking whatever I can get."

Nemerra turned away, but not fast enough to hide her smile. "Sometimes mamas have a hard time realizing what they think is best for their beloved children isn't always what their children want. She'll get used to the idea, eventually."

Zefra wrinkled her nose. "How long will it take?"

Nemerra laughed. "It depends on your mama. It might be easier while you're away, or missing you might make it worse."

"She sends me letters," Zefra said morosely. "Long letters, with lists of handsome men her neighbors' distant relatives know."

Nemerra covered her mouth with her hand. After a moment, she cleared her throat. "Did your mama work before she married?"

"She was a cartographer with her parents, but she quit to help Father with the horses. She keeps the records of their breeding program and the sales."

"What will you do about exploring when you start a family?" Nemerra asked. "Will you leave your family behind, take them with you, or switch professions?"

"I will have to leave them behind. I cannot take dependents on someone else's caravan."

"What about another profession, then?" Nemerra paid the bowing clerk.

Zefra stared at her. "This is all I ever wanted to do. I spent years learning and practicing. Why would I do something else?"

Nemerra shrugged. "Sometimes plans change."

Zefra pressed her aching stomach again. Must she sacrifice her dreams in order to eat?

2. MARKET
(CHISATO)

**The sixteen Iskrin districts have their own colors and emblems
to identify their clans.**
Iskrin Culture and History, vol 2

Just because Zefra had not found employment yet did not mean she
had failed. Somehow, she would find a way. Rain drizzled under her
collar and soaked through her shoulders. She took a deep breath and
hurried after Nemerra.

Her friend had paid for the infant clothes and was wandering through
tables of jewelry. Zefra caught up as Nemerra held a gold earring by the
small hoop in her right ear, checking the look in a mirror held by the
merchant. The Iskrin reached to hold the other earring by her left ear,
then pulled back at the sight of the unpierced lobe.

"I only need one." Nemerra switched from trade tongue to Iskrit.
Even if the merchant spoke trade tongue, which was possible but not
certain, using his native language was courteous.

To the confused merchant, Zefra quickly explained, "The Darrendrakar Cats pierce only one ear to indicate their married status."

The merchant lowered his widened eyes and bowed. "As you say."

Nemerra returned the earring with a smile and walked away. "Imagine," she murmured, "if you had explained about the Pigs' custom. I don't think he has any nose rings."

Zefra chuckled. "No, I imagine not. I did not know you spoke Iskrit."

"I've been here long enough to gain a basic understanding," Nemerra said, "though my trade tongue is much better. Ludik is nearly fluent in both, and the children already babble in three languages." She glanced through the rows of tents. "I have everything but flour now."

"Food is on the outer row." Zefra shifted the heavy basket in her arms and led the way to the closest farm stall, tilting her face to the rain.

Knowing trade tongue as well as Iskrit seemed sufficient when she intended to work in her home country, but perhaps it would be useful to learn another language or two. She should talk to Nia, her Nokai friend who spoke all languages.

This tent had a spacious canopy above crates of vegetables and baskets of fruit, and the open door revealed piles of grain sacks. As they waited, the patter of the raindrops on the stretched canvas slowed to a graceful syncopation.

An older woman spoke to a customer while a young man loaded food into the saddlebags of a horse with a high, arched neck and a flowing mane. The tall young man nodded at Nemerra and winked at Zefra, then turned away to finish loading.

Zefra glared. Who did he think she was, to be so familiar with her?

Nemerra wandered the row of produce while Zefra watched the insolent farmer from the corner of her eye. He finished his task and approached with a proper bow and a wide smile.

"Bright day, Zefra," he said in trade tongue. "Will you introduce me to your friend?"

Zefra's mouth dropped open, and she ran a hand along her scarf to check for betraying curls while she examined the young farmer from head to toe. The usual black hair and white skin, lighter brown eyes than her own, good-looking but not familiar. And she would remember his height and broad shoulders. Though not as muscular as her blacksmith brother, farming was obviously good exercise, and he was nearly as tall as Nemerra.

Nemerra's bow was almost as proper as the farmer's, though not as polished. "Bright day," she said in heavily accented Iskrit. "I am Nemerra.

How know you Zefra?" Her smile hovered between welcoming and protective.

"He does not know me," Zefra insisted. And with her unique hair properly hidden, he could not guess. His continued stare made her nervous, and she raised her hand without thinking, ready to call flame.

The farmer backed up and bowed again, rather hastily. "I recognized you, Khezekhori, from the Hotaru council two years ago. My father and I heard you tell of your quest for the missing gods. We supplied the ship for your last trip."

Nemerra relaxed. "I believe him."

Zefra narrowed her eyes at the farmer. "Why? He could have heard the story from someone else."

Nemerra smiled charmingly. "Even though your hair is covered, he's watching your empty hand like it wields a sword."

Oh. Zefra flexed her fingers. Few people knew of her fire, but those at the council were among them. She had not paid much attention to the visitors at the time. More important things had distracted her, like the fate of the world.

"I'm Tarakh Ekorov," the young man said. "I'm pleased to help you and your friend. Are you shopping for food today or merely getting out of the rain?"

"I need flour," Nemerra said. "I cannot seem to make bread fast enough to feed my family."

Tarakh grinned at her. "I have seen your little ones running outside the healer's tent. I do not know how you keep up with them."

"How do you know her family?" Zefra asked. "You asked for an introduction, so you have not met."

Tarakh bowed again. "Who does not know the foreign Shri whose healing powers impress even our own illustrious Tukiko? He treats the other outdwellers and the poor and any who ask. And we have all seen his lovely and distinctive wife, at least from a distance. The other outdwellers who come to visit or trade do not live among us, and few learn our language."

"Thank you for your kind words," Nemerra said. "My family and I appreciate the welcome we found in Devora. My children play happily with the Iskrin little ones and have learned to mind their claws. Though we are anxious to return home, we will remember our time here with fondness." She smiled warmly at Tarakh.

The tips of his ears turned pink.

The other customer mounted his horse and rode off, and the older woman joined Tarakh. "Bright day, ladies," she said. "Is Tarakh helping you with all you need?"

"He is quite gracious," Nemerra assured her, "and a fine employee."

The woman laughed. "He is a better son." She leaned against Tarakh for a moment, short enough that her shoulder reached only his biceps, but she had the same lighter eyes.

Tarakh put his arm around her. "May I introduce my mother, Hariskandra Ekorov? You already met my father, Devora's clan chieftain, in Hotaru. Mother, this is Zefra Ashvakosha of the Hotaru and Nemerra Moriko of Darrendra."

Zefra and Nemerra both bowed.

"'Tis a pleasure to meet you, lady," Zefra said.

"And to meet you." Hariskandra eyed Zefra's bracelets until Zefra clasped her hands behind her back. "Since Tarakh is taking care of you so well, I will leave you to him while I replenish my spices. Warmth to you." She patted her son's arm, grabbed a small basket, and headed into the market.

Tarakh turned to Nemerra with the serious expression appropriate to bargaining. "Now, I believe you said you need flour?"

While Zefra brushed sand from the dropped items and repacked the basket, Nemerra questioned him on the quality of his flour and the size of bags available, then haggled skillfully with a twinkle in her eyes.

Tarakh maintained his solemnity until they finished the bargain, then laughed. "You are a fine negotiator, lady. Will you take the flour with you, or shall I deliver it?"

Nemerra glanced at Zefra as she counted out the money. "You may bring it to our tent. Zefra, I have a little shopping left. Why don't you finish your business here and come for the evening meal? If you don't know where it is, I'm sure Tarakh can show you the way."

Before Zefra could react, Nemerra took the basket from her and strode through the crowd, which made way for her slender form as if she carried a bare sword.

Tarakh's wide grin crinkled the corners of his eyes. "May I get something else for you? Are you in need of produce?"

Zefra felt her nearly empty pouch again as her stomach rumbled. "I need work. Do you know anyone who is looking for a temporary helper? Or someone who needs a guide?"

Tarakh flicked a glance at her bracelets. "My father already has a caravan guide and an apprentice. I have not heard of a need elsewhere, but I will listen for one. I assume you have already asked in the caravan tents. Have you made a list of merchants to ask about temporary work?"

Zefra nodded. "But then Nemerra came, and the rains chased most of them inside. I will ask tomorrow."

"Have you considered other work? Do you have other skills?"

Zefra shook her head. "I know maps and horses, but I prefer to guide."

"I see. If you change your mind, let me know. There are more opportunities in the other fields, including with my father." Tarakh leaned on the table and smiled at her. His tan robe had dark brown embroidery around the collar and saffron beads along the sleeves as an understated display of his family's wealth and status. "Is your family with you?"

He picked a damaged fruit from a basket labeled, "Bargain! Buy now!" and peeled it with a finger-length knife. Though he carried no saif, a long dagger hung from his brown and saffron belt. The usual iron-bound staff, longer than Zefra's, leaned in a corner of the stall.

"I came alone to seek work," Zefra explained. "I camped in the desert outside the city borders. My brother, Izo, might visit, as will my friend, Ahjin, who is also coming here on business."

Tarakh's shoulder twitched. "I hope his business is unremarkable. I asked the storytellers for every tale they have of him, and many are too adventurous for my blood. As stories, though, they are impressive." He flashed a quick smile. "All his friends seem to attract trouble."

Zefra nodded sadly. "We do. Trouble has found us three times now. We have been fortunate to resolve it each time."

"Fortune grows grain in the well-irrigated field," Tarakh quoted. "I suspect you and your friends had more success than others would have found. Who else has rescued the gods, stopped a war, and destroyed an entire fleet of pirates?"

"I have remarkable friends," Zefra admitted.

"I find myself impressed with you, as well." Tarakh pressed half the peeled fruit into her reluctant hand, and the smile on his handsome face made her blush.

Tarakh smiled wider and ate his half of the fruit in three bites. "Eat. The fruit is old and going to waste. How fare your friends now?"

"Ahjin and Nia are in Arupa, dealing with the gods and their plans for the world. As for Ludik, you have apparently seen him more recently than I. If I find work, I look forward to staying here long enough to see all of them again."

He fixed his dark bronze gaze on her face. "I hope you stay longer, too."

Zefra lowered her eyes and tried not to blush. While she searched for a response, she nibbled at the fruit. The juice flooded her tongue with sweetness, and her stomach growled harder. Before she realized it, the rest of the fruit was gone and a sturdy hand held another half in front of her.

She looked for laughter or pity in Tarakh's face, but he merely smiled and bit into his half of the second fruit.

"'Tis good, is it not? You can tell the next customers." He held the fruit in front of her until she finally took it.

"Thank you. 'Tis delicious."

This one lasted a few seconds longer than the first, and by the time she finished, Tarakh had another ready.

"Will you stay with the Darrendrakar while you look for work," he asked, "or have you given up on our fair city?"

"I would like to stay." Zefra ate the third fruit. "'Tis still the most promising place for work in the area."

"Can I see you again?"

She furrowed her brows in confusion. "I will be here tomorrow, and you are not blind."

Tarakh grinned at her. "That is not what I mean."

Zefra choked on her last bite. "You mean..." She shoved her bracelets under her sleeve again.

Tarakh's mouth twitched. "Yes, I mean..."

"I will be busy." Zefra closed her inner eyelids as a subtle barrier.

"I know. I hope you are. I will not keep you from your business, and *when* you find a caravan to hire you, I will be happy for you. I merely wish to know you better."

Zefra took a step backward. "Why?"

Tarakh rearranged the fruit in the basket. "I admire you. You are brave and strong, talented and determined, smart and loyal."

"I am not beautiful," Zefra said.

Nia was beautiful, and Nemerra was lovely. Zefra knew herself to be scrawny, and though her nose was elegantly long, her mouth was too wide and thin for beauty.

Tarakh shrugged. "What is the value of beauty? 'Tis nothing but pleasure for the eyes. I would rather please my heart."

Zefra took another step backward. His heart was not her concern, and her heart was too busy. Before she could scold him, he shrugged again.

"But we are moving too fast. I told you, I wish to know you better. I want to be your friend. That is all for now." He smiled faintly, looking at the table instead of her face.

"Perhaps." Zefra tapped her slate. Friends would not complicate her plans.

Tarakh nodded. "You know where to find me." He looked over her shoulder. "Mother is returning. Would now be a good time to deliver Nemerra's flour?"

"I can carry the flour myself," Zefra said.

Tarakh laughed. "You will never surprise me with your abilities, but please, allow me to walk with you."

"Thank you," Zefra said, though his warm smile made her nervous.

He ducked in the tent, wrapped a large bag of flour in a waterproof canvas, and threw it over his strong shoulders. The rain had slowed to a trickle, and the crowds returned to the market behind her. A high voice complained about something, then laughed mockingly.

Shivers ran down Zefra's neck to her clenched fists. "I recognize that voice," she muttered to Tarakh, "but it could not be him."

"Who?"

"Lapwing." With her hand on her saif, she searched the market for pale brown wings.

Tarakh glanced at her hands, then put down the flour and picked up his staff. "Who is Lapwing?"

"Later. Look for black hair and tan wings."

Tarakh stopped to whisper to his mother, then caught up to Zefra with his longer stride.

The voice came again. Yes, the high-pitched whine was unmistakable. It came from the right, and Zefra pushed her way through the growing crowd.

"There," Tarakh said, from the vantage point of an extra span of height. "There is only one Iojif in the crowd, and he has tan wings."

Zefra pushed the customers harder, trying to force her way through. Someone shoved back, and Zefra fell against a post. Tarakh pulled her to her feet, but her scarf snagged on something and pulled free.

The woman who had pushed her yelled and swung her basket at Zefra. Tarakh blocked it as Zefra ducked. The commotion cleared a space in the crowd, and at the other side of the gap, Lapwing fingered a gold necklace in a display. He turned, and his eyes widened at the sight of her uncovered hair. He dropped the necklace and tried to run, but the crowd pressed too closely.

"Stop him," Zefra shouted.

She lunged across the gap toward Lapwing. The pirate tried to open his wings but failed to find space in the turbulent crowd. He shoved the table onto the ground, scattering jewelry through the mob. The merchant wailed and scrambled for his goods.

While Zefra dodged the table and the onlookers who discreetly reached for the scattered gold, Lapwing stepped into the cleared space and launched himself into the air.

Zefra skidded to a halt. She was too late. In a moment, the pirate disappeared into the cloud bank.

Tarakh appeared at her side, staff in one hand and her scarf in the other. "Now what?"

Zefra ducked her head as Iskrins pointed and gaped. "Resef hates me," she muttered. "I should dye my hair black again."

Tarakh smiled. "I like the red our god gave you. Now, who was that man?"

"When we destroyed the pirate fleet last spring, we killed the pirate general." Zefra said. "Lapwing was his second-in-command."

3. NEWS
(ARUPA; 8 DAYS EARLIER)

And established they The House of the Gods on Arupa. And lived there His Holiness, Ahjin the Great, first of the Mouths of the Gods.
A Comprehensive History of the Gods, vol. 7

Ahjin stretched his back and wings with a groan. Weeding even a kitchen garden was a pain, and Darravani's garden spanned the western edge of the small island. Getting help made his trip to Darrendra last year almost worth the trouble. Almost.

If he left now, he could bathe before dinner. He tromped carefully through the seedlings until he was far enough to not flick mud on his new gardeners as he sprang into the air. As he flew past the guest houses, he automatically looked for Nia, even though she wouldn't return until tomorrow. He missed her, but of course she needed to go home for her parents' wedding.

He didn't know why it had taken them nine months to wed. Nia's father had proposed as soon as he got home from the Dragon Isles last spring, and her mother had tearfully accepted. Maybe they needed to get acquainted again after a seventeen-year absence.

Ahjin still didn't understand the carefree Nokai attitude toward romance, though he had enough experience to drive him insane. Ever since Nia had finally decided she loved Ahjin, they disagreed on what to expect from their relationship. Three months ago, he'd asked her to marry him.

She turned him down.

Wasn't a six-month courtship long enough? Was marriage with him so terrible?

Below him, Kaito waited in front of Ahjin's house, brown hair and skin fading into the twilight. When Ahjin landed, the Darrendrakar Seal covered his eyes from the gust Ahjin's wings created. Kaito pointed at the setting sun and folded his arms across his colorful tunic.

"Fair winds, Kaito," Ahjin said. "I know it's almost time for dinner. Is everything ready?"

Since his parents and baby sister were currently in Ioj on an aerobatics tour with their troupe, dinner would only involve his top staff, and it was his turn to host.

Kaito looked to the sky and shook his head sadly.

"Never mind," Ahjin said. "I'm sorry I asked."

He ran into the house, which smelled of delicious food and hot bread. Kaito already had the tub filled, and since Ahjin lived alone, there was no competition for the steaming hot water. As he scrubbed, his thoughts inevitably returned to Nia. He didn't have to live alone, if she would marry him.

Ahjin grabbed a towel. What was wrong with marrying him, anyway? Marriage wasn't an insult even for a Nokai, and despite his scars, he didn't think he was ugly.

He put on a clean shirt and pants in the plain colors he preferred and finger-combed the tangles from his curls. He shoved his feet into his ankle-high boots just before someone knocked on the outside door.

As Ahjin put away the tub, Kaito let in Lyell and his daughter, Tala, both in their two-legged forms. Before Ahjin could ask why the dark-haired little girl wasn't her usual wolf-self, Kaito ushered everyone into the kitchen.

Lyell greeted the Seal, who said his typical nothing. Lyell was his usual amusing self, hampered only by keeping his daughter under control.

Kaito placed the platter of food on the table and gestured at the chairs. Once Tala was settled in her baby seat, Kaito grabbed the pitcher of cold water, and the adults took their chairs. As they passed plates and cups, they talked of Ahjin's upcoming trip to Iskra.

"Kassian wants me to check some records," Ahjin said, "Makana wants me to update myths, and everyone has a list of people to talk to. We'll leave as soon as Nia gets back tomorrow."

"With guards," Lyell said.

Ahjin glared at him. "With guards."

Kaito cleared his throat.

Ahjin groaned. "And servants. But only two."

"For a full diplomatic tour," Lyell said, "it will take one just to deal with your wardrobe."

Ahjin groaned again. He hated his formal wardrobe. "Kaito will help. How big do you think my yacht is? Or did you plan to help sail it?"

Lyell grinned a little too broadly, baring his teeth. "I don't care if you snip at me. I can bite back."

Ahjin stabbed his dessert with his fork. "You wouldn't. You live right behind me; do you think I don't hear you howl when you wake from your nightmares? I know how often you dream of biting Nemerra."

Lyell's glass clattered against his plate as he grabbed for a drink.

Ahjin sighed. "I'm sorry, Lyell. I meant, I know you'd never hurt me."

The door flew open, and the scent of the ocean flooded the house.

"I'm here," Nia called from the doorstep.

Ahjin dropped his fork and jumped to his feet. She was early — and soaked. Dripping braids clung past her curves to her knees, and her bare feet squelched mud.

"Nia, don't move." Lyell lunged for a dish towel. "Ahjin, pull out the tub. Kaito, more towels."

By the time Ahjin wrestled the tin tub out again, Nia was wrapped in a large towel while Kaito washed the mud from her dirty webbed feet. Shivers wracked all not-quite-five-feet of her from gills to toes.

"Why did you swim?" Ahjin asked. "I'd send the boat for you in the morning."

Nia shrugged. "It's only twenty miles."

Ahjin poured the hot water from the stove into the tub and added a bucket of cold. "Oh, that's certainly a reason to freeze."

"Don't be silly," Nia said. "It never freezes here." She shivered harder.

"And what about the mud?" Lyell asked.

"I cut through the fields," Nia admitted.

"Tomorrow you'd have shoes," Ahjin said.

"No, thanks." Nia's green eyes flashed, but her chattering teeth ruined her tart reply.

"Enough," Lyell said. "While Nia bathes, get something dry for her to wear." He glared and pushed the others outside into the night.

"I'm fastest." Ahjin launched himself into the air.

The large, golden moon gave enough light for him to find his way, even with the two tiny ones dark tonight. He landed on the domed roof of the Nokai guest house, then swung over the edge and through the window of the second-story. Unlike the underwater originals, it didn't use shark-grates and the bedroom was on the top floor.

Nia's closet was on the opposite wall, but the entire floor was littered with clothing and junk. Ahjin grabbed the first long-sleeved ocean suit he found.

He returned to his house and stood with one hand on the doorknob. With Nia in the tub, he couldn't go in, but without dry clothes, she would be stuck.

Lyell chuckled and swooped Tala to the doorstep. "Send it in with her."

"Me, me," Tala said.

Ahjin gave the pants to the little Wolf-girl, then cracked open the door with his back turned. As soon as she ran in, giggling, he shut the door. After a tiny knock on the inside, he cracked open the door again and dropped the shirt into Tala's arms.

Kaito waved and headed for the house he shared with Lyell and Tala. Lyell stared at the stars, then pushed himself upright when Tala knocked again.

When the little girl slipped out, giggling and yawning and rubbing her eyes under her fringe of black hair, he lifted her to his shoulders. "See you in the morning."

"Lyell..." Ahjin said.

His Chief of Staff waited. "What?" Lyell eventually asked. "Are you worried about tomorrow?"

"No," Ahjin said. "I'm just sorry. I shouldn't remind you of... things."

Lyell cleared his throat. "I remember my mistakes, no matter what you don't say. Sleep well."

He strolled toward his house, shoulders hunched. The moonlight glowed on the gray streaks in his dark hair and turned the brown mourning stripes on his Darrendran tunic to black. Though it had been over a year since his wife and other children died, he still sewed a narrow stripe around every neckline and four on every hem. The Wolf wore the stripes as a sign of his own broken heart, but they tore at Ahjin's conscience every time he saw them. If only he had gotten the gods to cooperate faster, they might have extinguished the forest fire in time to save Lyell's village and family.

Nia opened the door, and he followed her to a seat by the fire. She started combing her hair with a grimace.

"Here, let me." Ahjin took the comb and picked up the ends of her ankle-length locks. The lavender strands spread in ripples across the floor as he slowly untangled them.

"I can't do all those fancy braids, though," he said when he finished.

Nia smiled over her shoulder. "How about one?"

"I think you've made me practice enough for that." He tickled the back of her neck on purpose as he gathered her hair and split it into strands.

She giggled and swatted his hands. As she kept the lengths from tangling, he braided, and she handed him a soggy ribbon to tie it.

"Do you want to go on a walk?" Nia asked.

"Are you still cold?"

She wiggled her toes. "Toasty warm."

Ahjin took Nia's hand and held open the door. Lamplight flickered from one window of Lyell's house, but they walked south. Ahjin kept his gaze on her face and followed the road by the feel of the cobblestones under his soft ankle boots. Crickets chirped under the stars, but the buildings and market stalls running along two sides of the town square were quiet and empty. At the opposite corner was the miniature temple with its marble columns, but he ignored it to admire the glow of Nia's golden skin in the moonlight. Once they crossed the road that ran from the eastern docks to Darravani's garden, the guest houses were not far ahead. The town used to end there, but in the last year, barracks for the workers had sprouted beyond. Married housing was next, but land was scarce on the tiny island the gods had created for him, and Ahjin had yet to find a design he liked.

He wanted to encourage marriage, though. Which reminded him...

"Nia," Ahjin asked, squeezing her fingers, "why did you come back early?"

Nia wound her long braid around her arm. "I was tired of Kala throwing boys at me."

"Throwing?"

"Shoving, then. I keep telling them I already have a boy."

Ahjin glanced at the moons. "There's a way to make them back off."

"Oh, do tell."

Ahjin stopped and took her hands in his. "Marrying me would tell them you aren't interested in anyone else."

"Ahjin, I love you, but marriage is permanent."

Ahjin tightened his grip. "I thought you wanted only me."

"I do!" Nia pulled her hands free and yanked on her hair. "But marriage feels different. It feels... I don't know. I'm not ready. Someday, it will be a great idea. Pleasant journey, Ahjin."

She leaned up for a kiss and then scampered toward her house.

Ahjin shoved his hands into his pockets and dragged his feet home.

Much too early in the morning, Kaito banged on the door. While Ahjin ate breakfast by the still-dark window, the Seal laid out his formal attire. The gods had argued for a long time over which part of his uniform should represent whom. The results were terrible. His orange brocade robe clashed with a scarlet headband with three flames stamped in black, and neither coordinated with the lavender sash embroidered with purple waves and multi-colored dolphins, or the bright green boots. The only bit of official insignia that was discreet was the silver star medallion around his neck.

Ahjin held out his arms and let Kaito fuss with seams and wrinkles. Arguing only prolonged the misery, and he already had enough torment in his life. Although, since the gods had been behaving themselves for the past nine months, his biggest problems were personal.

Why wouldn't Nia marry him? She was seventeen now. Ahjin was almost eighteen. They'd been happily courting for nine months. True,

Nokai rarely married, but Iojif did. Why wouldn't she make allowances for his beliefs?

Kaito twitched the sash again, then waved toward the doorway.

Ahjin lowered his arms carefully. "Thank you, Kaito."

They cut past the kitchen garden to the plain wood door that led directly to the inner sanctuary at the back of the temple. While Kaito continued into the outer temple, Ahjin checked his desk. Lyell's daily reports already piled up. Except for married housing, it seemed the new workers had all settled in. Ahjin initialed the job requests and turned to his task list for the day.

Two pages. How could he get through two pages before he left for Iskra?

Lyell poked his head through the inside door. "The sun is rising."

Ahjin tucked the list inside his sash and tightened the leather strand that kept his hair more-or-less confined at the back of his neck.

He walked through the door Lyell held open and into the outer temple. Stained-glass windows in the roof and walls poured rainbow light across the floor. Each of the side walls had two shrines. The back had only one, with the sixth space occupied by his sanctuary door.

His communication with Resef the Omnificent, the Iskrin God of Fire, came first, with the rising sun. Ahjin lit a candle on the mantle of the collapsible kiln of interlocking clay tiles and sat cross-legged. Without any real messages today, he laid out a practice one with the obsidian runes, then rested his hands on his knees and prayed. The runes didn't change, so he put them away.

He moved to the polished metal statue of a dolphin balancing a bowl of water on its head. Makanavailea the Omniscient, Nokai Goddess of Water, didn't appear in the water to answer his call. Knowing her, she was probably at a party somewhere.

Darravani's shrine was dark wood, beautifully carved into a tree trunk, capped with a tray of dirt, miniature parchment scrolls, and a book on the language of flowers. After his prayers, the yellow zinnia that bloomed for Darravani the Omnifarious, the Darrendran Goddess of Earth, merely meant "daily remembrance."

At the altar of jeweled marble with gold veins, Ahjin steeled himself for telepathic contact with Irajahan the Omnipotent. The petty Iojif God of Air answered absented-mindedly, skipped his usual insults, and disappeared quickly from Ahjin's mind with a distinct whiff of gloating. That was disturbing.

Kassian the Omnipresent had never had his own people, though he planned to change that. As soon as Ahjin touched Kassian's glass pedestal, a clear block with white stars etched inside, a new sheet of paper appeared beside the blank paper, ink, and quill.

"Ahjin," it said, "I finished surveying the Dragon Isles and am ready to accept settlers. Please screen applicants. Also, I want my colleagues moved there. Please see to it. Kassian."

Colleagues? What colleagues?

Oh... Ahjin dropped the paper onto the altar. Kassian meant to move his monsters to the Isles. How could Ahjin do that? The kraken could swim there and the giant bats could fly, if he could explain it to them, which he couldn't. Makana had gifted Ahjin with the languages of every country, but she hadn't included animals. Ah, but Nia's birth gift was *all* languages. That would take care of half the problem, but no ship captain in the world would agree to carry knee-high spiders or panther-sized scorpions. And if he moved the monsters to the Isles, how would he persuade people to settle there?

Obviously, he needed to talk to Kassian.

Lyell peeked in again. "Are you ready? People are arriving."

Ahjin straightened his stupid sash again and sat in his ridiculously fancy chair. Lyell ushered in Kaito and his guards and then opened the double doors at the front.

"You may enter the presence of His Holiness, the Mouth of All the Gods," he intoned loudly.

Ahjin managed not to roll his eyes as people crept along the walls or strode through as if they owned the place. This would be a long day. At least the gods didn't have a current argument for him to mediate. He met diplomats, relayed messages to and from gods, and invited settlers to the Dragon Isles.

After hours of boredom, Lyell ushered out the last of the crowd. Ahjin sagged in his chair. The day wasn't even over yet. After lunch, he needed to leave for Iskra.

"Oh, Ahjin," Irajahan said in the back of his head, with the echo that meant he was speaking to all the gods. "I have a proposal. I suggest the

Mouth of the Gods be a hereditary position, passed from parent to natural-born child." There was a definite smirk in his tone.

The buzz in the back of Ahjin's mind intensified as Irajahan argued with his siblings.

What mischief was Irajahan up to now? If the Mouth was always Iojif, Irajahan might have a future advantage against the other gods. If Ahjin refused to go along with the idea, Irajahan might use the excuse to replace him with another Mouth. Not that he'd mind escaping this drudgery, but he still didn't trust anyone else to watch Irajahan well enough.

Natural-born. If he married Nia, he wouldn't have children-by-blood, since she was a different race.

If the other gods agreed, Irajahan would make Ahjin choose between Nia and watching the deceitful God of Air.

4. TOUR
(ARUPA AND CHISATO)

The Nokai have no divorce, so few of them marry. Despite this, they take their complicated, extensive families seriously.
Everything You Ever Wanted to Know about the Nokailana Islands but Were Too Lazy to Ask

Nia crammed the last of her clothes into her pack and tied the lumpy bundle shut with her extra hair ribbons. At least Ahjin had waited until a decent hour to leave. He was much too fond of early morning, and she was tired of traveling at sunrise.

There, she was ready to go, and he wasn't back from the temple yet. She frowned as she dragged her pack downstairs and across town. In front of Ahjin's house, Lyell and Kaito directed a stream of people carrying baskets and packs toward the dock. Kaito took Nia's bag and motioned toward the temple and the midday sun.

Nia sighed. All that fuss to be ready on time, and Ahjin still wasn't here. "I'll get him."

She squished through the winter mud in actual boots, thanks to Zefra and Nemerra, and banged on the back door of the temple. "Ahjin, we need to leave with the tide. Hurry!"

She kept pounding until the door finally opened.

Ahjin glared at her with reddened eyes. "Come in and be quiet."

He yanked off his regalia and threw it on his desk, leaving on his everyday shirt and pants and the silver star of Kassian hanging around his neck on her old hair ribbon. His curly hair stuck out as if he'd yanked on it.

"Why aren't you ready yet?" Nia nagged. She took another look. "Is something wrong?"

"Irajahan—" Ahjin swallowed.

"Never mind, I don't want to know what that fiend has done now."

"But—"

"You can tell me later," Nia said. "We have to *go*."

While he switched from his official boots to his ordinary ones, she rolled up his ceremonial clothes.

"You'll wrinkle them," Ahjin said.

"Kaito will fix it." Nia shouldered him toward the door. "Let's go."

Ahjin grabbed his fancy boots and held the door for her, then locked it behind him. They joined the last of the crowd streaming east. Kaito took the bundled regalia from Nia, and Lyell handed Ahjin a list to discuss.

Nia skipped cheerfully at the thought of visiting their friends between Ahjin's boring official business. It wasn't until they reached the ship that she realized Ahjin was answering Lyell in the shortest possible sentences.

She walked up the plank, hands on her hips. Something was really wrong, not mere annoyance at Irajahan. But before she could talk to him, Lyell sequestered him in his cabin with a stack of paperwork. Nia helped Kaito stow their supplies and shoo the extra help ashore before their small crew of sailors cast off.

It took six days to sail around the northeast corner of Iskra, and they were all the same from morning sunshine to afternoon rain. Nia sailed, and sang, and played with Tala, and cooked under the watchful eye of Kaito, but Ahjin stayed in his cabin doing paperwork except when he snuck out to fly above the ship. By the time they pulled into the large

Devoran harbor in early morning, Nia was ready to pluck his feathers to make him talk to her.

But a crowd waited politely on the shore, and Lyell crammed Ahjin into his fancy clothes and paraded him through the horde and into Chisato, talking nonstop about petitioners and checking records and other boring things. Nia was separated from Ahjin in the crush, and when she reached the stone building set aside for his visit, he was already closed up in the audience room with the local leaders.

Nia kicked the wall. She didn't know where to find Zefra or Ludik and Nemerra, and she couldn't wander the district looking for them. Until Ahjin got out, she was stuck here with nothing to do. She let a bowing Iskrin show her to her room to unpack and had half her clothes thrown on the floor when Kaito knocked on her open door and walked in.

The serious Darrendrakar took her purple divided skirt from her and pushed her gently into a chair. He carefully folded the skirt, her rainbow-embroidered blouse, and every outfit she'd tossed on the floor, shaking out the wrinkles and lining up every seam.

"You don't have to do that, Kaito," Nia mumbled half-heartedly. "They'll only get messed up again."

Kaito shrugged and stacked her clothes neatly on the shelf.

Nia sighed. "I suppose you already did this for Ahjin."

Kaito nodded and walked to the door. He tilted his head toward the hall and waited.

"I'm coming." Nia dragged herself to her feet. "Where are we going?"

Kaito led the way to a nearby suite of rooms, where barking alerted Nia to the identity of the occupants. As soon as Kaito opened the door, the black wolf pup darted through. Nia snatched her before she escaped.

"Oh, no, Tala, you stay here." She nuzzled Lyell's furry daughter. "You don't want to get caught in the middle of the boring talk."

Nia and Kaito took Tala into the suite and dismissed the frazzled Iskrin maid who had been watching the puppy. She bowed and left, her boot heels clicking faster and faster down the stone hall until the echo faded.

Nia burst into laughter and rubbed Tala's ears. "I think you scared her, sweetie."

Tala licked Nia's cheek and wriggled down to race around the room. Nia watched the fuzzy puppy with amused delight. While Tala was an adorable little girl when she chose, she usually took advantage of the extra mobility of four legs. Her indulgent father let her, probably because a lucky shift to wolf had saved her life when her siblings died.

"I guess we're waiting here for Ahjin and Lyell?" Nia asked Kaito.

Though the Seal-man understood trade tongue, she spoke in Darrendran Seal to be polite. Her birth gift of languages from Makana made it as natural to speak any foreign language as it was to speak her own Noki.

He nodded and sat on the floor to play with Tala. Nia joined them, and laughter and barking soon filled the room.

When Tala wore herself out and curled up to sleep, Nia slumped against the wall. "Ahjin proposed again."

Kaito nodded.

Nia gasped. "Did he tell you?"

Kaito shook his head with the smallest of grins.

Nia let her head fall against the cool stone. "I don't know how you know everything. I don't suppose you'll tell me, either?"

Kaito grinned wider and shook his head again.

"I said no."

He frowned.

"Stop that," Nia said. "Why does everyone do that? It's my decision."

The door opened behind them.

"We have plenty of time to marry later," Nia complained. "What's the hurry?"

"No hurry," Lyell said, closing the door, "but you're hurting Ahjin's feelings."

"That's ridiculous," Nia said. "He knows how I feel about marriage."

Lyell sat by Tala and rested a hand on his sleeping pup. He shrugged. "His brain knows. His heart has your aversion to marriage tangled up in your feelings for him. He thinks you don't want to take your relationship further than it is."

Nia smirked. "I'd be happy to take it further, if he'd relax and kiss me more."

Kaito banged his head on his knees.

Lyell shook his head. "You know he won't unless you marry him. Are you so culturally bound that you can't consider marriage? I liked being married." His hand shook as he touched Tala's paw. "Your parents married, and they're Nokai."

"That's not fair," Nia protested.

"And what you're doing to Ahjin is?" Lyell frowned at her. "Either tell him yes or let him go."

Nia jumped to her feet and stormed from the room. Her relationship with Ahjin was nobody else's concern, and she should have known better than to bring it up. Why wasn't anyone on her side?

Lyell was wrong, and Nia would prove it. It was time she and Ahjin had a talk.

She stomped through the building until she found a line of people winding through the halls toward a large room with armed guards outside the door. That looked like the sort of place to find Ahjin in his official capacity as His Fanciness.

Nia tried to slide through the doors, but people fussed and whined, and the Iskrin guards sent her to the back of the line despite her attempts to explain. It was a long line, and it took hours to reach the doorway. Inside the room, there were benches for the weary, though they were as hard as they were fancy. Nia threw herself onto one and watched Ahjin.

Dressed in his awful priestly outfit, he sat behind a polished table on a narrow-backed chair that looked more uncomfortable than the benches. Guards stood at intervals, and servants ran back and forth with messages and books. Ahjin spoke too quietly for Nia to hear, except when calling for the next petitioner. Scribes wrote down every word, and copies of each decision left with the satisfied or unhappy people. Ahjin's face was diplomatically smooth, but his wings revealed his feelings to Nia, cramping with difficult decisions, relaxing with happy ones.

She watched him for hours. He took occasional short breaks, during which she wasn't allowed to approach, but mostly he sat there and listened and researched and talked and listened some more. The pile of books and scrolls on his table grew higher and higher, and his wings twitched more often. Nia sat on the hard bench, or sprawled across it, or hung upside down and tapped her heels on the wall murals until a stern old woman made her stop.

Eventually, boredom put her to sleep, head resting on her folded arm.

"Nia," a tired voice said.

"Waiting for Ahjin," Nia mumbled.

"I'm finished. Let's go."

"Mhm."

"Let's go before someone else comes and I can't escape."

Someone tugged on her arm until she stood and opened her eyes.

"Let's go," Ahjin repeated.

He pulled her toward a discreet door in the back corner, yanking off his sash and headband as he walked. Nia struggled to move her sleepy feet fast enough to keep up. They slipped through the door ahead of the guards and servants, and Ahjin shut the door in their faces. While she rubbed her eyes and stretched, he leaned against the door, then grabbed her hand and jogged down the hall.

"My room is closer," he said, "and more private. One of the few perks of the job."

In fact, his room was only a few doors down once they turned a corner. He shut the door quietly and braced a chair under the doorknob. Wide awake now, Nia's irritation returned.

He tossed his priestly accessories on the bed. "Why were you waiting for me? I thought you'd be too bored in the audience hall. Didn't you visit Ludik and Nemerra while I was busy?"

"I'll find them later," Nia said. "I want to talk to you."

Ahjin kicked off his boots and pulled off his brocade robe, revealing his usual bland outfit beneath. He took a deep breath and sank on the bed. "I have to tell you what Irajahan said."

Nia slouched in the cushioned chair by the wall. "Who cares what that old skunkwind says? I want to talk to you about us."

Ahjin's mouth twisted. "Oddly enough, what I have to tell you is also about us."

Nia furrowed her eyebrows. "But you said... You mean, Irajahan is talking to you about us? He doesn't even like you. Or me. What does he want?"

Ahjin grimaced. "He wants the Mouth of the Gods to be a hereditary position."

"Fine, whatever," Nia said. "The next Holiness can pass his job to his children."

"No," Ahjin said. "He wants it to start now. He's trying to persuade the other gods to go along with him, and I'm afraid they'll agree."

Nia wrinkled her nose. "If you need to adopt children already, we can talk about how soon is soon enough."

"Children by *blood*," Ahjin emphasized.

Nia laughed. "But we can't have children together, silly. Is Irajahan too stupid to realize the races can't interbreed?"

"He wants to either force me to marry a nice Iojif girl with whom I can have children, or replace me with someone who will comply with his demands. He's still angry I ended his conscription of priests, among other things. I think he figures he can get me out of his way equally well by breaking my spirit or getting rid of me entirely."

Nia sat up in the chair and spluttered. "Why, that, that... How dare he!"

"He's a god," Ahjin drawled. "He dares much, and he likes getting his own way. I don't know why you're so upset. You already said you didn't want to marry me. Now you have a perfectly good excuse not to do so." He blinked hard and shoved his regalia onto the floor.

"I don't want to marry you *yet*," Nia protested. "That's different from *never*."

Ahjin shrugged. "If you've gotten tired of being with me, you don't have to pretend."

He yanked the hair tie from the back of his neck and threw it on the ground.

"What's wrong with you?" Nia wailed. She jumped from the chair and flopped onto the bed next to him. "I love you, birdbrain, but marriage is a big thing, especially for a Nokai. Why can't it wait until we're older?"

"You can wait as long as you want." Ahjin ran his fingers through his curls until they stuck up in all directions. "I can't marry you while I'm the Mouth."

Nia banged her head on the soft mattress. "What if you stopped being Your Holiness? You never wanted the job in the first place."

"I've considered it," Ahjin said. "I could skydance with my parents like I always wanted."

"It sounds wonderful," Nia said. "What's wrong with that idea?"

"Irajahan, of course." Ahjin lay down, cheek to cheek with Nia. "If I quit, who will watch Irajahan?"

"He's not that bad anymore," Nia protested. "He helped us escape the pirates last year."

Ahjin snorted. "No, he didn't. Irajahan sent us after your mother's ship when he *knew* there were more pirates below deck. He didn't want us in the Dragon Isles and thought a convenient skirmish would take care of us. He also stripped my invisibility on purpose, to get me killed."

Nia gasped. "The toad! You should tell the other gods what he did."

"I tried, but he convinced his siblings I misunderstood everything because of my head injury. My brain *was* a little... difficult at the time. I thought maybe he was right." Ahjin covered his eyes with his arm. "So, how many people do you know who don't think Irajahan is charming and trustworthy?"

"You, me, Ludik, and Zefra," Nia rattled off. "The other gods."

Ahjin shook his head. "The other gods know he's difficult, but they think he learned his lesson and will behave from now on. Can you see Ludik or Zefra being the Mouth of the Gods?"

Nia smothered a giggle. "No. Ludik has other priorities, and Zefra would explode."

"What about you, then?" Ahjin asked.

Nia burst out laughing.

"Then give me another name," Ahjin said.

"Um, Izo? Lyell? Kaito? Nemerra? Askari or Sayaka? My dad?" Nia listed everyone who had been on one of their adventures with them. With every name, she and Ahjin shook their heads.

"Amrafel?" She named Irajahan's high priest, the Typhoon, with desperation.

"He doesn't think Irajahan is perfect," Ahjin said, "but he won't fight against him, either. No one else watches Irajahan well enough. He *is* charming, when he wants to be. I think I'm stuck with the job." He turned his head to look in her eyes from a mere thumb-lengths distance. "Will you come to my wedding when Irajahan assigns me a pretty Iojif?"

Nia rolled onto her back. "That's not fair. What an awful thing to say."

Ahjin inhaled, then let out a ragged sigh.

Nia jumped to her feet. "There must be somebody who hasn't fallen for his act."

Ahjin flipped onto his stomach and turned his face away, covering his head with his wings.

Nia paced the room, thinking. Would the gods take Ahjin from her? Someone in the world must be able to replace him as Mouth. But who? Was her life with Ahjin doomed before it even got started?

She didn't have any answers by the time Kaito brought them supper.

5. HEALER

(NEAR CHISATO; DAY 1)

The best Iskrin healers come from the Tukiko clan. The most talented earn the title of Shri.
Iskrin Culture and History, vol. 3

L udik took the pile of letters from a skinny Iskrin girl and bowed in thanks. As she ran off, he ducked inside his healer's tent and flipped through the pile. One from his Mama and Papa and one from Nemerra's. Five from his siblings. Three more from relatives. Without opening them, he guessed everyone was excited he and Nemerra were bringing their family home soon. His fingers twitched on the pile before he put it down. Reading would have to wait until he finished seeing his patients.

His instruments clattered as Zurrahava rammed his table. And patients must wait until his children were out of the way. He shook Rurru's teeth off his ankle and swooped Zurrahava away.

"Children, go play outside." He held open the tent flap and counted the furry cubs as they exited. "One, two, three, four, five, six... Six?"

There had only been four in their litter. He laughed and looked for the hole allowing them to run back inside. After fixing it, he shooed his children outside again to their minder. They tumbled in a ball of black, white, and yellow and rolled to their feet, coated in sand.

Ludik shook his head and invited his next patient inside. After the Iskrin boy's mama set a clucking basket on the ground, he clung to her robes, sitting so close to her that Ludik couldn't look at the arm he cradled.

"He fell this morning," the woman explained, stroking her son's hair, "and now he will not use the arm."

Ludik reached for the boy's arm, but when the youngster flinched, he leaned back. "It must be scary in here."

The boy shook his head emphatically.

"Your arm hurts," Ludik continued, "and your mama wants a perfect stranger to look at it, who might be too young to be any good at healing." That was for mama's worries. He lowered his voice to a whisper. "And then the healer has *brown* skin!" He put his hand next to the woman's white one and shook his head in fake dismay. "What kind of person has brown skin?"

The boy glanced at his mama, then shrugged.

"I am Shri Ludik." Ludik waited for the boy to close his mouth. Most Iskrins were surprised at his title. "I have only nineteen years, but I studied with Shri Okechuku." He waited for the mouth again. Okechuku was understandably famous. "I also studied with Koray, because I am from Darrendra, across the ocean, so I need to understand animal bodies as well as two-legger ones."

"You're a shapeshifter?" the boy asked. His brown eyes were so wide they no longer showed the graceful Iskrin tilt.

"I am. Did you see those adorable kittens outside? Those are my children." Ludik kept his voice low and soothing.

The boy gasped, examining Ludik's face and bare arms as if they would sprout fur on the spot.

Ludik hid a smile. "Now, does that settle everything except your sore arm?" He held out his hands and waited.

After a minute, the boy carefully laid his arm in Ludik's hands. The problem was obvious, even without using magic.

"I am afraid you broke this," Ludik said. "I can fix it, but it will hurt. Can you be brave enough?"

The boy gulped and nodded, clutching his mama's hand. She held him firmly against her as Ludik realigned the bone despite the boy's wail.

"All done." While the boy cried, Ludik held the arm firmly, sending a spurt of healing into it, then wrapped it in a splint. "You will be as good as ever in a month. Try to be careful until then." He shared a smile with the woman, not envying her task of keeping the boy out of trouble for that long. At least he had cut the healing time.

The woman bowed deeply and gave him a speckled chicken. Ludik bowed in return, showed them out, and gave the chicken to the youngster assigned to clean the tent.

The next patient had a fever and exchanged a gold coin for standard herbs enhanced with Ludik's healing magic. He left bowing repeatedly, babbling thanks and good wishes for the outdweller healer.

The third was Nokai. Her bare foot was swollen and red around a deep slash.

"I heard you know how to heal others?" she asked. "The Iskrins will treat foreigners — for enough money — but they don't usually study anyone but their own kind." She tugged on one of her long, pink braids and fidgeted.

"I have studied all four races," Ludik assured her, washing the cut with hot water and disinfecting herbs. "Is that why you took so long to see a healer?"

Her foot twitched. "I did go to a healer, but he said I got dirt in the wound and it was too late unless I saw a Tukiko. I can't afford one of the Shri."

Ludik ran a finger slowly along the gash, burning away the infection and binding the tissue together. "You might have lost your foot."

The Nokai blinked back tears. "I'm only a common sailor. I'd never have enough money."

"Well, I've barely earned my title," Ludik said lightly. "I'll take what you can pay me." He wrapped the foot in a long bandage, then covered it in strips of leather. "I know you don't normally wear shoes, but please keep this covered until it heals."

She threw her arms around him. "Thank you, thank you." She pressed a beautiful shell into his hand and hobbled from the tent.

Ludik ducked outside. Only three more patients waited for him. By the time the last left at midday, Nemerra's voice filtered through the tent wall. He set a payment of fruit on a table and grabbed the letters, then headed for his sweetheart by their family tent.

He read the letters while the children scampered around her feet, pawing at her knees and jumping for the basket she carried. The little ones were nine months old now, and on four legs, they were enough trouble for anyone.

"Settle down," Nemerra said, "before I step on you."

Rurru spun in a circle so fast his spotted white fur turned into a pale gray blur, then he pounced on Kamakana and bit his sister's leopard ear. She squalled and clawed at his tail, and the two tumbled end over end in a wrestling match.

Terru sat on Nemerra's toes and clawed his way up her dress. "Paw-lease," the lion cub mewed, "show us."

Zurrahava curled into a deceptively peaceful ball and licked her tail. "Yes, Mama, new toys?"

Nemerra laughed. "Today I only got food and clothes. The clothes are for you, though. Do you want to see them?"

Terru dropped to the ground. "No. Eat?"

"See," Rurru and Zurrahava chorused.

Rurru turned away again when Kamakana bit his tail, so only the miniature black jaguar watched when Nemerra held the little outfits low.

When Terru ran through his mama's demonstration, his sister hot on his rump, Ludik scooped them both into his arms. Nemerra led the other two into the tent, and the four cubs tumbled into their basket for nap time. They had outgrown their old basket months ago and now slept in one of the large baskets Nemerra used on laundry day.

"Here, Nemerra, we got letters today." Ludik handed her the one from her parents first. "The one from Gurryon is amusing."

He put away the food while she read, following her progress by the rustle of pages and her quiet comments.

"You're right." Nemerra laughed. "Ilani is expecting, and Gurryon is a mess of nerves. Haider seems to be adjusting to marriage better."

Ludik had missed the wedding of both his littermates last summer due to the distance across the ocean. He hadn't seen his parents and siblings for almost two years, and letters took months to travel back and forth. As soon as Ahjin and Nia arrived for their conveniently timed visit, Ludik would be happily on his way home. Both sets of grandparents impatiently waited to meet the cubs, and his sister had asked about them in every letter.

Ludik smiled and glanced at the basket of black and yellow fur in the corner. Black and yellow, but no white.

"Nemerra, where is Rurru?" He dropped the letters and hurried for the tent flap.

As he ducked outside, he saw Rurru chasing a spinning tumbleweed across the sand. And past him, a hunter raised his bow and pointed an arrow at the white kitten.

"No!" Ludik shouted. "Rurru, run!" He pounded for the Iskrin as Nemerra headed for their cub.

Rurru abandoned the tumbleweed, tripping over his own paws as he ran through dips in the sand toward the tent.

The hunter drew back the string.

"What are you doing?" Ludik yelled.

As he slammed into the man's side and knocked him to the ground, the arrow loosed. Rurru cried out and then was silent.

"That is my son!" Ludik and the hunter tumbled, and when they rolled to a stop, Ludik was on top.

The man's mouth dropped open. "I — I did not know."

Ludik fumbled for the bow, growling until the Iskrin's white face turned gray. "Nemerra?"

Behind them, Rurru squeaked, "Mama, Mama, Mama."

"He's fine." Nemerra's voice was higher than usual as she soothed the cub.

Ludik sucked in a shuddering breath. "Never shoot an unsure target," he snarled. He itched to shift and bite the man but settled for snapping the weapon in half. "Be glad you missed."

The Iskrin slunk away without his broken bow, and Ludik rested his head on his shaking knees. If he had been a little slower... He stayed under the apricot sky until he no longer felt like killing something, then joined his family inside the tent.

Nemerra held Rurru on her lap, petting his fur and humming softly. She held her finger to her lips. The other three were still napping, somehow.

Ludik touched the bandage around Rurru's paw where the arrow had not missed entirely, letting healing trickle through the bandage.

"Leave it wrapped until tomorrow," he whispered. "We don't want him to tear it open again."

Nemerra put the shivering cub into the basket with his siblings. "Hush; I'm here," she whispered.

Though he wouldn't see any more patients today, Ludik forced himself to return to the healing tent to prepare for their departure. He made notes for the healer who would replace him, then sorted supplies into those to stay and those to go. By the end of the day, he needed to have everything packed.

"Are you available?" someone asked from the open tent flap. The Iskrin was a thin man, fairly young, with a sparse but tidy beard.

"I am afraid I am closed for the day," Ludik said.

"Oh." The man stepped into the tent, cradling his arm. "I hoped you could help me. The other healers are also closed."

They must be gone on calls. Ludik sighed and grabbed a bandage roll. "Come in. You hurt your arm?"

"Just a sprain, I hope." The Iskrin dropped the tent flap closed behind him and sat on the cot.

Ludik wrote the date and time on a sheet of parchment. "What is your name?"

The man looked sideways. "Is this visit confidential?"

Ludik glanced at the closed tent flap. "Only my supervisor will see the notes."

"Mmm." The man grimaced.

"You do not want me to mention your name at all?"

The man fidgeted on the cot. "How do I know you are a real healer?"

Ludik put down the pen. "I am fully qualified. I am Shri Ludik."

"Then you are the man I want to see." The man smiled oddly and held out his arm.

When Ludik leaned over to touch his arm, the Iskrin pulled a long cord from his pocket and whipped it around Ludik's neck. Before he could react, the Iskrin pulled the ends and twisted hard.

As the cord tightened, Ludik gasped for breath and struck at the man's arms.

The Iskrin spun past Ludik's shoulder and braced himself back-to-back, pulling harder.

Ludik grabbed at the cord, trying to wiggle his fingers underneath, but it was too tight. He leaned backward to loosen the cord. The man merely leaned forward to maintain the tension.

Ludik thrashed sideways, reaching for his scalpel or any weapon. The Iskrin kicked over the small table of Ludik's supplies, scattering them out of reach.

The cord cut into Ludik's throat. He threw himself sideways, but the man stayed with him.

Gray spots danced in Ludik's vision. In desperation, he shifted to jaguar. His tunic ripped, and the cord tightened even more around his larger neck. As his vision blackened, he clawed behind him but reached only fabric.

He kept clawing, growing weaker, and finally caught something that resisted more than cloth. Ludik pulled hard, and the man screamed.

The cord loosened a little, and Ludik clawed again. The cord slipped. Ludik ripped free of the Iskrin and whirled. He shook the cord free and gasped for breath, weaving to avoid recapture.

Spots dancing in his eyes, he pounced on his assassin. The man threw a bleeding arm across his face and screamed again.

Ludik thought of Nemerra and his four children in the next tent and crushed the assassin's skull with his jaws. When the man stopped twitching, Ludik crawled off the body, trembling.

His throat hurt too much to swallow, and his breath came in choking gasps. Despite the pain, he sucked air down his throat, pressing a healing hand to his throat until he could breathe better. It was always difficult to heal oneself, but if he didn't fix his neck enough to talk, Nemerra would panic.

Nemerra! Ludik shifted back, quickly wiping off the blood with his ruined tunic and grabbing a spare Iskrin robe and scarf from the storage chest. He dashed outside, wrapping the scarf around the bruises, and ducked into his home tent. Nemerra had put out the lamp so the children could sleep, and he blinked in the dim light.

His wife lay on the floor by the cubs, eyes closed, knife near her hand. A streak of red ran down the front of her dress.

Ludik fell to his knees. Had the man come here first? Was he too late? He reached with shaking fingers for the red. *Please, Darravani*, let him be able to heal her.

The red was solid, not liquid. He felt the silkiness again to be sure, then croaked a laugh. Nemerra had unpinned her russet braid, and in the dimness, it looked like blood.

Nemerra opened her eyes halfway. "Are you finished today?"

"Almost." Ludik whispered to disguise the damage to his voice. He couldn't tell her about this. The attack on Rurru already worried her.

Someone screamed outside.

"Stay here," Ludik said. "Protect the children."

He dashed out of the tent and crashed into his assistant, who waved her hands and screamed.

"He's dead—"

Ludik clapped his hand over her mouth. "Calm down," he croaked. When he shook her, she finally stopped screaming.

People ran from every tent in the vicinity. Behind them, a horse galloped toward town. Ludik sent his assistant to reassure Nemerra and the crowd before the constables arrived, and he went into his healing tent and stared at the body. The face was destroyed, and one sleeve was soaked in blood. Ludik pushed up the sleeve to see the shredded arm. Above the damage, the biceps was decorated with a complex tattoo.

Ludik was still examining the body when the guards arrived. They let themselves in the tent, shutting the flap in the faces of the avid crowd, then surrounded Ludik, hands on their weapons.

The tallest of the three crouched beside Ludik and turned the corpse's head from side to side. "What happened here?"

"He tried to kill me," Ludik wheezed, "so I killed him." He touched a hand to his throat and dribbled in a little more healing so he could speak.

"With what?" blurted one of the other guards.

"I am Darrendrakar."

"Yes?" the first guard said.

"My other shape is a jaguar."

"I still do not — Oh." He flinched back.

The third guard picked up the table and dumped healing supplies into a basket with no regard for order. "Why did he try to kill you?"

"He did not say," Ludik croaked, unwinding the scarf and tilting his chin for the guards to see his neck.

The second guard bit off an exclamation.

"Then who did you make into an enemy?" the third guard asked.

Ludik shrugged. "No one? I am a healer and leaving soon for home."

The second guard laughed bitterly. "A healer did this?"

Ludik clenched his fist around his walrus tusk necklace, a reminder of the cost of hate. He had wished to never kill again.

"I regret his death, but my family is in the next tent. Should I leave them in danger to spare a killer's life?"

The first guard stood. "We cannot question a corpse, and you did not leave a face to identify. You have not made it easy for us to investigate."

Ludik croaked a laugh. "He has a tattoo, and you can take his weapon. It is here somewhere."

All four searched the tent until they found the cord. Ludik piled scattered bandages and herbs on the cot to sort later. Most of them could be salvaged and left with his assistant to heal more patients. He caught himself scrubbing his hands against his robe and clenched them behind his back.

The first guard coiled the twine into his pocket while the other two picked up the body. "We will let you know if we find anything." But he shook his head as they left.

Ludik shut the tent flap and poured water into a bowl. As he washed his hands, he racked his brain for anyone he might have offended. Was this hatred for a foreigner or something personal? And if he didn't know the reason, how could he know if this was over or if another enemy lurked around the next corner?

At least Nemerra had seen nothing. If he kept his neck covered, he wouldn't worry her more before they left for home in a few days. He could keep his family safe until then.

6. ATTACK

(CHISATO)

The great fire mage Kezhekori evaporated a hurricane, fought monsters with his flaming hands, stopped a forest fire, and burned a pirate fleet single-handedly.

Legends of Iskra

"Lapwing is a wanted criminal," Zefra said. "I should tell Ahjin, but I do not think he and Nia are here yet. Will you show me where Ludik stays? Nemerra did not give me directions, but he can pass word to Ahjin."

"Certainly," Tarakh said. "Now that the rain has stopped, we need to deliver Nemerra's flour, anyway." He headed back to his tent, using his staff to subtly make a way through the crowd.

While they wove through the marketplace still teeming with shoppers irritated by Zefra's chase after Lapwing, she told Tarakh about being stranded on the Dragon Isles and fighting a pirate fleet. Just before his pirate general was killed, Lapwing had flown away. He had not been seen since, and while she had no proof he was up to mischief, he did not seem the sort to live quietly and comply with the law.

Tarakh made impressed noises at all the right moments, and Zefra began to enjoy telling the story. 'Twas not as dramatic as their first adventure with the gods, nor had it been fun to be marooned in a secret pirate refuge, but she reluctantly admitted their outnumbered battle made an exciting tale when she was not trapped in the middle of it, wondering if they would live or die.

"How did you hear about the pirates to know where to find them?" Tarakh asked. "None of the storytellers knew that detail."

"Oh, we did not know they were there. We went to Nokailana for Nia's coming-of-age party, then left to search for Nia's long-missing father and land for Kassian. Landing in the middle of pirates was only misfortune."

"A party?" Tarakh shook his head. "I do not know anyone else who can go for a party and end up defeating pirates."

Zefra grinned at him. "When we went to Darrendra for Ludik's wedding, we chased a murderer, escaped our own execution, ran through the middle of a forest fire, and discovered a lost kindred. The only time we had an adventure on purpose was when Ahjin needed help to rescue the gods." She paused. "And that was even more dangerous."

Tarakh whistled. "It is good you are able to defend yourself, since you seem determined to live an exciting life."

Zefra shrugged. "Explorers must be prepared for the unexpected."

Tarakh smiled. "You seem very prepared."

"If only the caravan masters agreed with you, they might hire me."

"Perhaps they are only worried about being in your next adventure."

Zefra glared at him, and he laughed.

When they reached the farmer's booth, he said, "Have another fruit while I get Nemerra's flour and my scarf." He flicked a glance at Zefra's still-uncovered hair.

Zefra blushed. She had forgotten about her own scarf. Everyone in the market might have seen her fiery hair by now. She set down her staff and wrapped her scarf properly around her hair, covering every strand of red. Resef's distinctive mark did her no favors.

As she finished, a stocky Nokai man in an Iskrin robe approached the booth. His hair was only a thumb long, dramatically short for a Nokai, and such a dark teal it might be mistaken for black from a distance. Only his golden skin advertised his origins until he got close enough to see his gills.

"You shouldn't cover your hair, my dear. Red hair is much prettier than black. I saw it across the market. I'd enjoy watching it gleam in the sunlight as you select fruit for me." He held out a large basket in his webbed hands.

Zefra turned away and ignored his rudeness. Strangers must be excused their ignorance, but they did not have to be indulged.

"Oh, come, now. I have Iskrin money, not just trade shells. Give me some fruit."

"I cannot help you," Zefra said.

"I know Iskrin customs," the Nokai said. "Women are not forbidden to talk to strangers." He edged closer to her. "If you spend a little time with me, you'll see I'm not that bad."

"I do not work here," Zefra explained.

The man smiled pleasantly. "Where do you work?"

She pressed her lips together, weighing her irrational dislike for the stranger with her need for information. After a minute, she admitted, "I am currently looking for employment. Do you know of a position for a guide?"

The man grinned. "How perfect. I can offer you a job."

Zefra wrinkled her nose in disgust, straightening it before the man noticed, she hoped. "Where are you headed?"

"South." He waved vaguely and moved closer. "We can discuss details later."

Zefra frowned. "Details are important. I need to know if I'm familiar with your route."

He smirked. "My route is undetermined, but I'm happy to follow you anywhere."

Zefra casually put a hand on her saif, glad yet again that Izo had insisted she have proper weapons in her size before leaving home. And this time, she would not overreact with her flame. A simple warning should suffice.

"As a qualified guide, 'tis my job to get clients to their destination, not lead them blindly through the desert." She felt her smile growing tighter, and she was afraid she was glaring, potential client or not.

His smirk grew. "If we get lost, I'm sure we can pass the time pleasantly."

Her smile died. She would apologize to Tarakh for chasing away his customer after she got rid of the pest buzzing around his fruit. "I have no interest in working for you. And I am a *guide*."

Tarakh exited his tent with Nemerra's flour over one shoulder. "Are you ready to go? You can tell me the story of Ludik's wedding as we walk." He saw the stranger and put down the covered sack. "This is my stall. How may I help you?"

"I was just talking to this girl. I can come back for fruit later."

"Go jump in a sand dune," Zefra said.

"Leave her alone," Tarakh ordered. He whistled shrilly and gestured at someone in the market square.

The stocky Nokai ignored Tarakh. "Now that I've found you, I can't let you go. I'm sorry."

Tarakh picked up his staff. "'Tis time for you to leave."

The stranger drew his knife. "My business with her does not concern you, farmer. Leave before you get hurt."

Zefra pulled on her sword hilt, but the man put his hand over hers to prevent her from drawing the weapon. "Let go of me."

She pulled backward, but he held on, yanking her hand free of her saif and reeling her toward him. As he wrapped her in his arms, trapping her hands, she stopped fighting and drew energy from the sun.

"Let me go before *you* get hurt," Zefra said.

The man sneered at Tarakh before turning back to Zefra. "I'm not afraid of him. He doesn't have a sword, and he can't fight me while I have you. He wouldn't want you to get hurt." The Nokai held the sharp knife against Zefra's neck, pricking her skin.

"I'm warning you," Zefra said, pulling harder on the sunlight, "let me go."

"Do you not know who this is?" Tarakh asked. "You should pick your victims more carefully."

"I have no choice." The man shook his head sadly. "Stay back, and I won't hurt you."

"Please stay back and keep everyone else *away*." Zefra spoke calmly, hoping Tarakh understood her emphasis.

Tarakh nodded once. "Because you are a stranger," he said, "and do not know about Iskrins with red hair, allow me to introduce you. This is Zefra Ashvakosha Kezhekori."

The Nokai blinked. "I don't care about her name."

Tarakh looked at Zefra and twitched an eyebrow. Zefra nodded. She was ready.

"In Iskra," Tarakh continued, "we care about names. They tell us something about the people we meet. Kezhekori means 'burning fire.'"

"I don't care what her name means," the Nokai said, "any more than I care what her name *is*."

"You should." Zefra called fire through her arm and sent it roaring into the Nokai.

His robe burst into flames, and her sleeve caught on fire. He screamed and let go of Zefra, beating at his burning clothes.

Zefra jumped away and smothered her sleeve with her fireproof hands.

The Nokai crashed into the produce table and knocked it over. Tarakh used his staff to push the blazing Nokai away from the market tents, then rolled him in the sand. Merchants from nearby stalls shouted and gaped while someone called for help.

Zefra drew her saif and watched Tarakh save the man who did not deserve the mercy.

When the fire was out, Tarakh let the Nokai sit. The man clutched his burned hands and cried. His face was gray with soot, and his robe was in scorched tatters over his blistered flesh. The arm that had been around Zefra was the worst burned, and its sleeve had turned to ash up to his shoulder, revealing a tattoo of intertwining lines between the blisters and charred streaks.

Tarakh leaned on his staff, looking unsympathetic. "I told you to leave her alone."

"She's just a little girl," the Nokai moaned. "They didn't say—" He clamped his mouth shut and whimpered.

"Who did not say what?" Zefra asked.

The Nokai closed his eyes and shook his head.

Tarakh and Zefra stood guard until the constables arrived on horseback. They were adequate horses, but not as good as her father's stock.

"Put away your weapons," the guards said.

Zefra sheathed her saif and folded her hands demurely. Tarakh's eyes crinkled as he leaned his staff against the tent.

While one guard tended to the Nokai, a second wrote down Tarakh's report, and a third wandered through the crowd taking down eyewitnesses' stories.

In her report, Zefra added a few details that Tarakh had not seen or heard and finished, "Since he would not let go of me, I set him on fire."

"With a lamp, I assume," the guard said in a bored voice as he made notes, "since flint and steel take too long. 'Tis dangerous to throw oil in a public place, young lady. Next time, let the grown men handle it." He nodded at Tarakh.

Tarakh shook his head. "I assure you, Kezhekori can burn exactly what she intends without harming innocent bystanders."

The guard lowered his slate. "Kezhekori? *The* Kezhekori, who rescued the gods and burned an entire fleet of pirate ships? Kezhekori is a powerful man, blessed by the Most Holy Flame. You're a little girl. I do not blame you for defending yourself, but there is no need to lie. Since the fire did not spread, you will not be charged with public endangerment. Where is the lamp you dumped on him?"

Tarakh covered his laugh with his hand.

Zefra sighed. Her mother assured her that *someday* she would look like a grown woman. "You heard the wrong stories."

She shook her dowry bracelet so it slid from under her sleeve and spun around her wrist, then removed her scarf to reveal the red hair that marked her as fire-touched. Once she had the guard's full attention — and the crowd's — she snapped her fingers and called flame to dance in her hand.

The Nokai whimpered, his guard cursed, and whispers spread like wildfire through the crowd.

The constable taking Zefra's report kept a straight face but dropped his chalk. He touched the fire in Zefra's hand and snatched back his finger, then picked up his chalk. "Kezhekori," he drawled, writing on the slate. "Anything else you want to add?"

Zefra thought for a minute. "He might have been looking for me specifically. He talked a lot about my red hair, said he had business with me, and mentioned someone who told him something about me. But he did not seem to have a real job and would not accept my refusal." Her face grew hot as she thought of his suggestion to spend time together.

"He was determined to take her, despite being in a public place." Tarakh frowned at the Nokai, his fingers twitching toward his staff.

The third guard returned with a stack of slates. "I have the reports from the crowd."

The first guard looked at Zefra and Tarakh again, and when they shook their heads, he tucked his slate into his pouch. "If I have more questions later, I will let you know."

The guards shoved the Nokai onto horseback, despite his whimpers, then tied his hands to the saddle, mounted themselves, and escorted him toward stone buildings in the middle of the city.

While he returned the table to its position, Tarakh glared at the crowd until the gaping shoppers dispersed in small groups of whispering gossips. Zefra covered her hair again, then helped him refill the baskets with his produce. By the time they finished, the crowd had moved to the far side of the market square, still watching and whispering.

Tarakh put the last onion into a basket and held out his hands to Zefra. "Give me your hands."

Zefra put her hands behind her back. "I thought you wanted to take time to get to know me."

Tarakh blushed like a campfire and cleared his throat twice. "I mean, I want to see if you are injured."

Zefra turned her unburned hands palm up in front of him. "My own fire does not burn me. Any fire must be much hotter before it damages me."

Tarakh brushed a finger across her scorched sleeve hem. "You worried me."

Zefra dropped her hands. "I'm surprised you let me handle that. Though we have women guards in both the cities and the caravans, most men think I'm too young and weak to protect myself."

"You have a sword *and* fire in your veins. I knew you could protect yourself and me, too, but I hope I do not offend you if I admit I wanted to hit the Nokai myself."

Zefra grinned. "I would have let you, were it not for his knife against my throat."

"If he were a little smarter, he would have let me hit him instead of contending with you." Tarakh shook his head. "I told him who you are; I even explained your name. The stories are everywhere. He must be very stupid."

"Jail will keep him out of my way," Zefra said, "and I have more important things to worry about than an insignificant miscreant. Are you ready to go tell Ludik about Lapwing?"

Tarakh motioned to someone to watch his stall. "Where did the flour go? Ah, there it is." He slung the bag effortlessly over his shoulder and picked up his staff. "Grab that small basket of berries as a gift from me to your friends, please. It will be a pleasant walk to the edge of Chisato. Now, you were going to tell me how Ludik's wedding turned into a hunt for a murderer."

"We arrived the day of the wedding and found two dead bodies," Zefra began.

7. HEARINGS

(CHISATO)

All of Irajahan's priests have telepathy, and all telepaths are in the priesthood. (Footnote: Priests are no longer drafted, by order of the gods and His Holiness.)
Handbook for Winds

The next day, Ahjin donned his ugly uniform, wishing he could join Nia to play with Tala. Now that most of his meetings with the leaders were over, the morning would be spent in official business with the public before the afternoon hearings.

Kaito carried Ahjin's basket of paperwork as they snuck through the back halls and the back door of the fancy audience hall. The room was so full of chattering people, Ahjin took his seat at the front and arranged his agenda without anyone noticing him. The Iskrins had kindly arranged for a chair with a narrow back that fit between his wings. When he was ready, he nodded at Kaito, who edged through the crowd and tugged on Lyell's arm.

"What, Kaito?" Lyell turned to look at the quiet Seal and saw Ahjin. He rubbed his forehead, then waved at one of the guards stationed around the room and pointed.

The guard followed his gesture, then snapped to attention and waved more guards to stand near Ahjin. Kaito returned to his customary place at Ahjin's side, and Lyell stood to one side of the long, polished table that served as Ahjin's desk.

"Bright day, people of Iskra," Lyell bellowed in his primitive Iskrit. After the crowd hushed, he continued. "I present to you His Holiness, the Mouth of All the Gods."

He bowed to Ahjin, and everyone but the guards copied him.

Ahjin tightened his shoulders to keep from flinching. He scanned his list, and when Lyell was upright again, asked, "Is anyone from the new international fleet here yet?"

Lyell whispered in the ear of a young Iskrin, too young for gender to be obvious in the robe and scarf they all wore. The child dashed through the crowd to the benches lining the walls and returned with a small mixed group of sailors.

The sailors looked rough, but they bowed with varying proficiency and politely introduced themselves as captains in the armada the gods had authorized to patrol neutral waters. No one wanted another pirate infestation.

The Nokai captain with hair the same emerald as Nia's eyes collected scrolls, slates, and large leaves from the other captains and put them on the table under the watchful eye of the guards.

"Here are the detailed reports," he said in trade tongue. "Most importantly, we have finally cleared out the pirates. The Dragon Isles are empty again, and the shipping lanes are clear. Any ships not destroyed have been returned to their country-of-origin."

He waited for the crowd to stop cheering. "We will continue our patrols. Your Chief of Staff knows how to contact us." He nodded at Lyell and bowed clumsily to Ahjin.

"Thank you, all of you," Ahjin said. "You have done well. I appreciate the safety you provide for ships and coasts alike." He nodded at each captain in turn, matching the appropriate farewell to their customs and switching languages for each. "Pleasant journey, keep well, and warmth to you."

The captains bowed again and left.

Ahjin stood. "With this good news, I can announce that Kassian, My Lord Celestial, eldest brother of the gods, has declared the Dragon Isles open for settlement and under his protection. If you are willing to live with people of different origins and customs, you may apply for colonization."

He conspicuously handed Lyell a sheaf of parchment. "My Chief of Staff has the instructions. You may see him after this meeting. One warning: Kassian has pets that might be alarming to you. Make sure you understand the details before you apply."

Ahjin sat again and checked his list. "Lyell, bring in the foreign diplomats, please."

Lyell sent more children dodging through the crowd. They returned in minutes, trailing non-Iskrins, and Ahjin stepped around the table to greet them.

The middle-aged Nokai wore an Iskrin robe and scarf, true, but in eye-popping colors that emphasized her golden skin, and the scarf was wrapped around the gills on her neck instead of her wine-red hair. She introduced herself with a long name he couldn't possibly remember and kissed him on both cheeks.

The Darrendrakar's customary long tunic had been dyed dark green until the prior designs were nothing but highlights. With his dark skin, he looked like a shadow in the crowd of pale-robed, white-skinned Iskrins. Ahjin couldn't tell if his bone-white hair was natural or the result of his old age. He introduced himself by name and Antelope kindred and clasped Ahjin's arm.

The young Iojif, maybe a few years older than Ahjin, wore an Iskrin robe in the usual drab colors, but she had wrapped the wrists tightly with embroidered cuffs, shortened it to knee-length, and added leggings underneath. Her blue-black hair was cut to chin length, and her wings were a startling bright yellow.

She wore a discreet pin from the same House as Ahjin's mother, and as she shook his hand, she nodded at his raised eyebrow. "We are distant cousins. My name is Sufa."

To his surprise, her voice echoed inside his head next. "Thank you for setting me free." Her handshake tightened, then she stepped back to join the other diplomats.

It took two telepaths to talk mentally, and until recently, all of the others had been Irajahan's priests. This was the first time he had met a priest freed from conscription by his bargain with the gods, the first time he knew his efforts to help had made a difference to someone.

"Fair winds, cousin," Ahjin said. He cleared his throat before mentally adding, "You're welcome."

"Welcome to Iskra," he said aloud to all three. "Thank you for serving your country by improving international relationships."

He chatted with the three diplomats in their own languages, asking about problems and successes and making a few notes until Lyell raised his eyebrows and subtly tilted his head toward the waiting crowd.

"I'll talk to you more later," Ahjin said, "but if you need me, you can reach me through Lyell." He motioned to his Chief of Staff.

While all three diplomats bowed, he sent a private message to Sufa's mind. "You can reach me directly. Let's talk sometime."

Sufa dipped her chin a fraction. The children led them away, and Ahjin took his seat, clearing his throat again.

Kaito filled a glass with water and thumped it in front of Ahjin.

Ahjin drank, mostly to stall for a minute.

"Besides showing you those who are working with you," he told the crowd, "I hoped to encourage anyone who is interested to join one of our new international committees. If you aren't a sailor, there are openings for ecumenical priests or craft training or cultural exchange or—"

He stopped when two Iskrin men pushed through the crowd, shoving anyone in their way. When the guards drew their swords, they screeched to a halt in front of the table.

"We want to apply for the priesthood," the taller one said, rubbing one biceps and panting for breath. As an afterthought, he pulled his friend into a low bow with him.

They rose again, and the short one glared at the guards as he smoothed his fine robes. "Yes, we are ready to join now. Let us tell you our qualifications."

Ahjin raised his hand for silence and squinted at the two of them. Somehow, they seemed familiar. While he stared at them, they fidgeted, smiling and nodding and rearranging their hands. It was their clutch toward their shiny pendants that jiggled the memory forward.

He leaned back in his seat and frowned. "We've already met, and this is still not the way to apply."

"Oh, no," the short one said. "Why, you just got here." He smiled, winced, and rubbed his arm.

"We met on Arupa," Ahjin said, "over a year ago. You hit my little sister."

The crowd gasped. Lyell growled and stepped forward. Ahjin waved him back, despite wishing to turn the Wolf loose on the bullies.

"No, no, no," the tall one said. "I barely touched—" He turned bright red.

Ahjin nodded. "Your application for the priesthood has already been denied. Your application for *anything* is denied. You are unworthy and can't be trusted. Guards, escort them out and list them as undesirables."

Four guards grabbed the Iskrins by the arms. Despite the two scoundrels' screams, the guards shoved them out as the Iskrins cradled their left arms, weeping.

Ahjin rubbed his forehead. Did they think he was so stupid he didn't recognize them from before? He motioned Kaito closer. "Is it time for lunch yet?" he whispered.

Kaito shook his head and tapped the list on the table.

Ahjin groaned. "Lunch had better be delicious."

Kaito refilled his glass, and Ahjin turned back to the crowd. "How many of you are here for one of the international committees?"

Half the crowd raised hands.

"Lyell, do we have somewhere for these people to go to learn more?"

Lyell slid him a list of room assignments, and Ahjin read the first one slowly out loud, repeating it in multiple languages. Though he could let interpreters relay, he preferred to take responsibility himself. He waited for each interested group to depart with one of his assistants before reading the next entry.

Finally, the last group left. A guard checked the hallway and let in the last few stragglers, then closed the doors. The room was still half-full, and after Ahjin finished here, he'd have to repeat it in the next district, and the next, and the next. Iskra would take months, and then he had to go to Nokailana and the Dragon Isles and Darrendra and Ioj. Years might pass before he got back to Arupa. And all without Nia as his wife.

Ahjin leaned on the table for support, reading his list as an excuse. Would it be better to give up his job now and let someone else deal with it?

But he was making progress. The gods were finally cooperating, most of the time. Irajahan had been surprisingly mild since their adventure last spring, until this recent ultimatum about heirs. Sufa and the vanquished pirates were proof Ahjin was making the world a better place. Now that things were falling into place, could someone else take over, or would it all break apart if Ahjin left?

Kaito nudged him with his foot, and Ahjin sat up. "It is time for individual requests."

Most of the people left in the room lined up.

They could pray perfectly well by themselves. Their gods listened and answered, or not, as inclined. But experience had shown Ahjin that people believed His Holiness could get them a better answer. He'd never convinced anyone that he was only helpful to talk to a different god than one's native deity.

Ahjin forced a smile on his face. "Who is first?"

A giggling girl approached with a message for Makanavailea. She mumbled something about love and a boy. Ahjin carefully explained that Makana was not the goddess of love, all while drowning the note upside-down in a bowl of water so Makana could read it.

After a few minutes, he gently said, "There is no answer. The gods usually leave such matters to us. Maybe you should talk to the boy?"

She turned bright red, fluttered her eyelashes at Ahjin, and stammered something even less intelligible.

Ahjin motioned for one of Lyell's endless urchins and dismissed the blushing girl. The next three petitioners were reasonable, and Ahjin resolved their problems. Then he got an entire string of flirting girls from all over the world, who had apparently come to Iskra to see if he wanted a wife.

If Nia were here, she'd either laugh or pick up a harpoon. He'd borrow the harpoon, if he could get away with it. Ahjin tried to send the girls away, but each one pretended his farewell was meant for someone else and pressed closer. He finally summoned his guards to escort them outside.

If the other gods listened to Irajahan, the situation would only get worse. If he had to pick an Iojif to marry, he wouldn't be allowed to ignore the girls. But how could he give up Nia? How could he convince the other gods that Irajahan was wrong? He was still their brother and a god.

The next man in line was sweating despite the cool weather, and his dark eyes were wide and hopeless in a square face. "Tell the gods to leave the world alone," the Iskrin said. "Tell them to go away."

"I can't do that," Ahjin said. "This is their world. They made it."

"You are the Mouth of the Gods," the stocky man insisted. "You can tell them what to do."

"Although I coordinate their efforts," Ahjin explained, "I still work for them."

"Please." The man dropped to his knees and crawled around the table to grovel at Ahjin's feet.

The guards stepped forward, and Ahjin waved them off.

"Please tell them to leave us alone," the man begged.

"I can't." Ahjin pushed his chair away from the table and stood. "Without their care, the world falls apart."

"I hate the gods," the man whispered. "I hate the gods," he shouted, jumping to his feet. He drew his knife and threw himself on Ahjin before anyone could stop him.

Ahjin blocked his assailant's arm with his own, struggling to keep the knife from his face. He forced the blade down, but the man twisted and ripped the knife across Ahjin's side.

Then the guards were on the man, dragging him away from Ahjin and forcing the crowd back.

Ahjin dropped back in his chair, panting and shaking. He ripped off his lavender sash and clutched his side, feeling for damage. The pain, he knew from past experience, would start any moment.

The man laughed, pointing at Ahjin, and when a guard tried to take his knife, he slashed it across his own chest. The guard twisted his arm until he dropped the weapon, but as he was forced to the ground, he convulsed.

"Do not touch that knife," the guard shouted.

Lyell's eyes widened. "Ahjin!" He ran over and shoved Ahjin's arm aside, revealing the long cut in the orange brocade robe.

"He missed me," Ahjin said. Air blew through the rent in his robe and the shirt he wore beneath. He hadn't missed by much.

The man on the floor laughed as froth bubbled from his mouth. "It only takes a scratch."

Lyell stuck a hand through the torn clothing and probed Ahjin's side. "Bring a healer!"

Ahjin patted Lyell's shoulder. "I'm fine." He took a deep breath, still shaking.

Lyell stared at his hand. "No blood." His voice cracked, and his shoulders slumped before he turned to the prisoner.

The man on the floor bent his head and wept, and then he died.

Ahjin took another deep breath and stood. The guards turned the dead prisoner face-up, and Ahjin crouched to look at him. "Send guards to ask—"

An arrow flew above his head, missing him by inches and bouncing off the stone walls.

Kaito knocked Ahjin to the floor next to the dead man, shielding him with his body.

People screamed, and the door slammed.

Lyell cursed. "Close the exits. Check everyone for weapons."

Two guards stood beside Ahjin and Kaito while the rest spread through the room.

From his position on the floor, Ahjin heard the crowd hum with speculation and fear. "Let me up, Kaito," he said.

Kaito remained silent and unmoving.

Ahjin tried pushing him off, but the Seal weighed at least twice as much and had his wings trapped. "Get off, Kaito!"

It was useless. Not until Lyell gave permission did the Seal finally pull Ahjin to his feet.

Ahjin brushed the dust off his stupid robe and scanned the room. The people stood against the walls, hands in the air, while the guards pointed weapons at them. His desk-table was now buried under an alarmingly large pile of weapons, though a second glance revealed they were mostly the finger-length eating knives everyone carried here.

"We can throw them all in jail," Lyell murmured.

"Did you find anyone with an actual weapon?" Ahjin asked. "Did anyone seem suspicious?"

Lyell shrugged.

"Don't be ridiculous," Ahjin said. "Let them go, and have the guards search for the archer as well as information on the knife man. We'll pick up again tomorrow, and yes, you may search everyone on the way in." He raised his voice. "There is no more danger. Send these people home."

He waved with fake cheer as everyone was escorted from the room.

Only when the audience was gone did he crouch by the dead man again. What had the gods done to make him hate them so thoroughly? Through the slashed robe, he saw the man's chest wound cutting through an elaborate brand. The slash wasn't deep enough to kill, but the edges were discolored and bubbling under the blood.

Ahjin swallowed hard and fingered his side through the tear in his own clothes, feeling for any scratch he might have missed. A little better aim or a little less fabric in the way, and he'd be as dead as this man.

Was the archer his accomplice or someone with a separate complaint? How long must Ahjin look over his shoulder for assassins?

8. GOSSIP
(NEAR CHISATO)

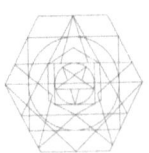

There is no such thing as an insignificant enemy.
Darrendran Proverb

Zefra finished telling about Ludik's wedding as she and Tarakh arrived at the healer's temporary complex outside Chisato's city limits.

Tarakh whistled. "I want to hear your version of the other stories later."

All three tents flew banners: one with the Tukiko amethyst-and-midnight crescent moon, one with a Devoran bee, and the farthest with a black jaguar. A line of people in various states of injury or illness waited by the amethyst banner. Zefra led the way to the panther tent, where Nemerra stirred a large pot on an outdoor ceramic stove. Four knee-high cubs ran between the tents.

Tarakh dodged the cubs. "Bright day, Nemerra. Here is your flour."

Nemerra wiped her hands on a towel and bowed elegantly. "Good to see you, Zefra, Tarakh. Put the flour there, please. Will you stay for the evening meal?"

"I would be pleased, lady." Tarakh bowed even more elegantly, setting down the flour as if it were part of the bow.

Nemerra laughed. "Would it bruise your dignity to occupy my children while I make the bread?"

Tarakh grinned. "I am at your service."

Zefra covered the berries to protect them from birds or mischievous children. "I need to talk to Ludik."

Nemerra peered at the amethyst tent. "Until the meal, it will be difficult to speak with him."

Something rammed into Zefra's calves. She whirled, hand on her saif, and discovered a lion cub at her feet.

Nemerra grabbed the cub and shook him. "Say you're sorry."

Zefra let go of her hilt. She was seeing enemies where none existed.

When the cub squeaked something, Nemerra put him down and crossed her arms. "If you behave, you children may stay on four legs until the food is ready. Otherwise, I'll make you shift early. Which do you choose?"

The miniature lion tilted his head to one side, then plopped on the sand at Zefra's feet. He squeaked again, and Nemerra chuckled. "He wants a story."

Zefra settled cross-legged into the warm sand, smoothed her robe over her knees, and thought of the stories she used to tell her little sisters.

When Tarakh sat, the two black and white cubs climbed into his lap. The lion cub climbed into Zefra's lap and rolled over, waving four paws in the air. The yellow leopard spun in circles on the sand, then stopped with her head on her paws. The lion dropped to his side and tapped Zefra's knee.

As Tarakh grinned, Zefra began the story.

Sometime during the third or fourth story, Zefra looked up and discovered she had a bigger audience.

Nia waved above the yellow leopard on her lap, and Ahjin smiled wryly as the black-and-white cub batted at his feathers with his uninjured paw. By the stove, Ludik helped Nemerra pat dough into shape. He wore his scarf around his neck instead of his head, even though Zefra had personally taught him how to wear it properly.

After Zefra finished the story, she greeted Ahjin with a bow and Nia with Nokai-style cheek kisses. Before they had a chance to talk, Ludik herded his children and Nia into the panther tent. Nemerra put Zefra and the men to work dishing food and distributing spoons and rugs, and by the time Ludik and Nia emerged with their arms full of two-legged babies, dinner was ready.

Nemerra put an adult with every child. Zefra found herself with a tawny-haired little boy on her lap. She looked into his silver eyes, and his one-toothed smile melted her heart. Ludik, holding a wiggly boy with copper hair and Nemerra's honey-brown eyes, grinned at her.

"Don't worry, Zefra," Nemerra said, "Terru is a good eater and will behave until he isn't hungry. Nia, don't let Zurrahava fool you. She can get in trouble before you know what happened."

Nia wrapped her arm more securely around the blonde little girl and cooed silly babble until the toddler giggled, her gray-green eyes a pale imitation of Nia's emerald but just as striking in her brown face.

Zefra hid a grin. Nia's charming smile could also be deceptive.

"And Ahjin," Nemerra continued, "you have Kamakana. She is well-behaved away from Rurru but needs more help eating."

Ahjin smiled. "I know who she is." He stretched one wing away from the grey-eyed little girl's pinching fingers and smoothed her wispy russet hair.

"You are Ahjin?" Tarakh jumped to his feet and bowed. "His Holiness, Ahjin, the Mouth of the Gods? Why did no one tell me? Let me take the baby so she does not mess up your clothes."

Nia burst into giggles. Zefra opened her mouth to reassure Tarakh, but Ahjin spoke first.

"His Holiness stayed in my room with my fancy clothes," Ahjin drawled. "Here, I'm just Ahjin Machol, visiting my friends and holding a baby like my little sister. Sit and introduce yourself."

Zefra tugged on Tarakh's robe, and when he glanced at her, she smiled and tilted her head toward his rug.

Tarakh slowly sat. "I'm Tarakh. I'm sure you do not remember, but I have seen Nia and Ludik before." He glanced at Ahjin again. "You were not at Zefra's meeting of the clans two years ago?"

"No," Ahjin agreed. "I was in the healer's tent."

"So," Nemerra said, "who is sharing their news first?"

"I will." Zefra fed Terru a bite. "I saw one of the pirates today. Lapwing."

"Crow's first mate?" Ahjin asked.

Nia gasped. "Didn't they catch that stinker?"

Zefra snatched a bite of her own soup before Terru reached for his spoon. She recited the story with a little help from Tarakh.

"Hmm." Ahjin expertly fed Kamakana, dodging the spoon around her tiny hands. "The armada captains told me they'd gotten rid of the pirates. I wonder where Lapwing hid all this time."

"I thought we finished that mess," Nia said. "Do you think he reformed?" She dropped the spoon into the bowl to drag the girl back on her lap. "Stay here, Zurra, supper isn't finished yet."

Nemerra drank half her soup and rose to put the bread in the oven.

"If he reformed," Tarakh asked, "would he not have told Zefra instead of running from her?"

Ludik wrestled Rurru into a position locked under his arm and crossed legs, then waved the spoon in front of his son's mouth. "Yes, his desperation to escape is suspicious."

"Perhaps he was afraid I would not believe him," Zefra suggested.

Ahjin shrugged. "Maybe. But I will have someone check. Lapwing isn't the only suspicious character from my past to show up. Nia, remember those two grandiose Iskrins that wanted to be Kassian's priests?"

"The ones I escorted off Arupa with my harpoon?" Nia giggled. "That was fun. Why?"

"They had to be dragged out of the hearings today."

"It's all your fault," Nia said. "You keep changing things in the world, and people want to be involved. Why do I miss the fun?" She dragged Zurrahava back onto her lap and pried the spoon from her little fingers.

"Oh, that wasn't even the fun part." Ahjin snorted. "After that—" He shut his mouth and fed Kamakana another spoonful.

"What was the fun part?" Nia asked.

Ahjin shoved a giant spoonful of soup into his mouth and shook his head.

Nia dumped Zurrahava into Tarakh's lap. "What was fun?"

Ahjin handed Kamakana to Tarakh, also. "Someone tried to kill me.

Two someones," he corrected. "One tried to stab me with a poisoned knife, and one shot an arrow at me."

Nia jumped to her feet. "Are you injured? Why didn't you tell me? Does Lyell know? Where are your guards? Did they catch the assassins? Why did they do it?"

Ahjin stood and caught Nia in a hug. "I'm unharmed. Lyell and Kaito are already planning horrible ways to keep me confined. The archer ran away, and the knife man killed himself. And my ugly regalia is being washed and mended. I guess some people are unhappy with the changes."

"Mended?" Nia screeched. "How close did they get?"

Ahjin rubbed his side absently, then quickly replaced his arm around Nia. "Not close enough."

Zefra narrowed her eyes. Ahjin uncharacteristically wore his surujin wrapped around his waist. He must be at least a little worried to bring his weighted throwing rope.

"You are an exciting group," Tarakah said. "Zefra magnificently defeated her other problem today."

Ahjin kissed Nia and pulled her to sit again. After they took back the babies, he asked, "Other than Lapwing?"

"'Twas nothing," Zefra said.

"He underestimated his target," Tarakh said, "but I would not call it nothing." He recited the story for the others, heaping praise on Zefra until her ears burned.

"Are Ludik and I the only ones people like?" Nia asked. "Or is everyone afraid of you two because of your power?"

Zefra sniffed. "I do not care what that imbecile in the market thinks."

"I don't care if people like me," Ahjin said. "I just want to do my job and deal with my own problems." He tucked one of Nia's braids behind her ear, then swung the baby in his arms upside-down.

Ludik looked at the amethyst tent and frowned.

"What is wrong?" Zefra asked.

Ludik glanced at Nemerra by the oven. "Nothing, and we are going home soon, anyway."

Ahjin raised an eyebrow, and Nia stopped wrestling Zurrahava to give him a skeptical look.

"Never mind," Ludik said. "What other news does anyone have? Zefra, did you find employment? Ahjin, what is the latest word from the gods? Nia, how was your parents' wedding? Oh, I have news. Gurryon will be a father soon." He laughed heartily. "I'm looking forward to watching him explode with anxiety." He wrestled Rurru back onto his lap.

"Ludik," Nemerra warned, sitting by him again. "Be nice. The bread will be ready soon. We have Tarakh to thank for the flour, dear. He even delivered it for us. I'm impressed with his service."

Tarakh dipped his head and blushed a little.

"As for the wedding," Nia said, "it was lovely. We rarely have one in Nokailana, so it's always a big occasion. Everyone from three islands came. Makana even stopped in for a few minutes to wish Mom and Dad a happy marriage."

Oddly, her ears also turned pink, and Zefra did not think 'twas from seeing her goddess. And Ahjin's mouth was tight. Something was up with those two. Zefra made a mental note to pester Nia later.

"I am still seeking employment." Zefra omitted the frustrating details. As an adult, she could handle her own problems and complete her own plans. Before Ahjin left, she would ask him about a letter, and tomorrow, she would visit every merchant in the square until she found a temporary job.

"I might have a lead for you," Ahjin said, "though it's in Sardad. You're welcome to travel with us, if you like. Talk to me later. Now, does everyone want the official news or the gossip?"

"The official news." Ludik hung a son upside-down until he giggled.

"The gossip." Nemerra winked at Ahjin.

"Everything!" Tarakh said.

"Everything, then." Ahjin's announcements and reports took a long time to discuss. By the time they finished, the children had shifted back to cubs to play, and Nemerra's bread was cooling under a clean cloth.

"How wonderful that you found a cousin," Nemerra said to Ahjin. "Do you plan to see her again?"

"If I can." Ahjin looked wistful.

"Surely Your Holiness can do anything you like," Tarakh said.

Ahjin grinned wryly. "Surprisingly, not true. Also... I might be replaced."

Zefra gasped along with everyone but Nia. The golden-skinned No-kai blinked rapidly and rubbed her nose, and Zefra added emphasis to her mental note to speak to her privately.

"Why would the gods replace you when you have served them so faithfully?" Tarakh asked.

His wide eyes looked almost as shocked as Zefra felt. Ahjin had been Mouth of the Gods for almost two years, and international affairs had never been so good.

"Irajahan wants to persuade his siblings that the position should be hereditary," Ahjin said.

"That makes sense." Tarakh nodded, then looked from Ahjin to Nia. "Oh. Ohhh."

"Oh, dear," Nemerra said. "What will you do?"

"I haven't decided yet." Ahjin did not look at Nia.

Zefra crossed off her mental note. She had no idea what to say to Nia. She would talk to Nemerra, instead, and see if the more experienced woman had advice.

"And the other gods agree?" Ludik asked. "Have they already forgotten what he's like?"

"They're still thinking," Ahjin said, "but Makana hasn't threatened to punch him yet."

Tarakh's eyes widened. "Should you say things like that about the gods?"

Zefra shrugged. "Why not? 'Tis the truth, and not the first time."

Tarakh gulped.

"Let me get you some nice, hot bread," Nemerra offered. "It might distract you from our shocking ways." She returned in a minute, hands and mouth full, and passed slices to everyone.

"I will be back." Ludik jumped to his feet and separated two of his children who were rolling through the sand in a growling, spitting ball of fur.

Zefra set her bread on her knee and waited for Ludik to return. The others followed her example, chatting with Nemerra about the children and their voyage home in a few days.

"We're very excited." Nemerra pressed her hand against her stomach. "The letters from our families are full of plans..." She bent over, wincing, and her brown skin turned ashen. "Ludik," she groaned, "help."

"Ludik," Ahjin bellowed, putting an arm around Nemerra. "Hurry."

As Ludik hurried back, arms full of squirming kittens, Zefra jumped up, dumping her bread on the ground. "Give us the children."

Ludik dropped a cub in her arms and one in Nia's and lunged for Nemerra. Tarakh scooped up the last two kittens while Ludik and Ahjin carried Nemerra into the amethyst tent.

Zefra waited anxiously with Nia and Tarakh, bouncing the squirming kitten and whispering soothing words she wished she believed.

After a few minutes, Ahjin emerged, face ashen and hands shaking. "She's been poisoned."

"None of the rest of us are sick," Nia protested.

"The bread!" Zefra jerked to look at Tarakh.

Saying he wanted to be friends was an excuse to get close to Ludik's family. She would burn the traitor to ashes.

"It could not have gone bad." Tarakh scratched his head. "She made it today."

Zefra handed the cub to Ahjin and called her flame. "She made it from *your* flour. What did you do to her? Put down Kamakana right now."

Tarakh handed the leopard cub to Nia, keeping his hands away from his knives. "I promise, I did nothing."

"Where is the rest of the flour?" Zefra asked.

Tarakh pointed to a large jar by the oven. The empty sack and the canvas wrapping lay nearby.

Zefra dug through the flour with her free hand but didn't find anything.

Tarakh squinted at the flour. "That looks odd." He stepped forward, then stopped when she waved the fire at him. "Please, let me help." He looked past Zefra. "Your Holiness, I swear by all the gods, I sold good flour."

Ahjin joined Zefra. "If he tries anything, can you defeat him?"

"Easily."

"Then let him look."

Zefra lowered her flame, keeping it ready.

Tarakh stirred the flour, rubbed it between his fingers, then brought it to his nose. "How did someone poison my flour?" he muttered to himself. "Is it in the whole batch? After I dropped it off? Ah! The flour is damp. They could have let it soak through the bag."

He stepped back, keeping an eye on Zefra, and picked up the discarded sack. After running his hands over the bag, he frowned more. "It does not seem moist."

Ahjin pointed to a design on the corner of the sack. "Is that your symbol?"

"The bee is mine."

"That is no bee." Ahjin showed the design to Zefra. The lines interlocked again and again, forming a lacy geometric.

"'Tis the same as the tattoo on the man who attacked me," Zefra said.

"What?" Tarakh stared at the design. "This is not my sack."

"It's also the same as the brand on the man who tried to stab me," Ahjin said grimly, unwinding his surujin.

Nia took a deep breath, squeezing the cubs in her arms until they yelped. Zefra called more fire until her hand blazed from fingertips to wrist.

"But how...?" Tarakh snapped his fingers. "The Nokai was nothing but a distraction. They must have switched the bags during Zefra's defense, and with the canvas over it, we did not notice."

Nia leaned against Ahjin's arm. "What if he's right? I think Tarakh is innocent."

"If the Nokai only needed to distract me," Zefra said, "he would have given up or settled for mere conversation. He tried very hard to take me from the market." She slowly let her flame die, hoping Nia was right about Tarakh's innocence. "But if both our attackers were marked by this, are they allied?"

"Go wash your hands," Ahjin told Tarakh. "Nia, find a lid for this jar. Zefra, collect the bread. We'll let the constables examine it."

He wrapped his fighting rope around his waist and kept the cubs away from the flour-tainted sand and bag while Zefra collected every slice and kicked sand over the crumbs. Nia ran back with a round basket she pounded over the lid to keep it sealed.

Tarakh returned with damp sleeves and picked up one of the kittens. His hands were red from the harsh soap, and Zefra felt an unexpected surge of relief at his innocence.

"I've been thinking," Ahjin said. "Those two mangy aspirants kept rubbing their arms. Now I wonder if I would have found this symbol on them."

"How far does this conspiracy go?" Zefra asked. "What do they want to accomplish?"

"I don't know the answer to your second question," Ludik said behind them, "but your first one should include me, also." He collected two of his children. "Before you ask, Nemerra will live. She was lucky she only ate a few bites and I was nearby."

"Good," Zefra said, as everyone exhaled with relief. "Now, how does this involve you?"

"This morning, someone tried to kill me, too," Ludik said. "Someone is after us all."

9. POISON
(CHISATO AND NEARBY)

Because some Iskrin districts get no rain for half the year and not much the other half, they dig wells wherever they can find underground water.
Iskrin Culture and History, vol 1

Nia hugged Ludik and his children, then Zefra and Tarakh. The cute Iskrin boy turned a lovely pink, so Nia added kisses on each cheek. After endless discussion, the party had ended with no explanations for the attempted assassinations, although Zefra had insisted on a plan for precautions. Fortunately for Zefra's peace of mind, Nia had a plan. Ahjin could worry about Irajahan; Nia would take care of assassins.

Ludik was going home in less than two weeks, and Ahjin had volunteered to send guards to protect his family until then. Tarakh wasn't a target, as far as anyone knew, and Ahjin and Nia would be moving on soon with more guards. Zefra had decided to travel with them to pursue a job, so nobody would be left unprotected.

As Nia and Ahjin headed back into Chisato, her head swam. Who wanted to kill them, and why? Ludik was a healer and Nemerra only a mother. Zefra was a caravan guide and explorer. And Ahjin... If anyone was hated, it was Ahjin. Irajahan was already campaigning to get rid of him. Their mysterious assassin ought to at least wait to see if the god succeeded first. She rolled her eyes. Oh, yes, a great idea. Why didn't they see if Irajahan or the assassin removed Ahjin first?

Ahjin had been walking quietly, brow furrowed in concentration and wings twitching, but now he patted her shoulder. "Lyell is already plotting with the guards. We'll be so surrounded, nobody will get close."

Nia crossed her arms. "Why aren't you surrounded now?"

Ahjin's ears grew pink. "I lied to Lyell about taking a nap so I could have a quiet visit with my friends."

Nia slapped her forehead. "You're an idiot!"

They turned the corner of the city wall. The Chisato guards in their sober brown were flanked at the gate by a sturdy Darrendrakar and a snarling black-and-gray wolf. Behind Lyell and Kaito, an entire troop of guards from Iskra and Arupa lined the streets.

"Uh-oh," Nia said. "They discovered you aren't sleeping."

"Fair winds. Sorry I'm late." Ahjin patted Lyell as he strolled through the gate.

Nia grinned as the Iskrin guards widened their eyes before snapping their attention to the front. Most dignitaries didn't wear faded trousers and patched shirts and pat growling wolves on the head before shoving their hands into their pockets.

Kaito silently followed Ahjin with the Arupan guards. Lyell shook his fur and took rear guard with Nia.

"Fool," Lyell growled.

"I know," Nia said. "I didn't realize he snuck away."

She told Lyell about the incidents with their friends and the commonality of the mark, then explained her ideas for protecting the dimwit, starting with the hearings the next day.

Someone on the street gasped, and Nia finally noticed they had an audience. Half of them watched Ahjin and his guards, but the other half watched Nia converse with a Wolf in his native language. She smiled sweetly and waved. Lyell ignored them all.

⁂

The next morning, Nia dressed in her most boring clothes and added a leather jerkin and her serrated knife. Kaito brought a short harpoon for her when he escorted her to Ahjin's room.

Ahjin was arguing with Lyell when Nia arrived. He wore his usual shirt and trousers and his official boots, and the rest of his fancy uniform lay on the bed. Lyell held the leather apron that served as Ahjin's armor.

Kaito shut the door and stood in front of it.

"For the fifth time, no." Ahjin sounded calm, but the angry set of his jaw made Nia step in front of Lyell.

"Here, let me tie it for you, Ahjin."

"No." Ahjin folded his arms.

"I also have his dagger, his arm bracers, and his slingshot," Lyell said. "I don't like the way the apron leaves his back unprotected, but it's better than nothing. We'll reach Sardad by the time more guards arrive from Arupa. In the meantime, I talked to Daz, his guard captain. We won't have a repeat of yesterday's events. *Any* of yesterday." Lyell glared at Ahjin.

"Good." Nia said. "Lift your arms, Ahjin."

"I don't need armor or weapons," Ahjin snapped. "Yesterday was a fluke, and even if it weren't, you'll have me so buried in guards, I won't have enough privacy to—" He glanced at Nia. "To blow my nose."

Nia dropped the apron onto the bed. "Look, I know how badly you hate this. I also know we can't make you wear armor."

Ahjin nodded, a smug grin creeping across his face.

Nia patted his arm. "Lyell, please tell the Iskrins the audiences are canceled today. Ahjin will take a day of rest in his room."

Ahjin groaned. "Why?"

Nia wrapped her arms around him. "I love you. If you won't keep yourself alive one way, I'll do it another." She squeezed him tighter until he finally hugged her back.

His sigh echoed through his chest. "Give me the stupid apron."

He added armor and weapons before covering everything with his regalia. Below the mended gash in his orange robe, a new slit allowed access to his knife under cover of the diagonal lavender sash.

Nia smoothed a wrinkle. "Your robe doesn't fall as nicely as I'd like over the apron. We'll work on it later. Are we ready?"

"We?" Ahjin asked. "You'll be bored to insanity. *I'm* bored."

Nia sighed. "I know. Politics are stodgy. Kaito, open the door."

The Seal bowed as Ahjin exited. The guards on either side of the doorway snapped to attention. One whistled, and the thump of boot-heels echoed down the hallway. In seconds, a troop of guards jogged around the corner and marched into position around Ahjin.

After one last glare at Nia and Lyell, Ahjin spun on his heel and strolled as calmly as if leaving for an afternoon swim. They walked through halls empty except for sentries and entered the audience hall. He took his seat, flanked by Nia and Kaito, while Lyell stood in front of the table and raised his hands for attention.

When the crowd quieted, Lyell lowered his hands. "His Holiness, the Mouth of All the Gods, has arrived. Please form a line if you wish to speak to him."

Someone in the crowd waved frantically. Nia got a glimpse of bright yellow wings as the person left.

Ahjin groaned under his breath. "Not your fault, Sufa," he whispered.

The first ten people to shove to the front were girls dressed in what must be their nicest dresses. Even the Iskrins wore their brightest belts and embroideries.

"Is it true?" the first one exclaimed, clasping her hands in front of her until her many dowry bracelets jingled. "The diplomat said Irajahan declared you are looking for a wife." She blushed so hard her Iskrin-white skin resembled a snapper.

Nia glared at the row of pretty girls. What brazenness! Ahjin was already taken.

"My Lord Omnipotent is a little premature," Ahjin said. "But if it comes to that, I would only consider Iojif women."

The girl pressed her quivering lips together. She bowed low and backed out of the room with some of the others.

Two Iojif girls stayed, wings fluttering nervously, despite Ahjin's raised eyebrow and Nia's most ferocious glare. They pressed around the table, batting their eyelashes and asking stupid questions. When they reached to touch Ahjin, Lyell motioned for the guards to escort them out. Even as they were removed, the girls flirted over their shoulders.

Nia banged her harpoon against the stone floor, wishing she had Zefra's fire to teach the hussies a lesson. Then Ahjin smiled at a pretty girl, and Nia's blood chilled like a winter typhoon. She scraped the butt of the harpoon across the floor and pointed the shark-killing end at the girl.

Lyell grabbed her arm and whispered, "Go to the kitchen and make sure lunch is poison-free."

Nia yanked free of Lyell and stomped to the back entrance, wishing for clacking boot-heels of her own. She had to settle for slamming the door behind her.

How dare Ahjin smile at other girls! He was hers! Never mind stupid Irajahan and his stupid ideas. Ahjin wouldn't listen to the windbag. She smacked the wall with the butt of her harpoon.

The long trip through the back halls gave her time to calm. When she walked into the kitchen, the cooks and their helpers gave her confused smiles.

"Are you lost, lady?" one asked. "Someone run and get an interpreter. Sit here, lady." He pushed a chair toward her.

Nia leaned her harpoon against the wall. "Do not bother. I speak Iskrit."

The cook's eyebrows rose. "And very well, lady. What can we do for you?"

"I'm with His Holiness, and I came to discuss his food."

All the bustle in the kitchen stopped.

"Is there a problem with his food, lady?" The cook glanced at the harpoon and motioned for the others to keep working. "We made only the finest dishes. Does he not care for Iskrin spices? Can you tell me his preferences?"

"Actually, I came to talk about poison."

Everyone froze again. Someone whimpered.

Sweat beaded on the cook's forehead. "No, lady! There has been no poison. Oh, Luminosity, I swear we have not wronged His Holiness."

"No, I'm not accusing you of poisoning him."

A heartfelt sigh echoed through the kitchen. Everyone leaned toward her.

Nia slumped into the chair. "Maybe we should talk privately?"

The cook escorted Nia toward a side door. They sat on tall stools in a mere closet of an office with walls lined with menus.

"Now, lady, tell me what is wrong." His voice shook a little.

"My name is Nia. I'm no lady."

"Very well, la— Nia." He winced. "How can I help you?"

"Someone tried to poison Ahjin today. His Holiness."

The cook jumped off his stool. "But you said—"

"Sit," Nia said. "We were outside Chisato, but I want no one here to get an opportunity."

The cook sat slowly. "No one here would harm His Holiness."

"The friend who made the poisoned bread did not realize her flour had been switched."

The cook's eyes grew wide. "I see."

"So, what about your supplies?"

The cook scratched his chin. "We take what is delivered each week, unless we order something special for a guest."

Nia shook her head. "Anything could be slipped into the order." She spun in circles on her stool. "Oh, I know. I will ask Zefra's friend, Tarakh, for suppliers he thinks are trustworthy." She frowned. "But who will cook when Ahjin leaves on the next part of his tour?"

"If you trust me, la— Nia, I will send my best assistant with you." He wiped sweat from his brow. "He can also taste the food for His Holiness."

Nia scrutinized him for guilt, then decided he was merely nervous. "I accept," she said, "and I hold you responsible."

His hands shook, but he bowed. "Of course, lady."

Nia bowed and took her harpoon back through the kitchen, waving at the workers as she left.

This was ridiculous. Who wanted to kill Ahjin? All the changes he made were approved by the gods, so his death wouldn't alter anything. And who knew Ahjin would eat with Ludik? Maybe Ahjin wasn't the target. Nia smacked the wall with her harpoon again. The poisoner could have killed all of them, including the children. When she found him, he'd never get an opportunity to harm children again. She loved Ludik's children as much as she would her own.

If she had any. And what difference did it make if Ahjin had children? Why must the Mouth be hereditary? Irajahan was stupid and mean.

Zefra was lucky. She could pick any boy she wanted and nobody would tell her no.

Nia's conscience twinged. If she had agreed to marry Ahjin earlier, could they have avoided this? Or would the gods have created a Nokai divorce law just to get rid of her?

She reached the audience hall and sat in the hall to wait for His Holiness. If she had to watch one more girl flirt with him, somebody would get hurt. She wasn't ready for marriage, but she did want to keep Ahjin, even though he apparently didn't believe she loved him, and Irajahan the All-Powerful Stink seemed determined to prevent their wedding. What could she do?

I n the morning, Nia woke much too early and packed for the next stop on Ahjin's official tour. Tarakh had agreed to oversee Ahjin's food, though Nia suspected the cute Iskrin had additional red-haired motives, which she was happy to encourage. With staff and guards and a nervous assistant cook, the group that showed up to escort Ahjin was absurdly large. The addition of pack animals grew the retinue to a small town.

"I don't know how to ride a horse," Nia told Zefra, eyeing the beautiful animal prancing on dangerous hooves. "I've only been on a pack pony."

"I know." Zefra used the hand not holding the horse's leather ribbons to pet its nose despite its big teeth. "I picked a mild-mannered one for you, and I will stay close."

"That's not mild," Nia protested, watching the tall legs dance around Zefra.

"Stop whining and climb up." Zefra stroked the dangerous animal again.

"Here," Tarakh said, doing a poor job of hiding his grin. "Step in my hands, and I will toss you up."

Zefra patted the beautiful monster until it held still. Nia took a deep breath, grabbed the seat, and put her sandaled foot into Tarakh's linked hands. Before she could exhale, she flew through the air and landed on top of the beast, a million fathoms high. The monster shifted, and Nia slid across the leather.

"Twisted tentacles," Nia swore, grabbing the nearest strap. "I'll die."

Zefra shook her head and swung onto her own horse, somehow holding her own ribbons and the ones for Nia's horse at the same time.

Tarakh laughed and jumped onto his horse. "You will be fine."

Ahjin pulled his monster next to them, looking only half as awkward as Nia felt. "Squeeze with your knees to stay on."

"And since when do you know how to ride a horse?" Nia readjusted her grip to a sturdy-looking piece of the seat, clutching hard enough to cramp her fingers. "Why aren't you flying?"

"I only have two Iojif guards here, which I've been informed isn't enough to protect me in the air." Ahjin rolled his eyes. "They gave me a riding lesson before you arrived, but Chiara will be within grabbing distance for the entire ride. Each novice has someone to watch them. Tarakh, who do you get?"

"Kaito, but he hasn't said a word to me. Does he not know trade tongue?"

Ahjin snorted. "He's never said a word to me in nine months, but he does listen to my trade tongue."

"Oh." Tarakh pursed his lips thoughtfully, then jogged after Kaito.

When Zefra lifted her ribbon-filled hands, Nia tightened her grasp and squeezed the monster with her knees. Before she felt secure on the seat, the entire group bounced down the road.

Zefra talked at Nia almost constantly, telling her to sit up straight and put her hands down and drop her heels so she'd stop kicking the poor animal. At each rest stop, the tyrant made Nia practice climbing on and off the horse until both Nia and the animal rebelled.

It took them three days to reach the first water source, and by the time they stopped for the night, Nia had never been so happy to volunteer for camp chores. Anything to get away from the monsters, hoofed or red-haired. While everyone else set up tents, Nia and Kaito grabbed water buckets and limped for the well, rubbing their sore riding muscles. The tiny camp wasn't even a real town, just a currently empty stop on the clan's regular migration.

"Look for a small pile of rocks," Nia said. "Zefra said it won't look like the city wells."

What caught her eye, though, was a streak of blue on the sand, fluttering in the breeze. Kaito broke into a run, and as Nia raced after him, the flutter settled into the shape of wings.

They fell to their knees beside an Iojif with blue wings outstretched and skin much too pale. Nia pulled her shirt over her nose. By the stench, he had been dead at least a day or two. Blood from his head streaked across the well rocks. One wing bent in the wrong direction.

"Oh, toothless shark." Nia turned her head and swallowed hard. His wing looked almost as bad as Ahjin's had two years ago.

They ran back to the camp, and Nia threw her arms around Ahjin, interrupting his conversation with Lyell. "Oh, Ahjin, we found a dead Iojif." She tightened her grip, trying to stop shaking.

The men exchanged shocked glances, then burst into motion. While Ahjin flew toward the well, Lyell roused Zefra and the guards. Nia dawdled as much as possible, and by the time she arrived, the others were examining the body. To avoid looking at his awful injuries again, she picked up pink and blue feathers from the sand.

"To hit with such force," Zefra explained, "he must have fallen from the air."

Ahjin frowned. "He doesn't look that old. Why would he fall?"

"If Ludik were here, we could ask him." Zefra shrugged. "Perhaps he had a bad heart?" She bent to look at something, then circled the well.

Ahjin shuffled his wings. "There's nothing to do but hold his funeral. We don't even know his name."

"We will file a description in the next town," Zefra said.

The guards carried off the body, and Lyell, Kaito, and Zefra followed.

Nia fought back tears. Seeing this dead Iojif reminded her too much of when Ahjin died rescuing the gods. And speaking of the gods...

She picked up a bucket of water and touched Ahjin's arm, ignoring the remaining guards. "If the gods don't like our relationship, would they kill one of us to stop it?"

Ahjin wrapped his arm around her. "Stop being so morbid. If this trip worries you so much, should I send you back to Chisato?"

Nia shook her head quickly. "I'm staying with you. You're right, I'm being silly."

But she still worried how the gods would enforce their decree if they ruled against Ahjin.

10. DEATH
(DEVORA DISTRICT)

If things are getting easier, maybe you're headed downstream.
Nokai Proverb

Z efra walked back to camp, stuffing an escaped curl under her scarf. Something was odd about the dead body.

"A stone marker," Lyell muttered, "a map for kin, a prayer from Ahjin. What else, Zefra?"

Bad news could not wait. "Something bothers me about the wound."

"Just a minute." Lyell grabbed a worn blanket and a shovel. "We should bury him away from the well."

Ahjin and Nia caught up, and the group traveled a stone's throw before the guards lowered the body and began digging.

"Now, Zefra, tell me what is wrong," Lyell said.

"Wrong with what?" Ahjin asked.

Zefra washed off the dried blood with water from the flask on her belt, then traced the wound. "Here is where he hit the well rocks. So what is this?" She pointed to a small, deep hole inside the dent.

"He hit a pointed rock?" Nia asked.

Zefra shook her head. "All the rocks around the well were fairly smooth."

Tarakh frowned. "But we know he hit the well."

"Oh, yes. But what else hit him, and when?" Zefra raised her eyebrows.

Ahjin lowered his voice. "You think this wasn't an accident?"

Zefra shrugged. "We know a winged criminal who might be responsible."

Lyell looked south. "Lapwing is a long way from here."

"Not that far with wings," Ahjin said.

"What could he gain from this?" Nia asked.

Kaito ran a finger down the dead man's shirt, along a crease from shoulder to waist. He repeated it along creases on the other side and the man's waist.

Lyell rolled the body so Zefra could slide the blanket under it. The creases continued under his wings.

"It looks like pack straps," Zefra said. "Perhaps someone killed him for the pack."

Nia laid a few pink feathers on the ground. "I found these by the well, but he doesn't have pink, and neither does Lapwing." She bit her lip.

Ahjin tugged on his curls. "What is going on?"

A guard dropped the shovel. "It's deep enough."

After the body was buried and the grave marked and added to Zefra's map, Ahjin bowed his head and said something in his own language for his fallen countryman.

Everyone ate a quiet dinner and went to bed.

As Zefra and Tarakh spent the next day teaching the outdwellers to ride a horse at a miserable walk, she jealously watched messengers on fast horses race in the distance. She missed her father's horses and the feel of the wind in her face as she thundered across the sand.

Kaito gradually improved until he earned control of his own reins. Ahjin also learned, though his keeper had to stay close enough to calm the horse if he forgot to hold his wings still. Lyell and Nia were hopeless. Whenever the Wolf rode instead of running on his own four legs, he sat worse than a sack of flour, and the horses shied at his scent in either form. His horse pranced in alarm every time Tala squirmed in the saddlebag. Nia continued to flinch, no matter how many times Zefra assured her the horse would not throw her off.

Finally, Zefra saddled the dullest horse. "This one hates moving fast and never prances."

Nia examined the horse from head to hoof. "Excellent."

"And in exchange," Zefra said, "I expect you to finally learn to sit properly and hold your own reins."

"Deal." Nia kissed Zefra's cheeks and climbed into the saddle as if the horse were a ladder.

Zefra sighed. "And how to mount. That was ridiculous."

Nia shrugged. "Do you want me to take the ribbons now?"

"Let us discuss your seat before I give you the reins."

They rode while Zefra explained — again — how to sit on a horse so both parties were comfortable.

The struggle to teach Nia to ride was a welcome distraction for Zefra, and though Nia often bit her lip when she looked at Ahjin, she also spoke only of casual subjects.

Two days later, Zefra and the others crossed a bridge spanning two rivers to reach Pramath, a permanent community of tents with a garden and a field of wheat, next scheduled for a visit from His Holiness.

Their group left the next day, after official business and restocking supplies. After only an hour, the guards shouted a warning and surrounded the group. Zefra stood on her saddle to peer over their heads until a guard pulled her down.

But she had already seen. "There is someone in the road, not moving."

After a few minutes, the guards escorted Ahjin to the body. Zefra and Tarakh followed. Though this Iskrin had died more recently, animals and insects had already found it. Zefra covered her mouth and nose and sought calm.

Ahjin asked, "What happened?"

A guard gingerly tilted the corpse's head to show a rope around her neck. "Her neck broke." His voice was impassive, but his face was tight.

Ahjin frowned. "Murder?"

Tarakh swallowed audibly, and Zefra touched his elbow in tentative comfort. When he nodded, she moved closer to the body.

The woman's boots were scuffed, and holes were worn in her robe. The exposed end of the rope had frayed. Zefra hooked a finger under it and pulled until the other end came free.

"A lead rope," Zefra said. "Look at her boots and robe. I think she had a training accident and was dragged by a horse until the rope snapped."

"The brown-and-saffron wheat design on her belt means she's local," Tarakh said.

Ahjin looked backward. "Let's take her home."

At Pramath, Ahjin explained the situation to the clan elders as the guards handed over the blanket-wrapped corpse.

"Did you find her child?" an elder asked, face gray under her saffron scarf. "He was only a little boy, barely walking."

Ahjin tightened his lips. "No, but there were scavengers in the area. I suspect..."

"I will tell her husband." The elder left without the customary bow.

Ahjin mounted with growing competence and silently led the way back into the desert. Zefra led Nia's horse, postponing another lesson. The Nokai patted her horse's neck as tears crept down her cheeks.

No one spoke until they reached the place of death again, and then only as they looked for the missing boy. Within an hour, they were joined by the locals, and everyone searched together until sunset stained the white sand blue. As the Devorans returned home, Ahjin's party traveled half a league farther and made camp.

Zefra lay on her mat next to Nia and stared at the dark ceiling, avoiding the memory of the day's events. Her tent was cramped for two, but when she married, her husband's tent would be sewn to hers. If she married, after she worked for a few years. Ahjin had said a caravan in Sardad needed a new assistant guide.

"Why do things like this happen?" Nia whispered.

Zefra had no answer.

I n the morning, they followed one of the rivers north. On the third night, while Zefra filled an armload of water bags, a flutter in the shadow of a dune caught her attention. The guards sent to investigate found another dead avian.

While the grave was dug, Zefra gave Tarakh a brief lesson in judging time of death based on temperature, rigidity, and insects, whispering to avoid protests from Nia, who sat with her back to the tragedy. This one had been dead several days, perhaps a week.

Tarakh shot Zefra an appalled look. "Where did you learn all that?"

"Ludik taught me when we found the third dead body in Darrendra."

"The *third?*"

"The first two were barely dead," Zefra explained. "Timing was obvious."

Tarakh inhaled sharply. "I have seen more dead people in two weeks with you than in my entire life. Do you sow trouble or does it hunt you down?"

"The favor of the gods is a lodestone for danger." Zefra refused to count how many dead she had seen, friends and foe alike. If she let grief cloud her mind, what good was she?

She wrapped her arms around herself, cold despite the harsh sun. Tarakh moved closer and put a hand on her shoulder.

"I don't understand," Ahjin said, looking at the Iojif lady with pretty pink and gray wings. Her dress was stained dark with blood around arrows. "She has pink feathers, but if she killed the man, who killed her? She couldn't have flown so far if *he* had shot her. Is someone targeting all Iojif?"

"Did they mistake her for you?" Nia asked through her tears.

"I don't look much like her," Ahjin said, "but as a winged shadow in the sky? Maybe."

He glanced south, and Zefra wondered if the same person — Lapwing? — was responsible for both deaths. This death, certainly, was no accident.

In the morning, Zefra helped Nia onto her horse and mounted her own.

Ahjin pointed at the fresh grave. "Let's pick up our pace and report this in Sardad."

Zefra nodded grimly. With two outdwellers dead, and at least one of them murdered, 'twas time for professionals to take over.

Even at a faster pace and riding through the afternoon rains, it took nearly two more days before Sardad appeared in the midst of the sand dunes. Between the city and the river, small fields of grain marked actual soil. Though half the size of Chisato, the city was big enough to have some stone buildings besides the constant tents.

Zefra practiced a speech for her prospective employer, determined to earn the position. She was fortunate to travel with Ahjin's group, and more fortunate — she patted her pouch to make sure 'twas still there — to present the caravan master with a recommendation from the Mouth of the Gods. Surely the letter would be convincing. She smoothed the pouch nervously.

A blur of movement caught her eye, and the guards surrounded their group, hands on their weapons.

"A single rider," Captain Daz reported. "Iskrin." After a few minutes, hoof beats became audible. "Male, armed."

Zefra reached for her saif and then grabbed Nia's reins instead.

The hoof beats slowed. "Bright day," a cheerful, familiar voice called. "I'm looking for His Holiness."

And what was *he* doing here? Zefra dropped Nia's reins, then urged her horse to the guards that blocked her from her loved one.

"Who are you, and what do you want with His Holiness?" Daz demanded, hand on his sword.

Zefra tapped his elbow. "He's my brother. Let me out." Her eagerness made her horse dance under her.

Daz jerked to look at her. "Are you sure?"

"I recognize his voice." Zefra smiled. "He is a young blacksmith, wears a belt embroidered with turquoise hammers, and rides a fine dappled gray mare with two white stockings. His saif is sheathed in pale yellow leather with black and turquoise lines below the hilt."

Daz squinted at the newcomer. "What is your sister's name?" he called.

"I have four younger sisters." Izo's voice was amused. "But I suspect you mean the oldest one, so either I found His Holiness, or my sister is in there, or both. Bright day, Ahjin or Zefra."

The guards relaxed their circle, and Zefra raced to her brother. They both dismounted, and she leaned into his strong embrace, inhaling his familiar scent of smoke and steel and horse.

"You look well, little sister," Izo said. "I'm glad I found you before you vanish on some caravan for years."

Zefra tightened her arms around him until a noise made her remember their audience and step away.

Nia slid off her horse clumsily. "Come give me a kiss."

Daz gasped, and Ahjin rolled his eyes.

Izo laughed and kissed Nia on both cheeks. "You look as beautiful as always."

Zefra shook her head at Nia's boldness, but at least Izo seemed to have recovered from his old attraction to her. He deserved someone who loved him in return.

Izo bowed to Ahjin, then reached for an Iojif handshake.

"What are you doing here?" Ahjin asked.

"I brought you something. I intended to leave it in Sardad until I heard you were almost here." Izo took a bag from his saddle, then froze when the hulking Bear guard poked him with a spear.

Ahjin took the bag with a cross look at the guard and peeked at its contents. "What's this?"

"A laminated linen breastplate," Izo said, "as I suggested when we first met. You can even wear it under your clothing."

Nia grabbed the bag. "Look how well he adapted it for your wings, Ahjin." She tossed a section from hand to hand. "It's lighter than your old leather apron. Take off your jacket, and I'll lace it for you."

"'Tis a good idea, brother." Zefra squeezed his hand, thankful for the gift and one more hour together.

"Good idea?" Nia stuck her fists on her hips. "It's a lifesaver. Put it on right now, Ahjin."

Izo narrowed his eyes. "Has something happened?"

Ahjin removed his jacket and shirt with a pained look. While Izo showed how to put the breastplate on Ahjin, Zefra recited the recent events.

Izo whistled. "How do you find so much trouble, sister?"

Zefra slugged his shoulder. "None of this is my fault!"

Tarakh laughed, then turned it into a cough behind his hand. His eyes crinkled more when Zefra glared.

Ahjin redressed over his armor and remounted. "Izo, will you travel with us?"

"I'm on my way to a commission, but since you were coming to Sardad, it seemed a good time to deliver the armor. I had no idea how well-timed!"

He hugged Zefra again for an inadequate minute, then handed her a pile of letters from his saddlebag. "Stay in one piece, Zefra. Warmth to you all."

Izo rode off the way Ahjin's group had come, and Zefra watched until he disappeared. It had been too long since she had seen any of her family. She squeezed the stack of letters, unsure when she would see her sisters or parents again. Her chosen path was a lonely one. If she were not sure she had chosen well, she might regret the cost. When she shook off her sorrow and mounted her horse, everyone else was ready to leave.

They entered Sardad a few hours later and headed directly to the city guard post. Ahjin described the deaths of the two Iojif and Lapwing's possible involvement, hands clenched so tightly his knuckles turned white. The officer on duty took brief notes with no trace of interest, then dismissed them.

Zefra left the others at the white sandstone inn and took Ahjin's letter to the caravan master he had recommended. If he would not hire her, she did not know where to go next. The short, gaunt man read the letter, quizzed her on her experience and skills, and made her demonstrate her flame-calling. After merely watching her while she bit her tongue and kept her face still, he snorted.

"We do not often get applicants with experience in both cartography and horses," he said. "We have never gotten new help with so much exploration behind them. I assume you will share your knowledge of the oasis with us?"

"I would share it with anyone." Zefra pressed her hands on her knees to quell the shaking. "Then — I'm hired?"

"We leave in two weeks. I expect you at the city limits at dawn." He rose and bowed, a faint smile lighting his serious face.

Zefra bolted to her feet and bowed. "I will be there. Thank you." She clamped her lips together before she babbled and made him change his mind.

She returned to the inn in a happy daze. Telling everyone the good news took enough time that she had barely opened her pack when a terrified scream echoed through the air. She and Nia leaned out the window in time to see Ahjin dash from the inn and fly farther into the city.

"Let's follow him!" Nia said. "Look, Ahjin's guards are going. Come on!"

Nia dashed out. Zefra followed, loosening her saif. Why did Nia never think before she rushed into danger?

The two women caught up near a high tower, and Zefra grabbed Nia's arm as they squirmed their way through the guards. Once at the front, they saw Ahjin facing a troop of city guards across a growing pool of red.

Nia took one look at the distinctively Nokai green hair in the middle of the blood and vomited.

Someone grabbed Zefra's elbow. She jerked away until she recognized Tarakh. He looked almost as green as Nia, and his hands shook as he pointed up. Zefra followed the gesture to a high window at the top of the tower. She traced the tower from the window to the ground, a very long way.

"We know you did this," the city officer barked at Ahjin in trade tongue. "This, and all the others. We have reports."

From the fast messengers that passed them in the desert? But who had sent them and why would they lie?

"You've made a mistake," Ahjin replied soothingly in the same language, though he spoke Iskrit fluently.

Was he doing it on purpose, Zefra wondered, or did he now respond automatically like Nia did? She had known trade tongue for longer, though not as flawlessly. How well would she need to know a foreign language before she spoke in it without thinking?

"You thought we would not notice if you killed your victims with different methods in different places," the Sardad captain sneered.

"I killed no one," Ahjin said.

The captain counted on his fingers. "Two Iojif in the desert, killed by your slingshot and bow. One Iskrin, neck snapped with your surujin."

Ahjin's eyebrows crept up his forehead. Zefra tightened her grip on Tarakh.

"And one Nokai pushed from a high window." The captain gestured to Ahjin's wings.

"I wasn't around when most of those people died," Ahjin protested. "I have witnesses. And why would I kill them?"

The captain gave him a withering look of scorn. "I'm sure your people would lie for you. How would I know why you kill? But you have swift wings, and where you go, death follows. You are under arrest."

Lyell and Nia protested. Kaito stepped in front of Ahjin. Zefra pulled the sunlight through her veins and waited for Ahjin's signal to throw flame.

Ahjin pulled Kaito aside. "I am the Mouth of All the Gods. If you don't let me go, the gods themselves will strike you. Let me help you determine what happened."

"If we let you go, more people will die. You're lucky we believe in a trial instead of immediate execution." The captain turned to his soldiers. "Take him to jail."

11. ARREST

(SARDAD)

As recompense, the Seals will send one-tenth of their people for five generations to help other kindreds or countries, including workers to His Holiness.

Darravani's decree after the Death of Kairri, first year of His Holiness, Ahjin the Great

As she stared at the city guards across the pool of blood, Zefra called a flame to her hand. The last time they had been arrested, they were almost executed. Ahjin was no murderer, so avoiding arrest entirely was smarter.

Ahjin's guards drew their weapons. The city guard drew their saifs in response.

"Stop!" Ahjin spread his wings to their full fifteen-cubit width between the groups. "As law-abiding people, we can settle this mistake without violence. The truth will come out at the trial, if not before."

Zefra released her fire slowly. The Iskrin courts were known for their justice, though such an obviously ridiculous charge should not even make it to court. But she would honor Ahjin's choice.

Ahjin's guards lowered their weapons, but the city guard did not. Ahjin folded his wings, and they pounced on him, tying his wrists together and winding rope around his wings.

Lyell growled, and Ahjin's guards twitched toward their weapons again. Zefra clenched her fists, feeling heat run through her veins.

Ahjin shook his head at Lyell. "That isn't necessary, Captain."

The captain grunted and wrapped another loop around the white wings.

Ahjin winced. "Careful of the feathers, please."

The captain leaned in, nose to nose. "When I prove you're responsible for those deaths, I will break your wings."

Zefra called her fire, then dropped it to grab Nia, who lunged for the captain with her serrated knife, swearing hysterically. The captain drew his sword as Zefra and Tarakh pulled Nia back.

"Nia," Ahjin said. "Nia, stop it. Nia!"

"It will not help if they take you, too," Zefra whispered.

Nia's curses dissolved into angry tears. Zefra wrapped her in a tight hug while Tarakh grabbed the knife.

"Nia!" Ahjin tried again. As the Sardad guards collected the dead Nokai and dragged Ahjin away, he called over his shoulder, "Zefra, Lyell, take care of Nia and look for answers."

And then he was gone, and only the sickening pool of blood was left in the street.

Nia collapsed on the ground and wailed. Lyell raked his hands through his hair until it stood on end. Heads poked tentatively out windows, then yanked back inside.

"Back to the inn!" Zefra dragged Nia to her feet. "Move it!"

Lyell shook his head in a wolfish gesture and grabbed Nia's other arm while Tarakh pulled Kaito. After questioning a few bystanders who had seen nothing, all sixteen guards surrounded them as they trotted back to the inn.

Zefra led everyone into her room. She tucked Nia into a blanket on her cot and faced the others. Half the guards sitting shoulder-to-shoulder on the floor were Iskrin, chosen for Ahjin's visit to their home country. The other half were from all over the world.

"I have failed His Holiness," Lyell said, his face gray and lined.

Kaito hid his face against his knees.

"Stop that," Zefra said. "'Tis not true, and worse, it does not help Ahjin."

"How could they arrest him?" Nia wailed. "He's the Mouth of the Gods."

"I'm sure the gods will settle this soon," Zefra said, "but in the meantime, we cannot just sit here."

Tarakh cleared his throat. "What can we possibly do?"

"We need to find the true killers," Zefra said. "If they were only looking for an Iojif, why did they not arrest the others?" She waved her hand at the winged guards.

And she only had two weeks if she wanted to keep her new employment. If she missed the caravan, where would she find another job? She squelched the selfish thought. It would not come to that, anyway. They had time to clear Ahjin before she had to leave.

"It's part of the plot," Nia sobbed. "First, the assassins tried to kill us. When that failed, they killed those poor people and framed Ahjin."

Captain Daz said, "That makes a certain twisted sense."

"Hmm." Zefra pondered the idea. "We already discussed the knife man and Ludik's strangler being connected because of their common mark."

"And maybe the archer and the two ambitious Iskrins," Nia mumbled into her blanket.

"This latest development is too timely to be a coincidence," Zefra decided. "The question is, who is responsible and why?"

Daz nodded. "Since we inconveniently survived, they might have changed tactics."

"Could Lapwing be connected with this," Zefra asked, "or is he a separate trouble?"

Lyell pounded his fists on his knees. "How do we untangle any of this?"

"We need help," Tarakh said. "Obviously, not from the city guard."

"I'm from this area," one guard said. "I can snoop if I tell my family I no longer work for His Holiness."

"A spy is a good idea." Zefra counted the Iskrins in the guard. "We have eight of you."

"Only four have local accents," Tarakh corrected. "I can talk to my father about trustworthy agents. He has people throughout the district."

"'Tis a start," Zefra said. "I wish more people had Ahjin's invisibility.

It would be useful to have ears in the midst of our enemies, once we find them."

Lyell straightened. "Invisible — or just unnoticed?"

"All right, you cunning Wolf," Zefra said, "what are you thinking?"

"What about Darrendrakar?"

"Darrendrakar are very noticeable," Tarakh protested. "Even in Devoran clothing, your coloring stands out like an oasis in the desert."

"Let me show you what I mean." Lyell hopped up, returning with Tala, still four-legged and furry. "Who is this?"

"Your daughter," Tarakh said, forehead wrinkled.

"*You* know that," Lyell said. "The innkeeper told me to make sure my little dog didn't make a mess on his clean floor."

"We cannot send your young daughter into trouble," Tarakh protested.

"He wants to send Darrendrakar in their alternate forms," Nia said wearily.

Zefra pursed her lips. "Who would pay attention to animals? Do we have volunteers?"

All six Darrendrakar raised their hands.

Zefra frowned at Lyell. "We need animals that will blend in. You are a Wolf."

"I can pass for a dog," he argued.

Nia threw off the blanket. "Don't be ridiculous. A waist-high wolf does *not* pass for a dog. Tala gets by because she's still a puppy. And Kaito can't go. Iskra doesn't have seals, and certainly not on land."

Zefra examined the rest of the Darrendrakar guard, all male. "What kindred are the rest of you?"

"I am from the Pinniped tithe," one said.

"In the guard?" Zefra asked. "What about Darravani's rule?"

"I am a Walrus and was not at Kairri. I am allowed to fight."

Zefra turned to the others.

"Bear."

"Jaguarrundi."

"Lion hound."

"Bear and Walrus will not work. What is jaguarrundi?"

"Cat." The slender Darrendrakar smiled. "Something like a miniature jaguar, though not really."

Zefra squinted at him. "May I see the cat and dog, please?"

The two Darrendrakar left. In a few minutes, a large dog nosed open the door, followed by a cat. The dog pranced into the room, toenails clicking on the luxurious wooden floor. His coat, a short, sleek reddish-wheat, grew backward up his spine.

"He's as large as I am," Lyell protested.

"But he looks nothing like a wolf," Zefra said. "He will do."

The dog nodded and left the room.

Zefra looked at the two-cubit-long cat, who yawned in her face and lashed his charcoal-gray tail. "Do the Darrendrakar not change to any *small* animals?"

The cat meowed, and Nia translated. "I'm smaller than your jaguar friend."

Lyell shook his head. "A fox is as small as we get, and our foxes are bigger than a mere animal. His fur will hide well at night, and, from a distance, he looks like a domestic cat."

The cat grinned, showing all his sharp teeth. Zefra waved the two Darrendrakar from the room.

"That gives us two, then," Zefra said, "plus the four Iskrin guards."

"I'll find more," Lyell promised. "There are more foreign visitors in Iskra than usual, thanks to His Holiness's visit." He jumped to his feet. "I'll take Tala into the market."

"I will go with you," Tarakh said. "Sooner planted, sooner harvested."

The two guards returned in their two-legged form, and Tala raced between their feet.

"Lyell," Zefra said, watching the energetic puppy, "Tala cannot stay here. 'Tis not safe. After you find Darrendrakar to help, you must take her back to Arupa."

"No." The Wolf bared his teeth at her.

"Yes. See what you can discover from the other lands and gods."

Lyell scooped up Tala and glared at Zefra. "I'll go, but I recommend we all pray to our own gods."

"We can't talk to the gods about this," Nia said. "They let Ahjin be arrested."

"We do not know what they were told," Zefra said.

"That's exactly my point," Nia said. "First, we have to figure out who is behind this, and if it's an honest mistake or someone's plot."

"I will be discreet," Lyell said. "How can we pass messages quickly?"

"I can lend you some of my father's messenger birds," Tarakh offered.

"A good idea for Arupa to here," Zefra said, "but none are trained to fly to Arupa."

"What about Ahjin's cousin, Sufa?" Nia asked. "She is a diplomat in Chisato. Lyell can look for another telepath to relay messages to her. It will take us a few days to find Sufa, anyway, and for him to get home."

Lyell pointed to one of the Iojif guards, a woman with long, tapered wings in a beautiful mottled brown. "Arasi, you are fastest. Fly back and ask Sufa to investigate in Chisato and then come here to help."

"Wait," Zefra said. "Let me send a message for Ludik with you." She pulled out an extra slate and summarized the disaster in trade script. "Give it directly to him and say 'tis urgent. Look for a tall Darrendrakar with gold hair, or a big black jaguar."

"Let me go with her," the other Iojif said. "While she's in Chisato, I will search the well site for clues. I can be back in days instead of weeks."

"Go," Zefra said.

Both saluted and left immediately.

"Come, Tarakh." Lyell bared his teeth at Zefra. "Since I must leave for Arupa soon, we have little time to find more spies."

The two walked out. Lyell kept his nose in the air, but Tarakh waved as he left.

Nia scrambled out of bed. "I'll talk to the Sardad captain."

Zefra grabbed her arm. "No, *you* will stay out of sight. First, as a No-kai, you are highly visible. Second, what would it do to Ahjin if you were harmed?"

She scanned the guards. One Nokai and three Iskrin were women. "You four," she pointed, "are assigned to keep Nia out of sight and trouble. Walrus and Bear, you're in charge of protecting the inn."

"They have names, you know," Nia muttered.

Zefra bowed low to hide the blush heating her cheeks. Even the stress of the situation did not excuse her extreme rudeness. "I apologize. What are your names?"

The Walrus grinned. "It doesn't hurt *our* feelings. You can worry about it later."

The Bear merely chuckled and stalked out the door.

Zefra glared at Nia and turned back to the other guards. "Who has a local accent?"

One of the four hands that went up belonged to a female.

Zefra tugged a stray curl. "Change your clothes and go gossip in the market square. Nia will have to make do with three guards for now."

Two of the female guards took posts by the window and door, and everyone else left. Nia curled under her blanket again and stared at nothing.

Zefra lay on her own cot and ran endless theories through her mind until their cook called her to the kitchen to discuss how to work without annoying the inn's cook. As they prepared dinner, Tarakh returned with Tala.

"You're just in time," Zefra said. "Where is Lyell?"

Tarakh glanced at the cook. "He decided to eat in the market so he can finish arrangements."

Zefra flickered her own glance at the cook. "Then we will see him when he returns," she said casually. "Did you wash your hands?"

Tarakh bowed with a grin. "Yes, Mother. I even washed Tala's paws, not that it helps."

Zefra threw a dish towel at him. "Go get everyone."

After dinner, Zefra took a walk around the inn with the guards, then sat under the lone tree in the yard and waited. They had discussed the gossip from the marketplace while they ate. Though dramatic, none was helpful or true.

After dark, Lyell returned in the back alley and sniffed the air. "Zefra?" he whispered.

Zefra rose to her feet and called a spark to her finger for a second. Lyell slunk over and took her elbow.

As the finest in town, the inn had three separate stables and a large corral. One of the stables had been reserved for Ahjin's group, but their horses now stood in the open corral. Lyell knocked on the stable door in a complicated pattern, then dragged Zefra through. In the darkness, she could barely see him one step in front of her. The sound of someone else breathing echoed off the stone walls. Something growled to the left, and teeth snapped on air.

Zefra's skin tingled as someone breathed on her neck. She called fire to her hand. In the sudden light, rows of eyes gleamed around the stable. "Calm down, everyone." Lyell pushed cold metal at Zefra. "Here."

She dropped the flame into the lantern and turned up the wick until the glow reached all but the back corners. Every stall was full of creatures, many with very long teeth. Behind her, a large golden cat balanced on a stall wall and smiled as if harmless, but its amber eyes glowed.

Lyell hung the lantern on a hook. "Everyone, this is Zefra. Zefra, these are our possible recruits."

A muscular spotted cat with long forelegs stalked from the far corner, waving a stubby tail, and approached slowly until it stood a mere hand from Zefra, close enough for its breath to heat her chest.

"She is one of our makarodont," Lyell said proudly.

Zefra watched the cat without blinking. She was bigger than Ludik as a panther, bigger than his tiger mother, and as she yawned, her mouth opened wide enough to bite off Zefra's head with teeth almost as long and curved as her saif.

"Lyell," she whispered, "what recruiting criteria did you use?"

"Friendliness to His Holiness and knowledge of trade tongue and Iskrit," Lyell said. "They can't spy if they can't understand the language and report to us."

"Both good points, but what about 'unremarkable?' If a wolf is too noticeable, what is a... makarodont?"

Lyell shrugged. "I thought you might let her guard Nia. I recruited a few others as guards, too."

Zefra stared at the long teeth. "A good idea. Could we separate them for consideration?"

Lyell pointed left — "Guards" — and right — "Spies," and the Darrendrakar in the stable rearranged themselves, except for the golden cat still breathing on Zefra's neck.

"Lyell, if you evaluate the fighters, I will speak to the others."

At Lyell's nod, Zefra headed right and sat on a bale of hay. There were not as many possible spies as it had first appeared. "You all wish to help Ahjin?"

Half nodded and half tipped their heads in inquiry.

"The Mouth of the Gods," Zefra clarified.

All nodded.

"You speak trade tongue and Iskrit?"

All nodded.

"Can any of you speak it *now*, in those forms?"

All shook their heads.

Zefra rubbed her face wearily. "Let me see these forms, and then you can shift to talk to me."

A small parade rotated in front of her. Zefra sent a few to Lyell's side of the stable, then waited for the others to shift in the stalls. When she faced a row of brown faces in colorful tunics and dresses, instead of a menagerie, she spoke again.

"Who are the Horses?"

Two hands went up. The man and woman looked like kin, despite the different hair colors.

"You look close enough to Iskrin horses," Zefra said. "Are you fast? Would you accept a rider?"

"We will take a rider without bit or spurs," the woman said, "and I won four of the last five cross-country races in our territory. I should have won all five."

The man snickered. "But you got lost without me to guide you."

She smacked his shoulder.

Zefra frowned at the man. "We do not usually send our stallions from the herd, only mares and geldings. You should go with Lyell, instead."

The man's eyebrows rose halfway up his forehead. "Riders are one thing; gelding is quite another. But I do not like leaving my sister alone. She might get lost."

His sister smacked him again.

"We will send someone with her," Zefra said. "Who are the Dogs?"

Two more hands went up.

"You are both approved. Who is left?"

Two hands raised. One of them belonged to a man with red-and-gray-streaked hair who smiled earnestly at Zefra.

"I know you," Zefra said. "We met in Darrendra, did we not? I should apologize for hitting your head. Why are you on this side? I sent you to Lyell."

The forester laughed. "I had quite a headache that day, but it was better than what your tall friend planned for me. And I came back because I am not a good warrior. Please, may I help? I owe Ahjin my life. I finally made it all the way here to thank him."

"A fox will not blend into the city," Zefra said.

"What about the desert?" the male Horse asked. "He could run messages between locations."

"Oh, yes," the Fox said. "That will do. Please, lady."

"Very well." Zefra rubbed her forehead and turned to the last woman. "I am afraid I do not remember you."

"Yes, you do." The woman bared her teeth in a grin.

Zefra took another look at the amber eyes. "You're the Cat." The hair on the back of her neck rose, remembering the hot breath in the dark.

"I am a karrakal," the woman said. "No need to sound disappointed."

Zefra questioned the Darrendrakar about their skills and rubbed her forehead again. "Let me think about your exact assignments. Get some sleep."

She sat on the hay bale and watched everyone slip into the night. Finally, only Lyell was left.

"Will this work?" Zefra asked him. "Can we discover who is behind this?"

Lyell blew out the lamp. "We must."

As Zefra closed the door, she wished to return to a time when her biggest problems were an empty stomach and no employment.

12. SEARCH

(NEAR CHISATO; DAY 15)

Adult Darrendrakar can shift from one form to the other in seconds.

A Brief Sketch of Mysterious Darrendra

"Rurru, get out of that box." Ludik scooped his son onto the ground and turned to close the lid.

From her perch on the blankets in the chest, Zurrahava smiled at him, whiskers twitching.

"Children," Ludik groaned. He grabbed Zurrahava, bumped the lid down with his elbow, and sat on it.

They had to get to the docks by nightfall to catch their ship home. They should have left two weeks ago, but the city guard asked him to testify about the strangler he killed. In deference to his position as Shri and his need to go home, they had hurried, but it still took time to declare the death self-defense. The reason for the attack had never been determined.

"Are the chests ready?" Nemerra called from outside. "We have to leave soon."

"Almost." Ludik fastened the straps around the trunk and moved to the next one.

One of the new Iskrin guards Ahjin had lent them came inside and carried out the first chest. Ludik had one strap fastened on the second when he heard a frantic meow from inside the chest.

"Furballs," he swore, scrambling to free the kitten trapped inside.

It was Rurru again, but when Ludik took out the little snow leopard, the other three cubs eyed the open chest with mischievous grins.

Ludik pointed. "Outside. Now."

All four kittens tilted their heads and smiled.

The guard returned and snickered. "Need help with the trunk?"

"Please take the children outside to play," Ludik growled.

The guard snickered again and pulled a cluster of feathers-on-a-string from his pocket. "Come on, cubs, 'tis time for pouncing practice."

The kittens raced outside after the feathers.

Ludik hurried to strap down every trunk while he had the chance. If they missed this ship, they must wait weeks longer. Now that his apprenticeship was finished, he itched to see his family. He and Nemerra had been gone for fifteen months, a long time for someone who never wanted to leave home.

Ludik's certificate of mastery was in a small chest with their few valuables. Shri Okechuku had signed it yesterday with many flourishes and an offer to host Ludik anytime he wanted to visit Iskra again. While it was a kind thought, Ludik planned to never return. He looked forward to finally staying home.

His hand strayed to the cord around his neck, where a small nose-ring hung next to a fragment of burned walrus tusk. Suid territory was at the far north of Darrendra, so he would have to travel enough to return the wedding hoop to the wife of the Pig that died helping him in the Dragon Isles. If he could find her.

He grabbed a chest, and the guards returned for the others.

"Children," he called in Darrendran. "Let's go."

No kittens returned.

Ludik growled. "This is not the time to play hide and hunt."

"They're too young to understand time." Nemerra called in Iskrit for the guards.

Everyone scattered, calling for the kittens and their guardian. Ludik and Nemerra looked inside every tent, basket, and trunk, and behind every sand dune and boulder. Still no kittens, and no answer.

Someone shouted in the distance, and everyone ran until they saw two guards returning, faces grim.

"Their guard is dead," one of the guards said.

Nemerra wobbled. Ludik put an arm around her, but his own knees felt weak. The guard's voice buzzed in his ears, and he blinked hard to focus.

"No sign of your children, Shri," the guard continued.

Ludik laughed bitterly. "Is that better or worse? Did they find another hunter who carried them away for their pelts?"

Nemerra dashed to the nearest tent. "Hurry, Ludik," she called. "We must track them."

Ludik followed her to the tent, where they shifted to jaguar and leopard. They bounded out and screeched to a halt by the guards.

"The body is this way." One led everyone toward Chisato.

They traveled farther than Ludik thought his little ones could go, especially in so little time. His pride at their speed mixed with anger at their disobedience. Over a tall dune, they reached a hidden pocket where the guard lay twisted on reddened sand. His blood-stained sword was nearby, and multiple wounds slashed his body.

Nemerra wailed and immediately sniffed the sand around the body. Ludik joined her, sorting the different scents. *There* was the guard's scent, and there, and there. For a while, everywhere the guard went, four kitten scents followed. Ludik remembered the feathered string and the promise of hunting practice.

Then more scents joined them. The kitten trails ran in one direction, and the guard and the new scents crisscrossed until the track ended at the guard's body. After that, the new scents went in the direction the kittens had run.

When the trails finally crossed, the kitten scents disappeared.

"No blood," Ludik said to Nemerra.

Relief flooded him, followed by the return of despair. Even if the children were still alive, how long would that last? Without knowing why they were taken, he had no way to predict. His heart pounded with fear, but he pushed it aside and lowered his nose to the ground again.

They turned toward the city and followed the kitnappers' scents for several furlongs. Once at the marketplace, the scents disappeared into a chaos of smells. Too many people, too many spices, too many animals.

Their guards spread out, some surrounding Ludik and Nemerra and assuring the crowd they weren't dangerous.

Others questioned the market customers. "Have you seen four big cubs?" "Have you seen a baby lion? A leopard? A spotted white cat?"

"Here," one shouted. "She saw a black cat."

Ludik and Nemerra ran to the young Iskrin girl and listened as the guard questioned her.

"It went that way," she pointed. "All black, yes."

Ludik and Nemerra pelted through in the direction she indicated, leaping over tables and dodging customers too slow to move.

Nothing. Still nothing.

Then a distressed meow.

Ludik spun on his hind legs and darted to the right. There, a movement in the shadows and a gleam of cat eyes. And in front of the cat, a pack of stalking dogs.

Ludik roared and pounced, sending the dogs flying in all directions with swipes of his claws. Their pained squeals echoed in the alley. Behind him, Nemerra chased away the injured dogs. Finally, they were gone.

So were the gleaming eyes.

Ludik searched again and found a black tail behind a piece of abandoned junk. "Zurrahava?" he called softly. "Come out; it's safe now."

Nemerra crept beside him, panting. "Zurrahava!"

The black tail disappeared behind the junk, and the eyes reappeared.

"Meow." The black cat emerged, and behind her, a tiny kitten wiggled into view.

Ludik dropped to the ground and covered his eyes, breathing hard. She was just a cat, not a Darrendrakar and certainly not Zurrahava.

Nemerra wailed softly and nudged her head into Ludik's side. "Where are our children?"

"I don't know," he whispered. He nuzzled her, heart breaking. Why would anyone take their children?

Behind them, half their guards pounded up, swords drawn.

Ludik pulled himself to his feet. "Come on, let's ask again. Someone had to have seen something."

They returned to the market, where the other half of their guards still questioned people.

It took an hour to talk to everyone in the market, and Ludik's heart sank lower with every negative response. No one had seen anything. None of the few Darrendrakar in the area had smelled anything, either. Half the day had passed, and still no sign of their children.

A swirl of wind rushed overhead, and the flap of wings made Ludik spin, looking for Lapwing. An Iojif landed next to Ludik, but her wings were brown-speckled instead of tan, and her hair was golden brown. Her uniform was marked with Ahjin's seven-curled wind badge.

"Shri, I've been looking all over for you," she said, swaying with exhaustion. "I have a message for you."

Ludik bumped his head into his guard's hip.

"Give it to me, please," the guard said. "I will have him read it as soon as we deal with an emergency."

Nemerra nudged the water bag hanging from the guard's belt until he poured water for the woman.

She gulped the water and handed back the cup. "Thank you. I have orders to give it directly to the Shri. Kezhekori said it was urgent."

"Why is Zefra sending messages with His Holiness's staff?"

"Everything is in the message. I must go." She handed him a slate and flew away.

Now what was Zefra doing? While the guard held the slate low, Ludik struggled through the message. Zefra's trade script was tidy, but Ludik's mastery of the written version was worse than his verbal understanding, and the chalk was smeared from transit. Nemerra was twitching impatiently before he finished the letter.

"Plague fleas," he swore.

"Ludik," Nemerra chided. "Watch your tongue."

"Ahjin's been arrested for multiple murders on the way to Sardad."

Nemerra's mouth gaped. She blinked several times and finally closed her mouth. "Really? What did the gods say about that?"

Ludik read the note again. "No word yet if they believe the charges. Zefra wants me to go help."

"There is nothing you can do," Nemerra argued. "And what about the children?"

"Zefra doesn't know they were taken. I don't know how I can help, but how can I abandon him?" Ludik snarled. What an impossible situation!

He paced while the guards returned to questioning customers and the sun sank lower in the sky. It was too late to catch their ship home, even if they found their kittens now. And what if they could not— No, they *would* find them.

Once the family was reunited, where could Ludik leave them safely while he went to help Ahjin? Maybe Shri Okechuku would have an idea. Or maybe they could take refuge in the palace Ahjin had used for his official visit. Ludik could leave all the guards with them and protect himself.

"Oh, yes, I saw something," a voice said. "Or, perhaps."

Ludik jerked his attention back to the interrogation in front of him.

"Will you explain, please?" one of the guards asked politely, beckoning his partners closer.

"I did not see any cats," the man said, "but I saw someone carrying a large basket into the desert. I noticed it because the lid kept bouncing as if it held a nest of vipers." He shrugged. "You can get a lot of strange things in the market."

"Can you show us where you saw it?" the guard asked, clenching his fist on his sword hilt.

"Hmm." The man tapped his chin. "Where was I? I was buying spices, and a dowry bracelet for my daughter. She's not old enough yet, but it never hurts to start early. She's a beauty, she is. When she's a little older, the boys will line outside our tent for leagues."

Ludik lowered his head to hide his bared teeth. When would the man get to the point?

Nemerra nudged the man's hand and blinked at him charmingly.

"Oh, yes. The basket," he said. "Where was I? Spices, bracelet, vegetables... Saddle! I was looking at the new saddles. It will have to wait for another day, but I found a lovely saddle right by the horse corrals. Well-cured leather, fine tooling, and it comes with matching saddlebags."

Ludik and Nemerra left the man extolling the virtues of the saddlebags and raced toward the corrals.

"Why our children?" Ludik asked. "There is no ransom note, and we have little money."

"They will grow too big for pets," Nemerra said. "Maybe a demand will come later. Why else could they want them?"

Ludik shrugged. He didn't want to remind her of the hunter who wanted Rurru's fur. Maybe someone wanted *bigger* fur and was willing to wait for it to grow. That was their mistake. Ludik would find his children before then.

"If we don't find the children quickly, would Ahjin help us after he is freed?" Nemerra asked as they ran.

"Maybe this is a distraction to keep me from helping Ahjin."

Nemerra lowered her head. "I feel sorry for Ahjin, but he has others who can help him."

Ludik nudged her shoulder. "Our children will always be my priority."

As they approached, guards trailing behind, the corral smelled of horses and hay. The horses whinnied in alarm and circled in a whirl of hooves and flying manes.

The owner exited his tent rapidly. "What are you doing to my horses?"

He saw the two giant cats and backed up rapidly, fumbling for a weapon. "Stop them," he cried, looking at the guard troop. "Why do you not kill them before they eat my horses?"

"They mean no harm," a guard said. "They are Darrendrakar looking for their children, not wild animals. Have you seen any cubs today?"

The man stopped moving, still clutching his knife. "No, no cubs."

"Did you sell a horse to a stranger?"

The merchant shook his head again. "I have not sold a horse since yesterday."

He edged toward the corral, clucking soothingly to the horses while he watched Ludik and Nemerra with wide eyes.

"Did you rent a horse to anyone, or board one?" the guard asked.

"No, and no. Business has been slow all week. I have only sold three horses, and one was to a friend. No one has rented or borrowed a horse, and no one has left one here." He shrugged. "Except for the two I sold yesterday. He did not pick them up until today, after he finished his other purchases."

"Tell us about your customer," the guard said.

The horseman shrugged. "Iskrin, middle-aged, taller. Very ordinary, with a non-clan, lacy badge on his shoulder. He haggled well for two steady hunting horses, then paid in gold for the horses, one saddle, and a week of feed, including the time he left the horses in my corral."

"When did he return?"

The man scratched his ear. "Maybe an hour ago."

An hour! Ludik growled. So long ago, and yet, maybe not too long. And was the "lacy badge" the same design as the one from the flour sack?

The horseman climbed on top of the corral fence and sat casually, but the fear in his scent spiked higher. "He had a large sack of provisions," he said, "and a basket of puppies for his children."

"Oh." The guard's shoulders slumped. "You saw the puppies?"

"No. When I noticed the lid bouncing, he told me about them. Fine hunting dogs, he said. The horse did not care much for the squirming, but I train my horses well. They departed with no issues."

And what if they were not pups, but cubs? Ludik snarled and looked helplessly into the desert.

Another guard spoke. "Did he ever put down the basket, other than on the horses?"

The horseman scratched his ear again. "Yes, he had to saddle the horse. He wanted me to do it, but I told him I was busy."

Ludik pricked up his ears.

"Where did he put it down?" the second guard asked.

"Where? What difference does that make?"

Ludik growled, a rumbling snarl from the bottom of his chest and stalked toward the insolent horseman.

"Over there," the man squeaked, pulling his feet to the top rail. "By the gate."

Ludik pounced across the yard with Nemerra and sniffed the dirt. Many people had been here, and many animals. The horseman had walked across the spot a hundred times.

Wait. "Here it is," he said. "The children were here."

Nemerra sniffed the dirt. Ludik moved farther away and found a faint trace of one of the people who had killed the cubs' guardian, but not of the others. For a furlong, they hunted together for another spot of odor, some hint at which way the kitnapper went, but found nothing more. The sun dropped to the horizon, turning the sky blue.

The children had disappeared into the desert with someone maybe wearing the poisoner's mark, and there was no way to follow.

13. SPIES

(SARDAD)

Follow the river and you will find the sea.
Nokai Proverb

Zefra woke in the inn, already spinning her bad dreams into plans. The sooner they proved Ahjin's innocence, the better, since the Sardad guard captain seemed over-eager to execute His Holiness. And why had the gods not already proclaimed his innocence?

To investigate every death and attempted murder, Zefra needed a lot of spies and messengers. With the other lands and gods to inspect, Lyell would need even more, but he also had all the resources of Arupa.

Nia was an unmoving lump in the next bed, and the window showed the dark blue sky of early dawn. Zefra climbed out of bed and dressed, minus scarf, belt, and sword. All she needed was something to eat while she thought. She tiptoed downstairs and ate bread and fruit while she made notes, rearranging assignments dozens of times. Finally, she pushed away her slate and took a long drink of water.

Tarakh sat across the table, smiling at Zefra. When had he arrived? He was also dressed in robe and boots but with combed hair. She had not even changed her simple bedtime plait to her proper braided coronet.

She put her hand over her messy braid. "When did you wake?"

"Bright day, Zefra. Farmers rise early. Did you sleep well?"

Zefra shook her head. "Last night, I dreamed about failing Ahjin and watching his execution. It was quite uncomfortable. I now understand Ahjin's guilt about the injuries we sustained in our earlier ventures."

Tarakh chewed half an apple before he spoke. "And do you agree with Ahjin's guilt?"

"Of course not." Zefra flexed her hands. "He did everything he could, and we made our own choices."

Tarakh raised his eyebrows.

Zefra twitched. "Agreement and emotion are different things."

"They are." He spun her slate to face him. "What are you doing?"

"Assigning investigators."

"You have more listed than I recall."

"Lyell introduced me to new candidates last night. You can meet them later today."

Tarakh grinned. "Good. I will need to know what they look like."

"I cannot ask you to help with this," Zefra said. "It will be dangerous, and I will not be here to protect you."

Tarakh folded his arms. "I think you just insulted me."

"I — no, you—" Zefra held her breath. "There is no need for you to endanger yourself in our mess."

Tarakh smiled. "I like His Holiness encouraging the gods to cooperate. I like the new worldwide interchange and the increased trade options. I like Ahjin. And I like you. Why should I not help?"

Zefra's cheeks grew hot.

Tarakh read the slate again and reached toward her chalk. "May I?" He kept eye contact until she dropped the chalk into his hand. "Five locations?"

"Six, if we can," Zefra said. "I would like to get ears inside the temple. And we need messengers."

"You want to spy on our god?" Tarakh sounded equally amused and appalled. "How?"

Zefra shrugged. "I thought the Cats might help. Resef is not *their* god, and cats are well known for their boldness. If they are caught, which is less likely, Resef might think twice before burning his sister's children. I will let Lyell worry about how to investigate the other gods."

Tarakh tapped the chalk on the slate before making a note. "Two Cats to the temple. What else?"

Zefra pointed to her notes. "I already sent our two Iojif guards to the well and to Chisato to find Sufa and Ludik. The Fox begged to carry messages. That leaves Pramath, the river, and here."

Tarakh checked off her note and moved to the next. "Who is Rozali?"

"A Horse I thought could investigate the horse-trainer's death in Pramath. Perhaps one of the guards might pass for a trainer."

"What about Chiara, who helped with the novice riders?" Tarakh asked. "But she's guarding Nia."

Zefra laughed. "Oh, I have a replacement for her now." She grinned in anticipation of Nia's reaction to long fangs.

"We could send Isako and the lion hound to the river." Tarakh sliced an apple and handed half to her.

"Yes, Ingo, the Darrendrakar guard with the red-blonde hair. Go ahead and note that."

"My father's agents will listen here in Sardad," Tarakh said. "It will be easier than explaining to them about the deaths and where to find the graves."

Zefra nodded with her mouth full. The apple was withered from winter storage, but 'twas still sweet. She licked the last bit of juice from her lips. "They can report to Daz, along with the new Dogs: a molossus, who is something like a mastiff, and a leopard dog."

Tarakh wrote on the slate, and they worked on more details until the cook entered the kitchen and pulled out a stack of pans. Zefra bowed an apology, put her dishes into the sink, and tiptoed upstairs with Tarakh.

Lyell let them into his room, still in his nightshirt, holding a finger to his lips. Tala slept curled in a black ball of furry puppy on his bed. The other two beds were empty but neatly made with packs at the ends. The Wolf sat beside his daughter while Zefra and Tarakh found seats on the floor.

"Most of the Darrendrakar need to make excuses to their lodging or caravan," Lyell murmured. "They will come to the stable later. I've arranged for Ahjin's boat to pick me up, probably later today. Will you be ready if I leave that early?"

"Certainly," Zefra whispered.

"I will help," Tarakh said softly.

Lyell studied the bronze-eyed Iskrin, then finally nodded. "I will have someone greet people in the stable as they arrive."

"Do you need me for anything right now," Tarakh asked, "or should I arrange for messenger birds and let you two get dressed?"

Zefra put her hands over her messy hair and blushed.

Lyell grinned and tapped his bare legs below his nightshirt. "Are you saying I knee-d better clothes?"

Tarakh covered his mouth and slipped out, shoulders shaking.

"Warmth to you." Zefra bowed, ignoring the joke and the bare legs. "Travel safely and send me word as often as you can."

Lyell clasped her arm. "Keep well, Zefra. Do your best for Ahjin, but keep yourself and Nia safe."

She did not remind him she would leave soon. "We will see you again when Ahjin is free."

"When Ahjin is free." He sat beside Tala again and subtly rubbed his eyes.

Zefra shut the door silently, returned to her room, and gathered a pile of slates. On each, she wrote a summary in trade tongue, then more details about the specific location for that team. After her attempts to draw the tattoo-mark turned into a tangled mess that would make a spider cry, she settled for describing it. By the time she finished, her fingers had cramped and Nia had dragged herself to breakfast with unbraided hair frizzing to her shins.

Zefra brushed her own hair and braided it in the coronet that marked her as an adult maiden, then wrapped her scarf around it. Too many people had already seen her in disarray this morning, and her spies needed to see her as competent. She tied her embroidered sash across her leather sword belt, fingering her younger sisters' stitches wistfully. But she had no time to miss her family now.

She gathered the slates and walked downstairs despite the itch on the back of her neck that insisted enemies lay around every corner, waving at the rest of her party in the dining hall. "I'll check on the horses. Nia, stay inside."

Chiara sat beside Nia, handing the sleepy Nokai another glass of water.

Zefra strolled toward the stable as if grooming horses was the only thing on her mind.

The Walrus in the yard stopped sharpening his knives, moved his spear off the stable door, and knocked in an intricate pattern. "I'll teach it to you later," he murmured, then opened the door and pushed her in.

Daylight shone through high windows to illuminate empty stalls. Chiyo, one of the Devoran guards, sat in the middle of the room chatting with a Darrendrakar man and woman.

The woman's hair was black, not the pale blonde of the Horse woman. Zefra recognized the man's odd eyes, half blue and half white, like cracked glass, and checked her slate for the names of the molossus and the leopard dog. "Bright day, Harita and Redell. Chiyo, please ask Daz to join us."

The guard slipped out, and Zefra sat on a scratchy hay bale and examined the Dogs' tiny packs, which held almost nothing besides a water bag and a flint. Chiyo returned with her fellow guard, and Zefra introduced Daz to his new partners. The Dogs subtly sniffed the air while the captain bowed.

"I'm sending the three of you into Sardad," Zefra said. "Look for the trail of the Nokai's killer, or evidence of a conspiracy, or that mark anywhere, or any clues. Daz, the Cats will also report to you. Harita and Redell, I'm sorry to make you shift already."

Redell laughed. "Our alternate forms are no hardship for us."

He and Harita headed for separate stalls in the back. In a moment, a massive black dog with green eyes exited, followed quickly by a multi-colored splotchy dog. Daz stuffed their tunics and packs into his own. Harita bowed her head at Zefra, but the spotted dog hung out his tongue and snickered. Daz kneed Redell's side and clicked his tongue, and all three disappeared.

Zefra waited with Chiyo, and before long, more people arrived to instruct.

Madden the Fox made Zefra read his slate to him twice, then let her buckle a loose collar around his neck with a small tube for messages and a tag marked with her clan's firefly, to identify him to the other spies.

"Your turn, Rozali," Zefra told the Horse, who had already changed from a pale-haired woman to a beautiful golden mare with three white stockings.

"I do not think I like this." Her brother, Zinon, wrapped his dark fingers in her pale mane, and Rozali bumped her nose against his shoulder.

"I promise to care well for her." Chiara strapped a blanket onto Rozali's back. "I ride well enough that she need not wear a saddle. We will practice before we reach Pramath, so my 'commands' look real without bothering her."

Zinon made a face. "I believe you, but I still do not like leaving her."

Chiyo put down the slate he had been reading. "Zefra, is Madden the only messenger?"

"I hope Sufa, Ahjin's cousin, will relay messages once Lyell reaches Arupa."

"But no one else between locations? Madden cannot go into Chisato to get messages or come into Sardad to deliver them to you."

"I planned to meet the Fox outside city limits," Zefra said. "I have no one else."

"Yes, but he is also limited in speed. What if I rode Zinon, with his permission, as an additional messenger? Madden can concentrate on the desert locations and pass messages to me, while Zinon could check on his sister as we pass."

"He's a stallion," Zefra said. "No one would believe he is wasted on a mere messenger."

Chiyo shrugged. "From a distance, who can tell? And within the cities, I will tell people I am delivering him to a new owner."

Zinon slammed a stall door shut, and a splotched brown and white head soon rose above the door.

Zefra made a note on her slate. "I suppose that answers the question of his permission."

Chiyo let out the pinto and arranged a blanket on his back. "Let me pack a saddlebag. Zefra, will you copy your master slate for me, please?"

He left the stable, and Chiara put Rozali's dress into her saddlebags. "We will see you in a few days, Zinon." She led out the palomino.

By the time Zefra copied her list, Chiyo returned. He took the slate, buckled his saddlebags across Zinon's blanket, and left Zefra with the last two guards, Isako and Ingo.

"You two are going to the spot on the river where the female Iojif died," Zefra explained. "I'm afraid you must go on foot, though."

Ingo shook his red-gold head. "It doesn't matter. I can run for hours."

Isako grinned crookedly. "I can walk all day, and that will have to be good enough."

"Besides you two, that only leaves the Cats," Zefra said. "Why am I not surprised they are late?"

"Gazanar is waiting with Nia," Isako said absently, reading his slate.

Someone chuckled. Zefra whirled, flame rising from her hand. In the back stall, two amber eyes shone.

"Good to see you," the karrakal woman said, rising from the darkest corner. Her dark skin faded into the shadows, but her eyes crinkled with amusement. "Jumpy, aren't you? Did you get a mouse up your skirt?"

Zefra held a deep breath. The fire in her hand wavered as she desperately considered how flammable hay was and how unhappy the innkeeper would be if she burned his stable.

Isako coughed. "I will get Gazanar." He fled, but not quickly enough to hide his booming laugh.

Zefra let the flame die. "Let me explain what I want you to do."

"No need," Varnika purred. "I heard it several times. Just tell me where to go and show me my partners."

"Then you can wait." Zefra added Chiyo and Zinon as messengers in her notes.

Varnika sat behind her and read over her shoulder. Zefra squeezed the slate until her fingers ached. As soon as Isako returned with Gazanar, Zefra shot to her feet.

"I want you two Cats to find a way into the temple of Resef and listen to his priests," she said. "See if you can discover if Resef has anything to do with this, or if you think he would help Ahjin. You will report to Daz. Gazanar, your gray fur makes you well-suited to night work. Varnika, that leaves day for you, if you can remain unseen?"

"Did you see me while you talked to the others?"

Zefra glanced at the dark corner and clenched her fist. "No."

"Then they won't see me in the temple." Varnika yawned.

Zefra stepped outside the stable and shut the door firmly.

They would free Ahjin. Two weeks was surely long enough to prove his innocence.

14.LIBRARY
(SARDAD)

Makanavailea the Omniscient lives with her Nokai in the ocean and personally gives each a birth gift from a wide variety of options.

Everything You Wanted to Know About the Nokailana Islands But Were Too Lazy to Ask

Nia clutched her pack and followed the horses down the dusty Sardad road. She had fought bureaucracy for two days to see Ahjin, then the innkeeper kicked them out for being in service to a murderer. Every inn they passed refused them entrance.

Now it was almost noon, and she was hungry, her feet hurt, and people were rude. "Now that is not nice at all."

"What do you mean?" Zefra asked.

"If an Iskrin knocks, the innkeepers say they have rooms until they see the rest of us. Then they claim they don't have enough space. If one of us foreigners knocks, the innkeeper's first words are a refusal." Nia smoothed her braids. "I feel unwelcome."

Zefra squinted at the most recent inn. "Why would they do that?"

They turned a corner and knocked again. By the end of the street, it was clear Nia was right. Mentioning Ahjin made doors slam faster, and soon there were no more inns.

Nia stopped for a drink. "We need to split up."

The guards protested, but Zefra nodded. "Iskrins, find housing and a job in the city. Do not say you serve His Holiness. Stay watchful. If you discover anything to help Ahjin, tell Captain Daz. I will take the out-dwellers into the desert."

"The Nokai guards should wait in the ocean," Nia said. "Without shelter and abundant water, they will dry out too much."

"I will go, too," the Walrus said. "It is close enough to report back."

"And Nia," Zefra said.

"I've survived the desert before." Nia stuck out her chin and glared at Zefra until the younger girl nodded.

One of the Iskrin guards stepped forward. "I can work on the docks. My southern accent will not matter there."

Alemanana, Kolina, and the Walrus followed him down the street.

Zefra turned to the two Iojif guards, who had returned yesterday and this morning. "You should go. Your wings are impossible to disguise."

"You might need my swift flying again," Arasi said. "We are no more noticeable than the Darrendrakar, and the desert is no more dangerous to us. We will stay, at least until Sufa arrives, but we should change to local clothing."

"I will take care of that," Tarakh said. "We have been here too long. People are staring."

"We will find you later." Daz and the last three Iskrin guards melted into the crowd with most of the horses.

Nia counted. Lyell and Tala had left already, and the cook walked away when the innkeeper evicted them. That left ten, including eight foreigners and Zefra's distinctive red hair. Zefra had better have a plan. Nia caught herself mid-snort. Of course Zefra had a plan.

"This way." Zefra led them south through town.

They left Tarakh with two horses to buy food while everyone else continued into the desert.

Zefra led them to the shade of the fourth dune. "Tomorrow, we can visit the city. There are enough outdwellers in town that no one should notice, if we separate."

Nia pulled a scarf from her pack, dripped water on it, and wrapped it around her gills. Tomorrow was a long time to wait to see Ahjin.

Even with everyone working on the tents, it took an hour to raise all four in the growing wind.

"The tarps we used last time were easier," Nia complained.

"Nights are too cold now." Zefra grunted, pulling a rope tight. "And the rain blows beneath." She tied the last knot as thunder rumbled in the cloudy sky. "You and I are in my tent," she told Nia.

The other three girls would take one tent, and the five men divided the last two.

"When I leave, I will take mine with me," Zefra said. "You will have to squeeze in with the women then."

"Aren't you staying?" Nia protested. "What about Ahjin?"

"I do not leave for two weeks." Zefra glanced at the cloudy sky. "Ahjin should be free before then. And if not, I trust you to defend him at his trial. This caravan is the only one willing to hire me. I cannot miss the chance."

"It won't matter," Nia said. "By then, Ahjin will be free."

Tarakh returned and hobbled the horses. "I have news."

"After the rain," Zefra ordered. "We cannot do anything until then, anyway. Grab the supplies."

While everyone else tossed packages into the tents, Tarakh set out buckets for his horses.

"The rain will fill them," he assured Nia.

Thunder roared, and the clouds dissolved into rain. Everyone but Nia ducked into the tents. Nia ripped off her scarf and raised her face to the sky, dancing on the wet sand. Ah, water, blessing of Makana, almost as good as the ocean.

A stack of buckets were passed out of a tent. Nia grabbed the pile and spread them out to catch rain. As they filled, she passed them through the tent doors. She filled each several times before the rains ended and the others emerged dressed in Iskrin robes and scarves. Except for their brown skin, the Darrendrakar fit in well. The Iojif looked hunchbacked with their wings covered, and Nia's heart cramped at the memory of Ahjin looking the same way.

When would she get him back? She wiped her tears off her face along with the last of the rain, then wrapped her soggy scarf around her neck. She tightened her quivering lip and took an Iskrin robe from Zefra.

"I have good news," Tarakh said. "I found a window to Ahjin's cell. If we're discreet, we can talk to him."

Nia gasped. "What did he say? Is he well?"

Tarakh raised both hands. "A guard was in his cell when I passed by, and I had to get here before the rains."

"Let's go there now. Put me on that horse!" Nia yanked the robe over her head.

"Ahjin told me to keep you safe," Zefra said. "Tomorrow, we will try to *safely* get close to him."

And that was the end of the conversation, no matter how much Nia argued.

In the morning, they divided into teams and walked into Sardad while Zefra lectured them on safety. Nia was stuck with Arasi and the new Darrendrakar woman. Etana was almost as big as the Bear, though Zefra had grinned and refused to tell Nia her alternate form.

Zefra vanished into the market crowd to track down Daz and the spies. Tarakh led Kaito, Nia, and her guards to the far side of the square. He chatted casually with people until Nia wanted to scream for him to hurry. When it was clear, they ducked around the corner behind a stone building.

"Here 'tis," Tarakh whispered, pointing to a small, barred window at street level. "I will keep watch." He and the guards stood at the ends of the alley.

Nia and Kaito threw themselves on their bellies and peered between the bars. It was dark inside, and all Nia could see was the edge of a cot outlined in sunlight.

"Ah—" Nia started, but Kaito put his hand over her mouth and held a finger to his lips.

Nia made a face at him but leaned closer to the bars and waited for her eyes to adjust.

Inside, the room was bare stone, barred at the front as well as at the window. More empty cells stretched beyond, though there were no guards at the moment. The narrow cot was the only furniture besides a covered pot that stank even from the street.

A white streak fluttered on the cot.

"Ahjin," Nia whispered fiercely. "Are you awake?" If she were trapped in such a terrible place, she'd sleep as much as she could.

The white froze. "Nia?" Ahjin climbed onto the cot and stretched toward the bars, wings trailing behind him. "Nia, Kaito, what are you doing here?"

"We came to see you," Nia said.

Ahjin's smile wavered. "I'm fine."

Nia bit her lip while Kaito lowered a handkerchief-wrapped package through the bars.

Ahjin immediately unwrapped it and shoved the fresh bread in his mouth. "Thank you," he mumbled.

Nia gasped. "Don't they feed you?"

Ahjin shrugged. "Sometimes." He swallowed the last bite as fast as he had the short rations on the Dragon Isles. "The captain doesn't like me."

"Zefra found a bunch of spies to investigate," Nia said. "Did the gods say anything?"

Ahjin shook his head. "I tried, but they haven't answered yet."

Tarakh whistled softly and kicked Nia's feet.

"Go." Ahjin dropped onto his cot.

No; they had barely had a minute together. It wasn't fair. Nia clung to the bars until Kaito dragged her to her feet. Tarakh had disappeared. Her guards were waiting, but it was too late.

Four city guardsmen lined the alley, hands on their weapons. "What are you doing?"

Nia fluttered her eyelashes and pulled out her best gushing voice instead of stabbing them with her serrated knife. "We heard you had a ferocious killer and wanted to see what he looked like. You're so brave." She smiled at the guards and put a hand on her chest. "I was terrified, but you captured him. I told my friend" — she grabbed Kaito and sidled toward the alley entrance — "we're perfectly safe in Iskra. But we have shopping to do in your lovely market, so we'll leave now. Thank you for keeping us safe."

She fluttered her eyelashes again and stepped around a bemused guard, still dragging Kaito.

The guard winked. "You're welcome, lady."

One of the other guards narrowed his eyes. "Have I seen you before?"

"Sorry, must go." Nia dropped Kaito's arm and ran.

Her guards pounded on their heels, and behind them, someone shouted, "Stop them!"

They ducked through the busy crowd in different directions. Arasi flew behind a building. Kaito rolled under a merchant's table and disappeared into a tent. Etana jerked Nia around a corner and bounded through a window as someone pulled Nia through a doorway and slammed her against the wall.

Nia opened her mouth to scream.

Tarakh pressed his hand over her mouth. "Hush, 'tis me."

Etana motioned for silence from her crouch under the window.

Outside, feet pounded and guards hollered.

Nia held her breath. Her knees shook, and she was grateful Tarakh braced her against the wall, hands clamped on her arms.

As the search continued past them, her pounding heart gradually settled.

When everything went silent, Tarakh let her go. "Forgive me, Nia, for mishandling you."

Nia waved her hand. "You have my permission to save me anytime."

Etana peeked out the window. "They're gone. I will escort you to the tent. Tarakh can listen to market gossip."

"That's not fair," Nia said, but Etana led her back to the tents and kept her there.

The next day, Nia woke in a cheerful mood, ready to visit Ahjin again.

Zefra, unsurprisingly, was less optimistic. "You almost got caught yesterday. Give the city guard time to forget about you."

"It would be safer," Tarakh said.

Nia threw her hands in the air. "I won't sit here and braid my hair all day."

Etana flicked Nia's braids. "You are distinctive."

Nia sniffed. "More than wings or brown skin? If my braids are the problem, I can fix that."

She pulled her special hairpins from her pouch and pinned her braids until they covered her head like a cap, then covered her hair like a proper Iskrin maiden. "There. Now I'm boring."

Her golden skin still branded her a Nokai, but without the lavender hair, no one knew which one. Too bad hiding her hair also hid her sparkly hairpins. At least she would have her lockpicks and finger-length stiletto in her hair.

"You still cannot visit Ahjin until we know 'tis safe." Zefra marched toward town alone.

Nia stuck out her tongue at Zefra's back.

Tarakh grinned. "What about waiting in the library? Outdwellers may visit, and it has many odd corners to conceal you. You might research the Iskrin legal system for anything to help Ahjin."

Nia rubbed her hands together. "Let's go."

At the market, Nia waited for Etana to check the street, then followed Tarakh through alleys to the back stairs of a majestic building.

"Now, act like you belong," Tarakh said, "and you should be fine."

"I assure you," Nia said in flawless Iskrit, "I can manage." She shut the door in their faces.

Inside, the long hallway was covered with tapestries woven with intricate pictures and runes along the edges. "The war between Heresa and Tetsuya," one said. "The evolution of sailing." "The bloodlines of the Achira horses."

When the tapestries ended, she stepped into a large room divided with shelves in every direction. Signs labeled sections by country, subject, and time period. The air smelled of ink and chalk dust. Occasional Iskrins shuffled by, arms piled with scrolls or slates or the new Iojif printed books, and more rarely, a foreigner hustled behind a librarian.

Nia strolled toward the legal section and started browsing. After hours of reading through dry legal cases and rules without finding anything useful, she looked for water and other necessary accommodations. She left a request at the librarian's desk for more useful information on the courts, then returned to the shelves.

In the mood for lighter reading, she went to the shelves of ancient history in the far corner. She snagged a ladder and climbed to the top shelf of the oldest section, history so old it was almost myth. It looked like a graveyard, scattered with crumbling parchment and broken slates and faded ink on disintegrating paper. A single Nokai leaf fell apart when she touched it.

Nia gently stacked the entire collection onto a large book for support and took it to a private nook with a lamp. The fragments were even older than the histories, and the languages were so ancient that even with her gift of universal translation, she noticed the difference.

After a few more hours, she rubbed her eyes and stretched. The librarians hadn't found her legal information yet, and though the old tales were fascinating, she was hungry and restless. A pale sketch on the next parchment caught her eye. She held the lamp closer until she saw a simple compass rose. From a small grove under a pattern of dots, a trail led to a hexagon. The map didn't show the country or any detail, but the label, in an archaic version of trade tongue, said "Irad, City of Witness."

Nia pursed her lips in a silent whistle. Irad was the lost city of the gods in the oldest of myths from the beginning of the world. Nobody knew where it had been or if it really existed. Zefra would love to add it to the legendary maps she said her clan collected.

Nia pulled out a slate and copied the map as exactly as she could. Next to the map, a poem filled the margins. It was as faded as the map, and Nia struggled to copy each line. When she finished, she held the map to the light to check her work. As she moved the faded parchment, the lamp-light shone through the back and cast a lacy pattern into the hexagon.

Nia cursed loudly.

A librarian hushed her, and Nia smiled sheepishly. "Sorry."

She flipped the parchment. On the back, exactly under the hexagon, was a design similar to the mysterious tangled mark from the flour sack. It was hard to tell if something so intricate was exactly the same, but what could Irad have to do with the murders or Ahjin? Maybe Zefra, trained in maps from childhood, could tell where Irad was, and then they might discover how it connected to their current troubles.

The librarian peeked over her shoulder. "Oh, no, where did you find those?" He tsked. "Those are too fragile for amateurs and are waiting for our scholars to work on these forgotten languages. That scribble is valuable for the sheer age of it. I thought these were already moved to the back room."

"'Tis a map of Irad," Nia exclaimed.

The librarian hushed her again, and someone peeked around the tall shelves.

"Nonsense," the librarian said. "If our scholars cannot read this, then you certainly cannot. Irad is a myth, and what kind of map looks like *this?*"

Nia slid her copy behind her back. Once the librarian gathered the ancient documents and left, she snagged another slate and retreated to the washroom to copy the map and poem again for Zefra. She'd keep her first slate to compose music for the poem.

When she emerged, the high windows showed a dark orange sky. The afternoon rains had already passed, and night would soon fall. Nia meandered down the tapestried hallway to the back door, humming melodies over her slate.

"Did you find something interesting?" a smooth voice asked.

Nia looked up and found a handsome Iskrin smiling at her. She smiled back politely.

"A beautiful lady like you should not walk alone," he said. "May I carry your things home?" He reached for the slate.

"No, thanks." Nia tucked the slate under her arm and pushed open the door. The only man she wanted to walk her home was currently in jail.

"Let me see that," he insisted, yanking her toward him.

"No." Nia grabbed her miniature knife-hairpin from under her scarf and stabbed him with it. When he yelped and let go, she ran down the stairs.

He pulled his sword and followed. "Give me that slate!"

Nia darted into the street and found herself in the almost-empty market. She dodged around a stall and turned to find the man right in front of her, swinging his sword.

Pain burned across Nia's face and chest. She screamed and fell as blood soaked her robe.

He raised his sword again, and Nia threw her arm across her face.

He stumbled forward, missing her entirely, and turned to face the enemy that had shoved him. A giant, spotted cat snarled and slashed his arm with razor claws.

He dropped his sword and rolled, grabbing the slate from Nia's numb hand. And then he was gone, blood dripping behind him.

Nia pressed her arm against her bleeding chest and waited to die. The monstrous cat leaned over Nia, growling, fangs stretching from Nia's chin to forehead.

"You're right, Etana," Nia said. "I should have waited for you."

And then darkness closed in.

15. JAIL

(SARDAD JAIL; DAY 20)

What can't be cured must be endured.
Iojif Proverb

As his stomach rumbled, Ahjin stared at his slice of window. It was so low to the ground and so high above him, he couldn't see the sky, just the bare stone of the building across the street. Sunbeams angled into the top of his cell, tempting him with warmth and freedom. He stood on his cot and stretched to let them wash over his face with a wisp of fresh air. His seconds of conversation with Nia yesterday had been the highlight of his imprisonment. The captain had cursed the guards for an hour for letting her elude them.

The first day, he'd tried to fly to look out, but he couldn't get close enough to the ceiling without smashing his wings into the stone. And when the guards discovered him flying, they threatened to break his wings if he tried again. His guards were surprisingly crude and violent, and he frequently wondered if he should have flown away instead of surrendering.

His cell was cold and dim for most of the day, and watching specks of dust dance in the sunlight against the ceiling was almost his only entertainment in his tiny cell. Though cells lined three walls, he was alone. When he'd first been put in the cell, there had been a few other people in the jail. Most had been released after paying a fine for a minor offense. The rest had been moved after Ahjin talked to them. It seemed the Sardad guard captain thought His Holiness was a bad influence.

Ahjin shook his head. His entire job was based on being a good influence, and despite the accusations, he hadn't killed anyone. His conscience twinged at the slight inaccuracy; he had killed a few pirates last year, but only to defend his friends. And who could blame him for fending off the madman with a knife? But he certainly hadn't killed any of the people they'd found dead on this trip. Imprisoning him was ridiculously unfair, and his upcoming trial was a farce.

He stretched toward the thin sunbeams again. No flying, no fresh air or sunlight on his face, little food, and nothing to do. Claustrophobia and insanity crept closer every hour he was trapped below ground.

The guards were under strict commands to keep him from talking, though it didn't stop them from taunting him. He was bored enough to read the gods' dreary religious books, if he had any with him, but they had taken his belongings, including his tools for communicating with the gods. Runes, seeds, paper, all gone. He couldn't even contact Makana, since he was only allowed water in an opaque bottle, impossible to see into, and if he emptied it into his bowl, it became too greasy to use.

Irajahan was the only god with whom Ahjin could initiate contact without supplies, and he had only responded the first day.

"Wait for the trial," he had said. "Everything will be well. We will talk to you later, but we're having a few minor difficulties right now."

When Ahjin had asked if he could help, Irajahan, surprisingly, had suggested he and his siblings try to settle it themselves, like adults. Ever since then, the god had steadfastly ignored Ahjin. Surely, if they needed his help, they would ask. On the other wing, Ahjin couldn't discuss the murders, his trial, or the proposed decree of heredity for the Mouth of Gods.

The longer he thought about it, the more he thought Irajahan's current obstinate inattention indicated trouble. When Nia came back, Ahjin needed to make sure she'd told the others about Irajahan's treachery at the Dragon Isles, taking back Ahjin's invisibility and setting them up to be killed. It was possible Irajahan had made another attempt to kill him and maybe the rest of them. Ahjin should have thought of it earlier, but he was so used to Irajahan's petty hatred, he hadn't made the connection. After all, if a god wanted him dead, he didn't have to resort to poison to accomplish the task. And why would Irajahan kill four random people? It didn't make any sense, and Ahjin couldn't afford to miss another enemy by focusing on a grudge.

The door to the guard station slammed open. "Oy, 'tis dinner time!"

Finally! Ahjin hadn't eaten since yesterday. He retreated to his cot as three guards clumped down the aisle. He'd learned the hard way that approaching the front invited the guards to poke spears between the bars.

Two of the guards watched him, spears lowered. The third slid a small bowl and a bottle into the cell.

"There, Yer Holiness," he sneered in trade tongue. "The finest cuisine."

He laughed and swaggered up the aisle. His companions backed away, not raising their spears until they were halfway to the door.

Ahjin remained on his cot until the door closed, then lunged for the food and water. The guards would return in a few minutes. Today, the "finest cuisine" meant a meat stew. During his first meal, the guards had joked in Iskrit about what kind of meat the prison cook used. Apparently, no one had warned them Ahjin spoke all languages, and they always addressed him in trade tongue. Keeping his ability secret seemed a good strategy, as Zefra would say, so he kept up the pretense in hopes of overhearing something more important.

But for now, he flicked the chunks of meat into his stinking cesspot. He was not yet hungry enough to eat rat. That day might come, but until then, he settled for the tepid broth and withered vegetables. He gulped his meal, trying not to let it linger on his tongue. It wasn't as nasty as the food in the Orrik jail had been, but it was bad enough to make hunger easier to bear.

He drank the water, holding the bottle upside-down to catch every drop. And just in time, for the door slammed open again. Ahjin laid the cup and bowl next to the bars and lay stiffly on the cot. He listened to the crude comments as the guards collected his empty dishes, in case they entered his cell again. Since he'd refused to admit to the murders, they'd questioned him every day with words and fists but hadn't answered one of his questions.

Ahjin had been promised a trial. He spiraled between impatience at the long, uncertain wait and the realization that the longer it took, the more time Zefra and Nia would have to discover what really happened. If he did have to prove his innocence, he needed more than his own word, and finding out who was behind the murders was their best tactic.

A tap against his bars jolted him to full alertness. Had the guards returned? The tap came again, above his head. Ahjin climbed on his cot. "Kaito, fair winds," he whispered. "Is Nia with you?"

Kaito shook his head and shoved a rolled paper between the bars.

Ahjin grabbed it with the tips of his fingers. He leaned against the wall and unrolled the paper. The bad sketch with round eyes and flirtatious smile was unmistakably Nia. Her hair, however, was a mess of crazy braids in the picture. Ahjin turned his chuckle into a cough.

Then he read the runes under the picture, fingers tightening until the paper wrinkled in his grasp. "Wanted for questioning. Reward for capture."

He whirled back to stare at Kaito. "What—"

Kaito pointed to the picture and flipped over his hand.

Ahjin turned over the paper. *Ahjin, Nia is safe. We're tracking gossip. Hold on, and see if you can learn anything from the gods. Zefra.*

Relief ruffled his feathers like a warm updraft. "Do you have anything to write with?"

Kaito vanished and reappeared with a chunk of coal. Ahjin scribbled a message about Irajahan in the compact Darrendran symbols for Nia to interpret.

"Here, Kaito." He shoved the paper back toward the window. "Take it to Zefra immediately."

Kaito nodded and left.

Ahjin's thoughts spun. Why did the authorities want Nia? More importantly, who was really at fault? How could the girls find the truth with Nia being hunted by the enemy?

Someone banged on his bars again, and he looked at the window. Nothing.

"Oy, stupid, there is no escape that way." The bars clanged behind him.

Ahjin whirled in time to see a guard unlock his cell. Four others waited with weapons and shackles.

"Hold out your hands," the first one commanded.

Ahjin let them snap the metal cuffs around his wrists. "Where are we going?"

The guard smirked. "You know the routine. 'Tis time for questions."

"I've already told you everything I know."

The guard crouched to add shackles to his ankles. "Why not tell us why you killed those poor people?"

Ahjin forced his panicked breathing to slow. "I didn't kill those people. I don't know who did."

Boot heels stamped into the room, and everyone turned to watch the captain enter.

"What is going on?" the captain roared.

"We're just asking a few questions," Ahjin's tormentor protested.

"I will ask the questions! Bring him out here." The captain tapped his dagger against his palm while Ahjin was dragged out of the cell.

The guards hauled Ahjin after the captain, who walked to a door in the corner. "The judge will go easier on your sentencing if you admit your guilt. Why do you make things difficult for yourself?"

"I told you, I didn't do anything."

"Oh, but we know you did." The captain opened the door, and the guards shoved Ahjin through. "We know how you killed them with your weapons and disguised them as accidents."

The room was windowless and dark until the captain lit a lantern.

"You thought your position protects you," the captain said, stretching to hang the lantern by the door. "But it does not."

The light revealed shackles chained to the wall and a table lined with knives and ominous tools.

Ahjin inhaled sharply. "I didn't even know the victims. Why would I kill them?"

The captain ignored him and rearranged the tools to line up exactly. "We do not normally get to do this sort of thing," he said. "I had to improvise."

Ahjin started talking rapidly. "I don't believe the deaths were accidents, either, but I had nothing to do with them. I ask again, let me go, and I will help you find out what happened."

Though he kept his shoulders square and his head erect, he folded his wings tightly enough to hurt. He took a half-step backward before the guards yanked him forward.

"I have divine permission to keep you here." The captain touched the edge of his dagger and grinned when a drop of blood ran down his finger. "Make it easy on yourself and confess now."

"Which god said you could arrest me?" If the gods had betrayed him, the chance of a real trial had suddenly crashed. As his throat tightened and his vision grew spotty, Ahjin kept his eyes on the captain instead of the table's glittering contents. "Did he or she say I was guilty, or only that you could keep me here? Did the other gods agree?"

"What difference does it make?" The captain stalked nearer, flipping his dagger.

Ahjin struggled to keep his breathing smooth. If he showed his panic, it would encourage the guards.

"You work for all the gods," the captain said. "If one is not satisfied, you are failing at your job."

"If some are satisfied," Ahjin countered, "I deserve a chance to improve." And unless the gods started talking to him, his only hope was convincing his jailer.

The captain shrugged. "Our instructions did not tell *us* who thinks you are guilty." He stopped next to Ahjin and leaned in, laying his dagger along Ahjin's neck. "And as soon as I get permission, I will bring you back to this room and *make* you confess." He stroked Ahjin's wing with his free hand. "I never had an Iojif in here before. I will yank out your pretty feathers before I break your bones."

Ahjin shuddered despite his attempt to hold still.

The captain grinned and sheathed his dagger. "Let him think about it for a while."

The guards dragged Ahjin to his cell so quickly that he couldn't get his chained feet to cooperate. They threw him on the floor and removed his shackles, then locked the gate and left, speculating how long Ahjin would last under various techniques.

Once they were out of sight, Ahjin wrapped his arms around his knees and let himself shake, his feathers rustling against the cold stone.

He'd been scheduled for beheading, attacked by assassins, and nearly cut in half by a giant scorpion. He'd broken his wings twice and nearly suffocated in a forest fire. He'd even broken his skull and lost control of his body and words, and burned all his feathers in a lightning storm that killed him. But this was the first time someone had gleefully offered to pluck him and break him to bits on purpose.

He chuckled despite his fear. That was almost true; Nia had threatened a similar fate several times. She didn't mean it, though, and he was sure the captain would enjoy the process. Ahjin shuddered again.

If the gods were convinced Ahjin was guilty, how long before they left him to the captain's not-so-tender mercies? How could they doubt his innocence?

Ahjin dragged himself to his cot and huddled in the thin blanket. The next time Nia visited, he'd ask about their progress, unless the gods answered him before then.

He closed his eyes and prayed desperately to each of the gods. Still no answer.

Things couldn't get worse.

They would get worse, if the Sardad captain had his way.

Ahjin pulled his blanket closer and imagined flying free in the sky. For an hour, he ran through each step of his old aerobatic routine in his mind. He had just reached the double-spiral triple-loop backwards-somersault when his bars rang again.

He'd barely had any time at all. Ahjin gathered his shredded courage and opened his eyes.

Nobody was there.

It took him a minute to remember the other bars. When he finally looked at the window, Kaito was back, surveying the street behind him, gasping for breath.

Ahjin climbed onto his cot. "It's only been a few hours since your last message. What's happened now?"

Kaito's hands tightened on the bars before he reached into his tunic, leaving bloody prints on the iron barricade.

"Kaito, are you hurt?" Ahjin leaned back for a better look.

Wide-eyed and shaking, Kaito shoved a short piece of rope through the bars and ran away.

The rope hit the cot and dripped red.

He *was* hurt! Ahjin picked up the rope and examined it for some message. As he turned it in the sunlight, he realized it wasn't rope, but someone's braided hair. Lavender hair.

But Zefra said Nia was safe.

Ahjin collapsed onto the cot, squeezing the braid until the blood dripped down his hand.

Obviously, something had happened. Nia was injured, probably badly. Ahjin gasped for breath. Ludik had gone back to Darrendra and couldn't heal her. But Zefra would find another healer. Sardad was a big city with several available. Nia would recover.

She had to recover. He still hoped to convince the gods to veto Irajahan's inheritance idea, and if he failed at that, he would stall long enough to find a replacement for Himself the Holiness. There must be someone he could trust to keep Irajahan in line. After he trained that someone, he'd happily spend the rest of his life persuading Nia to marry him.

Sufa! His cousin might do it, since she had left Irajahan's service when she had the chance. Yes, he would ask the gods if Sufa could replace him.

The door slammed open at the end of the room, and Ahjin jumped. He blinked away tears and shoved Nia's braid under his paper-thin mattress, wiping his hand on the underside. Whatever happened next, he had to survive, with or without wings, to return to Nia.

The captain and half a troop of guards marched in. Their uniform sleeves displayed new armbands. As they approached, Ahjin saw the same intricate design as the mark on the flour sack. Were they now under the command of whomever had tried to murder him?

Ahjin stood, hands clasped behind him under his wings. Had the gods abandoned him entirely? His fingers trembled, and he tightened his knees to keep them steady.

"Back already?" He tried to sound casual and bored, but his voice cracked as the guards lined up outside his cell.

"We want to know the name of your accomplice." Between the bars, the captain shoved one of the papers asking for news of Nia.

Ahjin swallowed hard. "She's no accomplice, and I don't know where she is."

The captain laughed. "Oh, we know she's not working for you. She was gathering evidence against you, and your accomplice murdered her."

16. CHASE

(DEVORA DISTRICT; DAY 15)

**For the use of those who wish to personally interpret the
messages of Darravani the Omnifarious, Goddess of Earth.**
Flowers and Their Meanings: A Guide for All Darrendrakar: Introduction

After their children's trail disappeared in the market, Ludik and
Nemerra made their way through the dark to their tent. Most of
their guards stayed with them, but two reported to their supervisor in
the city.

Trail or no trail, Ludik wasn't giving up. The guards were too slow, but
he didn't need them. He threw things from their luggage until he found
his old leather pack, travel-stained and ocean-damaged though it was.
Nemerra hadn't replaced it yet, and it was the only one that fit him as
both man or jaguar. He stuffed three water bags and a loaf of bread
inside, along with his boots, his healing kit, an ax, and a firestarter.

Nemerra grabbed her pack and added a blanket, a bucket, more water
bags, and the children's carry-harnesses.

"What are you doing?" Ludik asked.

"Packing." Nemerra looked at the mess and threw in a hairbrush and
a couple of ribbons.

"But—" Ludik started.

"You would never leave me behind while my children are in danger.

Would you?" She hefted the bag and added a package of dried meat. "Besides, how will you carry four children home by yourself? Or do you plan to run at their speed while their captors chase you?"

Ludik gave up the useless argument. He threw everything else back into their trunks and lay on his mat. "We have to wait for morning, anyway."

"No! The children need us now."

Ludik pulled her down beside him. "How can we find them in the dark?"

After a brief struggle to rise, she rested her head on his shoulder, tears dripping onto his tunic. The night dragged on as he imagined the terrible things that might be happening to the children.

Before dawn, they both rose and stuffed their clothing in their packs. After shifting, they wiggled them diagonally across their backs.

Ludik peeked outside. Most of the guards snored in the next tent. The one on watch looked toward the city, the most likely direction for danger. Nemerra nudged a note for them to a more visible position and joined him at the door.

Just outside the tent, a tall plant bloomed in the sand. Ludik sniffed the bell-like flowers. Since Darravani usually spoke to her children using the language of flowers, all Darrendrakar became familiar with plants and their meanings. This one meant "come to me."

"Darravani wants us home," Ludik murmured.

"But we can't leave our children," Nemerra protested.

"After we find them, we will go home. The trail and Ahjin are both west. If we don't find the children by then, we will help him so he can help us."

Nemerra nodded and crept from the tent.

Ludik followed on a parallel track, close enough to see her but far enough to catch different scents. Though their top pace was as fast as a horse could run, they went more slowly to check for scents and tracks. Fortunately, they could hunt on the move. They traveled until nightfall, ate a couple of desert hares, then slept behind a sand dune.

In the morning, they found another flower. *Come to me.*

"Doesn't she understand about the children?" Nemerra asked.

After another day of searching, they passed the scents of Ahjin and the others at a well, and a fresh grave in the sand. It smelled of feathers and blood, but not Ahjin's. Two sets of feathers, actually, though one was almost too faint to detect. The area was covered with the scents of many Iskrins, but not their children.

They continued until nightfall without spotting anyone else and slept the fitful sleep of worried parents.

The next day, they stopped to rest. After the afternoon rains, Ludik rolled in the sand to dry his fur. He rolled too far, flopping under a scrubby bush that was thriving in the rainy season, and his ears snagged on the thorns.

As he struggled to get free, Nemerra giggled. "Do you need help, darling?"

He inhaled to snap a reply, and a familiar scent hit his nose. "Rurru!"

"Where?"

"Under this bush."

Nemerra pulled the brambles from his ears and held the bush aside while he sniffed around. A couple of white hairs were snagged on the thorns. Rurru had definitely been here, and probably Kamakana, stinking of fear, but their scents were overlaid with those of several strange Iskrins and Nokai. Ludik memorized those scents. If he met them in person, they would pay.

"I think the children might have tried to escape." He held the bush while Nemerra learned the scents.

Nemerra blinked back tears. "Foolish, brave cubs. West again."

But the trail quickly vanished, and when they stopped for the night, they had learned nothing more.

By the next midday, they reached a small town by two rivers. In the wheat field, Ludik and Nemerra found the scent of another Darrendrakar. Not Cat, not Dog, not Seal. Antelope, maybe. Ahjin said the Darrendran diplomat to Iskra was Antelope.

Nemerra shifted and dressed, then wandered into town to charm the residents and ask gentle questions.

Ludik stayed on four legs and followed the trail of the Darrendrakar to the horse corrals. An Iskrin woman sat on the fence, chatting with a pale yellow horse who nodded or shook her head or scraped her hooves. Ludik crept along the fence, scanning for the Darrendrakar.

The horse whinnied, and the woman on the fence turned her head. "Bright day."

Ludik crouched low.

"I mean you, panther." The woman swung her legs over the rail. "Rozali tells me you are Darrendrakar, as if I could not tell by myself."

Ludik tilted his head to one side.

The woman laughed. "Animals do not wear packs. Go ahead and shift back. We will not look."

She and the horse turned away. As the breeze flickered, it carried the horse's scent to Ludik. No, the Horse. He had found the other Darrendrakar.

Ludik watched for a moment, but they stayed facing away. He quickly shifted and dressed, then joined them at the fence.

The woman looked both ways before continuing in a low voice. "Are you Ahjin's friend, the Shri?"

"I am. Who are you?"

"I am Chiara, one of Ahjin's guards. Did you get Zefra's message about his arrest? Zefra sent us to investigate a murder here."

"An avian brought word," Ludik said. "I regret I cannot help Ahjin, but my children were kitnapped. I trailed them here."

Chiara frowned. "That is quite a coincidence."

Rozali snorted and tossed her silver mane.

Ludik shrugged. "I found no evidence of them here. But the trail led west a day ago."

"As long as your trail coincides with Ahjin's, are you willing to help?"

"Zefra's message was very short. How can I help?"

Rozali whinnied, and Chiara motioned to Ludik. "Stay down; the townsfolk have been twitchy since their neighbor died."

"My wife went into town to ask questions and buy food." He raised his head, but the town was too far to see.

Chiara nibbled her lip. "That cannot be helped now. Let me tell you what we know." She reported on all the murders, though she didn't know the scents.

"I found the Iojif at the well, I think." Ludik said. "The grave smelled of feathers. But he must have been connected to the lady, because I smelled two sets of feathers."

Chiara shrugged. "At the time, we did not know of the lady. We hoped to find his pack to identify him, but we never did." Her white skin turned pink. "But I have one of *her* feathers. It was such a pretty pink, I

kept it. 'Twas loose," she added quickly. "Here, see if 'tis the same scent."
She pulled a single feather from her belt pouch.

It was indeed a lovely pink, but Ludik shook his head. "That is
neither of the scents."

"Really?" Chiara frowned. "Well, perhaps the other is the pirate Zefra
mentioned, that Limpwing."

"Lapwing," Ludik corrected. "Maybe so. I never got close enough in
the Dragon Isles to smell him."

"Rozali and I do not have good noses. We will find your wife and ask
more questions of the townspeople. While you look for your children,
please watch for the trail of the young Iskrin boy who disappeared when
his mother died. We fear the jackals got him, but it might comfort the
town to know."

She gave him directions to the place the horse trainer died and to her
grave, then swung onto Rozali's back and rode off.

Ludik tucked his pack by the fence and shifted back to jaguar. At the
grave, he picked up the scent, then smelled nothing for a long time as he
loped to the death site. There, he found traces of the woman and a horse
and a child young enough to smell of milk and diapers. The woman stank
of death, but he smelled no blood from the boy, as would certainly be the
case if vultures or jackals had killed him.

And then he found some of the kitnappers' scents. His fur stood on
end as he went over every inch of sand again. No, nothing of his children, but was that good news or bad? He carefully memorized the new
scents in the familiar and ran back to town.

The horse corral held only horses, so he shifted out of his fur and
dressed. Though every instinct screamed to hurry, he meandered toward
the tents, looking for Nemerra, Chiara, or the golden Horse.

At first, he saw no one but distant farmers, who looked up, sketchily
bowed, and frowned at Ludik. As he got closer, children raced by on
errands or in games, and by the time he passed the first tent, a crowd had
gathered.

"More strangers?" someone muttered in Iskrit. "What does he want?"

Nemerra walked into view, arms full of food and eyes wide. "There
you are, sweetheart," she said loudly in trade tongue. "Here, you take
these." She dumped half her load into his arms. "I got everything we
need, so we can continue on our trip now. Isn't that convenient?"

Behind her, Chiara wheeled Rozali into a trot toward the corral.

"Very convenient," Ludik agreed drily as the Iskrins watched them go, hands on staffs or daggers.

Nemerra dragged him back to the corrals, chattering in trade tongue about her purchases and the lovely merchants. Her fingernails, however, dug into his arm.

Ludik growled under his breath. "What did they do to you?"

Nemerra patted his elbow. "Nothing, but I didn't like the way everyone watched me. Let's just go."

Ludik glared over his shoulder at the villagers until Nemerra tugged on his arm. When they reached the corrals, Chiara and Rozali led them into the desert. Once out of sight of the town, Chiara dismounted.

"Pack your supplies," she said. "I underestimated how nervous everyone is. They barely tolerate me and will not stand your presence for long."

Nemerra dumped out her pack and Ludik's and rearranged the load with the new food.

"I have news for you," Ludik said.

"Good or bad?" Chiara asked.

"Both. I don't think the baby is dead, but according to the scents, he was taken by some of the same people who stole our children."

Nemerra gasped, and Ludik wrapped an arm around her. "No, I didn't smell our kittens." He turned back to Chiara. "I think they rescued the boy but didn't take him to the nearest settlement." He tightened his grip on Nemerra before he proposed his newest theory. "What if they didn't steal him because his mother died, but killed his mother to get him?"

Rozali reared on her hind legs and whinnied until Chiara shushed her.

"Oh, no," Nemerra said. "How terrible!" She picked up a baby harness and cradled it to her chest.

"I will pass this on to the village," Chiara said, "though they will not thank me for it."

Nemerra straightened the straps of the harness and rolled it.

"Wait," Chiara said. "What is that?"

Nemerra shook it out again. "A carrier for our children. They are still too small to keep up with us for long on their own feet. Don't you have anything like that?"

"We tend to put our children on a horse." Chiara tangled her hands in Rozali's mane. "How do Iojif carry their infants?"

Ludik tucked the second harness into his pack. "Ahjin said his parents use something similar. Why?"

"I told you we could not find that Iojif's pack. What if 'twas not a pack that creased his shirt, but a baby carrier, and we did not find it because his killer took it?" Chiara gulped. "What if the common factor in all these deaths was the presence of children?"

The hair on Ludik's neck stood on end. "But why?"

Chiara shrugged, wincing. "I must tell the village and send a message to Zefra so she can discover if the Nokai had a child with her."

"And we must keep looking for our children," Nemerra said. "Thank you for your help."

"Are you continuing west or turning north?" Chiara asked.

Ludik narrowed his eyes. "Why go north when the trail went west?"

Chiara shrugged. "The path has matched Ahjin's route so far, and he turned north from here."

Ludik cast a desperate glance at Nemerra and got an equally despairing one in return. Had the kitnappers continued west or changed direction? If they guessed incorrectly, they might never find their children.

He looked west and then north, heart aching. "If there is a connection with the other children, then we need more information. We will go north and see what Zefra has found."

Nemerra choked on a sob. "Thank you for your help, Chiara, Rozali. May Darravani bless you in your search."

"And in yours," Chiara said, and Rozali bobbed her head.

Ludik and Nemerra headed north along the river in a looping path that traveled westward before returning to the river and then circling out again.

At nightfall, they curled together in the sand and dreamed of their children. Had they lost the chance to find them when they changed direction? Why did their captors take them? Were they still alive?

They spent the next three days searching the desert, zigzagging west to east and back, following the course of the river northward. Each night, they camped, hopes dashed by a fruitless search. The same flowers sprouted each morning, but they could not obey Darravani's decree without their children.

A week after the children had been taken, the wind woke Ludik with an oddly familiar scent.

"Who is there?" he called in trade tongue.

No answer came.

"I smell you," Ludik growled. "Answer me, or I will come bite you."

A red pair of ears popped above a dune. "My goodness. Such bad manners."

Ludik squinted at the Fox. "Have we met before?"

"Oh, no, I hope not." A tag on the Fox's collar jingled.

Ludik sniffed the wind. "Yes, we have. I once accused you of murder."

The Fox's ears sagged. "Oh, it's you. Your fur hides you well at night. Well, now that you know I'm me, I'll be on my way."

Ludik squinted at the tag, which was a familiar firefly. "You are working for Zefra? I have a message for her and need her latest news." He nudged Nemerra awake.

The Fox slid down the dune. "My name is Madden. I just heard from Zinon, one of Zefra's spies. Yesterday, a Nokai discovered a map to the lost city of the gods, which bears the same mark as that tattoo they've been chasing, but someone stole it at swordpoint."

"Mongrel curs," Ludik swore. "Which Nokai? How badly was he — or she — hurt?"

He desperately wished the victim was one of the Nokai guards instead of Nia, but his friend had a habit of poking her nose into dangerous adventures.

Madden shrugged. "Zinon didn't know, but rumor says they died. Since no one has reported success in the other locations, Zefra is recalling all the spies to Sardad."

"What if it was Nia?" Ludik asked. He looked north, mentally cursing. "But we can't stop our search."

"There are other healers," Nemerra said, "but we should send our news."

"Plague fleas," Ludik cursed. He explained everything he had discovered at Pramath, as well as their theory about the children and the repeating call from Darravani.

"What if the children were taken to the lost city?" Nemerra asked.

"Maybe their captors were only heading west — or north — until they got further directions, and now they have the map, they turned to follow it?"

Ludik pounced on the Fox. "If you want to see dawn again, tell me how to reach Irad."

Madden bared his teeth despite the stench of fear that reached Ludik's nose.

"Stop it," Nemerra said. "Madden, if that is where they took the children, let us follow immediately while you gather the others."

"You won't find it," Madden squeaked under Ludik's paws. "You have to start at Zefra's oasis, and you don't know how to navigate by the stars."

"*Zefra's* oasis? I have been there before." Ludik let go of the Fox and slithered back into his pack straps, frantic to leave.

"But do you know how to get there from here?"

Ludik snarled. "Yes. Which way from the oasis?"

"Straight south," Madden said.

"Simple enough. Tell Zefra I'm ahead of her. And if he doesn't already know, tell Ahjin that Darravani is calling her children home."

"Keep well," Nemerra called as they ran southwest.

Ludik put his energy into running in the cool night. Now that they knew where to go — or hoped they knew — it was only a matter of time. As he ran, he prayed to Darravani for the unidentified Nokai's soul and the chance to save their children from a similar fate.

17.MURDER

(SARDAD; DAY 20)

Where there is life, there is hope.
Iskrin Proverb

Zefra glanced at the sun. Midday already, and she had nothing to show for wandering the city for hours. At least Nia was waiting safely in the desert after nearly getting caught visiting Ahjin yesterday. As soon as Zefra found a way for her to visit safely, she would go back for her. This morning, Zefra had searched for her spies, but the only word was a simple "nothing yet" wrapped around a stick the dogs dropped for a pretend game of toss-and-chase.

While she ate meat and vegetables off a roasting stick, she listened to gossip in the crowded market. The downfall of His Holiness was a popular topic, and speculation overflowed.

Zefra glanced at the notices on the wall reserved for public news, grinning at a few possible jobs she no longer needed, then jolted to a stop at Nia's picture, which declared her wanted for questioning about the murders. Once she broke the news to Nia that she could not risk visiting Ahjin, Zefra would have to put a day and night guard on her to make her obey. She grimaced. She did not look forward to the protests, but protecting her would be worth the hassle.

Hands clenched on her sword belt and staff, Zefra slipped away, heading for the dunes. Before she reached the city limits, she ran into Tarakh, who linked his arm through hers and swept her in a different direction with extravagant compliments and ridiculous endearments.

Zefra glared at the familiarity. She started to pull away, but stopped when he squeezed her hand more urgently than affectionately. He was up to something. With a glance at the people around them, she relaxed and forced a smile.

"And guess what, darling?" Tarakh continued. "I ran into an old friend of yours today. He wanted me to pass greetings from himself and mutual friends."

Tarakh raised an eyebrow, and Zefra nodded. Now she understood. He was wise not to speak openly when anyone in the crowded streets could be a spy for the enemy. She forced a smile and tried to look enamored. Judging by the crinkles around his dark bronze eyes, she was not entirely successful, but he proceeded with his report in carefully worded nonsense.

He had actually found Daz and gotten news of all their spies, who had all found people to spy on and a place to stay. "And he has the cutest new kitties," Tarakh said, "who bask in the sunlight." He tipped his head toward the temple of Resef.

Zefra turned a relieved sigh into a flirtatious one. The Cats had a dangerous assignment, right under the noses of Resef's priests.

"Tomorrow, will you take me to see the kitties?" She tried to sound breathlessly excited, like Nia on a ridiculously enthusiastic day — almost any day.

Tarakh laughed and patted Zefra's hand. "Anything to make you happy, dear."

"Did you find a way to visit friends?" Zefra tipped her head subtly toward the jail.

"I'm afraid not."

Zefra glanced toward the desert. "Disappointing."

"Yes. But you can meet my father. He and Mother came to town unexpectedly."

"I would like that," Zefra said sincerely.

"This way."

"Now?" Zefra pulled back on his arm. They had more important matters at the moment.

"Sweetheart, I'm sure you will not mind that his booth is set up next to the city guard station. 'Tis noisy with all their coming and going, but you can still visit while I tend to sales."

"Oh." Zefra blinked. "Yes, they are fortunate to have such a dutiful son."

Tarakh laughed again. He continued his disguise of courting chatter until they reached a brown-and-saffron striped canopy above long tables. A middle-aged couple served customers with polite bows, loading baskets with vegetables and handing over sacks of grain. Zefra recognized the elegant woman from her first meeting with Tarakh.

"Bright day, Mother," Tarakh said. "Father, may I make known my friend, Zefra Ashvakosha Kezhekori? Zefra, this is my father, Farukh Ekorov."

Farukh brushed off his hands and bowed, then clasped Zefra's hands. "Bright day, Zefra. Have you come for duty or pleasure?"

She bowed respectfully. "I came to Sardad to seek employment, but Tarakh has kindly escorted me today."

Tarakh's mother, Hariskandra, chuckled. "Come help me load baskets with fruits and vegetables while the men bargain with the soldiers."

Farukh leaned around his wife. "Tarakh told me of your skills. If you want a job as a mapmaker or horse handler with my caravans, you have only to ask. Alas, I do not currently need a guide."

Before Zefra could tell him she had already found a caravan position, Tarakh led her to a seat by his mother, where 'twas easy to overhear the guards as they strolled by or paused to look at the food. She glanced at Tarakh, who winked as he stacked sacks of wheat, then she turned her attention to her work and the chatter of the guards.

As the afternoon passed and the brief rain pattered on the canopy, the only useful information was a confirmation of Ahjin's continued good health from a disappointed soldier.

At dinner, they ate inside the tent. Tarakh was attentive, and his parents were kind, and Zefra's plate was refilled several times while they congratulated her on her new job. Tarakh's parents also expressed good wishes for Ahjin's freedom.

"Please," Farukh said, "if we can help in any way, tell us." His eyes, the same dark bronze as Tarakh's, were sincere. "I sent inquiries to my agents. His Holiness always served with honor and fidelity."

"He will be pleased to hear of your respect." Before Zefra could continue, people shouted outside the tent.

Tarakh cracked open the tent flap.

A city guardsman waved a flier to the crowd. "We have discovered another murder." Nia's picture was on the poster.

"Do they think she did it?" Zefra muttered. "When will this end?"

"This Nokai is dead at the command of Ahjin Machol," the guard continued.

Nia, dead? Zefra staggered to the doorway, clutching the tent flap to support herself. Her throat tightened, choking off her air. Tarakh wrapped an arm around her, and his parents gathered close behind.

"There is a reward for information of his accomplice, the Darrendra-kar called Kaito," the guard continued. "A reward will also be given for proof of their conspiracy or evidence of other collaborators. Until the murderer is caught, we will enforce a sundown curfew." He moved farther into the market and repeated his message to the next segment of babbling crowd.

Zefra sucked in a breath, then another. "Nia is *dead*," she whispered. "They found her in the desert." Her wobbly knees dropped her onto a mat. Zefra had failed to protect her.

Tarakh knelt beside her. "Zefra, I'm sorry. I took her to the library. I thought she would be safe there." His eyes shone with tears in the lamplight.

Zefra bit her quivering lip. "They could find her anywhere. I must go; I cannot endanger you."

"Nonsense," Farukh said. "We can protect you."

Zefra called flame to her hand. "I can protect myself." She let the fire die and climbed to her feet. "My sincere thanks for the meal and the offer of help."

She smoothed her robe, and Ahjin's letter crinkled in her pouch. Zefra paused. The caravan could take her far from here, far from sorrow, but Nia's death changed everything.

No matter how badly Zefra needed that job, she could not leave Ahjin's fate in the hands of hired guards and near-strangers. She had failed one friend already and did not even know if she could find Nia's body. Caravan or not, she would not abandon Ahjin.

"Do you have an extra slate I might buy?"

"Nonsense." Farukh handed her a slate. "You may have it."

Zefra scribbled a quick note to the caravan master. "I will try to meet you, but a vital problem has occurred. If I am late—" She paused before forcing herself to continue. "—Do not wait for me. I am sorry."

She handed the slate back to Tarakh's father. "Please, will you deliver this for me? I must return to the others."

Farukh took it and bowed.

Tarakh grabbed his staff. "I'm ready."

"Wait, your hair is showing." Hariskandra unwrapped Zefra's scarf, pinned her hair more securely, and re-covered it. "Stay safe, both of you."

Zefra bowed, then hugged Tarakh's parents. She and Tarakh crept out the back, and in the twilight, Zefra let her tears fall. Nia was dead. Her bubbly, ever-optimistic friend would never annoy her again.

Armed soldiers roamed everywhere, reminding the crowd of curfew. Some wore only the insignia of the Sardad guard, but some also wore armbands or necklaces or pins with the intricate geometric design from the sack of poisoned flour. Zefra gripped Tarakh's arm, and he shifted their route farther from those guards.

"Are they behind this?" she whispered. "How can we win if the enemy is openly in the city guard?"

Tarakh squeezed her fingers and agreed with a shocked passerby that events were terrible, terrible indeed.

As they left the market, someone yanked Zefra into the shadows. She called fire, and Tarakh, leaping after her, raised his staff.

Kaito ducked and motioned them to follow. In the growing darkness, they sprinted down alleys, dodging junk and putrid refuse in broken-down neighborhoods. Finally, Kaito wriggled between a pile of trash and a collapsing building.

Zefra and Tarakh followed and found themselves in a dark room where unseen things crunched under their boots. A small window let in a trickle of moonlight.

"Kaito?" someone croaked. "Did you find water?"

Zefra called a flame and nearly dropped it. Beneath ragged blankets, one of Nia's green eyes stared at her from a blood-streaked face.

Nia was alive! Tears burned in her eyes, but Zefra gulped and fought them back.

While the fire shook in Zefra's hand, Kaito knelt beside Nia and held a cup to her lips. Tarakh leaned his staff against the wall and pushed Zefra forward.

"Well met, Zefra." Nia closed her eye. "I'm hungry, Kaito."

Tarakh pulled an apple from his pouch and peeled it, lips clamped together.

Zefra sank beside Nia and ran her flame above her from head to toe. Filthy, bloody rags covered half the Nokai's face, and more were wrapped around her chest and stomach.

Tarakh stopped slicing the apple long enough to pull a candle from his pouch.

"They said you were dead," Zefra whispered, lighting the candle.

Nia laughed, then groaned. "Etana rescued me."

A soft growl from the corner alerted Zefra to the presence of the big Cat.

Zefra bowed to the glowing eyes in the dark. "Thank you."

"Here." Tarakh put a slice of apple in Nia's hand, then another and another as she ate.

"Kaito," Nia mumbled through her last bite, "where's my pouch?"

Kaito handed it to Zefra.

"I found a map at the library," Nia said. "You like maps. He stole my copy, but I had another." She sighed, and her head slid sideways. "And then I saw the mark on the back." Her voice faded into silence.

Zefra pressed a trembling hand against Nia's bloody neck. Her pulse still beat faintly.

Kaito shoved her hand away and dipped a semi-clean rag into water. He pointed at the pouch in Zefra's hand, then dabbed carefully at Nia's skin.

After another glance at her unconscious friend, Zefra pulled out an Iskrin slate. An arrow indicated north, and a dotted line ran straight south from a cluster of trees to a hexagon labeled "tattoo" in Nia's sprawling handwriting. The title said, "Irad, City of Witness," and a poem in a strange language was squeezed along the sides.

"Irad?" Tarakh leaned closer. "That is a legend. 'Tis only a scribble, not a real map. Nia interpreted it incorrectly."

Zefra turned the slate toward the candlelight. "Nia does not make mistakes with language, though she does not know maps well. She might have taken a story map for a real one. But look." She traced the dots above the trees. "This is a star notation, like the Hotaru use. Nia would not know that, but she copied it accurately." So accurately, Zefra recognized it immediately.

"Then 'tis real?" Tarakh leaned over her shoulder. "Where?"

Zefra swallowed. "The middle of the desert." She tapped the drawn trees. "According to the stars, this is the oasis I discovered."

Tarakh sat back. "That explains why no one has found the city. There are no roads and no water there. Until you discovered the oasis—"

"Rediscovered," Zefra corrected numbly.

He gripped her shoulder. "Until then, no one could survive that route."

"Irad, the lost city of the gods," Zefra marveled. "What does it have to do with any of this?"

"And why did Nia write 'tattoo' here?" Tarakh asked.

"She said she saw 'the mark.' The assassins' mark?" Zefra frowned. "I wish I had a copy to study."

"Here." Tarakh reached into his pouch and handed her a fragment of burlap. "I washed the poison from the flour sack."

"We should take this back to the others." Zefra stood, but Kaito tugged on her hem and pointed to the moon outside the window.

"He's right. With the curfew, we should wait for morning." Tarakh said.

"Will your parents not worry?"

Tarakh shrugged. "They know I am helping you."

Zefra tucked the burlap scrap into her pouch and helped Tarakh lay makeshift sleeping mats at Nia's feet. She left the candle for Kaito. Tarakh's soft breath echoed in the room as she pulled her cloak over herself. This was highly improper, though she could not sleep by Nia lest she disturb the wounded woman. At least there were abundant chaperones.

Cold air crept through the window, and Zefra shivered. She pushed heat into a rock and handed it to Kaito, who tucked it under Nia's arm. Zefra reached for another, but Kaito kicked it out of reach. He ignored her squeak of protest and lay down, sliding backwards until they nearly touched. Heat poured from him, and she sighed before she caught herself. When her teeth chattered, Kaito sat up enough to raise an eyebrow at Tarakh and jerk his chin toward Zefra.

Tarakh cleared his throat. "I'm sorry, Zefra. He's right. You should save your fire in case we're discovered."

He moved his mat next to Zefra's and lay close enough that she felt his body heat. Between the two men, she felt almost warm, and sleep snuck in while she debated the proprieties of survival.

Z efra woke at first light, too close to Tarakh's warm body, and yanked her arm back from around his waist. If she could blush so hotly at will, she would never be cold again.

When she sat up, he rolled over and smiled at her. "Bright day, Zefra. Should we find food and water and clean bandages?"

Zefra looked toward Nia's bundle of rags. "An excellent idea."

Etana lifted her head from her front paws and blinked at them, then went to sleep.

Zefra shook the wrinkles from her robe and unbraided her hair, setting her hairpins aside. She braided her hair into its proper coronet, and every time she reached for a hairpin, Tarakh was there, examining the hidden lockpicks or tiny knife before he handed each to her.

After she covered her hair with her scarf, Tarakh took his staff. They slipped from the broken building and snuck along back streets to his parents' tent. She stood guard until he exited with a loaded basket and four jugs. He gave her two jugs, and they strolled casually past the guard station. Once out of sight, they quickened their pace and returned to Kaito and Nia without meeting anyone but a sleepy street cleaner.

Zefra put the food on the remnants of a shelf, high enough that mice would have a harder time reaching it, and grabbed the bandage rolls and clean cloths. She handed a water jug to Kaito and knelt to help with Nia. Under the filthy bandages, a long slash crossed half of Nia's face, and a longer one sliced down her torso. Fortunately, neither of the cuts were deeper than the muscle, and some reached only through the skin. Most of the bleeding had stopped, though some trickled when Kaito gently cleaned the wounds. Nia was exhausted enough to sleep through it.

After the dirt was gone, Tarakh handed Zefra a small bottle of alcohol, face turned away from Nia's exposed skin. At the first touch, Nia woke cursing and tried to move away. Kaito held her down while Zefra dabbed alcohol on every thumb-length of the terrible cuts, then they worked together to wind clean bandages around her.

Tears streamed down Nia's face, and curses dripped quietly from her tongue, though fortunately in Noki instead of Iskrit.

As soon as Zefra and Kaito finished, Tarakh handed Nia a bowl full of food, then served the others.

Zefra placed the scrap of flour sack on the floor and pondered the intricate design as she ate. "Nia, you said this was on the map?"

"On the back." Nia twirled her finger from her half-reclined position. "When I held it to the light, it shone through right where the hexagon is."

"City of the gods," Tarakh mused. "The hexagon is Makanavailea's symbol, is it not?"

"There are two circles here," Zefra said. "For Irajahan?"

Kaito traced a square in the middle.

"And here is another square," Tarakh said. "Darravani?"

"Dozens of triangles." Zefra traced several of them.

"No, wait," Tarakh said. "This is another hexagon, here."

The design suddenly made sense. "And stars," Zefra said. "Look, Kassian's symbol here and here. It has the symbols for all the gods." She traced each one.

"But what does it have to do with Irad?" Nia asked, "and what in Kassian's blazing stars does it have to do with us?"

"If that mark means Irad," Zefra asked, "why is it being used by the Sardad guard and the murderers? And if I had not rediscovered the oasis, would Irad now be safely out of reach of the conspiracy?" For the first time, she was glad so few people had been interested in her discovery.

Tarakh stared at the map. "If we went there, perhaps we might find the answers. Imagine, the City of the Gods!"

"We're still waiting for reports from our spies in the other towns," Zefra said. "Before we tangle with the gods, we need Ahjin's help, which means proving his innocence."

Kaito slapped his forehead and rummaged through his pockets. He handed Zefra the message she had sent to Ahjin about Nia, with new Darrendran symbols scribbled on the back in smudged charcoal.

Nia translated. "Gods say wait for trial. Irajahan betrayed us at

Dragon, told gods I misheard. Tried to kill us again? Why now, why strangers?"

"Why *would* he kill random people?" Zefra asked. "How would he benefit?"

Kaito and Tarakh frowned, and Nia cradled her wound.

"I need to talk to Ahjin," Zefra said.

But when she snuck into the city, the citizens were almost rioting against the soldiers enforcing the new rules. Zefra could not approach the jail no matter how long she haunted the streets. And when she returned to Nia's hideout at nightfall, Tarakh had left and never returned.

18.CONDEMNED

(SARDAD JAIL)

One enemy can harm you more than a hundred friends can help.
Iojif Proverb

"Your accomplice murdered her." The guard's words echoed in the cold jail.

Ahjin's knees buckled, and he sat abruptly on his hard cot, gasping for breath.

Nia was dead. Kaito didn't bring her bloody braid to tell him she was injured, but to let him know she had been killed. With numb fingers, he clutched the blanket hiding the lavender evidence.

Nia was dead. He would never listen to her chatter or sing, never kiss her again. He'd never have a chance to talk her into marriage. She was gone, killed by someone who probably preferred to kill Ahjin, instead. Ahjin would have preferred to die.

Nia was dead, and Ahjin couldn't even go to her funeral. Though his aching heart still beat, his life was over.

"Who did you hire?" the guard asked. "How did you contact him from in here?"

His fellow soldiers glared at Ahjin.

"Nobody. I didn't. She was my friend." His heart wailed, *She was my beloved.*

The guard laughed. "Not much of a friend, if you killed her."

"How did she die?" Ahjin asked numbly, not sure he wanted to know but unable to avoid asking.

"What, you want to gloat?" The guard clicked his tongue. "I will not tell you. You will have to imagine how efficient your accomplice was."

Ahjin's imagination took flight, picturing terrible ways Nia could have been killed, all of them bloody. Was she sliced in half or was her throat merely cut? How long did it take her to die? How much did she suffer?

He clenched his fingers in his hair, but the guard kept talking.

"A witness saw it happen. The killer shouted your name before he ran away. We know you did it. Tell us where to find your accomplice."

"I didn't do it," Ahjin shouted. "How could I do anything from prison? You haven't let me have visitors."

The guard nodded. "That is why we want to know how you did it."

"Go away," Ahjin said. "Leave me with my grief."

The guard leaned on the bars and ran his dagger along them. Clink, clink, clink. "Why grieve for someone you ordered killed?" Clink, clink, clink. "Tell us who you hired and how you contacted them. Did you bribe someone? Throw a message out the window?" Clink, clink, clink. "Ah, I know! You have telepathy, like Irajahan's Winds. That explains everything. We should look for another Wind. We will arrest everyone with wings!" He banged the hilt of his dagger on the bars and then re-sheathed it triumphantly.

"No." Ahjin groaned. "Don't arrest anyone." He jumped to his feet, fists clenched. "I told you, I have no accomplice." His voice rose. "I killed no one and ordered no deaths. Not the people in the desert, not the woman in the city, and certainly not—" His knees gave out again, and he fell back to the cot with a sob. "Not Nia," he whispered. He gulped and forced his voice louder. "I tell you again, as I've said so many times before, I am innocent. You have the wrong man, and while I'm locked up, you're letting the real murderer wander free to kill again."

"You are a stubborn one, are you not? No fear, we will get a confession from you."

All the guards looked toward the far corner of the room and grinned.

Ahjin walked to the bars, covering his terror with sheer bluster. "Do you see these scars on my face? On my hands? I have scars all over my body," he drawled. "I've been through more torture than you can imagine. You can't break me."

He didn't mention most of the scars had come from a lightning storm and the rest had been from a giant scorpion's claws. If they thought he was impossibly brave, perhaps they would give up their plans to torture a confession from him.

The guard examined Ahjin from head to foot. "You are quite the character, I admit. I do not want to know how evil your background is. It might be harder to convince you, but I'm sure we can do it. The captain is looking forward to the chance. He will be disappointed if you do not put up a little resistance."

Ahjin laughed bitterly. The captain wanted to pluck Ahjin's feathers and break every bone in his wings. It wouldn't be the first time he was broken-winged, but the first two times, it had happened quickly. Once had been only his wingtips, which was bad enough. The second time, a crash-landing had shattered his wings until Darravani healed him. The captain was almost right. If he wanted to break Ahjin, destroying his wings might have been effective before. Now, in the face of Nia's death, he didn't even care. Death was a mercy, except he had others depending on him.

"Ask the gods," Ahjin said wearily. "They'll tell you I'm innocent."

"I will visit Resef's temple tomorrow," the guard said. "And when he says you're guilty, we will return."

Ahjin lay on his cot with his arms behind his head and closed his eyes, ignoring the audience. He concentrated on breathing smoothly until the guards left. Once he was alone, he curled in his measly blanket and covered his head for as much privacy as his cell allowed.

The chill settling into his bones was not only from the cold stone but from grief. If his friends were here, they could cry together. But if they were here, they might be used against him. He was better alone.

Since he could not attend her funeral, he ran through every memory of Nia, from their first meeting when she rescued him from the ocean, through their various adventures and the months she lived next to him on Arupa, until the last time he saw her peering into his jail window. As his cot grew damp from tears, her cheerful face danced through his mind, bubbling with eternal optimism and a never-ending quest for fun. Except for his flying and his pranks, Ahjin tended to be more serious, but Nia never let him get too boring. She was the source of happiness in his life, the love that made everything else worthwhile. He had dreamed of marrying her and spending the rest of his life with her.

And now she was gone. It no longer mattered if Irajahan made him marry someone else, though he would never love another girl. It no longer mattered what anyone did to him.

The guards did not return. By the time Ahjin ran out of memories, dawn peeked through his high window.

Nia would tell him each new day brought a chance for an exciting adventure. Ahjin wiped his eyes. Nia's adventures were over, but if Ahjin could get out of jail, he might still help his other friends escape this disaster. He ran through his prayers to every god, even without his supplies. After all, they could still hear *him*, he just couldn't hear anyone's responses but Irajahan. He didn't know why they had been ignoring him, but he was ready to beg.

He ignored his grumbling belly and spent hours praying, with no discernible response. Irajahan's neglect was unsurprising, but, up until this recent trip, he'd always gotten a response from the other gods for important matters. Were they angry at him? Had they abandoned him?

He paced his cell, back and forth, then threw himself onto his cot. They couldn't believe the charges, could they? Makana the Omniscient would know he had nothing to do with the murders. Resef kept an eye on his land and people. Irajahan could read Ahjin's mind, not that Ahjin wanted him to rifle through his thoughts. And surely Darravani and Kassian trusted he would never behave so horribly. He had served all of them faithfully for two years. How could they abandon him?

The door at the end of the room slammed open. The Sardad captain marched down the aisle, boot heels thumping. "We found your conspirator," he said.

Ahjin clenched his fists in the blanket. Which of his other friends had been blamed now? "I don't know what you are talking about. I have no conspirators, and I did nothing wrong."

The captain smirked at him. "I'm sure you thought your important friends could help, but if your position will not save you, what makes you think his would help him?"

Ahjin wrinkled his forehead. Which of his friends had an important position? Lyell, as Chief of Staff for Ahjin, perhaps? Ludik as a Shri healer?

"Farukh Ekorov spoke in support of you," the captain continued. "He was foolish to reveal his alliance with you. That brought him to our attention, and when we attempted to question him, a mob formed and someone killed him." He shook his head. "It did not have to happen that way. If you had only told us when we first asked, we could have let him join you here to await trial."

"I don't know who that is." Ahjin sent a prayer to Resef for the soul of the innocent man.

"Hmm. You claim you do not know the chieftain of Devora himself? I'm sure he would be disappointed to hear he does not merit your recognition. His death serves him right, anyway. He should have known better than to speak for a criminal. And now your support is fading. No one else wants to side with a murderer. No one will defend you. You are alone." The captain grinned maliciously.

"Have you heard from the gods yet? No? Then leave me alone. I don't need any of your so-called news." Ahjin turned his back and pretended to sleep, but his heart ached for the unknown man caught in this mess. At least he hadn't been one of his friends.

Wait. The chieftain of Devora. Ahjin finally remembered the introduction from Zefra's friend that day in Ludik's camp almost three weeks ago. The dead man was Tarakh's father. His death was Ahjin's fault, for the man would surely not have become involved without the distant connection from his son to Zefra to Ahjin.

Who would create so much chaos and damage so many lives?

None of the gods responded to his frequently repeated prayers. No guards came, which was entirely a blessing except they didn't bring any food or remove the full cesspot that made the cell reek.

In desperation, Ahjin reached his mind toward Sufa, his newly discovered cousin. He had barely touched her mind when something slammed a door shut between them. The same thing happened when he tried to contact Amrafel, Irajahan's high priest. Was Irajahan doing this as punishment for Ahjin's supposed crimes? Kassian had once blocked Irajahan's own telepathy. Did any of the other gods have the capability? Perhaps Sufa and Amrafel heard about his wild rampage of slaughter and closed their own minds to him.

Shouts occasionally funneled into his cell. The crowd outside sounded angry. Since it had been days since he was thrown in here, it probably wasn't outrage over his condition. He liked to think someone was protesting Nia's murder. Had anyone buried Nia, or was her body rotting under the sun?

And what of his other friends? Ahjin paced across his cold cell. He assumed Lyell had gotten Tala to a safe place, away from the violence and death, but Zefra and Kaito were still at risk. He wasn't safe, either. The Sardad courts still waited to hold his trial, unless they had changed their plan and decided to leave Ahjin to the merciless captain and his room of terror.

Why were the gods ignoring Ahjin? Unless something prevented them from responding. Irajahan said the gods were having difficulties but wanted to solve them by themselves. What could be terrible enough to distract them?

Kassian had been that terrible, when he first returned, but he'd seen no sign that the gods were fighting among themselves recently.

A muddled memory suddenly jumped to his mind. Last year, when he and his friends had been stranded in the Dragon Isles, they fought a fleet of pirates under the command of Captain Crow, a murderous Iojif with wings amputated for his crimes. Before Crow was killed, Ahjin thought he said he was conquering the world for the one true god. Irajahan had convinced Ahjin that his head injury and broken language skills had led him to misunderstand many things on that trip, so he had forgotten the conversation.

But what if Crow *had* been working with a god to conquer not just other lands, but the whole world, in a more ordinary way than a fight between the gods? Lapwing, his first mate, might be pursuing Crow's plans. That explained the sheer amount of chaos involved, and the disregard for mortal lives. With all of Kaiatan as the prize, a few dead people were insignificant.

And if one god was trying to conquer the world, the others would surely object. If they were not already fighting — and they might not be, since Kaiatan wasn't shaking apart the way it had before — then either they had not yet noticed because of some distraction, or they were arguing in an as-yet non-violent way. But if it continued, the crosswinds would swirl into a storm.

This was exactly the kind of situation Ahjin was supposed to prevent as Mouth of the Gods. All his tours and interventions with the mortals were secondary, something to do while the divine status was calm. But with him in jail and the gods either too distracted or too busy to reply, he didn't know how he could help. They should free him so he could arbitrate. What good did it do to leave him here?

Not until the next day did the guards finally return. The satisfied grin on the captain's face as he stood in front of Ahjin's bars was not encouraging.

"We got a message from the gods. I told you we would." He turned the paper to face the cell.

Ahjin sauntered to the bars as if he weren't worried, but his mind raced for a reason the cruel guard was so pleased. Had the gods finally given permission to torture a non-existent confession from him, or would they skip the trial and move directly to an execution?

"Ahjin is no longer Mouth of the Gods," the note said. "You may do what you like with him." It was signed, "Resef."

19.TRANSLATION
(SARDAD)

Bad is never good until worse happens.
Darrendran Proverb

After a full day of sleep, Nia tried to sit. The gash along her torso burned, and she moaned and relaxed on the floor, ignoring Kaito's despairing head shake as he helped her lean against a broken table.

"I'm so bored." Nia pressed her hand against her wound and desperately pretended it didn't hurt. "Give me something to do."

Kaito waved a hand at the empty room and dropped a pear into her lap.

He was right. If she didn't count dust and broken furniture and far too many bugs, there was nothing here. Even the window was too high for her to see anything but daylight and apricot sky. Dog barks and bird song filtered in, with the occasional ruckus in the far distance. Tarakh had never returned, and everyone else had left this morning.

Nia leaned her head against the table as she ate. "Where's Etana?"

Kaito pointed outside, raised several fingers, then shaded his eyes with a hand.

Nia thought for a minute. "Looking for the others?"

Nod.

"What about Zefra?"

Kaito imitated Tarakh's cocky grin, then rocked his arms like he was holding a baby. Then he pointed to himself and minced along, swinging an invisible skirt.

Nia giggled while she thought. "Oh, mom! Zefra went to talk to Tarakh's parents? Probably about his disappearance."

Nod.

Nia sighed. Kaito didn't even talk. Despite the pain yesterday, she had at least slept through most of the boring hours. She turned her head and found a colony of ants in the corner. Watching them weave in and out occupied her for an hour. Betting with herself on which beetle would reach an arbitrary finish line took a little longer. She lost the bet, and when she broke out of this miserable place, she would gladly pay herself a fresh fish with slices of juicy pineapple. Mmm, so delicious.

"Where do you think Tarakh went?" She threw a pear seed into the corner for the ants and watched them swarm.

Kaito shrugged, then dropped the map of Irad into Nia's lap.

"There? But he'd have to know where Zefra's oasis is to start the trek."

Kaito shot her a knowing look.

Nia laughed. "He does know an awful lot about her, doesn't he? Do you think she likes him?"

She closed her eyes and drifted into lovely daydreams of Zefra and Tarakh courting. But every time things started getting interesting, Zefra pulled out her slate and made a new plan. Finally, Nia gave up. Zefra was simply not fun. Poor Tarakh, with his interest fastened on someone who treated courtship like a caravan voyage. And speaking of voyages, Zefra would leave soon, and it might be a year before Tarakh saw her again. No romance for them.

Kaito approached her with a bowl of water, the flask of alcohol, and another roll of bandages.

"No, no, no." Nia pushed at him. "That's not necessary."

Kaito ignored her, setting his supplies on the floor and reaching for the end of her chest bandage.

Nia tried to wiggle away and almost screamed as collarbone to navel stung like she'd been split in half. Her face was almost as painful, and the alcohol would only make everything worse.

"Please, Kaito," she begged. "You washed everything yesterday. Please don't touch it."

Kaito tightened his lips and tugged on the bandage. When Nia pushed at his hands, he let her shove until she gasped, then moved back in. The first two layers unwound easily until he reached the ones stuck to her skin with dried blood. Kaito tugged gently, and the next layer ripped free.

Nia muffled her scream with her arm.

Kaito dabbed water on her chest bandage. When he pulled again, it came free slightly more easily. Red and brown streaked across her chest. She took one deep breath and another. She was cut in half and would be maimed for life, if infection didn't kill her. If her face looked this bad, she would be ugly, too.

"We need to find a mirror," Nia panted.

Kaito put a hand over her eyes. With his other hand, he patted her arm until she took a shuddering breath. He removed his hands and returned to his work.

Maybe he was right. If she didn't look, she could pretend it would all be well.

Then the alcohol's burning agony made her gasp and cover her mouth again. Tears ran down her face, stinging her cheek under the bandage. Kaito's hands were gentle, but it felt like an eternity of torture.

Then it all had to be repeated on her stomach and her face. By the time Kaito finally re-bandaged Nia, she was exhausted and fell into an uneasy sleep.

In her dreams, she wandered the library, looking for something she couldn't find while Makana told her to give up and go home. When she opened the books and unrolled the scrolls, they were filled with gibberish. She finally found her way out, only to enter a marketplace where people pointed and jeered in unknown languages. Then the swordsman appeared out of nowhere, waving his sword. When he slashed down, Nia's body split in half and all her blood ran into the gutter. Ahjin pointed at her, nose wrinkling in disgust. Then he walked away as the two halves of her body crumpled flat and dissolved.

She woke gasping and holding her stomach. After shivering for long minutes, she looked around the room. Still no Zefra, but Etana was back with the other Darrendrakar and Iojif guards, and everyone was staring at her.

"Sorry," she whispered.

Arasi gave her water and patted her shoulder, then returned to the whispered conversation.

Nia went back to watching the ants, desperate to forget her dreams.

"What about a healer?" someone said in a louder whisper.

"With the riots and the new soldiers," Arasi said, "we can't let anyone know we're here, and we can't trust anyone."

The conversation hushed again, but Nia stopped watching the ants and stared at the ceiling. No healer. Kaito was probably keeping her wounds clean enough to prevent infection, if she was lucky. Even if she didn't die, without a healer to smooth the edges and encourage correct healing, she would scar horribly. Now would be an excellent time for Ludik to be around, but he was lucky to be on his way home to Darrendra with his cute little children and beautiful wife.

Nia closed her eyes against more tears. She would settle for an ordinary healer and Ahjin to hold her hand.

What would Ahjin do if he were here? She snorted a half-laugh. He would find someone to confront, the idiot. He always charged at problems head on instead of finding a sideways route. And look at him, locked in jail, accused of murder, waiting for a trial — again.

If Ludik were here, he would heal her face and body and then look for someone else he could help. Nia would help if she could move. That would at least be more interesting than ants.

And Zefra? That was easy. She would make plans on her slate, over and over until Nia went insane. It couldn't be worse than boredom, though. Zefra was probably gathering information for plans right now, wherever she was. Then she would expect Nia to fulfill them for her. Unless those soldiers had caught Zefra.

Nia shifted painfully to a new position. She was wounded. Ahjin was in jail. Tarakh had disappeared to a lost city, if Kaito was correct. Zefra was in the middle of riots.

Ludik was lucky to be out of the whole mess.

When they started Ahjin's tour of Iskra, her biggest problem had been convincing him to wait for marriage. That now seemed such a tiny argument. She would gladly marry him. If he still wanted her, now that she was ugly and crippled.

Nia cleared her throat twice and blinked at the ceiling. Even boredom was better than such dreary thoughts. Despite the pain of moving her arm, she groped for the map she had copied from the library, to interpret the poem for Zefra and compose music to accompany it.

The chalk had smeared a little but was still legible. Nia stared at the ancient trade script for a while, just to get a feel for it.

"Hey, Kaito," she asked absently, "may I have a couple more slates, please?"

Hmm. On their first adventure to rescue the gods, they had discovered trade tongue had been invented by Kassian, and he'd been gone for thousands of years before he returned, so this poem was probably older than most civilizations.

"Thank you." She took the slates from him, then returned to pondering.

The poem had three verses, though two were pretty silly. One slate became vocabulary notes and rhyme suggestions, while the next gradually filled with more finished lines. She hummed as she worked, running tunes around the words.

After a while, Arasi handed her fresh bread with a sliver of fish on it. Nia stopped translating to pay proper attention to such a wonderful gift, but the music continued to run through her mind.

Zefra returned before supper was finished, dirty and sweaty and weapons drawn. She sheathed her sword and leaned her staff against the wall.

"Tarakh's father is dead." Her hands shook as she wiped them on her robe. "Those new soldiers killed him when he asked about Ahjin." She reached through the doorway behind her.

"Oh, no." Nia looked out the window, where the apricot sky darkened to rust with streaks of blue. "How is his mother?"

A middle-aged woman ducked into the room. "Still in one piece, thanks to Zefra." Her elegant robes were torn and dirty, and tear tracks ran through the dirt on her face.

Daz cursed. "Hariskandra, what are you doing here?"

"Here in Sardad, or here with you?" Tarakh's mother accepted food and water and sat gracefully cross-legged. "We came to help Tarakh, and when everyone went crazy in the riots today, I decided I was better off with Zefra."

Daz reached for her, and she raised her hand. "I do not wish to talk about it." She drained the water bag and bit into her bread.

Since Nia couldn't help and didn't want to think about more death, she returned to her song. "Can you open heaven's gate if it's closed to you? Will you forever wander, for eternity deprived?"

"What are you singing?" Zefra asked.

Nia held up the slate. "The song from your map."

"You translated it? Sing it again."

After only two lines, Zefra raised her hand. "You're singing it wrong."

"It didn't come with music," Nia protested. "How could it be wrong?"

"You do not even have the words right," Zefra said.

Nia huffed. "You can't read it, so how do you know?"

Zefra drained another water bag. "You have it partly right, enough to recognize. 'Tis one of the songs of legends my clan collects, along with the maps. We do not have that map, but we preserved the song. My grandparents taught it to me."

"If you're so smart, sing it the right way."

Zefra hummed a few notes, then sang the first verse in a moderately decent voice. "Can you enter heaven's gate if you find it is shut tight?

"Will you be forever lost, for eternity bereft?

"But your soul can find the way if you merely choose the right.

"Find the door and enter in; make your choice and turn thrice left."

"Hmph." Nia shuffled the slates to read her extensive notes. "I suppose it might go that way. But your music is odd. The notes don't go up and down where I expect."

Zefra shrugged. "I'm not a musician, but that is how I was taught to sing it."

"It's a really old song," Nia protested. "I don't see how it could possibly have been passed on accurately for thousands of years. And what legend does it go to? You might as well tell us the story."

Zefra turned up her nose. "The Hotaru take their responsibilities seriously. We do not have the legend or map the song goes with, but we *did* keep the words and music intact."

"If you say so. Why didn't you tell me in the first place that you already knew the song?"

Zefra waved at the slate. "As you said, I cannot read that language." She shrugged. "I did not recognize it until you translated it."

Nia pushed the slates off her lap. "At least it gave me something to do."

"How fortunate we have you," Zefra said, "and the enemy does not. Without you or a Hotaru cartographer-historian, the song will be gibberish to them."

Nia shook her head. "While my gift of languages isn't one of the most common birth gifts from Makana, I'm not unique. They might find another Nokai with the same gift and fewer scruples."

Zefra frowned and made a note on her slate.

Night fell, and more Iskrins and Darrendrakar squeezed into their now-crowded building. Kaito kept busy going through everyone's supplies and arranging food for all. Due to a shortage of bedding, some of the Darrendrakar stayed in their fur and curled in a warm pile.

Hariskandra sat on one side of Nia and Zefra on the other, and they pulled a blanket over the three of them. Finally warm, Nia fell asleep in the moonlight with the ancient song running through her mind.

For two days, Zefra and her spies branched out, seeking supplies and information about the new soldiers, Ahjin's trial, the murders, or the mark that seemed to represent the lost city of the gods.

Kaito, Etana, and Hariskandra stayed and cleaned the room as much as possible. Etana shifted Nia to clean behind and under her. They dumped junk and broken stones in the streets, leaving only the broken table to serve as Nia's backrest. Then they wiped the walls and every thumb-length of the floor. At the end, the blackened rags joined the junk in the street. The room couldn't be called clean, but at least the floor no longer crunched under their feet, and some insects fled for safer environments.

Nia kept them company by quietly singing Zefra's song again and again. Once she could sing it perfectly, she switched to a variety of songs from each country.

Lunch was scant leftovers, but Zefra returned by supper with a basketful of food.

"How is Ahjin?" Nia asked.

"I could not get close to the jail," Zefra said. "The streets are still full of riots and soldiers. But he is now a confirmed murderer, and his trial is scheduled in six days."

"Confirmed! But he didn't do anything!"

Zefra rubbed her face. "After what happened to Farukh, no one else will speak for him, which is considered proof of his guilt."

"That is ridiculous."

"It gets worse," Zefra said.

Before she could explain, the leopard hound, Redell, ran through their broken doorway and pounced on Nia's ankle. "Chiara and Rozali are coming, completely exhausted. Rozali needs a blanket, and both need food and water."

Nia relayed the message, and when the spies staggered down the street, Etana threw a blanket over the Horse's back. Rozali shifted, wrapping the blanket around herself, and ducked into the room with Chiara.

While Rozali dressed, Chiara reported. "Madden found us yesterday. He gave us your message, then left to tell the others. He saw Ludik, and so did we, and we need to pass on his messages."

"What?" Zefra said. "I thought he left for home."

"His children were stolen." Chiara waited for the exclamations to stop. "He's tracking the kidnappers, and he discovered they had something to do with the murders."

"How?" Nia asked.

"It's the—" Rozali coughed. After gulping half a water bag, she tried again. "It's the children. We already knew the Iskrin lady had a little boy who disappeared, but Ludik smelled an infant with the Iojifs, too. Someone took them as well as Ludik's cubs."

Hariskandra gasped. "That is terrible! What will they do with them?"

"We do not know," Chiara said. "But Ludik will investigate when he reaches Irad."

"What about the Nokai woman?" Nia asked. "The one pushed from the tower? Did she have a baby?"

"An excellent question," Zefra said. "Redell, will you come with me to investigate?"

The leopard hound nodded.

"If they killed the parents to take the children," Nia said, "why did they frame Ahjin?"

"Expediency," Zefra said. "Accomplishing two goals with one action. This way, they also get him out of the way. Are we ready to go?"

"Wait." Rozali glanced at the other Darrendrakar. "Ludik also said Darravani is calling her children home. I was busy with Chiara and didn't notice the flowers."

Etana shrugged. "I took it as a suggestion, and I'm busy."

"Why does she want you to leave?" Nia asked.

"She didn't say."

Nia frowned. "I had a nightmare earlier, and Makana told me to come home, too. I thought it was just a bad dream, but could it have been a message?"

"Could either goddess be behind the plot?" Hariskandra winced. "No offense meant if they are innocent."

Zefra scribbled a note on her slate. "We have no way to know."

Nia sniffled. "Ahjin would know."

Zefra tucked her red hair under her scarf. "Oh, I forgot to tell you, Ahjin is now accused of arranging your assassination."

"I'm not dead," Nia protested.

"But you cannot leave with your injuries," Zefra said, "and if someone is determined to use your death as proof, they might make sure they succeed next time."

She and Redell slipped out for a few last hours of spying, and Hariskandra bustled about, making Chiara and Rozali comfortable.

Nia squirmed into a more comfortable position. Not only had that nasty man tried to kill her, either he or one of his cronies blamed it on Ahjin. That wasn't nice at all.

She gasped. They must have told Ahjin she was dead!

Nia needed to prove her survival to Ahjin and the judge before Ahjin gave up entirely.

20. IRAD

(ISKRIN DESERT; DAY 25)

Darrendrakar infants mature faster than those of other races.
A Brief Sketch of Mysterious Darrendra

L udik checked that the southern constellation was at the correct
angle and ran faster. Nemerra raced beside him. Two of the three
moons shone tonight, though only the tiny lavender one was full. The
golden crescent was still bright enough to light their way. If they ran
almost exactly southwest, they should intersect Zefra's oasis. Even if they
were a little off, they could correct their path when they could see the
trees.

"If the kitnappers only discovered which way to go yesterday, they
can't be that far ahead of us," he told Nemerra.

"We don't know that," Nemerra said. "If they knew the general area
they wanted, they might still have a big head start. And what if they
aren't taking our children there?"

"We will keep looking for them, and so will Zefra." Ludik lifted his
nose to the cool wind, wishing for the scent of his cubs.

Once before, they had run like this, after escaping from jail. Then, it
was through a Darrendran forest with Ludik's brother and Lyell, with
Nia and Zefra riding on their backs and Ahjin flying overhead. Enemies
had hounded them for hours, and death had waited for them to fail.

Now their friends were behind them, different enemies lay ahead, and their children's freedom — or lives — depended on their stamina. They must run for days at a steady lope to balance speed with energy. And if they got lost or died, no one would ever find their bones in the desert.

Ludik checked the stars again and slowed his pace a trifle. Though it made his heart ache, they must not wear themselves out. He shoved his worries toward the stars and merely ran.

When the sun rose, they stopped to drink and rest briefly, shifting forms to handle the water bags. Ludik made Nemerra eat the last of the dried meat from their pack.

"What about you?" she asked.

"I'll catch something later."

Nemerra looked dubiously around the bare, white sand. "Catch what?"

"There is food here, if you aren't too picky. Zefra showed us the last time we traveled to her oasis, hunting for Resef's directions to rescue the gods."

Nemerra narrowed her eyes. "How not-picky will I have to be?"

Ludik laughed. "Ahjin only ate lizard and rat once before he started catching birds, and he refused to eat scorpions."

Nemerra shuddered. "Rat isn't bad, except for the skinny tail getting stuck between my teeth. I imagine lizard is about the same? As for scorpion... Ugh. But if it means getting my children back, I will eat any scorpion that crosses my path."

"I suspect rat and lizard will be the worst of it," Ludik reassured her. "In fact, we will probably still find hares."

Nemerra handed a water pouch to Ludik. "I'm ready whenever you are."

Ludik drained the water and packed the bag, then shifted to jaguar. "Let's go."

And then they ran again.

They stopped in the late morning to hunt and sleep during the hottest part of the day. When the rains woke them, they filled the bucket and their water bags and drank as much as they could hold. While rain shifted the sands underfoot, they walked. When the rain stopped, they ran again for hours. Nemerra didn't complain, though her head drooped and her legs staggered. Ludik slowed the pace again, finally calling a halt for another nap in the evening.

"Sleep now, run later." Ludik curled around her and put his head on Nemerra's shoulder.

She was asleep in minutes, and he slept soon after.

They woke in the dark, hunted desert rats, drank water, and set off at a faster speed. The cool air was pleasant, and the moons soon rose, making the white sands glow. The large, golden moon was still a mellow crescent, but its tiny, pale blue companion chased its lavender twin across the heavens.

Nemerra broke the silence for the first time that evening. "This is beautiful. I miss the forest, but I will miss the desert when we return home."

"At least this is the rainy season, or we would get thirsty. But it will be better when we can enjoy it with the children."

"Yes, dear." She smiled at him, lovely with the moonlight on her spotted fur, sleek muscles bunching and paws flashing over the sand. If they weren't on an urgent mission, he would stop and show her how much he loved her.

When he got his family home to Darrendra, life would be perfect.

They loped for two days, stopping at dawn for water and a brief rest, and again at midday. By evening on the second day, they still saw nothing. They should reach Zefra's oasis soon, unless they had missed it entirely. Should they turn farther south or farther west? If Ludik guessed wrong, they might be lost forever. He flattened his ears and kept going, carefully watching the horizon as his hopes dried like the sand.

"Look at those birds," Nemerra said. "They would be tastier than rats, if we could catch them."

"Birds! The only water for them in the middle of nowhere is the oasis. Thank Darravani!" Ludik adjusted his course to track them.

Within an hour, he saw a dot of green on the horizon, and by midday, they arrived. A narrow spring bubbled through the tall grass into a tiny pond. A dozen short trees clustered in thin groves, and rabbits hid in the scrubby bushes.

Nemerra and Ludik dipped their heads into the spring and drank until their stomachs ached, then slept. Around midnight, they hunted rabbits for their first good meal in days. Too exhausted to continue, they slept again.

At the first sign of dawn, Ludik and Nemerra drank again, filled their water bags, and left the oasis. They put the sun at their left shoulders and headed south into unknown territory. Their children might be ahead of them. If they were wrong... His fur stood on end, and he shook himself until it lay flat, hoping Nemerra hadn't noticed.

He was exhausted, and Nemerra ran with her paws dragging across the sand, but they couldn't stop as long as they had any chance to save their cubs. At least this part of the journey was simpler to navigate. Due south was easy under sun or stars, and just as well, since he had no idea what was at the other end of the path.

They ran into late night, slept briefly, and started again before dawn, running until Nemerra stumbled and rolled in the sand.

She tried to rise but couldn't. "Just a minute," she panted.

"Never mind," Ludik said. "We both need a rest. Sleep." He shifted and held a water bottle to her mouth until it was empty, then drained another himself.

He meant to only sleep for an hour, but he didn't wake until the afternoon rain sprinkled his fur.

"Wake up, Nemerra." He nudged her until she raised her head.

They caught a couple of lizards, drained their water, and ran south. All afternoon and evening, they saw nothing but sand and an occasional cactus and an even more rare animal scampering across the dunes.

"Are we lost?" Nemerra finally asked.

"I don't know," Ludik said. "Zefra's map only gave directions, not distance. All we can do is keep going."

Nemerra chuckled. "If we find the ocean, we know we've gone too far."

Ludik shook his head but grinned. "I think we'll know long before we cross the entire continent."

They stopped talking and ran through sunset and moonrise, always due south. If they missed their target this time, how would they know which way to go? Would they ever see their children again?

Ludik blinked away the tears that made the sand gleam, but the shimmer stayed, floating far ahead of him.

"Is that water?" Nemerra croaked.

"There's no water here."

"Then what?"

Ludik had no answer, but he quickened the pace a little. *Something* in the middle of nowhere might be their goal. Their children might be right in front of them.

Nemerra matched him step by step until the glimmer settled into the shine of moonlight on stone.

"I don't remember a city on any of the maps," Nemerra said.

"There isn't." Hope pushed Ludik faster.

They stopped at the top of the next dune and crouched low. Below them, the moonlight glimmered on stone walls built in an intricate, interlocking design. No actual buildings were apparent, only the walls. Most of the "city" was still covered by sand, some with the top of the wall exposed and some merely hinted at by lumps in the desert.

Nemerra tilted her head to the side. "Something looks familiar about that design."

Ludik scanned it from one side to the other. "I don't know how you can tell anything about that tangled mess."

"Oh, yes! You're brilliant," Nemerra said. "It's the mark from the flour sack."

Ludik laughed. "Someone is brilliant, but it isn't me." He licked her ear. "Let's go find our children."

He didn't mention how badly he worried about finding their children in a place that matched an assassin's badge.

They crept slowly down the hill, watching for sentries or any sign of life, but all was still. Finally, they huddled in the shadow of the uncovered wall, listening to the rustle of sand in the wind.

Ludik looked both directions along the bare, sand-pitted wall disappearing into the sand. He glanced at Nemerra and tipped his head left. She nodded, and, crouching low, they snuck through the shadows.

Halfway around the uncovered wall, he smelled something. He froze and inhaled, sucking the odors into his nostrils with hope and fear. That was the enemy who took his cubs. There was the second feather-scent from the grave by the well. The milk-and-diaper smell from Pramath. Numerous horses. Some odors were unfamiliar and thus worrisome. And there! He crouched lower. Somewhere close by were his children. He inhaled again. One, two, three — he couldn't tell if all four were there or not. His stomach cramped, and his fur stood on end. Were they too late to save one of their children?

Nemerra pressed against him, trembling. He nuzzled her cheek and pushed her back into the shadows, then crept forward, step by careful step. Another furlong, and he saw rows of tents set up near the wall, open tent flaps revealing no one was in them. Clothing was thrown carelessly on sleeping mats, and trays of half-eaten food sat on water barrels. Ludik's stomach growled at the thought of a full meal. Later. He could eat later, after he retrieved his children.

Ludik sniffed the door flap of one of the closed tents. Nothing. Two tents later, he barely heard quiet sniffles. He stuck his nose next to the crack in the tent fabric and sniffed. The scent that hit him almost made him cry. That was Rurru on the other side, filthy, stinky, and wonderful.

He looked back at Nemerra and nodded. She ducked her head for a minute, then stepped forward. He shook his head and pointed a paw around them, then to his eyes. She glared but lowered herself farther out of sight to keep watch.

Ludik listened again. Nothing but the sniffles. He carefully edged his head through the bottom corner of the tent flap. The vents at the top of the walls were open for air, and a little moonlight trickled through. He waited for his eyes to adjust, gradually picking out a shape here and a gleam there. Finally, the picture made sense. Someone had put his kittens in cages!

He needed fingers for the locks, so he dumped his pack and shifted, pulling his tunic quickly over his head. Then he slid through the door and tiptoed toward his children. His heart ached to free them, but silence was vital. As he got closer, he saw four cages, and to his surprise, three held two children each, huddled together in the bottom, and one held a little Iojif child with downy wings, shivering alone.

"Papa," Rurru squeaked, and his siblings echoed him. "Papa, Papa, Papa. Out!"

Ludik smiled but held a finger to his lips. In another minute, he would hold them again.

Something shifted in the corner. Ludik whirled to face the danger and found himself staring at dark bronze eyes reflecting the moonlight above a scarf-hidden mouth. He crouched, and the man shook his head fiercely. Ludik bared his teeth and crept forward, and the eyes grew wide, though the guard did not move forward. Then the coward's scent hit Ludik, and he paused. It was familiar, but not from his children's capture. He squinted at the man and realized the scarf was tied around his face, not merely wrapped, and the shadows nearly hid the ropes that bound him.

This was no guard, but another prisoner. Ludik relaxed, and the man sagged, then jerked his head toward the entrance. Ludik crept toward his children. The man jerked his head sideways harder, raising his eyebrows at Ludik.

Ludik frowned. He looked at the tent flap, and the man nodded vigorously. Ludik pointed, and the man nodded again. Ludik pointed at the children. The man twisted his body to expose tied hands.

Ludik pondered the risk, and despite not yet being able to place the man's scent, carefully untied the ropes. As soon as he stepped back, the man pushed himself up, hissing with pain. He rubbed his shoulders and pulled the scarf from his mouth.

"I will free the children," he breathed. "I got caught eavesdropping, but your dark skin will hide you. Find the others, discover what they are doing. Hurry!"

He rubbed his hands and wrists and headed for the cages at the back. When Ludik didn't move, the Iskrin gestured emphatically and turned back to the children. "Your children are not the only ones at risk. Go!"

Reluctantly, Ludik snuck out. He whispered an update to Nemerra, who nuzzled Ludik and headed for the prisoners' tent to help.

Ludik shifted again and crept farther through the shadows around the wall. By the time he saw the end of bare wall and the beginning of the still-buried section, he heard voices. Pressing himself low to the ground and narrowing his eyes to avoid their gleam giving him away, he crawled silently until he could see silhouettes and hear.

Ahead of him, many people with shovels tossed sand behind them.

"At least we finally found the door," one said.

"I thought we would have to excavate the entire thing," another whined.

"Stop yapping and keep digging," a third ordered. "We still have to get inside."

The first two hunched their shoulders, and as soon as the third walked away, shadowed wings waving, they continued their conversation in lower voices.

"Who died and let him rule?"

"Nobody yet." He cackled.

The other one chuckled. "But we will be in power when the gods are dead."

"Four of them, anyway."

The man glanced at the other diggers and lowered his voice even more. "Or all of them."

The other man stopped digging. "You mean—"

The first one shrugged. "Exactly. We have what we need."

"Hmm." The other leaned on his shovel before digging again. "If we find Kassian's potions tonight, we can start tomorrow. After we kill those squalling brats, we free ourselves."

Ludik crept backward until he was out of sight, then ran for the tent. He had to get his children away from here.

21.RESCUE
(SARDAD)

Resef the Omnificent is famed for both his mischief and his awesome fire.

Iskrin Culture and History, vol 1

Zefra followed Redell through the city, eyes open for soldiers and rioters. Some streets were deathly quiet, not a person visible despite the bright sunshine, and all windows shuttered tightly. Others teemed with angry or worried people. The leopard dog avoided those roads or led Zefra past them as quickly as possible.

Whenever Zefra asked where they were going, Redell merely lolled his tongue with a disgusting amount of cheer. She followed him halfway across the city to a large inn a few blocks from the temple. Instead of going inside, Redell pranced around to the stables.

Where the corral met the stable wall, a shadow rose. As it stalked to meet Redell, it separated from the real shadows and resolved into a black Dog, nearly as tall as Zefra's waist, with eyes as green as Nia's.

"Bright day, Harita," Zefra said. "We need to discover if the dead No-kai had a child. Is there somewhere we can speak privately?"

The molossus leaned on the stable latch and pushed open the door. Zefra followed both Dogs inside. This stable was full of horses, so Zefra sat in the middle and told Harita everything.

"So if we can confirm or deny the Nokai had a child," Zefra finished, "we will at least know if there is a pattern."

Harita barked at Redell, who nodded and let himself out. The leopard dog lolled his tongue again, then trotted down the road. Harita pawed Zefra on the thigh and headed in the other direction. Zefra followed her into a crowded street, one hand clenched on her sword belt and the other casually swinging her staff. The large black dog easily dodged citizens until they reached the Sardad temple of Resef.

Surprisingly, Resef's priests were preaching on the steps of the simple baked-clay building instead of inside as usual. Harita slowed until Zefra caught up, then subtly pressured Zefra to stand near a particular priest.

"And I say again," the priest called loudly, "Resef tells you not to trust the other gods. Do not trust their people. Watch for strangers, but do not speak to them. Report them to the priest and tell them nothing about our land."

Harita nudged Zefra to the priest a street away, who said nearly the same thing, with an additional exhortation to encourage outdwellers to shorten their visit and leave Iskra.

Zefra snorted. "I suppose 'tis a good thing that does not apply to dogs, hmm, Harita?"

Harita leaned against Zefra's knee, then trotted around the temple to the local market. The dog pushed Zefra to sit in the shade of a canopied stall and laid her black head in her lap. Harita closed her eyes, but her ears pricked toward the stall next to them. Zefra stroked the black fur and listened.

Market patron after patron came to the stall to hear news. Apparently, the vendor was well known for being the biggest gossip in the neighborhood. As she listened, Zefra was appalled.

Iskra was known for both the faithfulness of its own people and their acceptance of visitors' beliefs, and Sardad was big enough to have shrines to the other gods. Now, it seemed those shrines had been overturned or destroyed in the last few days. The outdweller priests each proclaimed that only their own god could be trusted. Only Kassian's few priests had not preached the same message. In the minds of the market customers, that was just as suspicious and surely a cover for his own nefarious deeds.

Riots had broken out over the new distrust of outdwellers, the enforced curfew, and the infamous serial murderer locked in the local jail.

"'Tis the fault of that so-called Mouth of the Gods," the vendor said. "If he did his job, the gods would not neglect us. He must be guilty for them to abandon him."

Zefra rubbed Harita's fur harder until the dog bumped her with her muzzle.

One of his Iskrin customers looked sideways at a nearby Nokai man and leaned toward the vendor. "None of the outdwellers can be trusted. How many were involved in the murders, hmm?" She raised her eyebrows and slipped away to whisper to a soldier wearing an armband with the ominous lacy pattern of Irad.

The soldier marched to the Nokai. "Come with me."

The Nokai protested, and the soldier lowered his spear. "I said, come. Must I put you in shackles?"

The Nokai raised his hands, but as he followed the soldier, he called a quick phrase in Noki. At the soldier's suspicious glare, he smiled innocently. Behind the guard, a Nokai woman vanished into the crowd.

Zefra pushed Harita off her lap and followed the woman. If she had something to do with the murders, Zefra would turn her in herself. If she was innocent, Zefra wanted to find out whatever she knew. The big black dog trotted on her heels, and shoppers made way almost automatically.

After losing sight of the woman, Zefra sent Harita to sniff her out. She followed the dog down several streets, turning through alleys and cutting across yards, before Harita pointed her nose at a closed door.

Zefra knocked politely on the door, but no one answered. She pounded harder and still got no response. Finally, she moved to the window and tried her limited Noki vocabulary. "Well met. I need to speak to you."

The door cracked open, and a flood of whispered Noki bubbled out.

Zefra bowed. "My apologies," she said in trade tongue. "That is all I speak. What do you know about the murders or the Mouth of the Gods?"

"None," the Nokai whispered fiercely, leaning back to shut the door.

Zefra put her boot in the doorway. "Why was that man arrested?"

"Nokai are strangers here, not trusted. My man hurt none." Tears ran down the woman's face. "Makana warn, but I not listen."

"Makana warned you about what?"

"She say go home, leave Iskra alone."

"Is that all?"

The Nokai nodded, lip quivering. "I wish I listen."

Zefra saw sorrow but no guilt in her face. Even though she knew nothing useful, she was clearly innocent of the conspiracy and deserved to escape. If Zefra could manage it.

"Then may I help you?" She moved her foot out of the way.

The door slammed shut.

Zefra shrugged at Harita and sat on the step, huddling close to the door to avoid the first sprinkles of the afternoon rain.

The door cracked open again. "How you help save us?" The trade tongue was heavily accented and ungrammatical, half-choked by tears.

Zefra petted Harita's back. "I cannot help your mate, but I can take you to the ocean."

The door shut again, quietly. Muffled sobs echoed through the stone.

Zefra pulled out her slate. The Nokai and the Walrus could take care of the woman. She needed a disguise and an excuse to be on the streets...

The door yanked open behind her, and hands pulled her inside. Zefra stumbled to her feet, hand on her knife, but stopped at the sight of the weeping Nokai. Two small children hid behind her back, and she had a loaded basket at her feet.

"He say 'go,'" she said. "Go now, save him later."

"An excellent idea." Zefra looked at the children and pursed her lips. This would be more difficult than she thought. "Do you have ink?"

The woman fed the children while Zefra drew a reasonable facsimile of the Irad symbol on a scrap of fabric, which she wound around her own arm. All three of the Nokai wrapped scarves around their colorful hair. While they changed into Iskrin robes, the mother quietly lectured her older child in Noki. Flour lightened their golden skin almost to an Iskrin color. The infant was bound to the mother's back until she was nothing but a lump, padded by clothing taken from the basket.

"Leave the food and water," Zefra said. "Take as little as you can."

The woman gulped and rummaged through the basket for a shell painted with a tiny picture. This she slipped into her pocket, and then she scooted the basket to the side. "Ready."

Zefra glanced out the window to where Harita still guarded. The deluge had slowed to a mere trickle. If they left now, the streets might be less crowded.

"First, we will just walk," Zefra said. "Pretend you are Iskrin but keep your head down. Stay between me and the dog. If we are stopped, let me do the talking. Whatever I say, do not argue and do not run until I say. Do you understand?"

The woman wrinkled her forehead. "Head down. Stay with dog. You talk. Run you say?"

"Close enough." Zefra peeked outside, and when Harita nodded, she led out the family.

The streets in this neighborhood were almost empty, and the few walkers avoided each other's gaze. Closer to the market, the crowd grew thicker. As a disguise, Zefra murmured a quiet stream of Iskrit comments about an imaginary shopping list, though the Nokai would not understand. The woman bravely smiled and nodded at Zefra, flour-whitened face lowered and one hand clenched around her son's wrist.

After the market, they passed the temple street, which now had newcomers at the far end. Though dressed similarly to Resef's priests, Irad's emblem was on their headbands. Zefra stumbled in shock as the first one preached against all the gods. The second warned against out-dwellers, but suggested they might be trusted and protected if they wore the symbol. The third scorned His Holiness, the Mouth of the Gods, and implied that anyone who followed his decrees would be subject to discipline.

Zefra pulled the Nokai faster. Ahjin had been in jail for less than two weeks, and already things had gotten this bad. How much worse could they get?

A dark-skinned Darrendrakar strolled by, an Irad pin blatantly on his chest. Zefra scanned the crowd and found more outdwellers wearing jewelry or armbands marked with the symbol. Some strolled proudly, while others accosted pedestrians in loud voices. This disease had spread far.

Who had the influence to pull in all four races? Was this merely a mortal problem, or were the gods involved? And which ones? Makana wanted her people out of Iskra, but was it to keep them away from dangerous others or to protect them from her own mischief?

Zefra desperately wanted to talk to Ahjin. She pulled the Nokai toward the road to the docks. They were almost there, almost safe.

And then a woman stepped in front of them. "Is that a Nokai? What are you doing with her?"

Zefra kept pulling the Nokai. "Getting her out of our country." She tried to sound hateful, turning her body to show the makeshift armband.

The woman's eyes narrowed. "You know we're confining them for now. Let me take her." She reached for the Nokai, who shrank away.

Zefra frowned. "That will not be necessary. I can handle the weakling." She shook the Nokai until she cried out.

The nasty Iskrin motioned at someone. "Come help me," she cried.

Zefra whispered, "Run, Harita," in trade tongue and shoved the Nokai toward the dog.

Harita ran with the Nokai and her son close on her heels.

Zefra whirled on the Irad-follower, blocking the way to the escaping fugitives. "Now look what you did! She believed I was helping her, and you ruined it. Do you know how hard it was to get her to trust me?"

She continued the tirade until a soldier grew close, then tucked her staff under her arm and ran for the pier.

Ahead of her, Harita bounded for the end of the dock, barking madly. In the ocean, a walrus-head popped up beside Ahjin's two colorful Nokai guards. The fugitive threw her child off the pier. One of the Nokai swam toward the child as the woman dove into the water, followed by Harita.

Zefra changed direction, dodged the guard, and ran into the city as fast as her legs could go. She dodged in and out of alleys and buildings for half an hour before she dared stop behind the tall library and catch her breath. When she noticed people staring, she slipped inside and wound her way through shelves, finding an empty window in the far corner from which to watch for Harita.

Almost an hour later, the big black molossus wandered down the street, sniffing the dust and waving her tail at random children. The splotchy, glass-eyed leopard dog trotted behind her.

Zefra dangled her hand out the window and waited. Soon, the dogs looked up. The smaller leopard dog backed up, ran at the window, and scrambled inside.

Zefra motioned, but Harita shook her head.

"Then shift," Zefra hissed, hanging her Irad armband outside.

The molossus snatched it and wandered away. Within a few minutes, a tall, green-eyed Darrendrakar in a slightly damp Iskrin robe and an Irad armband took the chair by Zefra.

Harita flashed a smile at Zefra. "That was exciting."

"Very," Zefra said drily.

The leopard dog licked Zefra's ankle.

"Stop that," Zefra hissed. "The Nokai escaped, then?"

"Slick as a squirrel up a tree," Harita murmured.

"How long will this take?" someone complained on the other side of a bookshelf. "'Twas supposed to be fast and easy. Nothing has gone as planned. The information is incomplete, promises are unfulfilled, and see what is happening here." The books thumped, and pages rustled.

Another voice said, "This is where that twit found the map. Have you found a translation?"

Zefra jerked to attention. Harita clenched her fists in her stolen robe.

The first man continued complaining. "No. And even the rapid communication is no blessing when all the news is bad. And I hate those terrible kittens!"

Zefra raised her eyebrows at Harita. Not the spies. Ludik's kittens? The women crept closer to the shelves and peeked around. One glance at two men with fancy Irad jewelry and gaudy robes, flipping through old books, and they pulled back, leaning toward the shelf to hear.

"I was so happy to send them on with Rada," one man continued, "though I galloped all day for a week. I ache like an old man, but I do not envy him dealing with them."

"From the stories, they are still as bad," the other man said. "The other children are properly respectful with a little encouragement, but those four..."

Four. They *must* mean Ludik's children. Zefra held her breath and leaned as close to the edge of the bookcase as she dared.

"If we could find replacements," the first man said, "I would throw those cubs into the desert."

"Patience," the other soothed. "You should be grateful they are so disobedient. If they had stayed by their parents, we would have needed to fight teeth and claws for them."

The first man sniffed. "A quiver of arrows would solve our problem and be quite enjoyable."

Zefra felt heat rising through her veins. She leaned against the book-shelf and took a deep breath.

"How long will this take?" the man asked again.

"Now that we have the map, we are almost there. We have our half of the ingredients. All we must do is keep the city distracted until they find the other half. It will take a day to mix the poison, and then you will not have to deal with your little monsters anymore. Then we return for His Holiness's execution." The second man sneered the title. "The gods will surely come for their favored servant's trial, and then our fearless leader will have his chance." He sneered "fearless leader," too.

Redell frantically licked Zefra's ankle, but whatever he wanted to say would have to wait. The men were still talking, and she craned to hear.

The first man cackled. "Then we will be free from the troublesome gods."

"Hush. Someone will overhear. Have you found a translation?"

Zefra and Harita turned their backs to the men.

Another book thumped. "There is nothing else useful. The little twit must have been lucky."

"Lucky for us." The other chuckled.

The two men swept regally from the building.

Redell yipped rapidly at Harita.

"They have Ludik's children," Zefra whispered, "but where? And — will they poison them?"

"Maybe," Harita said. "Redell recognized the scent of the one who urged patience, from Nia's attack and the tower where the Nokai died."

"Did Redell discover if that Nokai had a child?"

Harita shook her head. "Not for certain, but based on the conversation, it seems likely. All the children are in danger."

"And the gods." Zefra felt numb. Ahjin was in jail, Nia was injured, and Ludik was wandering through the desert. Even Tarakh had vanished. How could she save everyone alone?

22. QUESTIONS

(SARDAD)

Forewarned is forearmed.

Darrendran Proverb

As soon as she dared, Zefra leaned out the library window, hoping to see where the men went, but they were already out of sight. Her best tip was gone, and the cold ash of despair smothered her hopes.

Redell growled.

Harita whispered, "See if you can follow them."

Redell jumped out the window and disappeared.

"What do we do now?" Harita peered around the library stacks. "If the gods and the children are in danger, can we save them all?"

Zefra nibbled on her lip. "The gods can defend themselves if they are aware of the problem. Normally, Ahjin takes care of that, and they do not seem to be listening to us."

"What about the Cats?" Harita asked. "You sent them to spy on the temple. Maybe they found someone to trust, or at least some way to leave a message."

Zefra nodded. "You're right. I also need to ask them what they have learned." She eyed Harita's robe. "Do you need to return that before we go?"

Harita flashed a grin. "Anyone who leaves their laundry out during the rain deserves to have it 'washed away,' but I can return it. I'm safer as a dog, anyway. I will meet you at the corner." She walked out, ignoring stares at her bare feet.

Zefra strolled down the road, though her hands itched to call flame every time a guard looked her way. Soon, the big black dog joined her, dropping Zefra's fake armband into her hand.

During the trip to the main temple of Resef in the middle of Sardad, everyone stared at the band now back around Zefra's arm. Some people smiled, and some moved away from her, but no one ignored her. The attention made her skin crawl.

Who was behind this evil scheme that had made so many people suffer? *Free ourselves from the gods,* the man had said. Did they — whoever they were — think they could merely ignore the deities? They might be seeking independence somehow. Perhaps they planned to move to the Dragon Isles and had forgotten Kassian now claimed them. Or they might think Irad was exempt from the gods' influence. But if that were true, why did they not just go?

And what did all this have to do with the children?

When they reached the temple, Zefra sent Harita to search for the Cats and knelt at an altar to pray. She turned all the runes upside-down and closed her eyes.

Please, Resef, Most Holy Flame, light the way to understanding. Show us where to look for answers. Melt the hearts of our enemies to forgiveness, or burn them to ash. Please, Luminosity. She waited, churning questions in her mind.

When she opened her eyes, the runes were still upside down. Resef had nothing to say. She bowed her head in despair and caught a glimpse of the Irad-symbol on her armband.

Ashes! She wore the enemy's mark. Zefra whipped it into her pocket and prayed again, beginning with an apology and an explanation of her disguise.

This time, when she opened her eyes, five runes had turned upward. She puzzled over the first four and finally decided the most likely meaning of the set was gods, conflict, treachery, and the reversed rune for communication. That did not tell her much, except perhaps that the problems in the mortal world were linked to the gods. Zefra grimaced. Had they not dealt with the problems of the gods often enough?

And no communication. Do not talk? To whom? Or Resef would not
— or could not — communicate.

The fifth rune spoke of a journey. Was she supposed to go somewhere, or was someone else? Who, and where, and why? Zefra swept the
runes into their bowl.

A dog barked outside the temple, and Zefra climbed to her feet and
replaced her armband. When she exited, Redell guided her to a dark
alley where Harita waited with both Cats.

Zefra checked for eavesdroppers, then crouched beside the four Darrendrakar. "What did you discover?"

The golden cat tilted her head sideways and meowed.

Zefra almost cursed again. No Ahjin to talk to the gods, and no Nia
to talk to everyone else. And none of the Darrendrakar had clothing
with them, since Zefra had foolishly made Harita return the stolen robe.

"I'm sorry," she said. "I need to find clothes for one of you."

Gazanar shook his head. The dark gray cat *twisted* and suddenly, a
man crouched on the street, arms wrapped around his knees for the
barest of modesty.

Zefra looked away, face burning.

"Sorry, but we have little time," Gazanar said. "Please do not inter-
rupt. Resef isn't talking to the other gods, and his priests have instructions to share no information. His priests are frantically searching old
books for mentions of mazes. Old maps have been hung all over the
private interior of the temple, and the priests spend hours staring at
them. What else, Varnika?"

The golden cat meowed and hissed.

"Right. Any priest that shows up wearing that new symbol is immediately repudiated. Is that all?"

The other cat snarled.

"And Captain Daz didn't come for our last arranged meeting. We
don't know if something happened to him."

There was a long pause, and then a gray paw nudged Zefra's knee.

She cautiously peeked sideways and saw Cat whiskers instead of bare
skin. "Thank you, Gazanar. Can you and Varnika keep listening, or do
you need to get out?"

The two Cats meowed at each other, then slunk back to the temple.

Zefra turned to the Dogs. "Did you learn anything, Redell?"

The leopard dog shook his head and growled.

Zefra leaned against the building. "Too bad. We could use more information." She sighed. "Maps and mazes. Not talking to the other gods. Oh, that explains the reversed communication rune. I still do not understand the rest of it. And how can I help?"

Harita shrugged, and Redell lolled his tongue out of his mouth.

Zefra headed for their broken-down hideout. "Perhaps someone else will have an idea. Nia has plenty of time to think while she heals. And," she reluctantly admitted, "she's smarter than I am, when she bothers."

They had not traveled far when she recognized a pinto Horse and one of Ahjin's guards beside him in the crowd. Chiyo immediately turned toward the road out of the city, jerking his head for Zefra to follow.

Once outside the city, he said, "Hurry. This way."

He swung himself onto the Horse and pulled Zefra behind him. They galloped to their old camping spot with the Dogs loping behind. Two of the tents had fallen, but the third stood crookedly. Zefra should have taken care of them earlier, but she had forgotten about them when Nia was injured.

Someone peeked from the upright tent, then ducked low to avoid catching her bright yellow wings as she exited. The pretty Iojif lady had short black hair and wore leggings under a shortened Iskrin robe.

Chiyo and Zefra dismounted and bowed, and the Dogs relaxed in the sand.

The Iojif shot a skeptical glance at Zefra's armband.

"Zefra is a friend of Ahjin," Chiyo said. "In disguise."

The lady expertly bowed. "Bright day. I am Sufa, Ioj's diplomat to Iskra, and Ahjin's cousin."

Zefra shook Sufa's hand, extending her the same courtesy of using her own customs. "I am pleased to meet you, though I wish it were under better circumstances. Have you reached Ahjin? I desperately need to consult with him."

Sufa shook her head. "He called my name once, but when I replied, I was cut off."

"What about messages from Lyell or anyone on Arupa?"

"I'm having trouble contacting anyone," Sufa said. "All I got from Lyell was a quick message that all the gods have closed their borders. Please, let me tell you what I do know." She sat gracefully.

Zefra handed her water and sat cross-legged.

"Thank you." Sufa pointed to Zefra's fake armband. "In Chisato, that mark is now quite common, and its bearers are growing more powerful. Foreigners are unwelcome without the emblem, and even Iskrins are steering carefully in the changing winds. Clans arm themselves and their allies, and I fear war is on the horizon among the districts."

"But why?" Zefra groaned. "What will they gain from this?"

"Power," Chiyo said as he poured water into a bucket for Zinon. "'Tis always about power somehow."

"The officers and judges and officials wear that mark," Sufa said, "or were replaced with others who would. I stayed until I feared a later flight risked my life."

"You did well." Zefra closed her eyes to think. "If Iskra approaches civil war, I do not understand why Resef does not stop it. Though 'tis not just civil war. Outdwellers are unwelcome again. And how does this connect with the children and everything else?"

"Several days ago," Sufa said, "I hid on a roof in Chisato after following several newly influential people. They discussed their plans, in unfortunately vague terms, but then they argued about why they weren't finished yet. One accused another of taking too long to get the last 'little bits' vital for the plan, and the second one got his feathers in a knot, yelling about how long he'd spied on them until they were almost alone. The first one laughed and asked why he didn't take them no matter who was around, and the second practically screamed. 'Did you see what that black monster did? I like my face. Besides, until we have the map, we're wandering blindly. What is the hurry?' And then the first one accused him of being a coward for being conveniently busy and making someone else actually collect the 'pieces.' I thought perhaps the black monster was that panther friend of yours?"

"And the pieces are his children," Zefra said. "They are only children; what part can they play?"

"At least they are still missing information," Sufa said.

Zefra shook her head. "No longer. Nia found the map, and one of the conspirators stole it from her."

Sufa shrugged. "I imagine they would have found the way, eventually. Fortunately, you also know."

"I know nothing," Zefra grumbled under her breath.

"One more thing," Sufa continued. "On my flight here, I spotted some of your spies. I'm sorry, but one of them is dead and two are gravely wounded."

Zefra counted on her fingers. Chiara and Rozali had already returned, as had the two Iojif. Two Dogs were here with Chiyo and Zinon. The Cats were in the temple, and Daz, wherever he was, would not have had time to get far into the desert. That left Isako and Ingo from the guards, and Madden the Fox.

Or Tarakh.

Zefra sucked in her breath. "Who? Where? Why did you leave them?"

Sufa frowned. "I can't carry them, you know. I had no healing supplies, no food, and little water, and I knew you needed my report. I moved them to shelter, bandaged their wounds, and left my only water bag. What else should I have done?"

Zefra clenched her fists. "You were wise. But — who?"

"The dead dog had pretty fur, like a tanager's feathers."

"Ingo," Zefra said. Ahjin's guard had paid the final price.

"The Iskrin — I'm afraid your uniformity of coloring makes a description hard — he lost half an arm and had to use his belt for a tourniquet. When I arrived, he was unconscious. The Fox has broken bones and cuts. He changed form to talk to me, but he didn't know the Iskrin's name. He wanted me to tell you their attackers knew they were Darrendrakar and not animals. Also, the scents revealed the killers waited for their prey. They were not chance killings."

Zefra felt guilty for hoping Isako had stayed with his partner. Though wherever Tarakh was, he might be in no better shape than Isako. Or Ingo.

She forced her mind back to the problem. "But why?"

"I don't know, and I must return to them," Sufa said.

Chiyo unloaded a package from his saddlebags and handed it to Sufa. "I got most of what you wanted."

"Thank you," Sufa said. "Is there anything you want me to tell them?"

"There is nothing more they can do out there. Bring them in, if you can. If you do hear from Ahjin, fly back to let me know."

"It will take me a while," Sufa said. "The Fox can't walk, and the man can't carry him."

"Nothing is going well," Zefra said. "Do the best you can."

Sufa nodded and jumped into the air.

Zefra leaned her elbows on her knees and pulled a lock of hair free of her scarf. "What kind of mixed-up plot is this, Chiyo? A Nokai attacked me, and an Iskrin strangled Ludik. An Iskrin stabbed Ahjin, and another tried to kill Nia. Lapwing is back, and we do not know the race of the archer and whoever poisoned the flour. Someone knew how to identify our Darrendrakar in their other forms, and that is most likely another Darrendrakar. And yet, people of all the races have been killed, too, and their children stolen. What kind of conspiracy stretches across boundaries so?"

"'Tis odd," Chiyo admitted. "Ahjin did well convincing all four lands to cooperate. Who wants to destroy that?"

"If someone is throwing a giant temper tantrum, I suspect Irajahan," Zefra drawled. "But this is more subtle than his usual style, and I do not see what he would gain." She dusted the sand from her robe. "We cannot keep the outdwellers from conflict without Ahjin's help. Can we stop our clans?"

"If Farukh were alive, he could do it," Chiyo said. "Ask Hariskandra for ideas."

"Brilliant." Zefra mounted Zinon behind Ahjin's guard, and they returned to Sardad with the Dogs trotting behind.

Her worries itched at her like sand down her robe. Tarakh, and Nia, and Ahjin, and the dead and injured spies, and the threatened gods, and the secret enemy, and multiple assassins, and missing children, and the stolen map, and imminent civil war, and no way for her to help anyone. One grain piled on another until she felt buried in a collapsing sand dune.

When they arrived, Tarakh's mother was making everyone clean their hideout again while Nia sang "City of Witness" over and over, experimenting with the melody and harmony.

The Darrendrakar all shifted back, and everyone recited what they had heard and done since the last report. Everyone was horrified at the further news of the children.

"Farukh heard about the clans fighting before he died," Hariskandra said. "He went to talk to some people about it, and that is when he was killed, though the city guard says 'twas because he supported Ahjin. I'm afraid 'tis too late to stop the clans without some sort of proof or a state-ment from Resef." Hariskandra twisted her hands in her lap. "Tarakh went to Irad looking for proof of a conspiracy."

Nia nodded. "I thought so."

Zefra stared at them both.

"He told me to tell you," Tarakh's mother explained. "I had no chance to pass on his message yet."

"How did you know?" Zefra asked Nia, fighting an unexpected wave of jealousy.

"It seemed obvious." Nia shrugged. "I thought you knew, or I would have said something."

"Hmph. Anyway, Resef is not helping," Zefra said. "And we do not even know our enemies' goals, other than to destroy Ahjin and cause a war."

"They must have a reason they stole the map," Nia said, "and need the children for something."

Hariskandra nodded. "That is what Tarakh thought. Since he did not know where to find the children, he decided to follow the map and leave you to deal with the other problems."

"It will take him nearly two weeks to reach the oasis," Zefra said, "and even longer to find Irad. And anyone following him is already days behind."

"He took three of his best horses," Hariskandra said. "He will make better time than you think."

"We might catch up anyway," Rozali said. "I made it to Pramath in two days. I told you, we ran our cross-country race a dozen times, and I won four of them. One hundred and sixty leagues in four days. Zinon is nearly as fast, and as Darrendrakar and trained runners, we have more stamina than any of your ordinary horses. We can run all day if you switch between us and let us set the pace."

"The oasis alone is nearly a hundred and twenty leagues from here," Zefra said, "and if Irad were anywhere but the driest desert, it would have been found already."

"Cross-country race," Rozali repeated. "And it rains every afternoon."

"You're the best person," Nia said, "since we can't ask Kassian until we're sure he's not involved. You know how to get to the oasis, you know the song, and you have the best ride. You know to look for the weapon and not only the children."

"You might be right," Zefra said. "But even the Darrendrakar cannot run fast enough to get me back before Ahjin's trial in six days."

Zinon rocked his hand. "It depends how far Irad is beyond the oasis."

Nia rubbed her eyes, then forced a smile. "I'll take care of things in Sardad for you. Maybe you'll make it back, and if not, I'll try to stall the trial for a few days." She rubbed her hands together. "I'd love to create a little chaos."

Zefra's heart flipped. 'Twas a risky notion, indeed, but if she could get to Irad, could she save the gods? And perhaps, if Nia's idea worked, they might even save Ahjin. She reached for her slate to make notes.

23.ESCAPE

(IRAD; DAY 28)

Darrendrakar are born with the ability to shift to an alternate form, though they can't control the process until they are a little older.

A Brief Sketch of Mysterious Darrendra

L udik raced along the endless, pitted stone wall, staying in its shadows instead of cutting across the open ground. Though he could make better time in the open, the white sand would make his dark fur, usually so handy at night, show up like an ink blotch on parchment, and those at the wall or the other tents would surely see him.

He could not afford to be caught. He had to get his family away from here before the enemy found Kassian's potions in the maze of walls. Ludik didn't know what the potions were for or what they had to do with his children, and he didn't care.

The tent holding his children prisoners was only a few furlongs away, but it seemed a league. At least it was a short distance away from the other tents, possibly to keep the children's cries from bothering the enemy. Even that little gap increased his chance of a successful rescue.

As Ludik approached, he saw a light inside. The tent had been dark when he left the other prisoner to help Nemerra free the children. Foolish man! Why had he lit a lamp? What if someone saw the light?

They could not afford to be discovered now. They needed to sneak away before anyone knew they were here. It was the only way to rescue the children.

Crying reached his ears from inside the tent. Someone cursed loudly and hit something, and the crying got louder. Multiple high-pitched wails echoed the first.

Ludik moved his paws faster. If that man had hurt his children, he would be sorry.

An angry voice cursed again. "How did you get untied? Put that cub back into the cage."

Not the prisoner, then. Ludik's fur stood on end. They had been discovered, and all was lost. He'd been so close to rescuing his family, but now Nemerra was as much in danger as the children.

Ludik almost dashed into the tent before he realized the sight of a black jaguar would lead to an immediate fight and probably screams. He needed to quietly distract the enemy long enough for his family to escape, unless it was already too late. Outside the tent, he scrambled into his tunic, grabbed his ax, and burst into the tent. Lantern light blinded him, and he blinked furiously, smelling all the children, the prisoner, and a stranger.

When his eyes adjusted, he saw a lean Iskrin holding the prisoner at sword point while the prisoner cradled Kamakana in his arms. The miniature leopard growled until he put a hand over her muzzle. In the light, Ludik finally recognized the man as Zefra's friend, Tarakh. Movement at Tarakh's feet drew Ludik's attention downward to a shadow, nothing more than shining gray-green eyes in a fuzzy black mist.

Nemerra was nowhere in sight, alive or dead. Ludik chose to believe that was good news.

"Papa, bite?" Zurrahava's baby snarl was more cute than intimidating, and Ludik shook his head quickly.

"Leave them alone," Ludik demanded in Iskrit, waving the ax.

The other five children were still locked up. The Nokai and Iojif babies wailed vigorously in their cages, though the Iskrin was silent except for a weak cough. Ludik's sons alternated between snarls and whimpers, brave boys that they were.

"Go 'way," Terru demanded from his cage, baring his fangs at the swordsman.

"Where did you come from?" The Iskrin banged his sword on the bars until Terru and Rurru huddled at the back of the cage. He wore no scarf, and his black hair was sleep-rumpled.

Ludik ignored the question. "Let the children go. And the man."

The swordsman laughed. "No. We have plans for them." He waved the sword at Ludik before pointing it at Tarakh again.

Ludik clenched the ax handle until he felt the wood grain. "Killing them, like your friends at the wall said?" He edged farther into the tent.

"You have been by the wall? I am not impressed with our sentries." The man stepped closer to Tarakh. "I was told to keep the infants here. I do not know the details."

"What kind of monster are you?" Ludik stopped moving and glanced at Tarakh, down at his children, and back.

Obedient to the silent hint, Tarakh pulled Kamakana closer to him and crept backward, sliding Zurrahava with his feet. The blanket went with her, hooked on tiny claws.

Ludik switched his ax to his right hand as a distraction. His weapon had almost as much reach as the Iskrin's curved sword, though the blade was much smaller. But he kept it sharp, and it had served well against scorpions and other monsters. It would work against this one.

"Let them go, or I will kill you." He would rather tie up the Iskrin, but he hadn't always been a healer, and if someone had to die, it wouldn't be his family.

The man grinned. "You might try. I am an expert swordsman. I have won many duels in my career, though I never fought a Darrendrakar, or an ax man." He squinted at the wood-chopping ax Ludik held. "If you call that a battle weapon."

"It works fine on trees," Ludik said. "You do not even have bark." He twisted the ax, fingers itching. If only Tarakh could move his children back a little more...

The man snorted. "I would love to learn how to defeat your style of fighting, but I doubt you could touch me. 'Tis unfortunate I must kill you, but I cannot let you take the children."

"They are just babies."

The Iskrin smiled peacefully. "We are not doing this to be cruel. We need them to free ourselves from the gods." He squinted at Ludik as if assessing him. "Will you fight me?"

Tarakh slid Ludik's daughters another step farther away.

Ludik took another step forward to keep the swordsman's attention. "How can babies possibly help you?"

The man shrugged. "I told you, I do not know, and I do not care. I care only about achieving our goals. Will you fight? Be warned, I have not lost a duel in years."

"Oh, I will fight." When the time was right.

"I do not suppose you know the rules for a proper duel?" The man sounded disappointed.

"We do not have 'proper duels' in Darrendra." Ludik bared his teeth in a grin. "If we cannot agree with words, like civilized folk do, we fight with no rules, to the death or surrender."

"Such barbarians. If you die, you cannot improve your skills the next time. It wastes talent."

Ludik ran a finger along his ax head. "It is our way."

"Oh, for an ignorant barbarian like you, I can drop the rules and fight to the death, though it will distress me to kill you in front of your children."

"My children will enjoy watching me kill you," Ludik said. "But you may surrender now, if you wish." He swished his ax in crossing loops, trying to look impressive.

The swordsman watched the display and smirked. "Nonsense. Are you ready?"

For the first time, Tarakh spoke. "Take it outside. There is not enough room in here to swing your weapons properly. And hurry, before someone interrupts you and spoils your fun." He raised an eyebrow at Ludik.

Ludik wrinkled his forehead. What did he mean?

"An excellent idea," the swordsman said, "but first, put the cubs back into the cage." He moved his sword through the bars to threaten Terru.

Tarakh glanced at Ludik and put Kamakana into the stinking cage, then bent to detach Zurrahava's claws from the blanket.

Ludik's stomach churned as his second daughter was also imprisoned.

"Now, barbarian, bind that traitor, or I will eliminate this cub. Three will be plenty."

Three would *not* be enough. Ludik rested his ax against the tent wall and tied Tarakh's hands. "Sorry," he murmured.

Tarakh narrowed his eyes and sniffed, raising his eyebrow again.

"No need to cry, boy," the swordsman said.

Ludik inhaled. He smelled horses, and Nemerra, too. He dipped his chin to indicate understanding.

The swordsman held open the tent flap and motioned Ludik through. Ludik picked up his ax and ducked out of the tent into the night. The golden moon had set, and the only light was the small blue moon, barely enough to glint on the curved sword and the ax. The sand dipped in shadows and rose in gleaming mounds. Ludik squinted in the dim light. If he could stall until their eyes adjusted, he would have an advantage.

The swordsman backed up past the tent ropes. Ludik followed him to a clear space and straightened to his full height, almost a foot taller than his opponent. The Iskrin circled him, sword lowered. Ludik merely turned to watch him, ax held loosely in his right hand.

"Come get me," the man taunted. "If you do not kill me, your cubs will pay the price."

"I have chopped down many a tree." Shapes grew more clear. Just a little longer...

"But does the tree fight back?"

Ludik laughed. Once, he had fought a kraken and pretended it was nothing but a tree, and that tree had fought back, indeed. "You might be surprised."

"I would like to be surprised. So far, you are dreadfully dull." The swordsman swung at Ludik, who merely stepped backward. "Coward," the man spat.

Ludik's eyes had adjusted, so he switched the ax to his left hand and shifted it for a better grip.

"You are left-handed?" the Iskrin said. "At least that makes me work a little harder. I was afraid I would have to win this duel in my sleep."

Ludik inhaled the scents again. He had stalled long enough. It was time to end the fight before they were noticed. "If you are bored, should we skip further preliminaries? No rules and to the death. Unless you are ready to surrender."

Having no rules was all to his advantage, though the Iskrin obviously did not believe that.

The swordsman grinned. "On the count of three? One..."

"Two," Ludik said.

"Three." The Iskrin raised his curved sword and lunged.

Ludik sidestepped and dropped his ax in one motion. While the swordsman gaped in disbelief, Ludik shifted instantly to jaguar and pounced on the Iskrin. Before the man could scream, his throat was slashed.

Ludik stepped away from the corpse. Blood stained the white sand black in the moonlight, and the curved sword glinted by an empty hand.

"What you should learn from the ignorant barbarian," he growled, "is that I have the better weapons."

He shifted back, wrapped the torn remnants of his tunic around his waist, and dashed for the tent with his ax and pack. As he knew from the scent, Nemerra was back, and she had brought horses with her.

Inside the tent, a long gash opened the back wall, and two horses pranced beyond the gap. Nemerra, dress on inside-out, struggled with the lock on one cage while Tarakh fought with another.

Ludik dropped his bag. "Move." As soon as they were out of the way, he hacked the locks off all four cages with the ax.

"Can we get the potions?" Tarakh asked as he pulled the crying children from their prisons and set them gently on the floor. "I need them as proof for the clans, and we cannot leave them with those people."

"We need to escape now," Ludik said. "We can't wait for them to finish uncovering the door."

Nemerra lunged through the slit in the tent and grabbed her pack. "We have to take them all, but how?" She threw the two baby harnesses on the ground. "Tarakh, watch how I do this. Ludik, you first."

Ludik shifted into jaguar again, and Nemerra strapped the first harness around him. While she worked, they shared what they had learned at the wall and from the swordsman.

Nemerra bit her lip and worked faster. She stuffed Rurru into one pouch and Zurrahava into the other. "Children, stay still."

Rurru ducked his white head low. "Yes, Mama."

Zurrahava narrowed her gray-green eyes, but she lowered herself, too.

Ludik moved to the tent flap, careful of the cubs on his back, and peeked out. No sound or movement. The other tents were still dark, so maybe everyone was at the wall, too busy with the excavation to hear the children crying. *Please, Darravani, let them stay busy.*

"Here," Tarakh said. "Help me with the carrier the Iojif used." He and Nemerra sorted it so the empty baby seat rested on his chest.

"What about the other two children?" Nemerra asked.

"Oh, give me this." He grabbed Ludik's ruined tunic and the wailing Nokai baby and turned his back. "Tie her on my back. Hurry."

"That still leaves the Iskrin baby," Nemerra argued as she bundled the Nokai securely.

"I have an idea. You shift now, and I will help you with your carrier." Tarakh rummaged through the tent and stuffed an extra robe into Ludik's pack, then took all the packs and rushed to the horses while Nemerra shifted. He arranged the packs around one saddle to make a nest, then hurried back for the little Iskrin, who was too sick to even cry.

"At least he is familiar with horses," Tarakh whispered, tying on the boy with ropes and scarf, "and dividing the weight will help our speed."

He tucked Nemerra's abandoned dress over the little boy for warmth, then wrapped the other harness around her. Terru went on one side of her, with a comforting pat, and Kamakana on the other.

"Hurry." Ludik watched lamplight move through the tents, but it turned another way.

Careful of the downy wings, Tarakh stuffed the Iojif child in his chest carrier regardless of his cries and adjusted the harness and tunic-strips to balance the weight against the child on his back.

Everyone crept out the back of the tent, and Tarakh mounted the second horse. "Do you know the way home?"

Ludik nodded.

"Then pray we get a head start and move fast enough."

Ludik bounded into the night with Nemerra and the two horses close on his heels. The oasis, their nearest point of possible refuge, was seventy leagues to the north, and Sardad was even farther. Escape — and possibly the gods' lives — depended on their speed.

24. RACE

(SARDAD AND DESERT; DAY 26)

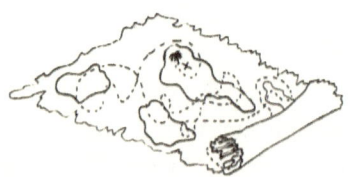

When in doubt, fly!
Iojif Proverb

Through the high window, the early morning light illuminated Zefra's saddlebags in the bare room. She had tried to leave last night, but by the time she returned to their hideout, 'twas too dark for the Horses.

Zefra stopped packing long enough to glare at Nia. "Stay out of trouble while I'm gone." Her friend was obviously not capable of defending herself, and yet she had no choice but to leave her at the mercy of the dangerous cult.

Nia smiled her most carefree, troublesome smile. "How can I get in trouble when I can't even move?"

"I do not know, but somehow, you always manage." Zefra transferred her glare to Kaito, who nodded, and Hariskandra, who smiled, having too little experience with Nia.

Despite much experience with Nia, Zefra wished she was healthy enough to travel and contribute her language abilities.

Nia passed Zefra a slate. "Here, I copied the map and song for you."

Zefra shook her head. "I have both memorized."

Nia shrugged. "You never know what you might need."

Zefra checked her bags and packed the slate. A bucket, her water bags, minimum food, and clothes for the Horses when they shifted. The blankets she would use instead of a saddle would also keep them warm at night. She carried her saif and knife on her belt and wore her cloak.

"Oh, no." She stared at the Horses in distress. "I have no grain for you."

Zinon laughed, despite being currently naked under a well-wrapped saddle blanket. "You forget we shift." He held up the bread and fruit Kaito had provided for breakfast.

"I planned to hunt rodents and lizards," Zefra said.

"Ick." Rozali made a face. "Cooked, I hope. We are not Cats or Dogs."

"Fair enough." Zefra hefted the bags. They were heavy, but most of the weight was water. "Are you ready?"

Zinon shoved the rest of his food into his mouth and followed her outside, blanket tight around his body. When he shifted, the blanket slid off the brown and white pinto. Zefra tied the blanket in place and added the saddle bags.

After Rozali shifted, Zefra fastened the other blanket over the pretty palomino. She led the horses through the back streets to the desert, then mounted Rozali and took her headings from the sun. Southwest to the oasis for one hundred and twenty leagues, then due south to Irad. Though her chances of finding proof of the conspiracy were slim, if she did nothing, she would certainly fail, and Ahjin would pay the cost.

She would not make it back in time to leave with the caravan. Though the least of her worries, she felt a pang of regret.

Zefra tucked her cloak around her and pointed. "That way."

She crouched low over Rozali's neck, gripping the mane as the Horses ran. She had ridden horses before she could walk, even bareback. These cantered smoothly, not as fast as her father's racehorses, but faster than Zefra expected with such a long race ahead of them. Their manes blew backward in the wind, and the hoof beats of both horses thudded almost in unison.

How strange that Zefra's long-lost oasis was the key to Irad. Had her discovery been the cause of the current problem, or had it merely provided the needed location? Either way, without knowing where her oasis was, Irad would have remained lost. Her gift might be a curse for the world.

She had hoped only for a shorter trade route and a chance to win her chosen profession. Instead of a job, she had found only trouble. The Irad-believers controlled Sardad and Chisato, and probably other places, and civil war threatened all of Iskra. If she did not find proof, the spark of intrigue would ignite war across the world.

She rocked loosely with Rozali's soothing motion, rising and falling at every stride. Those men in the library had seemed sure they could take down the gods. Kassian had almost beaten his siblings, but he was a god and had taken them by surprise. The current enemy appeared to be mortal. What weapon did Irad hold to defeat the gods, and how could Zefra stop something like that? In her first quest with Ahjin and the others, they had a map from Resef. Now, she was alone, and Resef's only message was unhelpful. Though she *was* on a journey she had not anticipated, so that part of the message was correct. Perhaps she was on the right track. Or perhaps not. Tarakh had already left, presumably for Irad, and he had not returned.

Nonsense; 'twas too early to worry. Tarakh had not been gone long enough to return, unless he turned back before Irad. And though the enemy had left before her, they could not travel as quickly with ordinary horses.

Zefra lowered her head against the wind and concentrated on the ride. After an hour, she watered the horses and herself during a brief rest, then switched the saddlebags to Rozali. Zinon's canter was choppier than his sister's, and Zefra gripped hard with her knees to move her weight off his back before they both ended up with bruises. They reached the top of another dune, and Zefra looked across the endless desert.

Every hour, she switched her mount, glad for Rozali's smooth gait between Zinon's bouncing. When the afternoon rains began, she leaned back in her seat to call a halt. She collected the water in her bucket and refilled her pouches, then left the Horses with the bucket and went hunting. Walking was easier on her legs than more riding, and the siblings needed a chance to rest.

In the hour she hunted, the rains stopped. Over a little winter grass, she cooked the rodents she caught. Rozali and Zinon ate with eloquent looks at each other, but they did not complain.

After lunch, Zefra rubbed her riding muscles and remounted. Rozali tossed her pale mane, and the Horses ran. Despite their obvious fatigue, they maintained the pace they had first set, league after league. As Zefra rode, her thoughts endlessly nagged.

Behind, she left chaos. Ahjin still faced his trial for murder. Nia lay injured, and Tarakh's father and Ingo were dead. Sufa was somewhere in the desert, trying to rescue Madden and Isako. Ludik's children were missing, and Lyell still had not sent any messages from Arupa, which seemed a bad sign.

Ahead of her lay uncertainty. Only five days were left before Ahjin's trial. How far to Irad? Once to the oasis, she could calculate their speed, but she did not know how far south they must go after that, so her figures would not help until their return trip. What would she find at the lost city? How many enemies lay in wait? Where was Tarakh?

Finally, desperate to stop fretting, she let the map song run through her mind to the rhythm of the pounding hooves. Over and over, she practiced the words to the tune Nia called peculiar. "Can you enter heaven's gate if you find it is shut tight?"

When the Horses stumbled to a stop, Zefra was surprised to discover darkness had fallen. Zinon whinnied and bit at the saddlebags on Rozali's back. Zefra dismounted and unloaded both Horses. She pulled out their clothing, turning to allow them modesty to shift.

"Why stop in the cool night?" she asked. "Do you prefer running in the heat?"

"Horses don't see well in the dark," Rozali said, "and we're tired. We timed our pace to end at nightfall."

Zefra turned to discover both Horses already drinking. She took a third water bag and drained it. "Then I will hunt again. You rest."

She left them behind and chased lizards. After eating, all three curled up for shared heat and slept.

For two more days, they ran and rested and ran again, until they reached the oasis in the third evening. Three days for one hundred and twenty leagues. The amazing speed proved their boasts to be fact.

While the Horses slept in the shade of the trees, Zefra snared rabbits and dug wild onions, using deadfall twigs to cook in her old fire pit. After they were done, she woke the siblings, and the three of them ate every bit and licked their fingers.

They curled up for the night with Rozali in the middle. The Horses fell asleep again almost immediately, but Zefra lay awake counting stars and worries until exhaustion buried her like a sandslide.

The next day, they ate breakfast and filled their water bags.

"How much farther?" Rozali asked.

"The map did not give distance," Zefra said. "It might be a day or a week or a month."

Zinon flinched. "A month!"

"'Tis not likely," Zefra said. "A month at your speed would take us to the southern Itziri mountains, and if Irad were there, we would know. But unless we reach it soon, we will cross into Tarvati territory."

Rozali and Zinon exchanged worried looks. "Will that be a problem?"

"No," Zefra said. "'Tis only empty desert. When the Tarvati bargained to add it to their territory, the Hotaru had no reason to say no." She frowned. "Did my clan have the song because Irad was in our territory before?"

"And if it was," Rozali asked, "how far could it be?"

"Only a hundred leagues," Zefra said.

They took off due south, running with periodic rests. At evening, they were still running, and Zefra scanned the horizon for any hint of Irad, as if she knew what it looked like. Four large blobs caught her attention.

"Look, is that Irad?"

The Horses sped up, racing toward the dark spots. They were smaller than she expected. Zefra laughed at herself. Why had she expected anything in particular?

Then the splotches moved. Two went left, one went right, and one headed straight for her. Rozali and Zinon curved their path, and the dark figure adjusted to match. Now the two on the left were obviously horses, though the other two were shorter. Twilight made it hard to tell what they might actually be.

Zefra leaned back, and Zinon slowed. She drew her saif and waved Rozali behind her. Out here, any horses were likely ridden by enemies. Perhaps they were sentries from Irad, or triumphantly returning to Sardad to defeat the gods with their mysterious weapon. If that was so, Zefra might be able to stop four of them, especially if Zinon and Rozali could fight. That would have been a good question to ask earlier.

The enemy horses on the left had stopped in the distance. The creature on the right had also stopped, nearly disappearing in the dim light. If Zefra and the Horses veered either direction, they would run into the watching foe.

The middle shadow continued straight for them, bounding over the sand in a very un-horse-like way. Somehow, it looked familiar, and Zefra squinted, pointing her saif toward the beast.

It growled a snarling rumble, and Zefra laughed. "Ludik!" She sheathed her saif and slid off Zinon.

The black panther jerked sideways right before he would have pounced on her.

"What are you doing out here?" Zefra touched his black fur before making a proper bow.

Ludik nodded at the straps around his sides. He bumped his head against Zefra, pushing her toward the other shadows. Rozali and Zinon followed at a distance.

Zefra stumbled across the sand, more tired than she had realized, until she reached a spotted leopard.

"Nemerra! And you found your children." There were two cubs in the pouches at Nemerra's side, and the other two staggered through the sand after their parents. "How wonderful!"

She bent, throwing her arms around Nemerra's neck and petting the closest kitten. In the midst of disaster, one thing had gone well, and it let her hope again.

And then the horses from the left caught up. Zefra saw a tiny boy tied on top of a horse drooping with exhaustion, and an empty saddle on an even more tired horse. Before she could scold someone for their poor care of the beasts, a man swept a strong arm around her waist. Her face pressed against a bundle of feathers on his chest, and a little foot kicked her side. She reached for her knife, then recognized the hoarse voice whispering her name.

"Tarakh!" He was alive! Zefra hugged him with an unexpected burst of joy, then pulled back in embarrassment. An Iojif infant slept in Tarakh's chest pouch, but a little Nokai child still kicked her. The Iskrin boy on the horse coughed and rubbed his eyes without waking. "Where did you find three extra children?"

"In Irad," Tarakh said. "Ludik, Nemerra, shall we stop for the night?"

Ludik nodded and removed one of the cubs in Nemerra's carrier by the nape of its neck.

"Irad! How far is it?" Zefra looked south, hand on her saif.

Tarakh untied the little boy and dumped him into her arms. The child was much too hot, and his body shook with his coughs. Tarakh tossed bags to Ludik and Nemerra and knelt to unbuckle their carrier straps.

"We have been running since last night," he said. "Running as much as we could, anyway. 'Tis hard with the children."

Rozali and Zinon edged into the group, already shifted. "Good to see you, Tarakh. Can we help?"

"Take the children, please." Tarakh turned his back, pulling at the knots of a bold Darrendran fabric holding the girl.

Rozali took the girl as she came free, and Zinon took the little avian boy, wincing nervously as he shifted his hold around his wings.

"But Irad," Zefra repeated.

"Yes, Zefra, I will tell you the story," Tarakh said. "Please, help us get the children settled first."

On two legs and dressed, Nemerra stepped from behind the Iskrin horses and smiled at Zefra. "Do you have food or water? Extra blankets?"

"Water, yes. Food, no. We can share our blankets, I think?" Zefra glanced at Rozali and Zinon, who nodded.

Nemerra poured water into a bucket for her children. "If there is no food — no, Zefra, don't fret what you can't help — then we should go to sleep. With adults on either side of the children, they will be well enough. Ludik and I can sleep as Cats with all four of ours. Ludik will take first watch, too."

"We can take these two." Rozali cuddled the little girl, who clung to her tightly.

Zinon shifted the Iojif boy on his hip and nodded.

"Good," Nemerra said. "I hoped Zefra would take the sick one. Do you have enough warmth left?"

Zefra nodded, then realized who was left to sleep on the other side of the boy and looked sideways in embarrassment.

Tarakh grinned as he pulled the saddle off his horse. "You can sleep with my mare, if you prefer, but she kicks." He hobbled both horses and gave them water.

"I will take my chances with our little chaperone between us." Zefra's cheeks burned so hot, she was glad the darkness hid her face.

Ludik's yawning children lay next to him in a heap of fuzzy black and white and yellow. Nemerra shifted again and lay on the other side of the cubs, and Tarakh spread their blanket over the family.

Rozali and Zinon lay on one of the horse blankets, pillowed their heads on Zefra's pack with the two babies between them, and pulled the other blanket over them all.

Tarakh spread his cloak on the sand and settled his pack at one end. "May I take your cloak?" He reached for her clasp but waited for her nod before he unfastened it. "What is your preference for a pillow, my lady? My pack or my arm?" His eyes crinkled at the corners.

"You are terrible." Zefra folded herself onto his cloak, careful of the infant in her arms, and laid her head on his pack. She closed her eyes as he lay beside her and covered the three of them with her cloak.

"Warmth to you, Zefra," he whispered, his breath warm on her cheek. "Let me know if you want to switch pillows."

"Does your mother know how you speak?" She sucked in a regretful breath and opened her eyes. "Oh, Tarakh, I need to tell you — your father was killed trying to stop the clans from fighting."

He closed his eyes and tightened his lips. "My mother?"

"She is with Kaito and Nia and the others. She is as safe as any of us." Zefra put a hand on his elbow.

He put his hand over hers. "Thank you." A tear leaked from under his thick eyelashes.

In the quiet, Zefra sent a prayer of thanks to Resef. Though Tarakh had lost his father and the caravan would leave tomorrow without her, seven children had been saved and she knew where to find Irad. Hope lay just around the corner.

She carefully turned up the heat in her arms until the little boy stopped shivering, then went to sleep, trusting Ludik to wake her if danger came.

25. DESPAIR

(SARDAD JAIL; DAY 30)

For the rest of their lives, everyone here, down to the smallest babe in arms, will never fight against another Darrendrakar, even in self-defense.

Darravani's decree after the Death of Kairri, first year of His Holiness, Ahjin the Great

Ahjin flapped his wings and jogged around his cell to keep his muscles fit, ignoring the pain as his arms brushed his torso. Resef had repudiated him six days ago, and the captain had waited only a day to drag him off for torture. To Ahjin's surprise, he had been subjected to only a taste of what the room contained. Perhaps the jailer feared Ahjin regaining his position. More likely, he was merely waiting for some signal or for the suspense to crack Ahjin. If the bloodthirsty captain had only known, mourning Nia was worse than anything they could do to him.

He'd been waiting for his promised trial three and a half weeks. His domain was limited to the cold, dingy walls, the unyielding bars of his cell, and the vicious taunts of the guards. This was the second time he'd been falsely imprisoned. Did he have a tattoo on his forehead that suggested he should be locked up?

Outside his window, people shouted. The normally quiet Iskrins had been noisy recently. He'd even seen a murder right outside, which his captors had grumpily cleaned up when he pointed it out. They hadn't chased the killer, which Ahjin found annoyingly ironic. At least they hadn't blamed that one on him.

A high-pitched squeak sounded like Lapwing, but he shouldn't be in Sardad. And if he were, why would the wanted criminal be wandering free?

Ahjin stood on his cot to peer out his window. At the head of the alley was Lapwing, indeed, wearing fancy robes and talking to the crowd. Next to him was the tall Iskrin that Ahjin had thrown out of the Chisato hearings. What were those two ruffians doing together? His feathers itched with worry.

He only heard bits and pieces, but it sounded like the two were preaching against the gods and predicting a new day of freedom. He, too, had thought the world was better off without the gods, but he'd been wrong. The world wouldn't survive without them. Cooperation and trust were the real road to freedom.

Despite the dangers of attracting attention, he rattled his bars. "Hey, captain," he shouted.

It took half an hour before anyone responded to his continued calls, and another ten minutes before a lowly guard returned with the Sardad captain.

"What is it now?" the captain asked, strolling in with his hand on his sword. "Are you ready to confess? Your trial is tomorrow, so you're running out of time."

"I can't confess to something I didn't do," Ahjin repeated for the thousandth time. "But you should question the Iojif with the tan wings and the tall Iskrin with him. There's some connection between them and the murders."

"Tan wings?" The captain rubbed his chin. "Do not worry about them. Things are changing, and some people know what is good for them." He patted his sword and leered at Ahjin. "Tell us what we want to know, and we could pardon you."

To distract himself from memories of the room in the corner, Ahjin examined the captain's new sword. The odd hilt seemed to be a lizard head. Where had Ahjin seen that before? No Iskrin clan had a lizard symbol. None of the Darrendrakar kindreds, either.

No! It was Crow's dragon-hilted sword that Ahjin had abandoned at the Dragon Isles. Captain Crow, who wanted to conquer the world. And now his sword was in the hands of Ahjin's jailer.

Ahjin didn't know how long the captain had been in the conspiracy, but there was certainly no chance of him arresting Lapwing or any of his cronies. And Ahjin was in even more trouble than he'd realized.

He shrugged. "Never mind. It seems I was mistaken. Thank you for coming when I called."

He lay on his cot and closed his eyes, listening hard to the sounds outside his cell. Would his jailer drag him back into the corner room?

The captain paced for a while, then left, slamming the door.

The situation was growing worse, beyond anything Ahjin could handle by himself. He grabbed a feather, wincing, and yanked it free. After pushing the blood-tipped quill toward Kassian with the tiny bit of magic that allowed him to send messages, the feather disappeared to the hands of the eldest god. Surely a bloody feather would convince Kassian that Ahjin desperately needed to speak to him.

And then Ahjin waited. He waited all day, but Kassian didn't reply. Resef had signed the note surrendering Ahjin to the captain, but perhaps he wasn't the only god in the plot. Perhaps none of the gods wanted Ahjin anymore. Or Kassian might be allied with Resef.

At least his friends were free. Ludik should be almost home, assuming good weather. Zefra, Kaito, and Lyell were working to get him out, and since the vigilant captain hadn't found them yet, they must be safely hidden. And Nia would never suffer again. Ahjin touched Nia's braid, and the dark stain on the lavender made his chest ache.

Working as a team, he and his friends had freed themselves from jail before. Izo even made lockpick hairpins for the girls, in case they were ever again imprisoned. Ahjin smiled. Zefra schemed to make her hair ornaments practical, and Nia wanted pretty *and* practical. If they were with him, they could pick the lock to escape.

Nia would never be with him again. Ahjin squeezed the braid, and something pricked his hand. He slowly parted the hairs until he found thin metal, which he held in the thin sunbeam from his window. It was a lockpick!

Forget holding on. Getting out seemed a much better idea.

Ahjin tucked Nia's braid inside his jacket and started practicing with the lockpick. Whenever a guard entered, he hid the hairpin and let the taunts wash over him. Nia had learned to pick locks so quickly, Ahjin had assumed it was easy. Her cheerful, superficial babble made it easy to underestimate her intelligence, and he loved both her optimism and her intellect.

Had loved.

His fingers spasmed, and he almost dropped the lockpick outside the cell. When the shaking eased, he stuck the hairpin into the lock again and twisted.

Snick. The lock clicked, and the cell door swung open. Ahjin tucked the hairpin into his pocket. Once out of the cell, trickery seemed the best tactic to escape the guards.

The next time a guard entered the jail, the cell door stood ajar, and nobody was in sight. The guard yelled for reinforcements, looking under the cot and along the ceiling, then ran back to the guard room.

Ahjin, invisible in the corner of the room, held his breath until the door slammed shut. He tiptoed to a new position next to the exit. Once they left to search the city, he could walk out. As a troop pounded into the room, Ahjin pressed himself against the wall. If even a feather rustled, they would find him.

The guards searched every cell, every bare cot, every inch of ceiling. By the time the captain strolled in, they were frantic.

"What is going on?" the captain roared, kicking the outer door shut.

The guards backed away. "He — he escaped."

The captain gripped the dragon-hilted sword. "Incompetents!" He scanned each wall slowly.

Ahjin held motionless.

"There." The captain pointed at him, grinning cruelly, hand still clenching the dragon hilt. "By the door."

The other soldiers stared blankly. "Where?"

The captain let go of his sword, then grabbed it again and marched toward Ahjin. He seized Ahjin's arm and yanked him forward as a splitting pain topped his normal invisibility-headache.

The soldiers gasped. "Where did he come from?"

Ahjin looked down and saw his boots. Somehow, the captain had seen through his invisibility and stripped it from him.

Many frustrated hands shoved him into his cell while the captain demanded, "How did you get out?"

Ahjin wiggled his fingers. "Magic, of course."

The captain narrowed his eyes. "Chain him to the bed." He patted his sword and marched out.

As a guard shackled Ahjin's ankle to his cot, he muttered, "We should take you back to the interrogation room."

Ahjin restrained his shudders until he was alone. No answer from the gods, no update from Zefra. No way out. He yanked on the shackle's chain until his cot shook.

At least his claim of magic had saved him from a search. He still had Nia's lockpick. The shackle had a different lock than the door, but he had time. He tried to pull his foot onto the cot and was pulled up short. That would make nighttime uncomfortable, too. Never mind that now. Ahjin slid to the floor and pulled out the lockpick. Since the gods had abandoned him, he didn't bother to pray.

He was still jiggling the thin metal when someone tapped on his window bars. Sliding the lockpick into his boot, Ahjin turned toward the high window.

"Kaito." Ahjin knelt on his cot, his chained foot dangling toward the floor. "Do you have another message from Zefra? Drop it; I can't get closer with this pretty anklet."

Kaito looked behind himself.

"Are Lapwing and that awful fake priest still there?" Ahjin said. "You should come back later." He jingled the shackle. "I'm not going anywhere."

Kaito cleared his throat. He tapped his forehead on the bars and winced. "Zefra is gone," he croaked in a hoarse voice.

Ahjin gaped at him. "You talk? Why didn't you talk before?"

"Nia is alive," Kaito said raspily.

Ahjin fell off the cot to the stone floor. "Ah, I'm dreaming. Go away, dream." He closed his eyes to block the tears.

"Nia is alive, and Zefra went to Irad three days ago."

Ahjin wept despite himself. "Wake up, Ahjin." He punched the cold stone floor.

"Listen," dream-Kaito croaked again. "Nia found a map to Irad. Zefra went to look for proof someone is plotting against the gods. Hold on."

"If you're real," Ahjin said, "and I don't believe you are, why didn't you ever talk before?"

The dream at the window kept rasping. "I set the fire at Durriel. I did not know it would spread. It is my fault Lyell's family died. I did not know how to tell him how sorry I am I murdered them."

Ahjin opened his eyes. Kaito was still there at the window, dark brown eyes filled with tears.

"You shouldn't have set the fire," Ahjin said automatically, "but did you mean to kill anyone?"

Kaito shook his head.

"Were you the one who killed the Dogs?"

Kaito shook his head harder.

"Then it was a bad decision but not murder. I'll help you talk to Lyell." Ahjin reached inside his jacket and squeezed Nia's braid. "You're not a dream?"

Kaito shook his head again.

"Nia is alive?"

Kaito nodded.

"But — the braid."

"Injured," Kaito croaked. "I had no time to explain and could not return until now."

"Ten days? You couldn't find time for ten whole days?" Ahjin pressed the braid against his chest.

Kaito shrugged. "Patrols are heavy, and I waited until I was sure Nia would live."

Ahjin closed his eyes and smiled. A noise came from the window, and when he looked up, Kaito was gone.

"Wait," he whispered. "Tell me more." He closed his eyes again and stroked the braid. Nia was alive. The cold stone under his back was real, and he wasn't dreaming.

"Is that comfortable, or do you prefer the bed?" Someone stepped over him and bounced on the cot. "Hmm. Not much difference."

Ahjin stared at the blue pants and plain leather shoes. Not the Iskrin guards then, with their red and black uniforms. He sat up. The slender man on his cot twirled a white feather between his fingers. His straight, brown hair was cut just above his ears, and his skin was uniquely tan, too pale for Darrendrakar and too brown for any other race.

"Kassian?" Ahjin blinked twice. "After all this time, I thought you'd forgotten me."

"I got your message. What's going on?" Kassian looked around the cell and furrowed his brows.

Ahjin jumped to his feet. "Haven't you gotten any of my other messages?"

"Just this one." Kassian held out the blood-tipped feather. "Until now, I've only gotten Resef's updates. He said you were safely protected until your trial, so I've been working on other problems."

Ahjin yanked on his thoroughly tangled curls. Nia would laugh and insist on combing them. Nia would laugh, because Nia was alive!

He forced his attention back to Kassian. "The trial is tomorrow, and I disagree with 'safe.' Did Resef tell you his captain tried to torture a confession from me for murders I didn't commit? Or that he signed a note giving permission?"

Kassian tapped his mouth with the feather. "No, I would have remembered that. Tell me everything."

Ahjin started from the beginning.

Kassian's frown grew darker as the tale continued. Finally, the god held up a hand. "Stop. We've been told many lies. I must discover why my brother did this."

"You say Resef lied," Ahjin said bitterly, "but if you asked me which of your brothers hates me this much, I wouldn't name *him*."

Kassian leaned back. "The messages were in Resef's handwriting, so I believed them. Now I wonder if Irajahan is a forger. It would explain a lot."

"Like what?"

"Somehow, despite our truce, my siblings and I have been fighting a lot lately. Irajahan wants to replace you, especially if you've killed multiple people, but it's more than that. Arguments have broken out all over, and none of us are talking to all of the rest of us. Except Irajahan, who has been a peacemaker."

Ahjin snorted.

"You're right," Kassian said. "That is suspicious. We were fools."

"Irajahan is very charming," Ahjin agreed. "When he exerts himself, he sounds utterly reasonable."

"He's worse when he's inside our heads," Kassian drawled. "He made a good case for your guilt. Since I based my doubt on your character rather than proof, he made me sound like an idiot. My sisters aren't arguing your case anymore. Resef is too angry to talk to any of us. His clans are on the verge of civil war, his temples have been sacked, and two of Darravani's Cats spied on his priests."

Ahjin winced. "Please ask him to let them go."

"Hmm. My sisters are angry about the deaths of their own people and the chaos spreading in their lands. Three of my siblings have called their people home and are expelling all foreigners. Only Irajahan still believes in cooperation."

Ahjin snorted. "That doesn't seem like him."

Kassian shrugged. "His land has always been the most open to other people. I thought you were having a good influence on him."

Ahjin rolled his eyes. "Then why is he trying to get rid of me?"

"He says it's to prevent future contention," Kassian said. "But just recently, I discovered he runs between us whispering of deceit. He almost persuaded me to keep his warnings to myself. Not until I talked to the others today did I discover he told Resef that Darravani's people, formerly so homebound, are coming to his land to spy rather than trade. He told Darravani that Makana wants to annex the Seals, since as water-creatures, they belong to her. He told Makana I only wanted the Dragon Isles as a base to conquer the world, and that my monsters have been spying for thousands of years. He told me Resef is hiding Irad and my old treasures from me. He told both sisters I was staying with Resef so we could plot together.

"Nobody trusts anybody anymore, and everybody thinks everyone else is gathering their people to attack. Irajahan is the only one still talking to anyone, and he's in our heads whether we like it or not, soothing and prodding and stirring currents. Once I got suspicious, it took me days to persuade the others to talk to me."

"Your last fight was also because of his lies," Ahjin said. "I don't know why any of you trust him."

Kassian sighed. "When you put it that way, I don't, either. But there is something about his voice in our heads that makes us think he has changed his ways. I imagine that's why you're in here — so you can't convince us otherwise."

"Changed his ways! Let me tell you what he did last spring." Ahjin recited how Irajahan stole his invisibility and left him to die. "And Crow said he was helping 'the one true god' conquer the world. For a while, I thought that might be you." He cleared his throat. "History repeating."

Kassian raised an eyebrow.

Ahjin shrugged. "Sorry. And then my jailers got the note from Resef, and I decided it was him. But based on what you told me, I now think Crow meant Irajahan."

"Why didn't you tell us about this earlier?"

Ahjin tapped his head. "My brain was broken; I couldn't even find words. When Darravani healed me, Irajahan convinced me I had misunderstood."

"Mmm. Irajahan makes himself look good while turning the rest of us against each other. In fact, I sneaked in here behind Resef's back. Irajahan assured me Resef was taking care of you, but after you sent me this feather, I wanted to see for myself."

Ahjin rattled his chain. "Either Resef doesn't care, or he doesn't know the reality."

"Irajahan wants me to believe Resef is lying to us and betraying you, but Resef used to be honorable." Kassian looked around the cold cell. "Without proof, I can't convince my siblings of Irajahan's mischief. I'm afraid we gods will fight again."

"Kaito says Zefra has gone to Irad for proof," Ahjin said.

"What does she think she'll find there?" Kassian frowned. "And without the key, she'll run into my deadly traps. Please forgive me for leaving you here. I can't have someone notice I freed you." He disappeared.

Ahjin went back to picking the lock on his shackle, but this time, he prayed.

26. MAZE
(TARVATI DESERT; DAY 30)

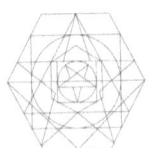

Gods sell knowledge for labor and honor for risk.
Iskrin Proverb

E arly in the morning, the children woke, crying from hunger. The
little boy in Zefra's arms did not cry, but his lip quivered and his
cough intensified. Rozali and Zinon bounced the children they held,
panicked looks in their eyes.

"There is no water between here and the oasis," Zefra said, "about
forty leagues north, if our pace was as regular as claimed." She looked at
the Horses, who nodded.

"Then just food." Nemerra bounded off, leaving Ludik to wrestle the
four cubs.

Tarakh returned Zefra's cloak. "After she finds breakfast, we should
leave in case someone pursues us. They did not check on the children
often, but good fortune expires faster than cabbages."

"Then while we wait," Zefra said, "tell me about Irad."

"Due south," Tarakh said. "I do not know how far. 'Twas too difficult
to determine our speed, and we had to stop often after the first two
hours. But why go? We saved the children and heard the enemy plans."

"We still need proof."

"Irad swarms with enemies. Our testimony will be good enough."

Zefra shook her head. "It will not, though please try if you return in time. Now, what do you know?"

Ludik growled something.

Tarakh threw his hands in the air. "You think I should go along with her crazy idea? You will find thick walls without buildings, twisting through the desert like, like—" He tapped the faked armband she still wore. "Like that. Around the walls are a city of tents and an army of people excavating the walls."

"What do they seek? I heard two of them discussing ingredients for poisoning the gods, but they did not say what kind."

"They want abandoned potions from Kassian," Tarakh said.

"If anything could harm the gods," Zefra said, "it would be something from another god." She patted the little boy's back and eyed the other children. "Where do the children fit into their plan?"

"They never explained," Tarakh said. "Perhaps to test the poisons?"

"Use a smaller dose to preserve more for the gods?" Zefra shrugged. "We cannot risk the chance they could still make their weapon. You take the children to the oasis. When you are rested, go to Sardad, whether or not I am back."

Tarakh folded his arms. "I cannot let you go alone."

"She isn't alone," Rozali said. "We can outrun trouble." She marched off with Zinon.

"Do not waste time," Zefra said. "They will be shifted in a minute, and you must take the children."

"I should go with you," Tarakh protested. "Ludik and Nemerra can take the children."

Zefra handed the little boy to Tarakh. "How can they carry all seven?"

His shoulders sagged. "Warmth to you, Zefra. Resef's blessings go with you."

Zefra loaded the Horses and mounted Rozali. She pushed her hairpins in securely and gathered her courage. "Travel swiftly."

Ludik raised a paw, and Tarakh bowed with the infant clutched against his chest.

Zefra rode south, faster and faster until the wind whipped through her hair. They ran for five hours, switching mounts every hour. After an hour's rest during the rain, they ran again. This time, Zefra switched her ride only once before distant shouting alerted them to the enemy. The Darrendrakar stopped and shifted back to two legs.

"This requires subtlety, not speed," Zefra said. "Keep watch, but do not follow. If I am captured, return to the oasis, straight north. Sardad is northeast of that, but you can go north to the coast or east to the river and then to the city."

Zinon nodded, and Rozali surprised her with a hug. "Be careful."

Zefra hung one water bag from her belt and left the others with the Horses. She shifted her sword belt and took a firmer grip on her staff. With a deep breath, she walked forward. By the time she crested the last hill, she was crawling with her nose brushing the sand.

Below her, stone gleamed, flanked by tents and flying banners. And that is where she stayed for hours, watching hundreds of people swarm the walls of Irad as she hummed "City of Witness" under her breath. Nia was a bad influence.

After a while, Zefra decided Tarakh was right. As the crisscrossing walls were exposed, perhaps twice the height of a man, they matched the symbol of Irad. The emblem of Irad was Irad itself. Nia's map was more accurate than she knew.

The southwest corner of Irad was busier than the others. Perhaps there was a door, because men gathered at the corner, then half disappeared. The other half waited and waited before shouting for a new group. Then the entire process repeated.

The people who went into Irad never came back out.

If the potions were inside the walls, the enemy was having no luck retrieving them.

Can you enter heaven's gate if you find it is shut tight? she hummed absently. *Will you be forever lost, for eternity bereft?* The enemy below her looked very lost. Zefra smiled grimly, enjoying their misfortune. Now if she only knew how to find the treasure in the maze.

Find the prize and win the fight. The third verse teased her before she returned to the beginning. *Can you enter heaven's gate?*

Can you enter heaven's gate! Irad, City of Witness, lost city of the gods, was heaven's gate.

Zefra smothered her exclamation. *But your soul can find the way if you merely choose the right. Find the door and enter in; make your choice and turn thrice left.* There were a lot of "right" and "left" words in the song, and a few "up" and "down."

Because the song told the directions to the maze! But the enemy had stolen a copy of the song with the map. Why had they not found the way yet?

Nia had interpreted the poem almost correctly, but not quite. Did the exact words matter? Zefra hummed the song mentally, again and again as more men vanished into the walls and did not return. They must have found another Nokai with the gift of languages to interpret the words and were trying variations. They still got lost. Why? It should be easy to interpret "right" and "left" in order.

They had the map. They had the song. They had only the words to the song! The music was obscure, known only to a few Hotaru historian-cartographers like her grandparents, and it had not been written with the map.

Unless the exact words were that important, something in the music must be the real key. But she was no musician. What had Nia said? Some nonsense about notes going up when they should go down. So if the enemy had only the words and still got lost — then Zefra should follow the notes. But which notes, and how could she follow music?

She hummed again. *Can you enter heaven's gate if you find it is shut tight? Will you be forever lost, for eternity bereft? But your soul can find the way if you merely choose the right. Find the door and enter in; make your choice and turn thrice left.*

If you put your right foot in and you follow with the left, Take your courage, raise it up, you will turn right, find the way. If you turn down all the wrong, there is only one path left. Make the turns and make them right, if you want to see the day.

Miss the key, get left behind. If you're left, then all is lost. Take a step right and beware; danger beckons on the right. Do not dare get left behind; who is left will pay the cost. On the left the danger burns. Find the prize and win the fight.

All nonsense.

Logic, Zefra, use logic. She had tuned out most of Nia's musical lecture, but she did remember that "choose the right" should apparently have ended in a lower note instead of a higher one. She pulled out Nia's slate, which had a question mark by that note.

Zefra hummed the entire song again three times. Some of the "right" and "left" words were on upward notes and some were on downward. Since the enemy below had yet to return from the maze, some of the words were obviously lying. How did she know which were correct?

Miss the key, get left behind. The key had to be in the song. In the notes. The words told which notes, but which direction did the notes mean?

Choose the right. Up note. Choose the right. Choose the up.

Zefra shook her head. That was wrong. While her brain spun with random directions, she took a drink. She capped her water pouch and paused. Choose the up? What if "up" meant "right?" And if up was right, did down mean left?

Zefra sang the song under her breath, noting each direction and the note on which it fell. Now, if she were right, she had the key and the directions. Nia's first translation, the one the enemy had stolen, was inaccurate. Even with the music, the exact words were important, since a word in the wrong place would indicate the wrong note and thus the wrong direction.

Down below, another group of people entered the maze. If they succeeded, her chance would be gone.

But after an hour, no one emerged. Those waiting at the outside corner threw their arms in the air and stomped away. Some rode off on horses, but most went into their tents and dropped the flaps. The smell of spicy meat filled the air, and Zefra pressed her arm against her growling stomach.

After waving cautiously to the Horses, she watched for another hour, but still nobody emerged. Twilight streaked the apricot sky with blue and purple until the sand lay in darkness, lit only by moonlight on the dune-tops. The lights in the tents went out, and silence fell.

Watching the tents, Zefra crept over the hill toward the half-buried city. She could see well enough in the dark to pick her way, but she missed the talents of her friends. Nia could eavesdrop on the enemy, either with her scrying or her language skills. Ahjin could fly invisibly, without the crunch of sand underfoot. If Ludik were here, his black fur would hide in the shadows. But she was alone and dared not fail.

Zefra snuck to the corner where the searchers had never emerged.

On one side, the uncovered wall gleamed into the distance. On the other, sand mounded over the wall. In front of her, a dark opening gaped in the white wall, beckoning her to enter.

Discarded slates littered the sand. Zefra picked up one written in curvy Noki script. The next two were written in Iskrit, with two variations of the poem. Neither was exactly correct. She estimated the number of slates at around twenty. A minimum of twenty attempts, and not one had succeeded. Even if her logic were correct, what if she had forgotten a word or a note and followed the wrong directions?

If her grandparents were here, they could keep Zefra in tune. And if wishes were water, there would be no desert.

She tightened her sword belt and loosened her saif in its sheath. Staff in her left hand, she stepped to the unlit doorway. After taking a deep breath, she took a single step in before calling fire to her right hand.

Instead of ending at solid rock, the door led into a tunnel which split into four narrow halls. One went directly to her left and two toward the right, while one continued straight ahead. Which should she take?

Her weak flame reflected off bare stone but did not illuminate far into the hallways, giving her no hints. Her only chance was the song.

Turn thrice left, the song said, on an up note that meant turn right instead, if she had deciphered the key correctly. Turn right three times? Or should she begin back farther with *choose the right* and turn right only once? Or did the first verse only warn and hold the key, while the directions were in the last two verses?

Zefra tightened her grip on her knife. She had to make a choice.

Make your choice and turn thrice left. No, *thrice right*, according to the tune. Very well, she would begin there. Three rights in a row. She turned to face the dark hall on her farthest right and lifted her foot.

Turn thrice right. Not right thrice? She hummed the music. There were two up notes in a row, so the words could be switched and still mean the same. Was it for the sake of rhyming with the earlier line? Probably so.

She took one step and paused again. The directions and the key must be the most important parts of the song. Surely the other lines had been rhymed with *them*. If it did not mean turn three times, what might it mean?

Four paths. One chance in four of guessing correctly, and that was just the first step. Zefra studied the lacy design on her armband. If every line was a tunnel inside the walls, there were many ways to go wrong.

Thrice right. The third right? Zefra swallowed hard and counted from her right. "One, two, three." The path that led straight ahead.

She took a step and then another, holding her fire to light the way. Nothing happened, though the tap of her boot heels echoed. The path was narrow enough to touch both sides if she stretched her arms. The unadorned walls were dusty, and sand grated under her boots.

Soon, she reached two hallways crossing. Dark gaps in the expanse of white stone meant another intersection was not far to her front right. And on the floor a few cubits in front of her, a dark red smear.

Someone had failed the maze. If she made a mistake, she might be next.

Zefra pressed her lips together. According to the first direction in the second verse, she should go right. She drew a discreet mark on the dusty wall and turned. That hallway had another intersection almost immediately. Before turning left, Zefra stretched her flaming hand down the hallway but saw nothing.

She kept following the song. Right, left, left, right, right, marking each turn with nearly invisible symbols. At the end of the first verse, as she made the last turn, the tunnel to the left was short enough to see a dead body on the floor. Perhaps fortunately, she could not see what had killed him.

At the next intersection, she followed the third verse and took the first right. That took her back to an intersection with her mark on the wall. She froze at the edge of the crossing halls, not daring to step forward. Had she gone the wrong way? Perhaps the traps let one go a little wrong before triggering, and her next step would be her last.

On her way in, she had come down the hallway in front of her and turned left, which was now on her right. She frantically rehearsed the song. If she had not already made a wrong turn, the song now directed her to turn the way she had not yet traveled.

Someone screamed in the distance, and the sound echoed in the stone tunnels.

Zefra let her fire go out and froze in place as the scream continued. Someone else had followed the wrong poem. It could have been her.

The scream cut off.

The silence was worse than the screams. Once she stopped shaking, Zefra called her flame and turned left. Her neck crawled, but nothing happened. Right, left, left, right, and the last right turn in the song. And still she was alive.

At the next intersection, she stopped before she put one foot into the opening. There were no more directions. She had missed something, and if she did not find the correct way, she would die like the others. *Find the prize and win the fight.* Where was the prize?

After a prayer, she held her little flame high. Though the hallway was only a short section between the two junctions, she scanned it three times before finding the hidden door, which was surrounded by stones that pressed inward. Another hour was spent finding how to open it using the same order of right and left to press on the moving stones. Zefra spent the entire hour praying.

Finally, the uneven door swung inward. Dust floated heavily through the air, and she covered her mouth with her scarf before she stepped inside.

The wall next to her was lined with shelves loaded with bottles of liquids and jars of powders. Everything was neatly labeled in a language she could not read. At the end of the wall, she turned at a sharp inward corner. The next wall held a long table, loaded with miniature stoves and odd equipment and at a comfortable height for her, so it had been used by someone not particularly tall.

Zefra turned another corner and found a wall full of books, all written in the same unfamiliar language. The more she stared at the titles, the more they almost made sense. As she reached the end of the wall and turned a third sharp corner, she found herself at the doorway.

She backed up and squinted at the books. If she was in Kassian's laboratory, then the writing might be trade script, since he was the author of that language, or perhaps the original language of the gods. After a little more staring, the writing finally clicked into place in her mind. 'Twas indeed trade tongue, though too ancient to be readable. She ran a finger down a dusty book. Nia could read these, if Zefra took them back.

But books were heavy and not what Zefra needed. She passed the doorway and stalked around the triangular room again, examining every label. In the first corner, hidden behind a pot, she found jars labeled with the emblems of the gods. She could not read the labels, but they must be what the enemy wanted. If she could identify the contents, she might discover how to use them as proof.

Zefra slid two jars into her belt pouch and tied the other three to her back with her scarf. If nothing else, she would keep them out of enemy hands.

27.RETURN

(OASIS AND SARDAD)

Though all the gods helped create the world, Kassian, the eldest, was the designer.

A Comprehensive History of the Gods, vol. 1, corrected footnote

Z efra feared she had spent all night wandering in the maze, but when she closed the secret room and retraced her steps to the outside, darkness still covered her flight. She crept through the desert until she found Rozali and Zinon, wrapped in blankets and keeping watch.

Zefra held her finger to her lips and motioned north. While the Horses modestly shifted behind her back, she put the jars into her pack, padded with her scarf. As soon as Zefra loaded their supplies onto Zinon and swung onto Rozali's back, the palomino bolted into the night, her brother at her heels.

The sun rose a few hours later, and as Zefra switched mounts, she looked behind. In the sunrise, the sand shone faintly blue, but no one followed. The enemy would keep searching uselessly in the maze, never finding what they sought.

Or they would see her tracks in the sand and follow to take what they wanted.

The uncertainty made her neck itch. Zefra bent low over Zinon's mane. If someone did chase them, they would find out if the Darrendra-kar could outrun Iskrin horses.

But they could not run fast enough to make the trial. *Please, Resef,* Zefra prayed, *help Nia save Ahjin.*

They reached the oasis before midday. As they thundered in, three shapes rose from the shade of the trees and reached for weapons.

"Friends," Zefra shouted, swerving Rozali left while Zinon dodged right.

"Zefra!" Tarakh dropped his staff and sprinted toward her.

Rozali stopped, and Zefra slid off wearily. Before she had a chance to retrieve her precious cargo, she was swung off her feet in an enthusiastic hug.

"Bright day, Tarakh," she croaked. "Put me down, please."

Tarakh swung her in another circle and lowered her to the spindly grass, tucking her stray curls behind her ears. "Are you well?"

Zefra nodded. "I found the proof," she croaked again.

"Here, Zefra." Nemerra reached around Tarakh with a full water jug.

While Zefra drank, Nemerra pulled the blanket off Rozali and held it as a shield for her to shift and dress. Ludik, dressed in a too-short Iskrin robe, did the same for Zinon.

"Come sit," Nemerra invited, drawing them into the shade.

She curled next to a pile of sleeping infants and scooted a daughter off the Iojif child's wings. Ludik pulled the Iskrin boy into his lap.

Tarakh divided a cooked rabbit three ways, and Zefra and the Horses eagerly ate. Fatigue pulled at Zefra, but a good meal was too precious to skip, even for sleep.

"I thought you would be farther along," Zefra said. "I hoped you might make it back in time for the trial."

Unless Nia had found a way to free Ahjin, they would return too late to save him. She tugged her sword belt tighter and fought back tears that helped no one.

"One of my horses died," Tarakh said, "and Ludik can heal the infant better while he's holding still."

"What happened at Irad?" Ludik said.

Zefra reached for her pack. "I found my way through the maze using the song as directions."

"Wait," Tarakh said. "What song?"

"The song on the map Nia found. The one they stole when they attacked her."

"What!" Nemerra leaned forward, then settled back when two of the children whimpered.

"You seem to have left out a lot of the story, Zefra." Ludik smoothed the wispy black hair off the Iskrin boy's hot forehead.

"How fares Nia?" Tarakh asked.

"She is still alive," Rozali said, "though she can't find a healer in the riots."

"Riots?" Ludik asked.

Zefra rubbed her face. With Rozali and Zinon's help, she recited the entire story. When she got to the tale of Irad, the Horses listened as intently as the others.

"So the music was the key," Zefra finished, "and without it, they could not avoid the traps in the maze."

"But what did you find?" Tarakh asked. "Can we use it to convince the clans to stop fighting?"

"Let me show you." Zefra reached for her pack.

"Yes, what did you take of mine?" a quiet voice said behind the trees.

Zefra reached for her saif and her fire while everyone else grabbed an infant or two.

A short, slight man walked around the trees, glaring at them. "I'd like my belongings back, please."

He carried no weapons but put his hands on a line of bottles hung on his belt. Though his plain green shirt and blue pants made him look like a common workman, he had the sharp visual edges of a god.

"Who are you?" Tarakh blurted.

Zefra pushed more heat into her handful of flame, though she knew 'twas useless. "Kassian." And if he was looking for the potions, he must be behind the plot.

"*The* Kassian?" Tarakh turned to protect the infant in his arm, fumbling for his staff with his free hand.

Rozali and Zinon backed away, arms full of crying children.

"Stop," Kassian warned, and they froze.

"We will not let you do this," Zefra said.

After a wide-eyed glance at her, Ludik handed the little boy to Zinon and flexed his fingers.

"Calm down. Do what exactly?" Kassian picked a bottle from his collection and shook it until it changed color. He held the glass toward the sun and shook it again.

Zefra raised her saif. "Use your potions to kill the other gods."

Kassian lowered the bottle and stared at her. "Excuse me?"

"We found your poisons. We know your plan."

"Hmm." Kassian returned his jar to his belt and crossed his arms. "My plan to kill the other gods. And you puny mortals stand in my way?"

Tarakh raised his staff, and Rozali and Zinon edged backward again.

"It would not be the first time," Ludik said.

Zefra tightened her lips to keep them from trembling as she lied. "We are not afraid of you."

Kassian laughed. "Yes, you are. Luckily, Ahjin sent me to find you." He sat against a tree and bit into an apple that appeared from nowhere. "Is anyone hungry?"

Tarakh raised his hand and sat, putting the infant behind him.

"You cannot," Zinon hissed. "What if—"

Tarakh shrugged. "He does not need to poison an apple to kill me."

Kassian grinned and threw another apple, which Tarakh bit into immediately. More apples flew to the adults. Zinon and Rozali grimaced at theirs, but Zefra ate her perfectly ripe fruit in six bites and licked the sweet juice from her fingers before she remembered 'twas bad manners.

"Thank you for the apples," Nemerra said. "How do we know Ahjin sent you?"

Kassian pulled a white feather from inside his shirt and handed it to Ludik. The end was stained red.

Ludik sniffed it, silver cat-eyes narrowed to slits. "It is Ahjin's, but we have no proof he gave it freely." He fingered the red stain and glared at the eldest god.

"No, you don't." Kassian held out his hand for the feather. Once Ludik gave it back, Kassian looked at Zefra. "Now, let's discuss what you took from Irad."

His appearance was so sharp-edged, it hurt to look at him. Zefra closed her inner eyelids as a thin barrier. Could she trust him? What if he lied about Ahjin and had tortured him for that feather? What if giving him the poisons meant death for the other gods?

He did not move, merely watched her with a raised eyebrow so like

Ahjin's habit that she missed her friend more than ever. After a minute, the obvious thought occurred, and she reached for her pack.

"But Zefra—" Rozali said.

"He could have already had them," Zefra said. "They were in *his* laboratory." She pulled out her bundled scarf and unwrapped each jar carefully.

Kassian hissed and reached for a bottle. "What are you doing with these?"

Zefra pulled it out of his reach. "The conspiracy searches for something to kill the gods. I could not read your labels, but these seemed a logical guess." She tapped Resef's emblem on a jar.

"I intended these as healing potions for my siblings and myself, but with the wrong ingredient corrupting them, they would be poison."

"Who knows that?" Zefra asked.

Kassian pursed his lips. "Any of my brothers and sisters. Hmm. Maybe a few priests or historians, though that's less likely."

"What is the wrong ingredient?" Tarakh asked.

Kassian glanced at the little boy in Ludik's lap. "The blood of their people. Younger blood is stronger, though any would do."

Nemerra gasped, and Zefra's blood ran as cold as if her fire deserted her.

"You mean they would cut the children?" Zefra asked. "How many drops would it take?"

"To make a strong enough poison to kill the gods instead of merely weaken them," Kassian said, "they need — all of it." He ran a finger down a fuzzy kitten ear.

Zefra rewrapped the jar slowly. "Then these and the kidnappings prove someone is trying to kill the gods. With these, I can convince the Iskrin clans to stop fighting."

"Will they think that is proof?" Kassian asked. "They aren't poison yet."

Zefra rubbed her forehead. "Perhaps I will bluff the new priests and see if they try to silence me. I can use that as proof, instead."

"If they had not found the potions yet," Tarakh asked, "why did they kidnap the children already? They certainly did not like taking care of them."

"To frame Ahjin," Ludik said.

Zefra frowned. "Yes, but also, few outdwellers bring their children here. They had little selection, I think, and surely wanted to be ready, accounting for travel time. Ahjin might have been only a bonus."

"But who is behind the conspiracy?" Ludik asked.

Kassian picked a different vial from his belt and rolled it in his hands. "If you take those back, people will think I'm behind the new cult. They *are* my potions, and the enemy wears the emblem of my Irad. And the new, so-called priests are a mix from every land, and I'm the one recruiting all over the world. The pirates had a base in the Dragon Isles, which is my new land. And I was the last god to attack the others. I look very suspicious, do I not? Here, give the baby this." He handed the vial to Ludik.

Ludik weighed the tiny jar in his hands. Finally, his eyebrows rose, and he dripped the contents into the Iskrin boy's mouth. The little boy coughed violently, then relaxed into a deep sleep. His breathing quieted, and his pink cheeks paled to a proper Iskrin white.

"Thank you," Ludik said.

"But I can tell you who might be in charge of the current disaster," Kassian continued.

Rozali nodded her head. "The gods know everything."

Kassian snorted. "You're mistaking me for my sister. Makana is omniscient, but even she has to look for the answer, and if we try hard enough, the rest of us can confuse her temporarily." He rocked his head from side to side. "The confusion doesn't last long. That's why I captured her second last time, right after Irajahan, the communications master."

Zinon held up a hand. "Then how do you know who is behind all this?"

"Ahjin and I worked it out. Isn't the answer obvious?"

"No," Zefra said. "We found evidence against all of you and a lot of mortals, too. All the gods are preaching against the other gods. No one wants to help us or let anyone cooperate. You all look suspicious."

"Ahjin isn't the only one who's been framed." Kassian crossed his arms and glanced south. "I can't believe I didn't suspect Irajahan from the beginning."

He recited a conversation he had with Ahjin, counting points on his fingers as he went. "Irajahan has always been after power," he finished, "and he doesn't know how to compromise. Ahjin merely made him try a more subtle plan. So how do we convince the others?"

Zefra slumped. "Irajahan excels at charming others. He will have an explanation for anything we say."

Kassian nodded. "We need to prove his involvement, but I'm highly suspicious. The other gods still barely speak to me."

"What about Ahjin?" Ludik asked.

"They aren't speaking to him, either, until his own innocence is proven."

"Then his trial is not over yet?" Zefra asked.

"Tonight," Kassian said.

Zefra clenched her fists. "Even at a dead run, Rozali and Zinon cannot go so fast."

Kassian smiled. "I can take you back with me."

"With you?" Nemerra turned green. "You mean... your way?" She waved her hand through the air.

Kassian's mouth twitched. "It's the only way I have."

"Oh, no, Zefra." Nemerra squeezed her black cub until the kitten woke and squalled. "Nobody should travel that way."

Ludik grinned. "Kassian *is* 'Nobody,' remember? But, Zefra, it's a terrifying way to travel."

"Humph," Kassian said. "I didn't drop *you*. I can take two, in fact."

Zefra gulped. "I'm Ahjin's only hope. Besides, if he takes me, Rozali and Zinon can help get the children to Sardad."

Kassian looked across the endless sand. "Unless I can arrange better transportation."

"But how will you persuade the others that Irajahan is behind this?" Tarakh asked.

"Too bad you don't have a potion for making him talk," Ludik muttered.

"I do, but he will never drink anything from me," Kassian said.

"Unless he thought he was winning..." Zefra peeked at the jars in her scarf. "I have a plan. Kassian, I will explain on the way." She gave Nemerra and Ludik quick hugs and bowed to Rozali and Zinon. "Keep the children safe."

Tarakh swept her into a tight hug. "Keep yourself safe. And take this." He pinned his salvaged Irad emblem on her robe.

"Does anyone else want to come?" After their head shakes, Kassian asked Zefra, "Are you ready? You'll feel safer if you put your arms around me, but I won't drop you. I won't go as high as usual, since it seems to make mortals uneasy." He cast an amused glance at Nemerra and Ludik and opened his arms.

Zefra pulled the hem of her robe between her legs and tucked it into her belt for modesty in the air. She slipped the wrapped jars into her pack and held out her hand. Before she had a chance to second-guess herself, Kassian grasped her hand firmly, and they vanished into nothingness.

She could see nothing but darkness and feel nothing but cold, biting to her bones. The scream vibrating in her throat was inaudible. Then they reappeared in the middle of the orange sky and fell.

Zefra's stomach shot into her mouth as they plummeted toward the ground. This time, she heard her scream as she threw her arms around Kassian's neck.

"How will we plan if you waste time screaming?" Kassian tightened his arms around her waist. "Ah, I can see our next spot."

They disappeared again into the cold darkness, and Zefra closed her mouth with a whimper.

When they reappeared in the sky, leagues farther north from the oasis, she blurted out five seconds of plan as they fell nauseatingly downward while Kassian picked his next jump point.

To calm her panic, she frantically calculated their travel time. The oasis was about one hundred and seventy leagues from Sardad. In the sky, Zefra estimated their height above ground. In the darkness, she calculated line of sight with the formula her mother had taught her. If her numbers were correct, they were jumping ten or fifteen leagues at a time. That gave her only fourteen or fifteen jumps to explain herself.

Each time Kassian took them into darkness, she swallowed her screams and planned her next sentence. Each time they fell, she fought her lurching stomach as she blurted out the next part of the plan.

By the time they landed outside Sardad, more than twenty jumps later, she had explained half the plan. Either her numbers were off or Kassian thought shorter jumps would be easier. If he had asked her, she would have voted for fewer, instead.

She removed her pack and fell onto the thankfully still sand, clutching her stomach. After a few deep breaths, she wrote notes as she finished explaining her plan.

"So if you deal with the potions, I will send someone to meet you behind the jail." She finished her explanation at the same time as her notes asking the gods to trust Kassian.

"Should I take you into town?" Kassian asked.

"I will walk from here, thank you." Zefra reeled toward Sardad, avoiding the noisy middle of town and slipping through the nearly empty back streets. As she walked, she finger-combed her windblown hair and re-braided it properly.

Ahjin's guard Aki was at the dock, eavesdropping on gossip while he waited to unload the next ship. Most of the conversation turned into "I will tell you later" as Zefra explained. Finally, Aki ran to meet Kassian.

Zefra stole a scarf from a laundry line, covering her hair as she walked. Now was a bad time for her infamous red hair to betray her. She elbowed through half the crowd in the market square by the jail until a broad set of shoulders struck her as familiar. Behind the brown-haired Darrendrakar hid a short figure in a hooded cloak. A lavender braid slid free of the hood until a small, webbed hand pushed it back.

Zefra wriggled toward her two friends, who were surrounded by familiar people hidden in Iskrin robes and hooded cloaks. Hariskandra stood with Sufa, and most of Ahjin's guards and Zefra's spies were scattered nearby.

As she passed her people, she whispered, "Whatever happens, do not react."

Once she reached Nia's side, she had a better view. At the right side of the high stairs leading to the jail, soldiers stood behind Ahjin. At the left, a row of archers pointed bows at him. His Holiness faced the crowd, coils of rope wrapped from shoulder to hip.

Had the trial already been held? Was she too late?

28. ANSWERS

(SARDAD)

Irajahan the Omnipotent is a jealous god and does not tolerate a divided loyalty.
Handbook for Winds

Nia pulled her hood lower and peeked around the man in front of her. Despite the crowd in the market square and the bandage covering half her face, she desperately did not want to be recognized. Equally desperately, she couldn't stay away.

Ahjin stood at the top of the stairs leading to the building, as dignified as if he weren't tied up and on trial. His unruly hair stuck out in all directions, and her fingers itched to comb his curls into order right after she smacked his guards. Oddly, he wore his favorite jacket, though the weather was pleasant enough that Nia wore her cloak only as a disguise.

She smothered a sob. Zefra wasn't back, and two rows of soldiers guarded Ahjin, looking ready to execute him before the trial was even held. She and Kaito and the others had made plans for a little chaos to delay the trial, but making the archers twitchy now seemed a bad idea.

Someone wiggled through the crowd and grabbed Nia's elbow.

"Bright day," Zefra whispered in Nia's ear. "Whatever happens, do not react."

Nia kept her gaze forward while she grabbed Zefra's hand and squeezed. *Oh, please, Makana, let Zefra have the proof they needed to win the trial.*

"They claim they chose a judge from another land to be neutral," Nia complained bitterly. "But look."

She nodded at the porch where an elderly Darrendrakar took a seat. The soft-eyed man waved at the crowd and smiled kindly, smoothing his wavy white hair.

Zefra gasped. "Is that the judge from Orrik?"

"Exactly." The judge had rightfully been removed from his position in the Darrendran town, and he shouldn't be in charge of Ahjin's trial when he had already sentenced him unfairly once before.

Zefra gripped Nia's hand harder and turned to search the crowd.

"What are you looking for?" Nia asked. "Did you find—"

"Shh," Zefra commanded.

A murmur rose in the crowd, and Nia turned forward again. Four of the gods exited the jail and took seats behind a long table, scooting as far from each other as they could. Irajahan smiled calmly, but the other three glared at each other.

"Where is Kassian?" Nia murmured. "Is he the one behind this, then?"

"Shh," Zefra hissed, nearly crushing Nia's hand.

"Silence," the judge said. "We begin the trial for Ahjin Machol, once His Holiness, Mouth of the Gods, now accused of multiple murders." He shook his head. "See how he has fallen from holiness."

Resef frowned at both Ahjin and the judge.

"Who will speak against this man?" the judge asked.

A guard stepped forward, one hand on his elaborate sword hilt. "I will." He introduced himself as the captain of the Sardad jail, then listed the evidence against Ahjin.

"He made that up," Nia sobbed. "Liar, liar."

Zefra wrapped an arm around her. "Hush."

"But, Zefra," Nia protested.

Zefra squeezed her tighter, though careful of her wounds. "Listen. Watch."

An Iskrin approached the stairs with a tray of glasses. Two guards blocked the way until he whispered in their ears and tapped something on his chest, then one ran to whisper to the judge.

The judge smiled. "We have refreshment for our beloved gods." He waved the Iskrin forward. "We hope you will enjoy the local delicacy of tart xaffac-berry juice."

The man with the tray climbed the stairs and bowed to the gods, then turned to Irajahan and tapped his chest again.

"Is that—" Nia mumbled. Zefra's hand tightened over her mouth.

Aki, one of Ahjin's guards, who shouldn't be serving at Ahjin's trial, gave Irajahan a tall glass of red liquid.

Zefra sighed. "He's his own worst enemy," she breathed in Nia's ear.

Aki or Irajahan? Nia squinted, trying to decide why Aki had betrayed Ahjin. Aki moved to Resef, who let go of his belt pouch to take the glass with his emblem on it. Makana tucked something into her neckline and took her marked glass. Darravani slipped a hand from her pocket and took hers. Aki set the starred glass in front of the empty chair meant for Kassian.

Irajahan held up his glass. "To a swift resolution." He tipped it to his lips.

"A swift resolution," Darravani said.

Three gods drained their glasses.

Irajahan watched them with narrowed eyes but waved at the judge. "Continue."

Nia shoved down Zefra's hand and wrapped her arms around herself. If Zefra wouldn't speak for Ahjin, Nia would have to disrupt the trial as soon as the archers relaxed a little.

"Is that all the evidence against Ahjin?" the judge asked.

"No," the captain continued. "Under questioning, he confessed to possession of weapons similar to those used in the murders. We did not have time to finish our interrogation, but we feel sure he would have admitted to the rest of it. His guilt is obvious."

"He *wouldn't* confess," Nia whispered fiercely. "He's innocent."

As the captain poked Ahjin's chest, Ahjin cringed like he was in pain. The captain grinned at each flinch.

Nia clenched her fists. "He hurt Ahjin. That rotten piranha. I'll debone him like a salmon."

Kaito gripped her arms, and Zefra's warm hand covered her mouth again.

"Be *quiet*," Zefra whispered.

"Who will speak for the accused?" the judge asked.

Nia tried to twist free, but Zefra and Kaito held on. Tears soaked the bandage across her face.

The judge shook his head sadly. "No one believes his innocence. But is His Holiness, favored of the gods, merely rotten or is someone behind him?"

Nia growled through Zefra's hand. Someone was obviously rotten, but not Ahjin.

"Who could urge him to such evil?" Irajahan asked. "Is it merely coincidence that Kassian didn't come today? Kassian, who so recently tried to steal the world from his siblings and their rightful peoples?"

"But—" Makana said. The word faded as she fell from her chair, arms stretched toward Ahjin.

Darravani slumped in her seat, and Resef collapsed across the table.

Irajahan groaned and held his stomach. "Kassian poisoned the drink! I'm fortunate I took only a sip."

The judge shot to his feet. "More proof of Ahjin's conspiracy! Three of the gods are dead and Kassian is a traitor."

Irajahan dragged himself to his feet, leaning on the table. "Stay here and execute my murdering ex-priest while I hunt Kassian to protect us all." He spread his oversized, mirror-bright silver wings and headed for the stairs.

Nia fought to reach Ahjin, but Kaito lifted her off her feet.

"No need to leave," a voice drawled. "Here I am."

The crowd gasped and parted from the edge of the marketplace to the stairs. Kaito put Nia down but kept his arms around her as she gaped at the newcomer.

Kassian strolled through the gap, hands on his potion-loaded belt. "I will speak for Ahjin."

The judge stood, and the soldiers drew their weapons.

Irajahan clenched his fists, and his face turned purple. "You're a rotten traitor and murderer," he blurted. "Where have you been while I —" He blinked and stopped talking.

Kassian stopped halfway up the stairs. "Who's a traitor?"

""You *and he*," Irajahan yelled, "are rotten traitors and murderers, taking what is rightfully—" He stopped before finishing. "Ours."

Nia looked wide-eyed at Zefra. What was wrong with Irajahan?

Kassian climbed to the top and faced the crowd. "Did you notice Irajahan barely drank? It's because he thought he knew what was in the glasses."

"How could *I* know?" Irajahan pressed a hand to his chest. "Wait, *thought* I knew?" He jerked his head to look at the dead gods and the empty glasses. "What do you mean? They're dead. *So* dead, and I—" He blinked again.

Aki ran up the stairs and pressed something into Kassian's hand, then slipped behind the archers.

"I thought he was a traitor," Nia whispered, and Zefra covered her mouth again.

Kassian held up a metal pin with a lacy design. "Thanks to this, Irajahan thought his allies had found his last weapon. Since his conspirators wouldn't poison him, he was safe tasting his juice, and it gave him an excuse to blame Ahjin and me."

Zefra let go of Nia's mouth, but she was too astonished to speak.

"Of course I blame you," Irajahan bellowed. "You killed our brother and sisters!" He pointed behind himself, glaring at Kassian. "Look!"

"Look at what?" Makana said. "Did I mess my hair when I fell?"

Irajahan jerked around. Makana rose and seated herself, smoothing her rainbow hair. Darravani sat up and placed her hands neatly in her lap. Resef pushed himself to his elbows and rested his chin on his hands.

None of them were dead. When Zefra tapped her chin, Nia finally closed her mouth.

"But — they were dead," Irajahan sputtered. He sniffed the closest glass. "You poisoned them. You've always held a grudge against us. This is the second time you've tried to conquer the world, and I hate—" He touched his lips with trembling fingers.

Nia squinted at him. Nothing looked wrong with his mouth, but he kept one finger pressed against his lips.

Kassian uncoiled the rope around Ahjin. "I forgave you two years ago. You're the one with a grudge. We discovered your plan, stole the potions from your cronies, and *didn't* add the ingredient to turn my nice healing potions into poisons. I warned my siblings to go along with our little deceit, and here we are."

The other gods pulled notes from their belt pouch, pocket, or bodice and waved them at Irajahan.

The judge tiptoed into the jail, only to return, hands in the air, with Aki behind him.

"You've made a mistake." Irajahan pronounced each word carefully. "You have no proof." He spread his wings again.

Kassian and the other three gods surrounded Irajahan.

"We are not finished with this discussion," Resef said.

"You can't stop me," Irajahan hissed.

Resef reached toward the sky, and a bolt of lightning shot into his hand. Above the screams of the crowd, he said, "Oh, I think we can."

As most of the watching crowd ran away, Nia held firm. "You knew about this?" she asked Zefra. "You could have explained."

"What if someone overheard me?"

"Hmph. I'm going to Ahjin." Nia took a step forward until Zefra jerked her to a halt.

"Wait a little more." Then, very unfairly, Zefra marched to the front. Nia closed her gaping-fish mouth and stomped after her.

"I have proof," Zefra said. "I heard two of the fake priests say they were stirring up conflict as a distraction from their search for the potions, which they planned to use at Ahjin's trial for their leader's sake. They even admitted to kidnapping the children."

"That's not proof of anything but poor recruits," Irajahan huffed. "My priests do anything I—" He pressed his lips together.

"Nia found a map to Irad," Zefra continued, "which Tarakh followed to the lost city of the gods, looking for evidence of the conspiracy. He and Ludik rescued the children whose blood was intended to poison the gods."

The crowd gasped, and Nia covered her mouth with horror.

"When I reached Irad," Zefra said, "I found my way inside Kassian's fortress and stole the potions the enemy sought. Kassian brought me back here, and we arranged for Irajahan to think he had killed his siblings. He obviously expected the poison."

"There's obviously a conspiracy," Irajahan screamed, "but Kassian is behind it. He tried to conquer the world before and failed, and now he's trying again. Stop listening to his minions!"

He pointed his finger at Zefra, and a gust of wind shot toward her. As Zefra staggered in the gale, Darravani struck Irajahan's arm. The wind died, and Nia pressed forward to Zefra's side, ready to support her if Ira-jahan tried again.

Ahjin threw off the last of the rope. "While I was in jail, I almost escaped with my invisibility, but our good jailor had the sword of the pirate Captain Crow, which oddly let him see me anyway."

Kassian tapped his chin. "And what is the significance of that?"

"Since Irajahan gifted me the power of invisibility," Ahjin said, "he's the only one who can counteract it."

"That's true," Makana said.

"So Irajahan is responsible for the failure of my magic." Ahjin turned to the jailor. "And here's our lovely captain, wielding a sword with magic that can only be given by his master, Irajahan. And Crow's sword means Irajahan was 'the one true god' who hired the pirates earlier to conquer the world."

The onlookers gasped again.

"None of this is proof," Irajahan spat. "You're the one on trial here. You don't have the right to try me for doing—" He clenched his jaw so tightly that Nia saw the muscles strain. "It's not *proof*." He immediately clamped his mouth shut again.

"Ahjin, I hate to ask you to bleed more," Kassian said, "but may I steal a little for Irajahan's glass?"

More? Nia searched Ahjin from head to foot while Kassian held out the cup.

"If I may borrow a knife," Ahjin said. "My weapons haven't been returned yet." He glared at the Sardad captain, who glowered back.

Nia snickered. Trouble couldn't come to a better captain.

Darravani drew her knife, and Ahjin sliced a finger above the drink Kassian held. When he returned her knife, she held his hand for a moment, healing it.

Kassian pushed the glass toward Irajahan. "Prove I'm wrong. Drink."

"No."

Resef lowered his lightning sword toward his younger brother's head. "Are you scared to drink?"

"Why are you all so cruel to me?" Irajahan whined.

"Cruel?" Darravani crossed her arms. "Cruel, like the lies you've told? Cruel, like murdering people or poisoning us? Cruel, like turning babies into poison? Cruel, like trying to kill Ahjin and framing him for murder and letting him be tortured? Is that what you mean by cruel?"

Tortured? Nia's chest cramped. Darravani meant that as a metaphor, didn't she? Nia scanned Ahjin again.

Irajahan pouted. "Are a few lives worth losing the world?"

"Drink," Kassian said.

"But it's poison! I know what Zefra found—" Irajahan snapped his mouth closed.

Kassian grinned slowly. "You know that what Zefra found in Irad would poison you if mixed with the blood of an Iojif. We have our proof."

"No, you don't. I know what was in Irad because I know what *you* planned. I was saving us all!"

Makana tapped Kassian on the shoulder and whispered in his ear. He rubbed his chin, watching Irajahan.

"That's not a bad idea, sister. Ahjin, come here, please. And — what's your cousin's name?"

"Sufa?" Ahjin looked over the crowd.

Not far from Nia, someone threw off a cloak. Bright yellow wings headed for the stairs. When Sufa reached the top, she bowed to the gods, keeping her black head lowered after she straightened. "Yes, My Lord Celestial?"

"Do you trust me?" Kassian asked.

Sufa glanced at Ahjin, who nodded. "Yes, Lord," she said.

Kassian looked at his siblings. "Do you trust me?"

"No," Irajahan said.

"Yes," the other three chorused.

Kassian pulled a vial from his belt. "I'll need a little more blood."

Ahjin held out his hand to Darravani, but Kassian pointed to Irajahan. "His."

It took three gods to hold Irajahan still enough for Darravani to prick his finger and let a few drops of blood drip into Kassian's potion.

Kassian shook the vial and handed it to Ahjin. "Half for you and half for Sufa. It will temporarily combine your minds and allow you to read his. His earlier sip already had something in it to make him talk, but work quickly."

Irajahan clapped his hand over his mouth and glared.

Nia's eyes widened. How clever of Kassian. No poison in the juice, but now Irajahan's frequent verbal slips made sense.

"I hoped to never touch his mind again," Sufa said.

"If I'm right," Ahjin said, "this will be the last time he'll bother anyone."

"You can't do this," Irajahan protested through his fingers.

With his free hand, Resef shook his lightning sword until sparks danced.

Sufa bowed her head for a moment, then raised her chin high. "I'll do it."

Ahjin took Sufa's hand. "I can nearly guarantee this won't be pleasant. Are you sure?"

Sufa nodded, and as soon as Ahjin drank half the potion, she downed the rest. Both of them shook, wings vibrating, as they reached toward Irajahan in strange unison. Irajahan tried to duck, but the other gods held him still.

Ahjin and Sufa put their hands on Irajahan's head. They bowed their heads for a moment and then spoke in unison. "My world. All mine. No more siblings taking my share. No more Mouth telling me what to do. All my people, all my rule. Kill anyone who opposes me. All mine."

They staggered and fell to the ground, shaking.

The crowd burst into horrified chatter, and the guards lowered their bows.

Nia bolted forward, but Zefra grabbed her arm. "Stay out of the way."

Before Nia could hit Zefra, Darravani bent over the two Iojif. "They'll be well in a few minutes."

"You stand condemned from your own thoughts, brother," Resef said sadly. "What do you say now?"

"I deserve this world." Irajahan nearly sobbed with rage. "I'm the best, the most powerful."

"But the world doesn't deserve you." The voice was so faint Nia almost didn't recognize it as Ahjin's. He pushed himself to a seated position, leaning on quivering arms.

"So," Kassian said, "in judgment for your treachery, we condemn you to death. Ahjin, you are free and reinstated."

Nia ripped herself free and scrambled up the stairs as fast as her injuries allowed. She flopped on the ground and threw her arms around

Ahjin, hiding her face against his chest. The embrace hurt the gash on her chest and face, but the feel of his arms surrounding her was the best healing in the world.

She wanted him and only him. Why had she fought his proposal so long? For him, marriage was a sacred expression of love. Just because she was reared differently didn't mean he was wrong.

"Will you marry me?" she blurted.

Ahjin jerked back to stare at her, and she ducked her head to hide her wounded face again.

"Ooh, that's a problem," Makana said. "I'm sorry, but Irajahan was right about one thing in this whole mess. It causes too much conflict to argue about who is the Mouth of the Gods. I'm afraid we'll have to make it hereditary, anyway. We can't let Ahjin marry someone who can't have children with him."

29. CHANGE
(SARDAD)

Patience is bitter, but the fruit is sweet.
Nokai Proverb

As Ahjin sat on the stairs with Nia, his heart plummeted. Now that she finally wanted to marry him, the gods still insisted he pick an Iojif wife so his children could inherit his position. Irajahan had ruined the best day of his life.

Ahjin glared at Irajahan, still in his siblings' grip, and tightened his arms around Nia despite the pain it triggered on his chest. "Then I resign. Without Irajahan stirring the currents, someone else can handle the job."

"That puts us back in the same position," Darravani said quietly. "We can't afford to argue this issue."

"It doesn't matter," Nia mumbled into Ahjin's jacket. "I forgot you won't want me anymore."

"What?" Ahjin rocked backward and tried to look in her eyes, but she ducked her head. "Why not?"

Nia backed up. "I'm ugly now."

Ahjin jumped to his feet. "I don't understand."

For the first time, Nia raised her head. She lowered her hood to reveal bandages around half her face. "The slash goes all down my face and doesn't end until here." She waved her hand across her stomach. "I can't even stand to look at myself."

Ahjin reached for her, fighting tears. No wonder her severed braid had been soaked in blood. She was lucky to have survived. "I don't care what you look like. I'll always love you."

She dodged his hands. "You can't look at *this* every day." She pulled off the bandages.

Ahjin recoiled in sympathy for the livid cut on her face, barely closed and still glowing red and white. And it continued down her body — how could she still move?

"That's terrible," he blurted.

Nia sobbed and turned toward the stairs. "I know."

Ahjin lunged for her, carefully turning her to face him. "I have scars, too."

Nia touched his face where the lightning scars still branched faintly. "Not like mine."

Ahjin winced at the crowd's avid stares. Couldn't they have this conversation in private? His cheeks burned as he unfastened his jacket and reached for his shirt buttons.

Nia's eyes widened. "What are you doing, bird brain?" She squinted. "Why is there blood on your shirt?"

"I convinced the lovely captain that since I'd broken my wings twice, it wouldn't bother me if he broke them again." He raised an eyebrow at Nia's snort. "I know. So he tried a different persuasion." Twice, but he wouldn't tell her that.

He took a deep breath and opened his shirt, turning so that only Nia and the gods could see. As her emerald gaze moved from his face to his chest, her eyes welled with tears and her lip quivered.

"Oh, Ahjin," she whispered, touching the cuts and burns with feather-soft fingers.

Behind them, Makana cursed and ordered someone to arrest the captain.

Ahjin touched his forehead to Nia's while he fumbled with the buttons. "Yes, I will marry you. We'll find a way. When?"

Nia scrubbed tears from her uninjured cheek. "As soon as we can."

"Next month," Ahjin suggested.

"You can't." Behind them, Darravani sighed. "Unless Nia intends to let you have children with another woman after you're married."

"Shredded fins, no." Nia fastened his jacket with angry jerks. "He's mine."

Ahjin put his arm around her and turned to face the gods. "You let me be jailed and accused of murder."

"Since we could not send you home like we tried with the other out-dwellers," Resef said, "we thought you would be safer with walls and guards between you and the enemy."

Ahjin patted his chest. "Was I?"

The lightning sword flickered.

"If you don't trust yourselves to choose the next Mouth together," Ahjin said, "why don't you let me pick my successor?"

"That is an interesting idea," Darravani said, "but imagine the polit-ical wrangling."

"If you don't trust me, I can't do my job."

Makana shrugged. "We trust you as much as we can, but there must be boundaries."

Ahjin glared at the gods. "It's not fair to punish me for something that isn't my fault. I've worked hard for you and will continue to do so for the rest of my life. I live where you tell me to live; I do what you tell me to do; I go where you tell me to go. Must I give up even love for you?"

"I have an idea," Kassian said.

Every head swivelled to face him.

He looked at the rapt crowd. "Which we should discuss in private. Resef, may we borrow your temple?"

"Certainly, brother." Resef turned to the crowd. "My thanks for coming today. The trial is ended, and His Holiness is innocent. The conflict is over." He shook his lightning sword for emphasis.

"Go home and apologize to your neighbors. Welcome visitors. If you find someone unwilling to keep the peace, report to the temple rather than handling it yourselves. Warmth to you. Guards, put this judge and your prior captain in the cells where they belong."

While the other gods kept Irajahan under control, the swordsmen surrounded the Orrik judge and the Sardad captain. Ahjin watched them escorted into the jail with an embarrassing amount of glee. He pressed a hand against his chest and made a mental note to have Resef sort through the rest of the guard for troublemakers who had been happy to follow their captain. And he wanted his armor back.

Most of the crowd trickled away, watching over their shoulders for any last-minute drama. Nia stayed with Ahjin, arms around his waist and fists clenched in his jacket. In the market square, Zefra spoke with many of the people before they left, some familiar to Ahjin and some not. She was the last to leave, hauling Kaito with her and glaring fiercely.

When the market was empty except for the gods, Ahjin, and Nia, Resef dragged Irajahan down the stairs. "This way."

They walked in silence for several minutes. The streets were empty, but heads peered out windows. Irajahan glowered, and Ahjin and the other gods steadfastly ignored the watchers, but Nia waved and blew kisses from under her hood. Obviously, Kassian's hint at a solution had restored her normal cheerful mood.

Resef turned at a simple brick building. "Here we are." He dragged Irajahan up the stairs, inside, and past the simple shrines to an inner room, where he shoved his brother into a padded leather chair and stood behind him. "Please, make yourselves comfortable. We have a lot to discuss."

Darravani poured water from a jug on a side table and handed around cups while Makana passed out fruit and nuts.

Ahjin picked a wide chair with low arms and pulled Nia onto his lap. He drained his water and set the empty cup on the floor, then picked at berries from the bowl Nia held. "Kassian, what is your idea?"

Kassian leaned against the windowsill and crossed his arms. "Biology keeps the species separate on purpose. But we created you — we can change you."

Nia gasped. "You mean we can have children together?"

Kassian nodded. "But it will take all of us working together."

Irajahan sneered. "Why should I help any of you? You condemned me to die."

"Help us, or you can die right now." Resef laid his lightning sword across Irajahan's neck.

Irajahan sneered. "Your unhappiness will flavor my death."

Darravani held up her hand. "A bargain, then? You help, and we'll change your sentence to imprisonment instead of death. We'll even give you the opportunity to win your freedom later. This is your one chance for mercy, brother."

Irajahan glared at her. "I hate all of you."

Makana laughed. "That is perfectly obvious. Will you take mercy or choke on your hate?"

Irajahan glared. "I accept your mercy and hope you choke on it."

"Oh, Ahjin," Nia said. "Imagine cute little babies with wings and gills."

Irajahan snickered. "Despite what Kassian said, you can't mix Iojif and Nokai. They can change you, but it comes with a cost. Are you ready, Your *Holiness*, to give up your wings for this... this *fish*? Or will you sacrifice her gills and her beloved ocean?"

"That's not fair," Makana said.

Kassian stepped quickly to her side and whispered in her ear.

Ahjin sucked in a breath. Never fly again? His wings twitched with the memory of rustling wind cradling him, but he pulled Nia closer. It would be worth it.

"Which?" he asked. "My wings or Nia's gills?"

Makana glared at Kassian before answering. "It's a risk you'll have to take. Do you love her enough to risk your wings? Oh, and we haven't mentioned yet, this might kill either of you."

Nia wrapped her hands over Ahjin's arms and squeezed until she whimpered in pain at the pressure on her wound.

Ahjin whispered in her ear. "I don't want you to risk losing the ocean forever. Go home and find someone who is less trouble. Izo still loves you, or you could find a nice Nokai man."

Nia smiled sweetly. She didn't bother to whisper. "I don't love Izo. I'm not leaving you, so you might as well hush, feather brain." She turned back to Makana. "I love Ahjin enough to risk my gills and my life."

"Even with help, it will take me until tomorrow afternoon to get everything ready," Kassian said. "Until then, do you want to visit with your friends?"

"They left," Ahjin said.

Makana laughed. "They're waiting outside."

Nia squealed and bolted from the room. Ahjin bowed deeply to the gods before following her. By the time he exited the temple, Nia was in the middle of a small crowd, hugging Zefra. Ahjin saw Kaito, Sufa, and most of Ahjin's guards, along with several unfamiliar Darrendrakar and an elegantly mature Iskrin lady.

Kaito clasped Ahjin's arm in greeting, then slowly wrapped him in a gentle hug. Ahjin patted his back until the Seal let go. "I'm glad to see you, too, Kaito. Would someone introduce me to our newcomers?"

The Iskrin lady bowed. "Allow me, Your Holiness. I'm Hariskandra, Tarakh's mother."

She escorted him from person to person, telling not only their names but also what they had done to help.

Ahjin thanked each of them in their own language. During the introductions, two more Darrendrakar exited the temple, wearing Iskrin robes and slightly wide-eyed expressions. The man, Gazanar, was one of Ahjin's Darrendrakar guards, and he hurried an amber-eyed woman ahead of him down the steps.

Nia pulled away from Zefra's fussing and rushed to embrace the two Cats. "Oh, good, Resef let you go. If he hurt you, I'll smack him."

Gazanar chuckled. "We're a little intimidated, but he didn't hurt us."

The woman huffed. "*You* might be intimidated. I'm annoyed."

Nia fidgeted while Zefra finished re-bandaging her. "Has anyone seen Daz? Zefra, where are Ludik, Nemerra, and Tarakh? Did they save the kittens? How did you find Kassian's potions? What was Irad like?"

Hariskandra looked at the avid onlookers. "All good questions, but we should find a private place to discuss them. Zefra, do we have anywhere better to go than our retreat?"

"Did you change inns?" Ahjin asked.

Nia wrinkled her nose. "When you were arrested, the innkeeper decided we were a bad influence. We've moved several times, but you don't want to see our current residence." She shuddered.

Ahjin straightened his jacket. "I've been restored to my position. Any inn in town should welcome us."

Nia grinned. "Then we should go back to our old one. I'd love to see the innkeeper's face."

"No," Zefra said. "Pick one nearby and spare us the walk. When he hears we went elsewhere, it will punish him enough."

Ahjin turned to Hariskandra. "Perhaps you could recommend one, lady?"

"Farukh likes—" She swallowed. "My husband liked the second one on that street."

In a short time, a fawning innkeeper had assigned rooms for everyone, with baths and food arranged.

Kaito bullied Ahjin into the first bath and waited, back turned, to bandage Ahjin's chest after he put on clean pants. Ahjin distracted himself from the lengthy treatment by listening to Nia sing and splash in her own bath next door. The curses that followed assured him her wounds were also being treated.

Kaito handed Ahjin his shirt and ushered him out the door. Before he had a chance to feel lost, Hariskandra beckoned Ahjin into a large room down the hall. Her damp hair was freshly braided, and she wore a clean robe.

"We will meet here," she said. "The innkeeper already brought fruit and water, and he will bring a hot meal soon. Please, sit and rest until the others are ready."

She bowed and smiled and made pleasant talk about nothing until Nia and Zefra emerged with wet hair, followed shortly by Kaito and Arasi.

Ahjin held Nia's hands, and the group chatted until everyone in their large group had bathed and settled on mats.

"Now 'tis time to answer your questions, Nia," Zefra said. "Where shall we begin?"

"In order," Ahjin said. "What happened after I was arrested?"

They were less than halfway through the tale by the time dinner arrived, and the whole story took until late into the night. Some questions, such as where Captain Daz was, what happened to Lapwing, or when Ludik's group would arrive, remained unanswered when everyone tumbled into bed.

In the morning, a Shri healer arrived to treat the injuries. After Ahjin's healing session, he found Nia, who wore fresh bandages and stunk of ointment.

"When do you think Kassian will be ready?" Nia asked.

Ahjin squeezed her hand. "I don't know. Are you sure about this?"

Nia slugged his shoulder. "Stop asking me that. Let's go for a walk." She handed him a basket of food and slung a water jug over her shoulder.

They spent the rest of the day walking and talking, sharing things they hadn't told the others and catching up on almost three weeks of separation. Sometimes daring pedestrians stopped to talk, but most people only watched as the two wound through the city.

At dinnertime, they returned to the inn.

"Hurry and eat," Zefra said. "Kassian sent word he will be ready soon."

Ahjin accepted a plate but picked at the rice and vegetables. It was almost time, and all he knew was that this *might* work, at the cost of his wings or Nia's gills, or it *might* kill them.

Nia ate all her food and asked for more. When Ahjin raised an eyebrow at her, she shrugged. "Why suffer with an empty stomach?"

On their way out, she grabbed a sweet pastry, arriving at the temple with sticky fingers and a satisfied smile.

All five gods were waiting. After the briefest of greetings, Kassian handed them each a glass jar filled with a swirling rainbow liquid. "Take this with you. After you drink, concentrate on what you want."

"Ahjin over here," Resef said.

"Nia in this room," Makana said.

"Can't we stay together?" Ahjin asked.

Makana smiled sweetly. "We don't want you distracted by the other person screaming." She shut the door in Nia's face.

Resef shook his head. "Drink whenever you're ready." He shut Ahjin's door, leaving him alone in a small room.

Ahjin flexed his hands. Screaming? He looked toward the wall of Nia's room. His brave sweetheart was probably drinking right now, and here he dithered like a coward. He gulped the potion, which tasted even nastier than he anticipated.

Concentrate on what you want, Kassian had said.

Make it so we can have children together. Please, please take my wings instead of Nia's gills. Don't hurt her.

The liquid swirling in his stomach expanded, winding through his veins and soaking into every part of his body. Then it became aching cold and melting fire and tingling lightning. Stabbing needles tore his innards apart. His knees buckled, and he fell to the ground, shaking.

Ahjin started to scream and then remembered Nia. He must not let her hear. He curled into a ball and clamped his arm across his mouth as pain struck in currents, worse than the guard captain's torture, worse than breaking his wings, worse than being struck by lightning.

Please, Ahjin prayed, *save Nia and end this.*

The misery went on and on, rising and falling in drowning waves until Ahjin couldn't breathe.

And then it stopped, leaving only an empty ache in every muscle.

Ahjin moved his arms. They seemed still attached. His legs moved, too. He opened his eyes and stretched the muscles that used to move his wings.

His wings moved, feathers rustling. Sheer relief poured through him.

In the next room, Nia screamed.

Guilt replaced the relief as he scrambled to his feet. It should have been him. It was his fault they were in this situation. He would make it up to her somehow. Teaching her to fly would be a good start.

Ahjin threw open his door and then Nia's. He dropped to the floor where she knelt, hands over her eyes, and wrapped his arms around her.

"I'm here," he whispered. "I'm here."

"I'm sorry, Ahjin. It's not fair. I tried to concentrate, but the pain made me forget."

Ahjin pulled back a little and examined her. She looked almost the same. Same skin. Same hair, and he brushed it off the same gills. Same webbed fingers. She had ripped off her face bandage in her agony, and the only difference was a new white scar in place of the gash.

It hadn't worked.

"We'll figure out something." He hugged her tightly.

"It should have been me," she said. "I asked for you to keep your wings."

Ahjin tickled her with his feathers. "The change didn't work."

Nia opened her eyes and reached for one wing.

"Yes, it did," Kassian said behind him.

"But how? I don't understand?" Ahjin fluttered his wings and pulled back Nia's hair to show her gills. "Irajahan said we'd have to change, give up our race."

Makana pushed Kassian inside the room. "Irajahan is a jerk, but we had to see if you were committed enough. Really, we don't have to change you, just the stuff inside you."

"So we can have kids with wings and gills?" Nia asked.

"No." Darravani leaned through the doorway. "Your children will look like *one* of you. Nothing we can do will let you mix races, but we made it so your children can be copied from one parent. The other parent will only provide — never mind, you wouldn't understand the details."

Ahjin pulled Nia to her feet. "Why let Irajahan say those things to us?"

"We had to be sure you wanted this enough," Resef said over Darravani's shoulder. "If your determination failed, the change would not work."

"It shouldn't have worked," Irajahan whined from the other room.

"Kassian!" someone yelled from outside. "Kassiaaaaaaan! Your scorpions are invading!"

30.FAREWELL
(SARDAD)

One meets his destiny often in the road he takes to avoid it.
Iskrin Proverb

Z efra flattened herself against the building and peered down the
road at the monsters. In an earlier adventure, a dozen of Kassian's
scorpions had nearly killed her. Now twice that number poured in from
the desert, and the citizens of Sardad hid instead of preparing to fight.
Not that she blamed them. Most of them were not warriors, and the
panther-sized monsters were terrifying.

The three Iojif swooped overhead.

"They aren't stopping, Zefra," Arasi called down. "I have the ambush
set for the next street back."

"Kassian," Zefra bellowed again.

A line of gods ran out, with Ahjin and Nia at the back. She did not
know if they had already finished, and right now, she did not care.

"Kassian, tell the scorpions to stop," she commanded.

Kassian raised an eyebrow. "Is that a command, little lady?"

"No, no." Zefra quickly bowed. "Please, Lord Celestial, if you would
be so kind as to stop your monsters from attacking Sardad before they
hurt someone." She left her hand on her sword hilt.

"They aren't attacking." Kassian put two fingers to his lips and whistled loudly.

Most of the scorpions skittered back to the desert. Two slowed to a walk and kept coming.

Zefra drew her saif.

"Oh, put that away," Kassian said. "I thought you, of all people, would understand. Didn't I tell you I'd try to get Ludik home faster?"

"Ludik?" Nia said behind Zefra, then ran toward the scorpions.

"Don't make them think you're attacking them," Kassian called after her, laughing.

Zefra sheathed her weapon and followed with Ahjin. Now that they were closer, she saw two scorpions each carried a rider and several bundles. There should be five riders. Who had been left behind?

Zefra got close enough to see the dark skin of the riders. No Tarakh, then. Had he decided to ride his horse? It would take him days to return. Had he not risked enough to investigate the conspiracy and rescue the children? Why had Ludik abandoned him? Rozali and Zinon were also missing.

Ludik and Nemerra slid off the scorpions and hugged Nia, careful to avoid squishing the children strapped to their chests. As soon as Zefra and Ahjin caught up, the Darrendrakar greeted them, too.

"I'm so glad you made it," Zefra said, "but scorpions?"

Her skin crawled, though both monsters held still and kept their stingers and claws lowered. Their torsos were coiled with rope holding baby carriers across their backs. The four Darrendrakar children, back in their two-legged shapes, giggled happily and drummed on the hard shells.

Nemerra shuddered. "I know. But they walked all night long and all day to get us here. Whenever one tired, we switched to another. Here, help us with the children."

She plucked the little Iojif boy from the carrier on her chest and handed him to Ahjin. Ludik handed the Iskrin boy to Zefra. Nemerra took her daughters from the carrier strapped to the scorpion, while Ludik turned so Nia could remove the sleepy Nokai girl from his back.

"But where are Tarakh and the Horse siblings?" Zefra asked. "Did you lose them somewhere?"

"They are coming," Ludik said, "I have a message for you from Tar-akh."

He scooped his sons from their scorpion-seats and passed them to willing hands, then gave Zefra a slate and reached for the packs with the help of Ahjin's guards.

Zefra, the note said, *After you save Resef, remember to have him deal with the warring clans. I trust you to stop them faster than I could find the battles. The horses, my own and the Darrendrakar, were terrified of the scorpions, so I stayed to guide them home. I will arrive in a few days. I hope you will stay long enough to see me again. Tarakh.*

Did she want to see him again? He was brash and over-friendly and much too personal. But he was also kind and cheerful and trusting. And the things he said to her... Zefra tucked the slate into her belt pouch to think about later.

After unwrapping the harnesses, Ludik tapped the scorpions. "Nia, please thank them and send them home."

Nia clicked a string of hard consonants, and the scorpions scurried into the desert.

Ludik threw tawny Terru onto his shoulders and tucked copper-haired Rurru under his arm. "I see Ahjin is free. Did you stop the conspiracy? Can we go home?"

Nemerra shifted blonde Zurrahava higher on her hip and let Etana take Kamakana, the russet-headed wiggler. "I would love food and a long nap. What do we do with the other children?"

Zefra pinched her lips together. "The gods can stir themselves to help, since they made such a mess of things."

She tightened her grip on the boy and marched to Resef. Ahjin and Nia followed with the other outdweller children.

Zefra bowed to Resef. "This infant's mother was killed in the conspiracy against you. What will you do with him?"

Resef kept one hand on Irajahan and beckoned one of his priests with his lightning sword. "I will send a message to his father in Pramath. My priests will care for him until his father arrives."

The priest smiled ruefully at Zefra and took the infant.

Makana cooed and waved at the little Nokai girl. "Such a pretty thing. Too bad about her mom, but I'll find someone to take care of her."

She beckoned Ahjin's Nokai guards. "Until then, I'm assigning her to you two."

"Who will take this one?" Ahjin cradled the wispy-winged Iojif boy against his chest.

"We will." His Iojif guards stepped forward and took the infant. "If we may be excused from your service temporarily?"

"Of course," Ahjin said.

"And if everything else is settled, now it's time to deal with Irajahan," Kassian said.

Resef grinned and raised his lightning sword. Darravani and Makanavailea held Irajahan's arms.

"You promised not to kill me," Irajahan squealed.

"Coward," Makana muttered.

"We won't kill you," Darravani said. "We thought of something much better. You will have plenty of time to consider your mistakes."

Irajahan glowered at Ahjin. "Agreeing to keep *that* pest in my life was a mistake."

Makanavailea clicked her tongue. "That's exactly the sort of thing we're talking about. Resef, Kassian, are you ready?"

Resef let go of his sword, and the lightning zapped into the sky. He held up his hands, stretching toward the sky, and Kassian copied him.

And then nothing happened.

Zefra waited, and still nothing happened. Nia fidgeted, tapping her fingers on her leg and humming. Ahjin widened his stance and clasped his hands behind his back, under his wings. Ludik and Nemerra rearranged their children in their arms.

Hands still raised, Resef and Kassian did not move.

Irajahan twisted free of his sisters and bolted down the street. A wall of dirt shot up in his face, and when he bounced off, Makanavailea pounced on his back and pushed his face into the ground.

"Ah, here it is," Resef said as a comet streaked through the sky, right toward them.

Nia squeaked, and several people in nearby buildings screamed. Zefra clenched her fists and watched Resef.

The comet screeched to a halt, towering twice as tall as the gods. Zefra backed up five steps from the heat. Everyone else but the gods backed up twenty and shaded their eyes.

Resef stuck his hands into the comet's fire and closed his eyes. The flames wavered and shrank until they disappeared, leaving a steaming clump of metal on the scorched ground.

Resef yanked Irajahan to his feet. "Come, dear brother, stand with me while our siblings do their work."

Makanavailea brushed off her hands and circled the comet. "Kassian, take left, Darravani, right." After the two gods shifted to either side of the comet, Makanavailea squinted. "Are you ready?"

Darravani and Kassian reached toward the comet and froze, not quite touching it.

"Ready," Darravani said.

Makanavailea took a deep breath and raised her hands slowly. An underground rumbling grew louder until a water spout erupted with a roar. Makanavailea waved her hands in an arc, and the water poured over the extinguished comet, exploding in a cloud of steam.

Kassian and Darravani jerked their hands backward as if pulling on a rope.

When the steam cleared and the water drained back into the sand, the comet sat on the earth, broken in half and rocking slightly. The core was hollow, pitted and scarred, a little taller than a man.

Ahjin shrugged his wings and stepped forward. "Irajahan, you have been judged worthy of death, but in mercy, we have provided another way."

Resef pressed Irajahan forward with his arms bent behind his back. Irajahan howled and kicked and cursed. Zefra shook her head in disgust, but behind her, Nia repeated some of the most colorful phrases as if to memorize them.

When the frantic God of Air head-butted Resef's nose, the other three gods stepped to help. Despite Irajahan's struggles, they crammed him into the middle of the comet.

"Makana, Resef," Kassian said, "hold him still." He punched Irajahan in the stomach to fold him back into the hollow.

"Got it," Resef said.

Makanavailea again created her waterspout, soaking all the gods.

Resef wiped his face and stepped back, black curls still dripping. "And — now!"

Kassian and the goddesses lunged backward while Resef waved his hands. The air suddenly got much colder. Zefra shivered and drew fire through her veins.

Momentarily unrestrained, Irajahan climbed from the hollow comet. He did not get far. As ice covered his skin, he slowed to a crawl. The ice thickened and spread until Irajahan looked like a shiny sculpture, caught half out of his new prison. His face was contorted in anger, and his fists were clenched.

Darravani grabbed a frozen arm and tipped her brother gently backward until he rested inside the comet.

Makana pointed to an extended foot. "He won't fit."

Resef put his hand on Irajahan's knee and melted the ice until the leg sagged. He tucked the foot inside and sighed. "Brother, this could have been avoided."

The other gods stepped forward. Each touched Irajahan briefly and murmured something. Finally, they backed up and nodded at Ahjin.

Ahjin spread his wings. "Irajahan, you are hereby condemned to circle the heavens for a hundred years. At the end, you will be tried again. If you have repented, you will be freed. If not, you will be returned for another hundred years, and another, and another, until you learn your lesson and are ready to care for your responsibilities instead of seeking only your own way."

Ahjin looked at the other gods. "I'm assuming you already have a plan to compensate for the god of air being absent."

Kassian nodded. "I'll take care of his work, with a bit of help from the others. The world will be safe this time."

He and Darravani settled the other half of the comet over Irajahan's frozen face. They ran their hands along the seam, fusing the halves together, and then the gods put their hands on the comet. It glowed brighter and brighter until Zefra had to shield her eyes with her arm.

Something whooshed, and the light faded. Zefra uncovered her face. The comet, once more burning, rose into the sky, higher and higher until it curved toward the sun and beyond.

Nia cheered.

Ahjin's diplomatic mask cracked a little as the corner of his lips turned up.

Zefra kept her face smooth but could not help the relief that warmed her. She turned to Resef. "Luminosity, will you please tell the clans to stop fighting now?"

Resef raised an eyebrow. "You are a bossy thing."

Zefra bowed low, lips pressed tightly together to avoid arguing.

"But you are right and a worthy wielder of my flame." A warm hand touched her head, and then she heard the woosh of a comet arriving.

She stood, knees shaky, in time to see Resef jump aboard and fly south. Warmth spread from her head to her heart, and she took a deep breath before turning back to the others.

Makanavailea linked her arm through Darravani's. "Well done, everyone. Let's go home and tell our children to behave."

Ahjin bowed to Kassian. "Excuse me, please." His voice cracked. "I have a favor to beg of you."

Kassian raised an eyebrow. "Another one? You're keeping your sweetheart and your position and losing Irajahan."

Zefra turned to beam at Nia. Keeping his sweetheart? 'Twas wonderful!

"It's not for me," Ahjin said. "It's for Ioj."

Kassian narrowed his eyes. "This sounds interesting."

Ahjin's wings twitched. "Although Irajahan wasn't a particularly good god, his absence leaves us without any."

"I thought you'd like that," Nia muttered.

Ahjin shrugged. "There are many Iojif that will feel bereft."

"What does this have to do with me?" Kassian asked.

"On behalf of Ioj," Ahjin said, "I request you act as their god, until such time as Irajahan returns."

"I already said I would take care of the air," Kassian said.

Ahjin stood straighter. "I'm talking about the people."

"You forget," Kassian said. "I just took ownership of the Dragon Isles."

"Make it a land free of gods," Nia suggested, "at least for required worship."

Makanavailea stuck her hands on her hips. "Why would we want to do that?"

Nia flicked a glance at Ahjin. "Some people prefer to ignore the gods. The Pinnipeds are an excellent example."

Darravani pursed her lips. "Yes, I'm sure they would love to be a little farther from Darrendra."

"I've already approved a long list of colonists," Kassian said.

"They can choose if they still want to come," Ahjin said.

Kassian tapped his chin. "On one condition."

Ahjin squared his shoulders. "What?"

"I'm tired of seeing Irajahan's badge on you, as if you were only his priest. Create something better to show you belong to all of us."

Ahjin's shoulders relaxed. "My pleasure."

Kassian clapped him on the shoulder. "We'll talk about the details later. I believe it falls under your job description."

Ahjin grinned. "It does, doesn't it?" He wrapped an arm around Nia and turned.

"Wait." Zefra hurried to catch up to Ahjin before lowering her voice. "What happened with you two inside the temple?"

Nia rolled her shoulders with a wince. "They said we can marry."

"But — how? Did they change their mind about inheriting the position?"

Ahjin rolled his eyes. "Apparently, we wouldn't understand the technical explanation, and I don't want to talk about the experience. All we know is that the two of us can have children now."

Zefra blinked. "Wings and gills?"

Nia shook her head. "They said that won't happen. I guess we'll have to see."

Ahjin raised her hand and kissed her fingers. "After we're married."

"And how soon is that?" Nia leaned toward him.

"I need to send a force after the rebels, including Lapwing, wherever the stinker is. And I want to retrieve my armor from a certain captain and then take Kaito to talk to Lyell first."

Nia laughed. "Kaito doesn't talk, silly, and he already communicates without your help."

"It's complicated. I'll explain later."

Their conversation deteriorated into teasing and flirting, and Zefra let them pull ahead with their guards. Ludik had his family back and would presumably go home as soon as possible, though for now, they followed Ahjin and Nia to the inn.

Zefra, on the other hand, still had nowhere to go and no job. The caravan had left without her this morning.

She had been so close, and he was the only employer who believed she had enough experience. Despite helping Ahjin rescue the gods, stopping a Darrendran blood feud, defeating pirates, and bringing Irajahan's conspiracy to an end, she was still viewed as a little girl. Her friends, family, and Tarakh were the only ones to view her as a grown woman.

She fanned her suddenly burning face. A handsome face did not make it Tarakh's affair how grown she was.

The gods disappeared, and the city returned to normal busy patterns. Zefra was the only person still standing in the middle of the street like a lost colt.

She squared her shoulders. 'Twas past time to solve her problem. She still had Ahjin's letter. Where could she go now to look for employment? The next district south had such a well-established trade route that they did not need guides, and they did not stray off the path into the empty desert. She would have to go all the way to the east or west coasts before heading south.

Why did nothing work the way she planned? She tried so hard, but everyone kept telling her to compromise her perfect plans.

Zefra tilted her head and looked at the comet arcing into space. At least Irajahan's plans had not worked, either.

She narrowed her eyes. He also thought he had good plans and refused to compromise. Look where that had gotten him.

Perhaps she should pursue her goals with a little more flexibility. She had many skills; did it matter if she became a guide now or later? A few years learning versatility might increase her value in the eyes of future employers.

"Are you coming back to the inn?"

Zefra turned around.

Hariskandra smiled and motioned down the street. "A good meal will prepare you for your next journey."

Zefra clasped her hands behind her back and walked with the older woman for a few minutes while she gathered her thoughts. Perhaps she should follow her brother's advice and strike where the iron glowed. She did have *one* offer.

She squared her shoulders and faced Tarakh's mother. "Your husband once offered me employment. So did Tarakh. Is the offer still available?"

Beetles of nervousness crawled in her stomach as she mentioned Tarakh. She pressed her belt pouch against her leg until she felt the edges of both slates, hers and his. This was about employment, not his silly compliments, she told herself sternly.

Hariskandra pursed her lips. "Certainly, either as mapmaker or horsewoman."

Maps and horses would do for now. She might even agree to be Tala's guardian. When an opportunity arose for a guide, Zefra would be ready. Plans did not solve every problem, and when life changed, she could adjust.

She patted the slates again. She needed to thank Tarakh for helping her. As an extra benefit, working for his mother would ensure she was around when he returned.

She nodded. "Then let us eat and discuss that job."

And if she ever wanted personal opportunities, *she* would decide when she was ready, charming smile or no.

Hariskandra laughed and linked arms with Zefra. "That sounds like a wonderful plan."

YOU HAVE TORTURED ALL OF OUR
HEROES, DEAR AUTHOR, SO THIS MUST
BE THE HAPPY ENDING AT LONG
LAST. YAY!

You don't want any more, dear reader?

OF COURSE I DO. BUT WHAT ELSE IS
THERE?

So glad you asked.
I've written a collection of short stories. Turn the page for info about **Tales of Kaiatan**, wherein we see our beloved heroes and meet new ones.

TALES OF KAIATAN

From a meticulously built world brimming with wonder, courage, and heart, find backstories to the **Unexpected Heroes** novels, as well as prequels, sequels, and side quests. Enjoy a diverse and compelling cast with new and old characters, including minor actors who insisted on telling their own story. All are waiting for you to join them in their adventures, romances, challenges, joys, friendships, and secrets...

*Tales of Kaiatan is the fifth book in the **Unexpected Heroes** series of clean YA secondary world fantasy and is best read in order for the most enjoyment, though you can also weave it into the first four books by story chronology.*

Check my website MCLeeBooks for links to buy the next story or get the entire series at once.

Still want more? Get free stories by joining my newsletter. Every two weeks, I chat about my current writing or my life & offer book news and deals. And did I mention free stories?

Sign up at MCLeeBooks.com

Free Story: The Cat's Fortune

On another world, so long ago that truth faded into legend, a cat and a boy seek their fortune together.

Orphaned and homeless, young Aktar travels to the city of Rapata for a better life.

But it seems the rumors of gold-paved streets are false. Can he find a home and a job before he starves? Maybe with the help of a foundling kitten.

A retelling of Puss in Boots and Dick Whittington, with timeless themes of belonging, courage, and self-discovery, set on the fantasy world of Kaiatan, home of the **Unexpected Heroes**.

Please leave an honest review on any retailer or reader site. Seriously, it would really help me. :)

If you found a typo, you're welcome to report it at mcleebooks.com/report-a-typo/

CHARACTER LIST AND PRONUNCIATION GUIDE

IF YOU ARE INTERESTED IN THE MEANINGS OF THE NAMES, PLEASE SEE MCLEEBOOKS.COM

Name (Pronunciation) Identity
  <u>People</u>

Ahjin Machol (AH-jzin MACK-ole) Iojif, 17.5 years old, skydancer

Alemana, Nokai guard to Ahjin

Amrafel (AHM-rah-fell) Iojif, chief priest in Vasi

Arasi (uh-RAHS-ee) Iojif, one of Ahjin's guards

Askari (Uh-SCAR-ee) Iskrin, guard

Chiara (Chee-AHR-uh) Iskrin, one of Ahjin's guards

Chiyo (CHIE-oe) Iskrin, one of Ahjin's guards

Crow (CROE) Nickname of Iojif serial killer/pirate captain

Darravani the Omnifarious (DAR-uh-VAHN-ee) Darrendrakar Goddess of Earth

Daz (DAZZ) Iskrin, one of Ahjin's guards

Etana (EH-tah-nuh) Darrendrakar, makarodont, Nia's guard

Farukh Ekorov (Fuh-ROOK) Iskrin, Devoran chieftain, Tarakh's father

Gazanar (GAH-zan-aur) Darrendrakar, Cat spy, jaguarrundi

Gurryon Moriko (GURR-yon) Darrendrakar, Ludik's brother

Haider Moriko (HIE-der) Darrendrakar, Ludik's brother

Hariskandra Ekorov (Hahr-is-CAN-druh) Iskrin, Devoran, Tarakh's mother

Harita (Huh-REET-uh) Darrendrakar, Dog spy, molossus

Ilani (Ill-AHN-ee) Darrendrakar, Gurryon's fiancé

Ingo (EENG-oe) Darrendrakar, Dog spy, lion hound

Irajahan the Omnipotent (Ear-AH-jzuh-han) Iojif God of Air

Isako (ISS-uh-koe) Iskrin, one of Ahjin's guards

Izo Ashvakosha (EE-zoe) Iskrin, Zefra's older brother

Kaito (KAY-toe) Darrendrakar, seal

Kalalamoanani (Kah-LA-la-moe-uh-NAHN-ee or KAH-la) Nokai, Nia's older near-sister

Kamakana Moriko (KAH-mah-KAH-nuh) Darrendrakar, Ludik's daughter, second, leopard

Kassian (KASS-ee-an) Eldest god, architect of world

Kolina, Nokai guard to Ahjin

Koray (CORE-ay) Iskrin, Rikatsu healer

Lapwing (Lap-wing) Nickname of Crow's former first mate

Ludik Moriko (LUD-ick) Darrendrakar, 19 years old, hunter

Lyell Ulriksin (LIE-el UL-rick-sin) Darrendrakar wolf, Ahjin's chief of staff

Madden (MAD-dun) Darrendrakar, forester Fox

Makanavailea the Omniscient (Mah-KAHN-uh-vie-LEE-uh) Nokai Goddess of Water

Nemerra (Neh-MERR-uh) Darrendrakar, Ludik's wife

Niamolenulanami (NEE-ah-moe-LEN-noo-la-NAHM-ee) Nokai, 17 years old, singer

Rada (RAH-duh) "Success, lightning" Iskrin, priest applicant

Redell (RED-ell) Darrendrakar, Dog spy, leopard dog

Resef the Omnificent (RES-eff) Iskrin God of Fire

Rozali (Roe-ZALL-ee) Darrendrakar, Horse spy

Rurru Moriko (ROO-rroo) Darrendrakar, Ludik's son, first, snow leopard

Sayaka Ruchi (Sae-YAHK-uh RUE-chee) Iskrin, guard

Shri Okechuku (SHREE OH-keh-CHOO-koo) Iskrin, Tukiko healer

Sufa (SUE-fuh) Iojif, released priestess, Ahjin's distant cousin on mother's side

Tala Lyelldin (TALL-uh LIE-ul-din) Darrendrakar, Lyell's daughter

Tarakh Ekorov (Tah-ROCK ECK-uh-rov) Iskrin, Devoran farmer

Terru Moriko (TERR-oo) Darrendrakar, Ludik's son, third, lion

Varnika (VAR-nuh-kuh) Darrendrakar, Cat spy, karrakal

Zefra Ashvakosha Kezhekori (ZEF-ruh ASH-vah-KOASH-uh KEZ-eh-KORE-ee) Iskrin, 16 years old, Hotaru guide
Zinon (ZINE-un) Darrendrakar, Horse spy
Zurrahava Moriko (ZURR-ah-HAH-vuh) Darrendrakar, Ludik's daughter, 4th, black jaguar

<u>Groups, Locations, Languages</u>

Achira (Uh-CHEER-uh) "Horse" Iskrin clan, specialty: horses
Arupa (Uh-RUPE-uh) Island
Chisato (Chih-SAT-oe) Largest city in Devora, Iskra
Darrendra (Duh-RREND-druh) Northern country
Darrendrakar (Duh-RREND-druh-car) People of Darrendra, shapeshifters
Darrendran (Duh-RREND-drun) Darrendrakar language
Devora (Dev-OH-ruh) Iskrin clan, specialty: grain
Heresa (Herr-ESS-uh) "Ruler of diamonds" Iskrin clan, speciality: gems, precious metals
Hotaru (Hoe-TARE-oo) Iskrin tribe, specialty: maps
Ioj (EYE-ojze) Eastern country
Iojif (Eye-OH-jziff) People of Ioj, avians
Iojo (Eye-OH-jzo) Iojif language
Irad (EYE-rad) Lost city of gods
Iskra(ISK-ruh) Southern country
Iskrin (ISK-ree)People of Iskra, desert-dwellers
Iskrit (ISK-rit) Iskrin language
Kairri (KERR-ree) "Ocean village" Village in Canid tribe
Nokai (NO-kie) People of Nokailana, aquastrians
Nokailana (NO-kie-LAHN-uh) Western islands
Noki (NO-kee) Nokai language
Pramath (PRAHM-uth) Small village in Devora, Iskra
Rikatsu (Rick-AT-soo) Iskrin clan, speciality: ships
Sardad (SAHR-dad) Medium-sized city in Devora, Iskra
Tetsuya (Tet-SOO-yuh) Iskrin clan, specialty: weapons & metalwork
Vasi (VAHS-ee) Capital of Ioj

ACKNOWLEDGMENTS

Thanks to my Day Group,
Carol Malone, Cheree Myatt, Donna Gonzales, and Gail Porter, for their
excellent advice,
and to my extraordinary alpha and beta readers,
Amy Vaudreuil, Laura Drake, Lea Carter, Matt Peel, Molly Morrison,
Phylicia Joannis, Robin Cranney, and Virginia Cummings

Special thanks to Laura Dotson and Skylie Cheney for musical help.

ABOUT THE AUTHOR

Marty C. Lee told stories for most of her life, but never took them seriously until her daughter asked her to write this one. Between writing and spending time with her family, she reads, embroiders, paints-by-number, and gardens.

She has lived in five states, seven cities, and ten houses so far. She currently lives in the West, but not in a tropical paradise. She doesn't like flying, even in an airplane. She wishes she could produce her own fire to warm her hands. She's glad she didn't have to wait a year to marry her sweetheart, who also wishes she could warm her hands.

You can find her at
    MCLeeBooks.com and on Facebook and book sites

www.ingramcontent.com/pod-product-compliance
Lightning Source LLC
Chambersburg PA
CBHW031214020726
47499CB00002B/579